ENDORSE

"In *A Christmas Journey Home*, Macias melds a poignant Nativity story with life's gritty reality to portray Christ's hope even in the most desperate situations. A must for your Christmas list!"
—**Patti Lacy**, author of *The Rhythm of Secrets* and *What the Bayou Saw*

"Suspenseful and bittersweet, with *A Christmas Journey Home* Kathi Macias has given us a new kind of Christmas story taken straight from the headlines, a poignant and compelling reminder that it took a baby in a manger to show us how to truly love our neighbors as we love ourselves."
—**Athol Dickson**, Christy and Audie Award-winning author of *Lost Mission* and *The Opposite of Art*

"Kathi Macias has earned a reputation for crafting stories that feature believable characters who face true-to-life situations, and she does it again in *A Christmas Journey Home*. Readers will quickly identify with Isabella and Miriam—very different women, forever changed by heartache and loss—and find themselves forever changed by Macias's powerful, spirit-charged story. Definitely a 'keeper!'"
—**Loree Lough**, award-winning author of 80 books, including *From Ashes to Honor*

"Kathi Macias has written a stirring story of sacrifice, loss, and grace, found in her beautiful new novel, *A Christmas Journey Home*. Miriam and Isabella, women as different from one another as night and day, separately and together discover the true meaning of Christ's birth through a shared experience of love given and received."
—**Karen O'Connor**, award-winning author of 70 published books, including *The Upside of Downsizing*

A CHRISTMAS JOURNEY HOME

KATHI MACIAS

NEW HOPE
PUBLISHERS
Birmingham, Alabama

New Hope® Publishers
P. O. Box 12065
Birmingham, AL 35202-2065
www.newhopedigital.com
New Hope Publishers is a division of WMU®.

Library of Congress Cataloging-in-Publication Data

Macias, Kathi, 1948-
 A Christmas journey home / Kathi Macias.
    p. cm.
 ISBN 978-1-59669-328-9 (sc)
 1. Christmas stories. I. Title.
 PS3563.I42319C47 2011
 813'.54--dc22

                                   2011016854

ISBN-10: 1-59669-328-2
ISBN-13: 978-1-59669-328-9

N124135 • 1011 • 5M1

DEDICATION

I humbly dedicate this book
to the One who came to pay a debt He didn't owe…
because we owed a debt we couldn't pay. Thank You.

And to my husband, Al,
and my children and grandchildren,
thank you for your gift of sharing my earthly journey.

PROLOGUE

ISABELLA SHIVERED, HER TEETH CHATTERING AS SHE HUDDLED AGAINST the frigid night air, doing her best to burrow her backside into Francisco's embrace. How could her *esposo* sleep in such harsh conditions? She and her husband had not eaten in nearly three days, they were almost out of water, and now she felt as if they would surely freeze to death before morning. And yet his even breathing, blowing warm against the back of her neck, assured her that her beloved had indeed escaped their dilemma for at least a few hours.

Isabella wished she could do the same. During the daylight hours, when her feet burned with each tortuous step, she imagined that she could fall asleep in an instant if given half the chance. But when the desert sun, still hot in midautumn, finally sank below the flat, dismal horizon and the night winds blew mercilessly upon them, sleep eluded her. True, Francisco did everything he could to protect her from the elements, even using his body to shield her as they sought meager shelter under a small rock overhang or behind a sand dune, but it was never enough. They were going to die; she was sure of it. She and her husband of eleven months would perish in the middle of the Arizona desert, with only the scavengers to dispose of their remains.

A slight flutter in her stomach reminded her that death would come to three of them, not just two. The baby that had been growing in her stomach for seven months, and that less than a week earlier had kicked with strength and determination, now grew weaker by the day.

Perhaps it is best, she told herself. *It was a foolish dream to think we could escape the violence and poverty of our home country and find a new life here, north of the border. My* abuelo *meant well, but we should never have listened to him . . . should never have taken his money and given it to the* coyote.

The ominous glare of the *coyote*, the man who had promised to take them safely to the United States but who instead had stolen their money and left them to die in the desert, danced through her memory, but she pushed it aside. Instead she focused on the beloved face of her grandfather, her *abuelo*, and fought the hot tears that stung her eyes as she wished yet again that she and Francisco were back in Don Alfredo's *casita*, sharing a simple meal of *tortillas* and *frijoles* with the leathery-skinned old man Isabella had adored since she was a tiny girl.

Despite her discomfort, the memory of her *abuelo's* face brought a smile to her lips, as she snuggled closer into her *esposo's* embrace. But then another memory, the horror of what had driven Don Alfredo to the point of pleading with them to flee across the border, wiped away her smile and once again brought tears to Isabella's weary eyes.

CHAPTER 1

NEWLYWEDS FRANCISCO AND ISABELLA ALCÁNTARA HAD LIVED in their tiny one-room home on the outskirts of Ensenada, Mexico, for about six months when their world exploded around them. Isabella had just begun to suspect that she might be pregnant, though she had yet to break the news to her *esposo*. It was important to be certain before speaking such life-changing words, words that would bring both joy and concern to Francisco's heart. As it was, he scarcely found enough work to pay the rent and keep them supplied with the most meager rations of food; a newborn would only add to the pressure he already felt to provide for his family, as well as his frustration at wondering how he was to do so.

Had they made a mistake getting married so young, particularly at a time when unemployment was rampant in their native country and violence from the drug wars encroached on their humble existence? Isabella had just turned nineteen a couple of weeks before the wedding, and Francisco had celebrated his twenty-second birthday a month later. On their wedding day they had been so hopeful, with

Francisco having found what seemed to be steady employment at a small factory within walking distance of their home. But the job had ended less than a week later, and he had been scrambling for any sort of day-labor jobs he could find ever since. Some days he found them; other days he came home empty-handed.

A baby, Isabella mused, her mind racing even as her heart melted at the thought. *A child, born of our love, as I've dreamed of almost from the day Francisco asked me to be his bride. But now? How will we manage? What if Francisco can no longer find enough work, or—?*

The pounding at the door had interrupted her thoughts, jolting her into a fearful state that warned her of evil tidings. The cries that accompanied the pounding could mean nothing but bad news. But how bad? Had something happened to Francisco? To her parents or siblings? Or perhaps to her dear old *abuelo*, who was in his eighties now?

Her heart beat a frightful tattoo against her rib cage as she approached the door with trembling, scarcely able to lift the latch and pull it open. When she did she was shocked to see Constancia, her parents' nearest neighbor, leaning against the doorjamb and wailing as if she had just peeked into hell itself.

"What is it?" Isabella whispered, surprised that her voice worked at all as she stepped back to let Constancia inside. "What has happened?" Before the woman could speak, Isabella knew the news somehow involved her family and that it was even worse than she had imagined.

"Your parents," the woman sobbed, nearly falling into the house, her wide, horrified eyes fixed on Isabella. "Your whole family," she cried, collapsing into Isabella's arms and weeping warm, wet tears that quickly soaked the plain cotton cloth that covered the younger woman's shoulder. "They're dead—all of them! They killed them all. They came with guns and—"

Isabella's heart froze. What was Constancia saying? Guns? Who came with guns? Surely she was mistaken. Who would want to kill her family? Why?

Taking her former neighbor's arms in her hands and pushing back so she could look into the woman's face, Isabella forced herself to breathe deeply and then asked, "What are you saying, Constancia? What has happened to my family? Calm down and tell me. Surely you are wrong. They cannot be dead. It is not possible. I just saw them this morning when I went to visit."

Constancia paused, and Isabella could see that she was struggling to calm herself. It was not working. "They are dead, I tell you," she repeated between sobs, her voice slightly softer this time. "I wish with all my heart that they were not, but they are. They have to be. The men in the car drove by and...and they shot and shot and shot until there was not a spot in the walls without bullet holes. They have to be dead, Isabella. No one could have survived that. No one."

Isabella tried to focus, tried to make sense of the woman's words, but all she knew at that moment was that she needed to go there, to the home where she had grown up and where she had gone that morning to visit. She had to see for herself that Constancia was wrong, that her *familia* was alive and all was as it had been when she left just a few hours earlier.

As if the woman's flesh were on fire, Isabella released Constancia's arms and spun toward the door, hurrying out into the afternoon sunlight and increasing her pace as she scurried along the familiar pathway toward her family's home, just a few blocks away. The faces of her beloved parents, as well as her little brothers, Antonio and Miguel, and her only sister, Teresa, danced in front of her eyes. Constancia's screams to stop only spurred her into a dead run, as she prayed to an impersonal God she did not know very well but whom she hoped was listening and would somehow answer.

Isabella's memory skipped the horror of what she had found at her parents' home, confirming in the worst possible way that everything Constancia had told her was true, though to this day she had no real answers as to why. Some said it was because her father refused to bow and scrape to the *bandidos* and *criminales* who had invaded their neighborhood; others said it could have been a mistake, the wrong house; still others said *los malos*, the bad ones, needed no reason—they killed because they were killers. Whatever the reason, Isabella's family was dead, the police had made no arrests, and the grieving young woman was certain her heart would never be whole again.

Now, still shivering in the bone-chilling cold of the desert night while her husband held her in his sleep, she forced her mind past the carnage at her family's home to one of the last times she had sat at the rough, round table in her *abuelo's casita*, sipping his strong coffee and sharing a piece of *pan dulce* as she searched for reasons to turn down his stunning offer. The memory of that small piece of sweet bread made her mouth water, as her stomach growled at the thought. What she wouldn't give to have just one *pan dulce*—or even a plain *tortilla*—to share with her husband right now!

"I . . . we can't do it, *Abuelo*," she had argued that day just a few weeks earlier, still reeling from the revelation that her grandfather had somehow managed to save several hundred dollars over the years and that he would now offer it to her and Francisco.

"You must," he had countered, his lined face and gnarled hands tearing at Isabella's heart. How could she even consider leaving this beloved man and fleeing with Francisco to a strange and foreign land where they scarcely spoke or understood the language? Even if they were successful in their attempt to cross the border and find employment on the other side, what would happen to her *abuelo*, Don Alfredo Montiel, the respected patriarch of their *familia* who had held them together for so many years, long after the death of his wife?

"If not for yourself and Francisco," Don Alfredo continued, "then you must do it for your *bebito*, who will be born before you know it. Since the murder of . . ." His voice trailed off, and his rheumy eyes watered as he fought for composure. "Since that horrible day, the violence has only become worse, and it will continue to do so. Do you really want your little one exposed to such danger? And you cannot argue that Francisco is having a more difficult time finding work every day. Besides, both you and Francisco have learned enough English through the years to get by north of the border, so it only makes sense for you to try to go."

"But what about you?" Isabella too was fighting tears. "We cannot leave you here to face such dangers by yourself, especially if you give us all your savings. How will you live, *Abuelo*? Who will care for you?"

Though his eyes still shone, Don Alfredo smiled and reached across the table to cover Isabella's small hand with his own. "*Gracias a Dios*," he whispered. "Thanks to God, I don't have to worry about that. He is the One who has cared for me all these years, and He is the One who will see me safely home when my days here are finished. You do not need to worry, *mijita*. Just as you are my little one and I wish to care for you, so *El Señor* considers me His *mijito* and wishes to care for me. You must always remember that, wherever you go." He paused. "*Comprendes*? Do you understand?"

Isabella doubted that she did, but she did not want to hurt her *abuelo's* feelings or cause him any undue concern. She nodded. "*Sí, Abuelo*. I understand."

"Good. Then it is settled."

"No," she argued. "It is not settled. Even if we agree to take the money to pay the *coyotes* to take us across the border, what will we do then?"

Don Alfredo's eyes narrowed, and his face became serious. "You must trust *El Señor* each step of the way. Pray before approaching a *coyote*, as many of them are dishonest and even dangerous. And pray once you are there as well. God will guide your steps if you will let Him."

"But, *Abuelo*," Isabella had pleaded, "why can't you come with us? I do not want to go without you."

Don Alfredo patted his granddaughter's hand. "Francisco is your family now—and the *bebito* in your tummy. You must make a new life for yourselves while you are still young. I am too old to go with you; I would only hold you back. Besides, my days are nearly over. God has numbered them, and soon I will go to be with Him. It will be a glorious day, and I look forward to it, but until then, I must stay here and pray for you as you go on without me."

"But, *Abuelo*—"

"No more," Don Alfredo said, shaking his head. "It is finished. You and Francisco make your plans, and when you are ready, I will give you the money. Now go. Talk to your *esposo*. God will go with you, *mijita*. Remember that."

As the mournful howl of what Isabella hoped was not a hungry wolf echoed in the starlit sky, the young pregnant woman remembered her *abuelo's* words but was having more and more trouble believing them with each passing minute.

Miriam couldn't sleep—again. This was getting to be a bad habit, but there seemed to be nothing she could do about it. When David was alive...

Her heart squeezed against the pain of remembering, and she blinked away the tears she refused to allow herself to shed. She had cried enough—rivers and oceans enough—and nothing had changed. David was dead, and that was that. Final. Finished. Futile. And all because of some slime-ball who wanted to smuggle drugs across the border.

When would the government learn? Worse yet, when would they do something to stop the illegal activity that had already taken so many lives? Deep down, Miriam suspected they already knew how bad it was, but for whatever reason they simply weren't willing to deal with it. And that's what made her so angry.

The night was cold, but the stars shone bright in the Arizona sky, as a wolf howled at a sliver of the moon. Wrapped in a blanket and sipping the last of a once-hot cup of coffee, Miriam sat curled up in a wicker rocking chair on the broad porch that nearly surrounded the old farmhouse where she and David had begun their married life eight years earlier. They'd had so many dreams then, so many plans. They just hadn't had enough time to see them come to pass—except for Davey.

Her long legs tucked under her tall, five-feet-eight frame, Miriam clasped the mug in her hands and stared out over the barely visible expanse of the small spread she had grown to love but that now seemed so alien to her. If it weren't for her six-year-old son, who bore his father's name not to mention his good looks, she would sell this place for whatever she could get for it and move as far away as possible. But Davey loved it here; it was the only home he had ever known, and he had already lost too much in his short life. Miriam couldn't bear to take any more from him.

And so she had stayed, after that devastating night when the news had arrived at her front door in the form of two border patrol agents, men David had known and worked with for years and whose wives were acquaintances of Miriam's. She had known the moment she opened the door and saw them standing there—maybe even before that, when she first heard the knock so many hours before daylight. David was gone, killed in the line of duty, murdered by some lowlife drug smuggler who had no business crossing the border with guns and narcotics and no papers giving him permission to even be here. How she hated him for that! She hoped he rotted in prison and went straight to hell from there.

An owl hooted from the roof of the nearby barn, and she took a last sip of lukewarm coffee. David was never able to drink anything with caffeine late in the day if he wanted to get any sleep at all, but it didn't bother Miriam. Before her life had been ripped apart eight months earlier, she could drink an entire pot of strong coffee and go straight to bed and sleep like a baby; now she spent most of her nights tossing and turning and cursing the God who had abandoned her.

Miriam's mother, Carolyn Sinclair, had come to stay with Miriam and Davey when David died, and had seemingly dedicated herself to trying to convince Miriam that God never abandoned anyone. "He has promised never to leave or forsake us," she told Miriam, time and again. "He's just a prayer away."

But Miriam didn't believe her. Even now, with no one to see, she shook her head as if to emphasize the thought, her long red-gold ponytail swishing from the movement. She might have believed it at one time, but not now—now that a so-called loving God had taken away the only man she had ever cared about, the finest man who ever lived, and for what? For a common criminal who wasn't good enough to wipe the sweat from her husband's brow.

Miriam loved her mother, but she no longer put any stock in anything the woman said. God had not only abandoned her, but He had betrayed her as well...and no one was going to convince her otherwise.

CHAPTER 2

DON ALFREDO HAD PASSED THE NIGHT IN COMMUNION WITH GOD. Since his wife had died nearly fifteen years earlier, *El Señor* had been his constant companion. Pouring out his heart to the faithful One and listening for His response had become such a habit to the old man that he could not imagine living any other way.

The early hints of morning light were just beginning to tease the sky and infiltrate the window beside the bed where he had once slept with Esmerelda, often lying awake to listen to her even breathing and to marvel that he would be so blessed as to share his life with such a beautiful woman. Even now, these many years later, the memories of their life together sparked a melancholy longing in his heart that only increased his yearning to leave this world and go home to be with *El Señor*.

But it was not so much the thoughts of Esmerelda that had kept him awake throughout the long, dark night, but rather concerns for his precious *nieta*, his granddaughter Isabella, and her *esposo*, Francisco.

And their bebito, he reminded himself. *A tiny life, fashioned and purposed by* El Señor Himself. *Surely, Lord, You will protect that helpless little one, that entire family that is only now beginning their life together. Mercy to them, Father! Protection and blessings,* por favor! *Please,* Señor, *guide and provide for them this day. Do not let their trip be in vain.*

With yet another prayer for his loved ones echoing in his heart, the old man ignored the arthritis that complained as he pulled himself from the warm comfort of his bed and rubbed his heavy eyes. Perhaps he would sleep later, dozing in the noonday sun in his favorite chair in front of his *casita*. It was his favorite place to pass the day, as he caught up on sleep he often missed during the night and greeted an occasional friend and neighbor as they passed by. Once in a while, one or two of them stopped to visit and to share a cool drink with him on a warm day, but mostly they just nodded and called out a greeting or offered a word of sympathy or consolation as they went about their business. It was enough. Don Alfredo did not need a lot of companionship, though he dearly missed his son and daughter-in-law, not to mention their three younger children who were killed along with their parents in the senseless attack.

Thank God that at least Isabella was spared! If she had not already been married and living elsewhere with Francisco, she too would undoubtedly have been listed among the dead. Don Alfredo's faith was strong, but he could not imagine enduring an even deeper level of grief than was already his to bear. He rejoiced to know that he would certainly see his family again, as they had all been dedicated to *Jesucristo*, but oh, the pain of waiting until that time!

Isabella, he thought, rummaging through his nearly bare icebox for a couple of leftover tortillas to warm and have with his reheated coffee from the day before. *My beautiful* nieta, *the only one in her family whose faith was not steadfast as the others, the only one who sometimes questions the truth of* El Señor *and His Word and never gave her heart and life to His Son. Of course she had to be spared! The others' destiny was sure; Isabella's was not. May it be so very, very soon, Father . . . regardless of the price.*

He flinched at the implications of his own prayer, not because he doubted that *El Señor* would answer, but because he was certain He would. Don Alfredo was well acquainted with the faithfulness of God, but he also knew that the road to fulfillment of His purposes was nearly always costly to those who traveled there.

Isabella awoke to the realization that her *esposo* was no longer wrapped around her, though she recognized immediately that his jacket was spread over her shoulders. She opened her burning eyes and wondered just how dry and scratchy they would get before they became permanently like the gritty dirt and sand they trudged through during the day and slept on at night.

Her stomach heavy and devoid of movement, she lifted herself to a sitting position, leaning on one arm while she searched for Francisco in the morning light. She did not have to look far. As she had seen him more than once these last few days, she observed him now, shivering in his shirtsleeves as he knelt on the ground and mumbled his petitions to God. Her heart contracted with love and gratitude to think that he was praying for her and their child, and she hoped above all reason that *El Señor* would pay more attention to her *esposo's* prayers than He had to hers when her family was killed.

Standing carefully on shaky legs and still aching feet, she hobbled to Francisco's side. When he did not look up or acknowledge her presence, she laid a whisper-touch of her fingers on his shoulder. Still he did not move but continued to pray, though she could scarcely make out his words. She took his jacket from her own shoulders and spread it across his back, and at last he said "amen" and lifted his head. His smile warmed her heart more than the sun that even now began its steady climb into the heavens.

"Good morning, *mi amor*," he said, standing to his feet. "Did you sleep well, my love?"

She nodded. "*Sí*," she lied, knowing he did not believe her.

He stood nearly a head taller than she, and as she looked up into the face she loved so deeply, she was shocked to realize how much weight he had lost in such a short time. Did he see the same thing in her? The way her clothes had begun to hang on her, even around her middle where the baby should be filling them out, convinced her that he not only realized how thin she had become but had been praying about the situation as well.

"We will find food today," he whispered, pulling her close. "I am sure of it. I have prayed, and *El Señor* will answer."

Isabella wanted to ask why *El Señor* had not answered when both she and Francisco had prayed the same thing the day before, but she clamped her mouth shut and leaned into her husband's chest, relishing the feel of his strong arms pulling her close. But how long could he remain strong if they did not find food very soon?

She sighed and closed her eyes, letting Francisco bear her weight as she relaxed in his embrace. Better not to say anything, she thought. After all, her husband's faith was so much stronger than her own—nearly as strong as her parents' had been and her *abuelo's* was even now.

Her *familia*—mother, father, brothers, and sister—all gone now, except for her *abuelo* . . . and Francisco and the *bebito*, of course. But *Abuelo* was old and would soon go to join his *esposa* in heaven—at least, that is what he had told her many, many times. And unless things changed quickly, she and Francisco and the baby would all die together, miles from anyone who knew or cared about them. It seemed a sad and pointless way to have lived and died, she decided, not yet ready to let go of the tiny thread of hope that *El Señor* would hear and answer—and rescue them before it was too late.

Davey was glad there was no school that day. The first-grader liked his teacher and enjoyed playing with his friends at recess, but a day at home was always better than a day at school. He just wished his father were still alive so they could do something together.

Bouncing out of bed, he slid his feet into the scuffed cowboy boots that were his constant companions. His dad had bought them just before he died, and Davey had been so proud. Now he had boots like his father! When they rode the horses across their thirty acres under the Arizona sun, he knew he wanted to be like his dad when he grew up. But it was the last time they had ridden together. His mom took him out occasionally, but he knew she didn't share his passion for horses the way his father had.

He pushed and squeezed until his feet were jammed into the pointed-toe contraptions that his mother insisted were too small for him to continue wearing. But there was no way he was going to give them up. He'd wear them until there was absolutely no way to get them over his feet, and then he'd make a special place for them on top of his dresser so he could see them every night before he went to sleep and every morning when he woke up.

Blinking away tears at the thought, he clunked his way across the hardwood floor from his room to the kitchen. His dad had been the first one up when he was home and not working the night shift, and he always made coffee for himself and Davey's mom, and hot chocolate for Davey. No hot chocolate awaited him this morning, though. The kitchen was cold and empty, and Davey was pretty sure he knew why. He had heard his mother roaming around during the night, no doubt making coffee and going out to sit on the front porch to drink it. Now she was catching a little bit of sleep. The only thing that bothered Davey more than his dad being gone was how angry his mom seemed to be since it happened. He pushed the thought aside and climbed up onto the counter to reach the cupboards. Before he could open them, he heard a voice from behind.

"Hey, sport."

Davey turned and grinned. Mom might still be catching a little shut-eye, but at least Grandma was up. Her short, reddish-gold hair was as neat as it ever was, though the gray streaks looked shinier under the kitchen lights. Davey wondered why her hair didn't stick up in frizzes and cowlicks like his did when he woke up.

"Hungry?" she asked.

Though he still felt a pang of guilt when he admitted to being hungry, somehow believing he shouldn't be thinking about food since his dad died, he nodded. "Starved," he admitted. "I was looking for some cereal."

Carolyn Sinclair smiled, her green eyes twinkling, and Davey thought again how much his grandma and mom looked alike—but how different they were inside. He loved them both and was really glad his grandmother had come to live with them after his dad died. But Grandma Carolyn was so calm and peaceful, while his mom—at least since his dad died—seemed ready to spin around the room and spit and scream if he said the wrong thing. As a result, he reserved most of his talking for his grandma, unless his mom seemed in a rare, quiet mood.

"Forget the cereal," his grandma said, wrapping her arms around his waist and lifting him down from the countertop. "What we need this morning is some nice hot chocolate and pancakes with lots of syrup. What do you say?"

As she set him down on the floor, he looked up and nodded, once again blinking away the tears that came at the reminder of the father he missed so very much. "That would be great. I love hot chocolate and pancakes."

Carolyn laughed and ruffled his already mussed brown curls. "I know you do," she said, and then bent down and winked. "Don't tell anyone, but so do I. So let's get busy, shall we?"

For a brief moment the ever-present ache in Davey's heart lightened and he giggled. Even without his dad here to share it with him, this was going to be a good day.

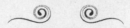

CHAPTER 3

M IRIAM HEARD THE VOICES COMING FROM THE KITCHEN AND
sighed with mixed emotions. She was grateful to have her
mother there to help with Davey, but she couldn't help but feel
guilty about the situation.

I should be the one out there making breakfast for my son, she thought,
as she huddled under the covers on the far right side of the
sprawling king-sized bed. Before David died she had always slept
on the left side, but since that first night when she'd been told of
her husband's death, she had instinctively curled up on his side,
clutching his pillow and sobbing as she tried to hold on to his
smell as long as possible. The thought that she might forget it—or
worse yet, forget the sound of his voice or the way he smiled—was
too terrifying to contemplate. She knew she could always watch
an old home video to see and hear him, but she couldn't bear to
think that she'd have to do so in order not to forget him.

Missing his touch was the hardest part. No matter how hard a
day they might have had or even if they'd argued before coming
to bed, once there they always seemed to end up back in one

another's arms, usually with her head resting on his broad, strong shoulder as they drifted off to sleep. Her handsome border patrol agent husband had, of necessity, kept himself in excellent physical condition, and Miriam had wanted to believe he was invincible. Quite obviously she had been wrong.

Laughter from the kitchen pierced her heart, even as the rising sun pushed against the heavy, dark drapes of her lonely bedroom. They were expecting another warm day—not summertime warm, but certainly well into the low nineties. Hard to believe when the cool, early morning air kept her lolling in bed under the covers.

Wait a minute. She frowned and peered at the alarm clock beside her bed. Why hadn't it gone off? And then she remembered. No school today. That was the reason her son and mother were spending so much time in the kitchen, preparing what her nose told her was a large breakfast rather than gulping down a bowl of cereal. She could smell the bacon and had no doubt that pancakes were bubbling on the griddle right beside the meaty strips.

She sighed and threw back the covers, sitting up and sliding her feet into her well-worn slippers. Might as well get started with her day. There was plenty to be done, even on a small thirty-acre spread. And though she had a little income in the form of widow's benefits, she wasn't about to waste it by hiring someone to mend fences or feed the cows. She'd do all that herself, as well as carve out some time for her advertising business, which she did from home on a very part-time basis. Thankfully her mother had taken over the majority of the household chores, and one day Davey would be old enough to do more than straighten up his room and take out the trash. Until then, she'd better get busy and quit lying around in bed feeling sorry for herself.

"Nopalitos."

Isabella paused in her torturous trek, following in Francisco's footsteps. What had her husband said? Nopalitos? She knew it meant some sort of cactus, for she had even eaten some on occasion at her *abuelo's* house. But why had her *esposo* mentioned them?

Francisco stopped in front of her, and she stepped up beside him. "What is it?" she asked, praying their prolonged exposure and lack of nutrition weren't taking a toll on her husband's sanity.

He lifted a hand and pointed. "*Nopalitos*," he repeated. "There. Look."

She followed the direction of his finger and saw the stand of flowered cacti just a few yards in front of them. Were those desert plants with their many needles the same as the *nopalitos* her *abuelo* cooked and ate with eggs? She had never been crazy about *huevos* and *nopalitos*, but if the plants she was staring at were indeed the same as the ones her *abuelo* loved to eat, then perhaps they would not starve to death as she had expected.

"Are you sure?" she said. "Are they the ones my *abuelo* eats?"

Francisco shrugged. "I think so. I have never seen them except when he served them to me on a plate a few months ago, but I have seen pictures of them." He looked down at her, his dark eyes hopeful for the first time in days. "If that is what they are, we can get moisture out of them and food too."

Isabella's stomach growled just as her *bebito* stirred for the first time that morning. So he was still alive after all. She nodded. "Let's try it. But how will we get past those awful stickers?"

Francisco dug a small knife from his pocket and held it up for her to see. It glistened in the sunlight, as he smiled and then bent down to kiss her on the forehead. "*Con mucho cuidado*," he said. "Very carefully." And she almost laughed with delight.

Don Alfredo nodded to the young family that walked by in front of his house as he sat in his favorite old chair under the noonday sun. He had seen them pass by often but had never conversed with them beyond a brief greeting or a casual comment about the weather. He had observed, however, that they were one of the few families that still walked the streets of their neighborhood on a regular basis. Most had taken to staying off the streets unless absolutely necessary, but a handful seemed determined to defy the growing violence and carry on with their lives.

The weather was nearly always pleasant in and around Ensenada—in all of Baja, for that matter—and today was no exception. But as Don Alfredo listened to the excited chatter of the two younger children skipping along in the company of their parents and teenage sister, the old man could not help but wonder what it was like for Isabella and Francisco who, by now, should be at the safe house outside of Phoenix.

Had they arrived safely? Was Isabella feeling all right? And the *bebito*? What about Francisco? Had he found a job? How long until he heard from them? And what if he never did? It had certainly happened before. Families split up as one or more members dared to cross the border into the United States in hope of finding a better life, promising to send money home to those who stayed behind. Occasionally it happened that way; most of the time, it did not. Much more common were the stories of those who were caught by border patrol agents and returned to Mexico, heartbroken at their failure to successfully make the crossing and more destitute than ever after giving every *centavo* they had to unscrupulous *coyotes*. But the saddest stories were of those who left, full of hopes and dreams, never to return or be heard from again. How he prayed his *nieta* and her *esposo* would not be among them!

"*Señor*," he whispered, closing his eyes against the gentle breeze that cooled his brow beneath the wide-brimmed straw hat that was his trademark anytime he stepped outside, "forgive me for worrying. I know they are in Your hands, and there is no safer place to be. You are our only hope . . . and that is all we need. Just You, Lord. Just You."

The children's voices died away, leaving only the sound of a dog barking in the distance to penetrate the old man's silence. He kept his eyes closed. Perhaps he could doze a bit as he passed yet another day alone except for the presence of the One who never left his side.

CHAPTER 4

ISABELLA'S STOMACH FELT SLIGHTLY MORE COMFORTABLE NOW, THOUGH the *nopalitos* had not been nearly as good uncooked as they had been when she ate them with her *abuelo*—and she had not been particularly fond of them then. But at least she and Francisco had received some much needed nourishment to help them press on in their trek through this ugly, endless desert. And she had promised Francisco to watch for more of the flowered cacti with their life-preserving qualities. Perhaps the prickly plants would keep them alive long enough to reach some sort of civilization, though what they would do when they arrived she had no idea, and she did not imagine that Francisco did either.

Francisco, she thought, as she watched her husband trudge ahead of her by a couple of paces. *My poor esposo! You tried to be careful, but still you ended up with many stickers in your hands. You said they don't hurt much, but I know you too well to believe that. I see the pain in your face, and yet you keep going, praying and doing everything you can to protect me and our little one. Though I am still not sure El Señor had anything to do with us finding the nopalitos, I am grateful to Him for allowing me to be your esposa.*

The sun was nearly directly overhead now, and Isabella wondered how they would survive another day in the heat. Apparently Francisco wondered the same thing, for he stopped his journey and turned to her, a halfhearted smile only slightly masking his pain and concern.

"There is a rock overhang ahead, big enough that I think we can rest in its shade until the sun goes down a little and the heat is not so bad. We should stay there for a couple of hours."

Isabella nodded. She knew it was her *esposo's* concern for her and the *bebito* that spurred him to make such a suggestion, on his own he would continue on until he could not take another step. Her aching feet and weary back were grateful for his suggestion. In moments they were once again huddled together, taking refuge in a sliver of shade. This time she had no problem falling asleep.

Carolyn Sinclair sat in the relatively cool shade of the front porch, concerned only slightly that for the third time in as many days she found herself feeling short of breath. She dismissed it as a natural part of the early aging process and instead focused on watching her only grandchild practice throwing a lasso over a tree stump in the front yard. The family's aging golden lab, Rocky, lazed in the sunshine, occasionally opening one eye to check on Davey's activities. Carolyn knew it was Davey's father who had sparked the interest in the boy to ride horses and throw a rope and mend a fence and any of the other dozen or more things that needed doing to run even a small farm in the Arizona desert. She knew too that her daughter, Miriam, had little or no interest in such things since her husband died but that she continued to try to keep the place going for Davey's sake.

I wish Davey were old enough to understand that, she thought, watching the warm afternoon sunshine sparkle on the boy's light brown curls. The determination in his face each time he tossed the rope, even though he had yet to do any more than graze the stump, squeezed her heart. Though the boy was so much like his father, he had a lot of his mother in him too. Miriam had also been a determined child, more headstrong than Davey, perhaps, but a delight nonetheless. Now it seemed she was angry at the world—and certainly at God—for taking away her husband. Carolyn understood the pain of grief, as she too had lost her husband only a few years earlier, but she was concerned that Miriam's loss was driving her to bitterness and despair. Poor Davey didn't realize that his mother's anger wasn't directed at him, and Carolyn had no idea how to help him understand that fact.

But You know, Lord, she prayed. *You know how to help Davey see what's really going on in his mother's heart and how much she loves him. You know too how to reach Miriam and heal her pain—and most of all, bring her back to You. Oh, Father, please help us all! Bring something good out of this terrible loss, as only You can do.*

Don Alfredo awoke to what sounded like gunfire. Jerking himself upward in the chair where he had passed most of the afternoon, napping and praying, his eyes widened as he strained to zero in on his surroundings. When the sound repeated, he realized it was a car, backfiring, and his shoulders relaxed.

Since the shooting of his family, the violence that had invaded their once peaceful neighborhood had become a reality that kept not only Don Alfredo but others on edge as well. From the stance of his neighbor across the street, which was actually a pothole-filled dirt road, Don Alfredo realized he was not the only one who mistook the car's backfiring for a rifle report. Don Felipe, who was only slightly younger than Don Alfredo, had stopped hoeing his small garden and straightened to attention, but now he too relaxed and waved in Don Alfredo's direction.

The old man returned the gesture and then slowly pulled himself to his feet. He had been in the sunshine long enough, and he was thirsty. He shuffled into the little two-room *casita* that had been his home almost his entire adult life and poured a glass of cool water from the pitcher that sat in the middle of the table.

Sitting down to sip from the glass, he savored the taste and feel of the soothing liquid and was surprised to find himself wondering if Francisco and Isabella had enough water to drink.

Surely they do, he thought. *They should have made it through the desert days ago and already be at the safe house, settled in as they begin their new life in America.* He closed his eyes. "*Por favor*, Señor," he whispered, "please, may that be true. I cannot let myself think that anything could have happened to them, that they might be hurt or suffering or..."

Tears burned his eyes, as a sob shook his still broad shoulders. For the first time he allowed himself to consider that he might have made a terrible mistake by urging the young couple to try to escape across the border. He knew there were many dangers along the way, and always there was the thought that perhaps *El Señor* would not bless them because they were doing something illegal. A stream of tears trickled down his face then, tracing the wrinkles that had settled there over the years. "If I was wrong," he prayed, his head bowed now as he set his glass down and folded his hands in supplication, "let the consequences be on me, *Señor*... not them. *Por favor*, protect and bless them. They are so young, while I... I am just an old man, a *viejo*, whose life on earth is behind me now. Forgive me if I was wrong to send them away. I only wanted to help them, to give them and their *bebito* a chance."

He sobbed again, as he waited for an answer he knew from experience might not come as quickly as he would like.

A Christmas Journey Home

CHAPTER 5

THE WORST OF THE AFTERNOON HEAT WAS OVER BY THE TIME Isabella awoke. Francisco sat beside her, picking at the stickers from the *nopalitos*. She remembered her *abuelo* saying those stickers weren't as bad as the ones from other types of cacti, so long as you removed them quickly. All her *esposo* had to work with was his knife, when what he really needed was a pair of tweezers.

She reached out and gently laid her hand on his arm. Francisco raised his head and smiled at her. "You slept well," he observed, and she nodded. He closed the knife and returned it to his pocket before standing to his feet and reaching down to take her hand and help her up. Isabella felt a surge of strength from his touch, and she was encouraged that perhaps their refreshment from the *nopalitos* had renewed them enough to go on. And though the afternoon sun had cooled, they still had enough time before dark to cover a few miles.

Which is good if we are headed in the right direction, she thought, brushing the dirt from the back of her long, filthy skirt. *Francisco says he knows which way to go by watching the sun. I pray he is right.*

Her own words snagged her thoughts, as she realized that once again she was praying. But was *El Señor* listening? And even if He heard, would He answer? Why should He? She certainly had not been a faithful follower during her lifetime, limiting her few communications with Him to times like these—when she was in trouble or danger.

Am I the only one who prays when I need help, even if at no other time? The question bothered her more than it ever had before. Her *abuelo*, her parents and siblings, and even her *esposo* had always talked with *El Señor* as if they knew Him personally. How was that possible? It did not even make sense, and yet—

Francisco had already stepped out onto the seemingly never-ending sand and begun their late afternoon trek into the desert, and she realized she had better do the same before he got too far ahead of her. Moving from the shade of the rock that had been their shelter as she slept, she followed the man she loved and trusted, wishing she had the same sort of confidence in *El Señor* Himself.

Nightfall came far too soon, and Isabella wondered how much progress, if any, they had made toward their destination of Phoenix, Arizona. The question of what they would do if and when they got there danced around the edges of her mind, though she refused to allow it a place in her conscious thoughts for fear that she would have to admit they had no answer. She had heard Phoenix was a very large city, larger even than Ensenada, and that most people there were not too welcoming to her kind. Would they be arrested and put in jail? Sent back to Mexico? Worse yet, hurt or killed? Was this exhausting and terrifying trip across the desert a useless venture that would only take them to a worse fate? She reminded herself that at least she and Francisco spoke enough of the language to get by, which was an advantage over many of those who tried to sneak into America. Having lived in a border town filled with tourists from the United States had nearly ensured

A Christmas Journey Home

Ensenada citizens of learning English if they applied themselves and paid attention, but those from deeper within Mexico had little or no chance of learning English unless they were wealthy enough to attend the best of schools.

At last Francisco stopped, and she had been following so closely to him as the sky darkened above them that she nearly ran into him. He turned and took her into his arms. "You are tired, are you not, *mi amor?*"

Though she did not want to admit her weariness and prevent them from going on if that was his desire, she nearly melted at his term of endearment. She loved it when he called her *novia*, sweetheart, before they were married, and *mi querida*, my dear, but her favorite was *mi amor*, my love. Isabella knew she belonged to Francisco, and he to her. She could not imagine her life without him. The very thought forced a shiver up her back, one she knew her *esposo* could not have missed.

Francisco pulled her close. "You are getting cold, as well as tired," he whispered. "We will find a place to spend the night."

Another night in this terrible place, Isabella thought. *How much longer can we survive? Will anyone ever find us or rescue us? It would be so much easier just to go to sleep and never wake up.*

She was ashamed at her thoughts. After all, she had a baby to think about. But she was so very tired, despite her brief nap earlier that afternoon.

"Here," Francisco said, stepping back and leading her by the arm to a spot where at least the sand appeared to be clear of rocks. "We will sleep here tonight."

Isabella nodded, too exhausted to argue. Besides, what difference did it make where they stopped for the night? Anywhere in the desert was cold once the sun disappeared, making sound sleep nearly impossible. But for her husband's sake—and the child's—she would try.

Soon the two of them were curled up in their familiar position, with Francisco wrapped around Isabella's backside in an attempt to keep her as warm as possible. Nearly certain that sleep would never come, she closed her eyes, grateful for her *esposo's* presence.

If they were to die, they would do so together. There was at least some peace in that.

Miriam was bone tired, every muscle in her body aching. And that was a good thing, she decided. It at least gave her hope that she might be able to sleep tonight and not spend the long, dark hours drinking coffee and staring at the starlit sky from her lonely porch.

She had accomplished a lot—nearly everything she had hoped to do that day, including mending a couple of fences and locating a stray calf that had become separated from its mother. David had hoped to add to their collection of animals—one dog, two barn cats, twelve cows, two pigs, three horses, and an assortment of chickens, roosters, and ducks. Miriam was glad he hadn't had a chance to do so before he died. The handful they had was more than enough to keep her busy. In fact, she had seriously considered selling off the majority of them—all but Rocky, of course, who was Davey's devoted companion, and the barn cats who kept the mice population from exploding. But each time she broached the subject, her son became so emotional at the very thought that she quickly changed the subject, not willing to put the boy through any more trauma.

"Are you going to tuck me in, or is Grandma?"

The hesitant voice caught her attention as she passed the open door to Davey's room. Was he really already bathed and tucked in bed? Apparently so—and no thanks to her. How she appreciated her mother's presence and help, but how it cut her to the heart when she realized how she was neglecting her own son.

She stopped and turned to stand in the doorway. Smiling, she said, "I'll do it tonight. I think Grandma might be tired by now."

Davey appeared unsure, but nodded. "She probably is. She's been taking care of me all day."

Miriam's heart felt as if it would implode from the impact of the innocently spoken but deeply cutting words. Of course her mother had been taking care of Davey all day. Who else would do it? Miriam would if she could, but there were so many other things to do, and—

She stopped herself mid-thought and stepped into Davey's room, still smiling down at him. His return gesture seemed apprehensive. What had she done to scare the poor child? Had she really become such a shrew that her own son was afraid of her outbursts?

Miriam sighed as she sat down on the edge of the bed. There was no denying it. She was angry and hurt, frustrated and exhausted—and not just once in a while but nearly all the time. And though she told herself each morning that she wasn't going to take out her pain on Davey or her mother, inevitably she found herself doing just that.

She laid a hand on her son's forehead and brushed back a stray curl. "How was your day? Did you and Grandma do anything interesting?"

Davey nodded. "Grandma watched me while I practiced lassoing the stump, and then later she took me into town for a hamburger and fries. We even had chocolate shakes."

Miriam felt her smile widen. "Sounds delicious. Wish I could have joined you."

A hint of sadness passed through Davey's dark blue eyes before he answered. "Me too," he said. "And Daddy."

His voice trailed off, as Miriam processed the end of his unspoken sentence. *And Daddy too. Yes, Daddy too. If only he were still here, we could all have gone, and your grandma wouldn't have had to give up her entire life and rent out her condo just to move here and help take care of you. But Daddy isn't here. He'll never be here again.*

She could feel her anger and sadness mounting, as they wrestled with one another for prominence. Best to banish them both.

"I'm glad you and Grandma had a good day," she said, reaching for a book on the nightstand. "But now it's bedtime. How about if I read your favorite book to you, and then you hit the hay. Just because you got to stay home from school today doesn't mean you have another day off tomorrow. It's up bright and early in the morning."

Davey nodded again, his smile back in place. "Yes, read to me, Mom. I'd like that. And then I promise to go to sleep."

Miriam's heart constricted, and she leaned down to kiss him on the forehead. Then she opened the book and began to read.

CHAPTER 6

THE MORNING SUN HAD BARELY RISEN ENOUGH TO STREAK THE edge of the horizon when Isabella was jolted out of a restless, nightmare-filled sleep. An angry voice assaulted them in both English and Spanish as she felt Francisco's grip tighten around her.

"*Quien eres?*" the male voice demanded. "Who are you? What is your name, and what are you doing out here?"

Isabella could feel Francisco's heart thumping against her back, and she held her breath so she would not cry out. At last her *esposo* spoke.

"We are Francisco and Isabella Alcántara," he said, his voice amazingly steady. "And who are you?"

A snicker in the semidarkness set off alarm bells in Isabella's thoughts. She had begun to hope they had been rescued and would get help, but now she was not so sure.

"No doubt you are American citizens," the voice sneered. "Just some innocent young couple who decided to spend a night in the desert, eh?"

Isabella sensed that Francisco had swallowed before answering again. "We are not hurting anyone," he answered. "We just want to be left alone."

As the morning light grew slightly brighter in the distance and Isabella's eyes became more accustomed to the lingering darkness, she made out the look of contempt on the face of the man who stood nearest them. Everyone else appeared as shadows standing behind him. How many were there? Eight? Ten? Maybe even a dozen? Some appeared smaller than others. Was it possible there were children among them? If so, perhaps they were families and were not as dangerous as she suspected from their leader's aggressive attitude.

"I think maybe you are like the rest of us," the man continued, his voice slightly softer now. "*Mexicanos* trying to reach a safe house in Phoenix. That is the truth, is it not?"

Isabella remained silent as she waited for her husband to answer. She felt the resignation in his shoulders as he slumped against her and relaxed his grip. "*Sí. Es la verdad.* What you say is the truth."

Isabella's heart raced. What would happen to them now? The man had indicated that he and his companions were here for the same reason as she and Francisco, but did she dare believe him? What if it was a trick?

The smile in the man's voice was evident now, as he chuckled and offered a hand to help them to their feet. "It seems we have found you just in time," he said. "It is not safe out here in the desert, not on your own or without a guide. How long have you been out here?"

Francisco accepted the man's gesture and allowed himself to be pulled to a standing position before reaching down and helping Isabella to do the same. "This is our fourth night," he answered. "Our guide took our money and deserted us. We have survived only on some *nopalitos* we found earlier today." He paused then, as he put his arm around Isabella and drew her close to his side. "Please," he said, his voice low. "My wife is pregnant. She needs food and shelter."

Isabella saw the man glance at her stomach before returning his gaze to Francisco. "We will help you," he said. "I am guiding these people behind me to a safe house, and you are welcome to come along. We have enough food and water to share with you until we get there."

So the man who had confronted them was a *coyote!* *Gracias a Dios* that he was not like the one who had stolen their money and left them to die. So there were decent *coyotes* after all!

Relief washed over Isabella as she realized they were not going to die in the desert as she had come to believe—not from exposure to the elements and not at the hands of violent thugs. The thought flashed through her mind that *El Señor* had heard their prayers and sent these people to rescue them. She was not sure if that was true, but she was willing at least to consider it. When her *bebito* kicked with vigor, she wondered if he somehow knew they were going to be all right.

Renewed hope surged in Francisco's heart as he felt his strength returning. A humble meal of *tortillas* and *frijoles* had never tasted so good, and the cool water from the *coyote's* canteen was the most refreshing he could imagine. Best of all, he could tell that Isabella felt stronger as well. The light in her eyes had come back, and he nearly cried at the sight.

Even the midmorning sun, shining almost directly overhead as they walked, did not seem so threatening as it had just the day before. Their stomachs were at least somewhat full, and their leader, whose name was Alberto, had assured them they would all arrive at the safe house by nightfall.

No more nights in the desert, Francisco thought. *No more nights of trying to protect my* esposa *and our* bebito *from the freezing wind and wondering if we would die before the sun rose again. ¡Gracias, Señor! ¡Gracias! You have heard our prayers and answered.*

Isabella walked beside him now, as he no longer felt the need to walk ahead of her, watching for snakes and other dangers so prevalent in the desert. He turned to look at her and found she was watching him as they continued forward. When their eyes met, she smiled.

"*Te amo*," she whispered. "I love you."

Francisco nodded before patting her protruding stomach. "And I love you, *mi querida*—and our *bebito* too." He raised his eyes from her middle where his hand still rested and focused back on the beautiful face of his beloved. "We are going to make it," he said, his heart warming as her smile widened.

"*Sí, mi amor*," she smiled taking his hand from her stomach and clasping it in her own as they trudged on behind the group, which they now knew consisted of four men, including the leader, three women, and four children, the oldest being a couple of teenage girls. "We are going to make it. We will find our new life here, and maybe even bring *Abuelo* to join us one day."

Francisco doubted her *abuelo* would ever leave his home in Mexico, but he was not about to say that to Isabella. He simply nodded again and walked on, anxious to reach their destination and find work so he could at last support his family.

The safe house appeared to be somewhat larger than the one Isabella had grown up in, and only slightly better in its condition. But it would at least be shelter, a place where they could lay their heads at night and know they would be safe. For that reason, as they waited in a nearby stand of trees for nightfall before approaching the house, Isabella thought it looked like a mansion.

She smiled at the thought. She had seen mansions before, beautiful, sprawling homes that rested in faraway neighborhoods and on the hillsides surrounding Ensenada and that seemed too big for one family to inhabit. But her parents had assured her that they were owned by only one family, not several. How rich those families must have been! Of course, such places were nowhere near the little *casita* where she lived with her parents and siblings, or the even smaller one where her *abuelo* lived. But sometimes, when her *papa* had earned a little extra *dinero*, he would treat his *familia* to a bus ride across town. There they would walk the streets and view these huge homes and wonder what it must be like to live in them. But always her *papa* would remind them that they needed to pray for the people who lived in those big houses exactly the same way they prayed for those who lived in the little ones like their own—and even those who lived in cardboard shacks or on the street.

"Everyone needs *Jesucristo*," he would tell them. "What you have here on earth means nothing when you breathe your last and go to stand in front of *El Señor*. The only thing He will ask of you is what you did about the great Gift He gave us through His Son. *El Señor* does not care about money or possessions, or how successful or popular you were on earth. He cares only if you know and love *Jesus*."

Strangely her father's words came back clearly to her this evening, as they huddled together and watched the dying rays of sunshine signal that the time was nearly here to cross the stretch of dirt beyond the trees and enter the safe house. For some reason she had expected the house to be in the middle of a populated neighborhood. Perhaps some were; this one was not. It seemed to be nearly out in the country, though Alberto had assured them they were close enough to Phoenix to get to work each day.

As their guide motioned for them to step out of the trees and head for the house, her heart raced at the thought they were so close to the new life her *abuelo* so desperately wanted for them. How much better she would feel about it all if she could be certain that her father's words about knowing and loving *Jesucristo* were really true.

CHAPTER 7

Don Alfredo cocked his head to the side, sensing that something was not right. He sat in his favorite chair in the sun once again, dozing and praying. Another day had come and gone, and still no word from Francisco and Isabella. Not that he expected anything quite so soon, but he would certainly rest easier once he knew they had arrived safely at their destination.

What was it that nagged at him now? What was it he listened for? Though his eyes were dim, his hearing was still good, but the only sounds that reached his ears were those of children playing in a yard nearby, and traffic passing in the distance. Not even a breath of wind blew past on this warm November day, and his cotton shirt clung to him as a result.

Still, he listened. When the whisper came, he knew it was *El Señor*, calling him to pray. Something was wrong. He had sensed it for days, but now it was stronger. Certainly it had to do with Francisco and Isabella. Had something happened to them? Were they in danger?

Pulling himself from the chair, he limped into the house, shaking his right foot as he walked, amazed at how quickly his blood flow stopped on its way to his limbs now that he was such a *viejo*. But it did not matter. His foot would reawaken in time. For now he must focus on praying for his little *familia*, wherever they were and whatever they were doing. *Gracias a Dios* that even though he did not have the answers or know the details, *El Señor* did—and He was calling his servant to battle. Don Alfredo would be faithful to answer the call.

Nearly a full day had passed since Francisco and Isabella had arrived with the others at the safe house. Though Isabella tried to tell herself that the conditions she found there were normal—not to mention temporary until she and her *esposo* could get a place of their own—she was already beginning to have her doubts. Something just did not seem right.

For one thing, the house had only three bedrooms and two bathrooms for the nearly thirty-five people currently staying there. One bedroom and bathroom were reserved solely for the owners of the home; another bedroom was strictly for the teenaged girls, while the remaining adults and children slept side by side on the floor in the third bedroom. When they had arrived the night before, Isabella had watched as the families who had come with them expressed concern over parents being separated from their daughters. Their complaints were ignored, and one of the mothers had cried for her daughter nearly all night. Muffled sounds of girls crying as well had drifted through the wall separating the two rooms, and Isabella had found herself feeling thankful that her own child was not yet born and could therefore not be taken from her for any reason.

She had frowned at the thought, even as the long hours of darkness crept by and several men kept her awake with their snoring. As they had in the desert, Francisco and Isabella lay spoon-fashion, though there was no longer any need for Francisco to shield her from icy winds. Still, Isabella had noticed that her *esposo* had not slept much better than she. The idea had danced through her thoughts for hours that if they were still at the safe house when their *bebito* was born, he might not be safe. The thought made her want to wake Francisco and beg him to take her back to Mexico immediately.

Of course she had not. Francisco needed his sleep so he could go out to find work in the morning. Alberto had told them he knew of day-labor jobs close by, and though Francisco's right hand still bothered him from the cactus needles, he assured Alberto that he would be ready for work as early as he needed to be.

The men, including Francisco, had left with Alberto before sunup, and Isabella had found herself thwarted in her attempts to start conversations with the women who had been there awhile. She was curious about what to expect and tried to ask questions, but it seemed the women were afraid to answer. And so she had stuck as close as possible to the three women from the group she had met the day before, all of whom seemed as puzzled and frightened as she.

What is it about this place, she wondered as she prepared a large pot of stew in the kitchen as she had been instructed by the woman who lived in the home and was apparently in charge of any other females staying there. The woman's name was Olivia. She appeared to be somewhere in her forties, with salt-and-pepper hair pulled back in a clasp at the nape of her neck. It seemed to Isabella that the woman had a scowl permanently painted on her pudgy, unpleasant face.

I do not like it here, she mused, *but I cannot say why. After all, what did I expect? This is a strange country with strange ways, and these people are allowing us to stay here until we find jobs and homes of our own, so I suppose I should be grateful. But something just does not feel right.*

She stirred the stew, trying to assure herself that she would feel much better when Francisco got home that evening and they could talk about his job and plan their future. Sensing Olivia's icy stare, she turned to find the woman standing just feet behind her.

Isabella turned back to her work and wished she were somewhere else—anywhere, even back in the desert.

Miriam drove the beat-up old Ford pickup down the dusty road toward home, the bed of the truck filled with hay. The amount of food those animals, particularly the horses, consumed was reason enough to get rid of them, but she just couldn't bring herself to do it. Davey loved each one of them, so why break his heart again? She knew one day she might have to if the money ran out, but she'd hold off until then.

It had been another warm late autumn day, and she clung to the remnants of the season with a vengeance, not wanting to let go and allow the holidays to overwhelm her. Thanksgiving was just days away, and she could probably survive that one with her mother's help. But Christmas, the day that had been David's very favorite? Never. Though she knew she had no choice but to observe the day for her son's sake, she simply could not imagine getting through it without breaking down.

Memories of the previous Christmas danced in her head and tugged at her heart, forcing hot, burning tears into her eyes. David had gone all-out, as he always did, decorating the house and the barn, even lining the fences with tinsel and streamers to celebrate the Christ Child's birthday. Miriam hadn't minded a bit, and had even joined in with her husband and son as they sat on the porch on Christmas Eve, sipping hot chocolate and singing carols. Life had been nearly perfect then.

Then. The reminder pierced her heart, and she blinked away the tears and pressed on the gas. No time for sentimentality and self-pity; she needed to get the hay unloaded before dark, and until Davey was a few years older, the job would remain squarely on her own shoulders.

CHAPTER 8

FRANCISCO HAD RETURNED HOME WITH THE OTHER MEN NOT LONG after dark, looking exhausted and discouraged. Isabella watched him closely, wishing they could escape at least to the backyard where they could talk privately. But it seemed they were watched everywhere they went. They had even been told not to go outside without permission. If Isabella had not known better, she would have thought they were in some sort of prison.

At last they were able to curl up together in a far corner of the bedroom they shared with so many others. Muffling their voices as much as they could, Isabella and Francisco whispered to one another in the sweat-scented darkness. Other couples did the same.

"What sort of work did you do today?" Isabella asked, her lips pressed up against her *esposo's* ear.

"Digging," he whispered back. "There is some sort of construction going on not far from here, and while the *Americanos* work on the buildings, we *Mexicanos* dig and haul out dirt in wheelbarrows. It is hard work, but I do not mind that part. What

I do not like is that I saw the boss give *dinero* to Alberto at the end of the day, but when we who worked in the heat with nothing but a tiny flask of water and two dry *tortillas* asked for our wages, he said we would not get paid until the job was done." He shook his head. "I do not like that at all. The job could take weeks, maybe even months."

Isabella felt her heart jump. Months? If they did not get paid for months, they might still be in the safe house when their *bebito* was born. What would happen then? Surely they would not separate a newborn from its mother!

She started to voice her concerns, and then stopped. Francisco had enough to deal with already; he did not need her adding to his burden. She kissed his cheek. "It will be all right, *mi amor*. Surely they will pay you soon, and then we can find somewhere else to live."

She reached for his hand, but when she touched it he jerked away, a slight cry escaping his lips.

"What is it?" she asked, her concern mounting. "What is wrong, Francisco?"

He shook his head again. "It is nothing," he assured her. "Just the needles from the *nopalitos*. There are only a few I have not been able to dig out. I am fine. *Por favor*, do not worry. Alberto saw it today and said he would take care of it in the morning."

Isabella felt her eyes widen, and the thought that her husband's hand might be infected crossed her mind. "Do you think he will take you to a doctor?"

She felt her husband shrug his shoulders. "I do not know. He did not say what he intended to do, but he assured me he would fix me up first thing so it would be easier for me to work."

"So you will work again tomorrow?"

"Every day, *sí*. From what Alberto and the others say, every day except Sunday, when the construction site is closed." His voice softened. "I hope that means we can go to church on Sunday. I would like very much to gather with other followers of *Jesucristo* and to thank *El Señor* for getting us here safely—also to ask Him for direction and much wisdom about what to do next."

Isabella was not so certain that *El Señor* had brought them to safety after all, but she certainly hoped that He would answer her *esposo's* request for direction and wisdom. It had become quite obvious to her that unless things changed, they could not remain where they were much longer, but she had no idea where else they might go.

The men had left for work before sunup, and Isabella and a couple of other women were ordered to help in the garden beside the house. Though it had been chilly when they first started, the rising sun was already warming her as she hoed the weeds around the pumpkins and squash. Though they had never been her favorite foods, she was glad for the variety they gave to their otherwise boring diet of *tortillas, frijoles,* and fried potatoes. And at least she was outside in the fresh air.

She glanced at the woman who worked closest to her. Isabella had heard someone call her Lupe. The morning sun shone on her long dark hair, and Isabella thought the woman who appeared old enough to be Isabella's mother was probably quite attractive at one time. *She might still be,* Isabella mused, watching her bend down to yank on a stubborn weed, *if she was not so sad.*

It struck her then that all the workers who already lived at the safe house when she and Francisco and the others arrived looked sad. A jolt of fear pierced her heart at the thought. Why would they all be sad? One or two, maybe—leaving family behind, homesick for Mexico, personal problems. But all of them? It did not make sense, unless . . .

She shook her head and turned away from watching Lupe. She would concentrate on her work and not allow her thoughts to wander and to create problems that might not exist. Faint memories of stories she had overheard while still in Mexico about slave labor floated on the edges of reality, begging to be recognized, but she refused them. Those stories were just that—stories, not truth. Surely such a thing did not truly exist! And if it did, she and Francisco would never be caught up in it. They had come to America for a better life, to give their *bebito* a chance to survive and to grow up to make something of himself. It was not possible that they had taken every *centavo* her *abuelo* had saved over his lifetime just to lose it and end up in a worse condition than before they had left.

The memory of their tiny *casita* just outside Ensenada nearly broke her, as she felt her knees weaken and tears spring into her eyes. But she refused to yield to her emotions. If Francisco could work in the heat of the day, digging ditches with an injured hand and scarcely any food, then she could carry on with her simple task. At least she could relax a little, knowing that Alberto had promised to take care of Francisco's injury today. She could not bear to think that her *esposo* would work another day while still in pain. A sense of gratitude washed over her at the reminder that today was going better for him than the day before. Perhaps tomorrow would be even better still.

Fire shot through Francisco's right arm with each shovelful he dug and threw over his shoulder. Yesterday had been bad enough, with his right hand throbbing from the remaining cactus stickers, but he had been encouraged when Alberto told him he would take care of the situation for him first thing in the morning. In a way, he had, but not as Francisco had expected. Alberto had heated a knife in the fire and then told two of the stronger men to hold Francisco down while he lanced his hand. True, the remaining stickers were now gone, and Francisco was hopeful that the wound would heal quickly, but the pain was excruciating. When he had asked for something to dull the agony that had spread from his hand up his arm and into his shoulder, Alberto laughed and told him to be a man and get back to work.

And so he had, praying to *El Señor* for strength with each movement of his arm. Each time he pushed the shovel into the ground, the pain intensified, and he gritted his teeth, focusing on

Isabella and the *bebito*, and reminding himself how important it was to work hard so the three of them could move away from the safe house into a little place of their own. But as the sun continued to rise in the sky, standing directly overhead by noon when they were finally given a fifteen-minute break to drink their water and eat their *tortillas*, Francisco was seriously concerned that he might not make it until quitting time.

CHAPTER 9

As much as Isabella enjoyed being outside, her back was beginning to ache and she was drenched with sweat by the time the woman named Olivia came to call them inside. From the position of the sun, Isabella imagined it was just past noon, and she had long since used up the tiny bottle of water they had given her when she began her work hours earlier. She was more than ready to go back inside for a little refreshment and, hopefully, a rest.

The refreshment was limited to another small portion of cool water, which she drank greedily, and some leftover potatoes wrapped in a *tortilla*. But she ate it gratefully, relieved to feel her *bebito* kick in response.

There was to be no rest, however. Lupe ordered all the women who were new arrivals to sit down in the kitchen and pay close attention to her instructions.

"We go easy on you in the beginning," she said, her deep-set dark eyes scanning their faces as she spoke. "But now it is time that you understand what is expected of you while you are here. You left your country and came here to work, and work is exactly what you will do—no exceptions." She glanced briefly at Isabella's stomach before continuing. "What we really do not need around here is another mouth to feed, but babies are born and there is nothing to be done about it."

Her eyes returned to Isabella, causing a chill to pass over the frightened girl. Why was the woman singling her out? What was to become of her and her little one?

"When your time comes, you will be given a couple of days off to regain your strength. Then it is back to work with everyone else. If you can carry your baby in a sling around your neck and still carry your workload, fine. If not, we will have to make other arrangements."

Isabella felt her eyes widen. Other arrangements? What did that mean? But her throat closed up, and she could not utter a word. Heart racing, she waited for the woman to explain further, but the topic was quickly changed.

"Now," Olivia said, once again allowing her gaze to rove from one woman to the next, "in addition to cooking, cleaning, laundry, and working in the garden, you will be expected to turn your eyes and keep your mouth shut about anything you see going on in this house."

She paused for effect, and Isabella thought she felt an icy wind blow through the otherwise stifling kitchen. She shivered and sat very still, terrified at what might come next.

Olivia pursed her lips and raised her dark eyebrows. "We sometimes have *visitors* here, clients who . . . pay for certain services from our young female residents. You may hear or see them coming in and out at various times throughout the day or night hours, going into the girls' room. No matter what you hear or see or what anyone—including the girls—tells you, you are to say nothing. Do you understand?"

She paused again, and Isabella's ears rang as she held her breath, hoping she was misunderstanding what the woman was saying. Surely she did not mean—

Before she could finish her thought, Olivia continued. "You will say nothing about what goes on here, and you will do nothing."

She squinted her eyes and leaned forward slightly as she spoke. "If you do, there will be very, very bad consequences—for you and anyone else involved—especially the girls. Do you understand?"

One more time she paused, waiting, but no one moved or said a word. At last Olivia raised her voice and demanded, "Do you understand?"

Slight murmurs and nods followed, until at last Olivia dismissed them. "Now get back to work. Those who worked outside this morning will work in the kitchen and laundry room this afternoon. The rest of you, finish the cleaning assigned you this morning and then go back to the gardening outside." When no one moved, she shooed them with her hands. "Go on," she ordered. "Get to work—now! There are no free rides around here."

A sob from one of the women who had arrived at the home with Isabella broke the silence as they all rose from their chairs and began to make their way toward their assigned duties. Isabella realized the woman who was crying was the mother of the two teenage girls who had also come with their group. The implications shot what felt like a jagged bolt of lightning directly through Isabella's chest.

Don Alfredo was heartbroken. Another shooting had ripped through their neighborhood, only a couple of blocks from his own little *casita* and very near where his family had been killed a few months earlier. All this violence and for what? Drugs? Turf wars? Revenge?

The old man had spent most of the morning sitting in front of his house in the sun, but it had become too warm to stay there any longer. It was unusually warm for late *Noviembre*, though certainly not unheard of. Don Alfredo could even remember a few times at *Navidad* when the sun burned so brightly that his little *casita* sweltered from the heat, even as they celebrated the birth of *Jesucristo*. But he was getting older and his skin thinner, so both heat and cold bothered him more than when he was young. As a result, he had abandoned his outside perch and come back inside where at least he was not directly in the sun.

A cup of cool water soothed his dry throat as he reflected on the two deaths that had resulted from the most recent shooting. He had heard from several sources that there had been no known gang activity among the victims, reinforcing people's fears that innocent bystanders were being picked off as often as those actively involved in criminal activity. No one was safe, even in their own homes. And though Don Alfredo still agonized over the fact that he had yet to hear from Isabella and Francisco, and he continued to pray for them daily as he still sensed that things were not right with them, he was indeed glad that he had urged them to leave this place. The once peaceful neighborhood where he and Esmerelda had married and started their family so many years before was now a battleground, where families hesitated before stepping outside to take a stroll or send their children off to school.

The weight of evil nearly crushed the old man's heart until he fell on his knees beside his bed and bowed his weary head. *"Señor,"* he begged, *"¡ayúdame!* Help me! Let me feel Your love so that this fear may be driven from me. I am fearful for myself, for my neighbors, for Isabella and Francisco and their *bebito,* yet I know You are greater than anything that can come against us. *Por favor, Señor,* deliver me from this fear that I might be free to praise You and trust You!"

Praise Me first, came the whisper from deep within his heart, *and the fear will melt away.*

Don Alfredo nodded. Of course. How easily and often he forgot that simple truth! Choose to trust and praise and love God, regardless of what went on around him, and peace would drive out the fear.

"Gracias a Dios," he whispered. "Thank You for Your patience with me, *Señor.* Thank You for reminding me to praise and trust You, no matter what I see or feel. I do trust You, and I want to trust You more. Teach me to do that—to turn to You first—in everything. I am an old man, but I still have so very much to learn.

Help me to learn from You what You want me to know—and teach my beloved Isabella and Francisco the same, while they are still young and have many years ahead to serve You."

Isabella thought the day would never end. When at last she heard the van pull up in front of the house, she felt as if her heart would burst with relief. Along with the other women, she waited anxiously for the men to enter. When the door opened and the exhausted workers piled in, all Isabella could see was the pain-etched face of her beloved Francisco, his right hand bandaged as his sad eyes called to her. It was obvious he had been through a lot that day; how could she burden him with more bad news? And yet he had to know what a horrible place this was and how very much they needed to escape.

Francisco's smile was stiff as he opened his arms and gathered her to his chest. He smelled of earth and sweat, but she imagined that she did as well. Neither of them had been allowed to shower except the very first night they arrived. After that they were told they could bathe once a week, as there were too many people in the house for anything more.

Fried potatoes and *frijoles* awaited them on the table, with stacks of warm *tortillas* and cool pitchers of water. Pans of baked yellow squash made the offering almost festive, and the men helped themselves first, with the women and children following close behind, all of them ravenous after a long and strenuous day.

Except for the ones who have "clients," Isabella thought, remembering the two men who had come in earlier and made their way to the girls' bedroom after handing money to Lupe. Isabella noticed that one of the teenage girls who had arrived with them a couple of nights earlier was not standing in line for the food. One look at the girl's mother and it was obvious that her daughter was indeed being forced to "entertain" a client in the other room. The thought made Isabella's stomach churn.

Sickened, she took only a small portion of food and went to sit on the living room floor beside Francisco, who smiled at her in welcome. Sooner or later she was going to have to inform him about what went on in that house, but right now she could tell his hand was bothering him worse than it had the day before. He could scarcely hold his plate and feed himself, and her heart broke at the realization. Oh, what a terrible mistake they had made to leave their home in Mexico! Yes, it was dangerous there, but at least they knew the customs, and they had her *abuelo* who loved them. Here they had only one another—nothing more. Would that be enough? She wanted to believe it would be, but the sight of her struggling *esposo* made her doubt it very much.

Wordlessly, she set down her plate and reached out to help Francisco, who resisted only momentarily before smiling and accepting her assistance. It was obvious to Isabella that they were going to have to work together every step of the way if they were going to get out of here alive. The memory of her *abuelo* on his knees praying, as she had seen him do so very many times, offered her a brief ray of hope. Maybe she and Francisco weren't alone after all. If *El Señor* helped them, they just might have a chance.

CHAPTER 10

I SABELLA DOZED FITFULLY THROUGHOUT THE NIGHT, ARGUING WITH herself about whether or not to tell Francisco what she had learned about the things that went on in the girls' room. How many girls were actually in that room, being forced to participate? As best she had been able to estimate, there were about a dozen or so, sleeping in that room, some as young as eleven or twelve. Surely it was only the older ones who were forced into such vile acts! Yet even if that were true, she thought, the younger ones were bound to be as damaged by it as the others, simply because they were present when it happened. Now she understood the unusual amount of crying she often heard coming from the other bedroom. How could anyone be so cruel and sadistic as to make money off the suffering of children? It was nearly more than Isabella could imagine, let alone comprehend.

Francisco would want to know—wouldn't he? She was nearly certain he would, but was it right to awaken the poor, exhausted man when he so obviously needed the rest so he could return to work the next day?

Isabella's head lay on his shoulder, and she listened to his soft, even breathing. Her *esposo* did not snore as did some of the others in the room, men and women included. She had nearly decided that it was easier to sleep in the cold desert wind, lying on a bed of sand, than here in this house where the people in charge were more fearsome than the wolves and mountain lions that prowled the wilderness at night.

Just after dinner, when she and Francisco had come to their bedroom with the others, she had asked about his hand. He dismissed it as being "a little sore" from the incision Alberto had made to lance the infection, but she knew her husband was downplaying the pain. She only hoped it would heal quickly, though she could not imagine how that would happen when he had to use it for so many hours each day while he dug ditches and hauled dirt. At least her assigned duties were manageable and even light in comparison to what Francisco endured. She worried, though, about how well she would be able to continue her labors as the time neared for her *bebito* to be born.

Her heart constricted at the thought, and she squeezed her eyes shut to stop the tears at the possibility of her little one entering the world in such a horrible place. *We must be gone from here before that time comes*, she told herself, her mind turning to the One her *abuelo* and *esposo* prayed to daily.

"Are you listening, *Señor?*" she whispered, so softly she hoped He was the only One who could hear, and yet she felt compelled to speak the words. *"Por favor*, You must help us. We must escape this terrible place before our *bebito* comes into this world. Show us, *Señor*. Guide us and make a way for us to get out of here."

The tears squeezed from her closed eyes then, spilling hot drops down her cheeks and into her hair and ears. This was not at all what they had planned when they left their homeland and began their journey. Though they knew there could be dangers along the way, never had they imagined anything so horrifying as this! Would *El Señor* hear and answer her prayers? She hoped so, for there was no other way they would survive their ordeal. She hoped too that both her *esposo* and *abuelo* were repeating similar prayers; perhaps *El Señor* would be more likely to answer them, as she knew they were so much more faithful than she.

Carolyn awoke feeling sluggish, as if she hadn't slept at all, though she scarcely remembered falling into bed the night before. She hadn't wanted to concern Miriam, so she didn't mention the fact that she hadn't felt well all evening, but she was relieved when Miriam once again took the lead in getting Davey tucked into bed, freeing Carolyn to retire to her own room. There was nothing she liked better than spending time with her grandson, but yesterday she had grown more and more tired as the day progressed. She had been so sure that a good night's sleep was all she needed. So why didn't she feel better now that the morning light was pressing through her curtained window and she knew she'd slept a minimum of nine hours?

Good morning, Lord, she prayed silently, closing her eyes as she lay very still on her back. *Thank You for such a wonderful rest, but I must confess that I don't feel rested at all—and I haven't even gotten out of bed yet! What's wrong with me, Father? Do I need some vitamins or something? Or am I just making a mountain out of a molehill, as I so often do?*

Shaking her head, she opened her eyes and sat up, immediately alarmed at the dizziness and shortness of breath that swept over her. Was she coming down with something? It was the time of year for all sorts of colds and flu; perhaps, despite her precautions, she'd caught something. If that was the case, she certainly didn't want to pass it on to Miriam or Davey. She'd get up and let them know how she was feeling and then make a cup of tea and come back to bed. The two of them would just have to get along without her today.

Once her vision had cleared and she was feeling slightly more stable, she stood to her feet, grabbed her robe, and slowly made her way to the kitchen. Relief swept over her when she realized Miriam was already up and fixing a quick breakfast of cereal and toast for Davey. One day of bedrest would surely take care of the problem, and then she'd be back on duty as "grandma of the house," filling in where her daughter simply didn't have the time to do all that needed to be done. The thought warmed her heart as she smiled at Miriam and went to the stove to heat the kettle.

Miriam was concerned. As far back as she could remember, her mother had been a pillar of health. She exercised, ate balanced meals with little or no junk food, and almost never got sick. But this morning she had taken her tea and gone back to bed, informing Miriam and Davey that she just needed a day to rest and she'd be back to her usual energetic self.

Sure hope she's right, Miriam fretted as she drove the old pickup down the bumpy road with Davey and his backpack bouncing along beside her. Her son felt he was old enough to walk the long driveway to and from his school bus on his own, but Miriam wasn't convinced. Carolyn often walked with him in the morning and kept him company until the bus arrived and also met him when it returned, but obviously that wasn't going to happen today, so Miriam had opted to take him in the truck instead.

"We'll wait in the truck until the bus comes," she'd told him, "and I'll be there to pick you up at the end of the day."

A stab of guilt pierced her heart as he eyed her suspiciously. "Are you sure?" he'd asked. "Grandma always gets here on time, but what if you're busy and forget to come? Does that mean I can walk home by myself?"

"No, it does not," Miriam had insisted. "You know I've told you many times that I'm just not comfortable with you doing that yet. It's a long walk, with far too many critters along the way."

"But we could train Rocky to come down and meet me," he'd argued.

Miriam had smiled in spite of herself. "I'm sure we could," she'd admitted. "And maybe we'll work on that. But for now, I'll pick you up in the truck until Grandma is feeling better and can come and get you herself."

"But what if one of the critters bothers Grandma?"

"Grandma can take care of herself, and you know she always brings Rocky with her."

"So why don't you walk instead of coming in the truck?"

Miriam sighed. "You don't give up easy, do you?"

Davey had grinned, his blue eyes shining. "Nope."

Returning his grin she said, "I drive instead of walking because I'm very busy. I have a lot to do, and I just don't have time to walk that far and back twice a day."

"It would be good for you."

Miriam laughed, surprised at how good it felt to do so and at the realization of how seldom she did it. Serious again, she fixed her eyes on her son as they came to a stop at the edge of the road. "And if you know what's good for you, young man, you'll stop arguing and just look for me here this afternoon—in the truck. Got it?"

He sighed and nodded. "I got it."

He dropped his eyes and then raised them again. "What's wrong with Grandma?" he asked, the suddenness of his question catching Miriam off guard.

Miriam swallowed before answering. "Nothing serious," she said, hoping she sounded more convincing than she felt. "She's just . . . tired, that's all. You have to remember that Grandma's in her fifties now, and she gets tired easier than she used to."

Davey frowned. "Grandma told me the other day that today's fifty is yesterday's forty. I didn't understand what she meant, but she said it means she's still young. So why should she be tired?"

The sound of the bus gearing down for a stop was a welcome interruption, as Miriam handed Davey his backpack and shooed him out the door of the truck. "We'll talk about it later," she said. "Right now you have a bus to catch. See you this afternoon."

The tears she so dreaded and fought with every ounce of her strength threatened again as she watched the miniature version of her husband scamper toward the school bus, his backpack bouncing over his shoulders and his brown hair shining in the morning sun. Davey and her mother were all she had left in this world. If anything happened to either of them, she couldn't imagine how she'd ever go on.

CHAPTER 11

DON ALFREDO SLEPT LATER THAN USUAL THAT MORNING. THE sun was already beating against his window by the time he opened his eyes, and he tried to remember how long it had been since he had slept past dawn.

"I am indeed getting old, *Señor*," he said as he pulled his stiff body from the bed. "I have slept past our early-morning meeting time. I am sorry to have kept You waiting."

Despite the sunlight filtering through the window, the old man felt the cold in his bones and wondered how many more days he would awake at all. His time on earth would end soon, and he longed for the day He awoke in the presence of *Jesucristo*. Meanwhile, he could only assume that *El Señor* still had a purpose for him here in this world.

"I cannot imagine what it is besides prayer," Don Alfredo said, smiling as he took a seat at the table where he had passed so many hours. His *Biblia* lay open where he had been reading the previous day, and he caressed the worn pages with a gnarled finger. He sensed he would spend many hours in communion with *El Señor* that day, and he anticipated it with joy. That was the greatest advantage of getting old, he decided. Though he loved what little was left of his *familia* here on earth and prayed for them and his friends daily, his heart was already on the other side. He had cut the strings that kept him earthbound and was ready to soar when the call from heaven came. Selfishly, he hoped it would not be long. So many had gone on ahead of him, and he wanted desperately to see them again.

"Speak to me this day, *Señor*," he prayed. "Lead me in prayer and show me who needs my intercession today."

Listening with his heart, Don Alfredo waited patiently for the answer he knew would come.

The day was nearly over, and Francisco pushed himself to finish the last hours of his labor. His hand hurt as badly as it had the day before, but at least it was not worse, so perhaps it would heal soon, and then his work would not be as difficult.

His heart ached at the memory of Isabella's face as he left that morning. The sadness and fear in her eyes made him want to grab her and run far from the place where they now lived, but the fact that they had no money and nowhere to go held him back.

Soon, he told himself with each shovelful of dirt, as his shoulders ached nearly as badly as his hand. *Por favor*, Señor, *let it be soon that they pay us and we can leave this place. Guide us and rescue us, please!*

"Stop the daydreaming and get back to work!"

The sharp reprimand and a slap to the back of his head from Alberto yanked Francisco back from his thoughts. He had not realized he had stopped working. He must be more careful in the future, or he would lose his job and the only shelter he and Isabella and their *bebito* had for now. Surely *El Señor* would answer his prayers and take them to a better place soon! He could not bear to see his *esposa* so frightened and miserable much longer.

Though Carolyn would not admit it, concern was beginning to creep around the edges of her heart. She had spent most of the day in bed and only awoke when she heard voices in the kitchen. Was it dinnertime already? Apparently Miriam had picked up Davey from the bus stop and brought him home hours ago. How was it possible she hadn't heard them? No doubt Miriam had asked Davey to play quietly so his grandmother could sleep. Now Miriam was in the kitchen, cooking as she and Davey chatted. Carolyn wondered briefly what Miriam was fixing her son for dinner and then quickly reprimanded herself for thinking that she would undoubtedly have given him something more nutritious.

Stop that, Carolyn, she scolded herself. *Miriam is the boy's mother, not you! Your need to be needed is clouding your vision and marring your perspective. You should be glad that Miriam is spending more time with her son. Who knows? Maybe God allowed you to have a low-energy day so you could get out of the way and let that happen.*

Still, she thought, dragging herself to a sitting position, *you can't stay in bed forever. You can at least get up and wash your face and put some clothes on so you can join your family at the table.*

On shaky legs she managed to hobble to the bathroom that sat between her bedroom and Davey's, with a door leading to each. She locked the door that led to Davey's room and then turned and looked in the mirror over the sink. Her eyes widened, as she wondered if she had aged twenty years overnight.

"I look terrible," she said aloud. "My skin is gray, and my eyes are puffy." She shook her head, relieved that at least the swelling she'd noticed in her feet and ankles the evening before now seemed to have cleared up. "There is no way I'm letting Davey see me like this. This calls for a shower and some serious makeup before I head out there to join them for dinner."

Summoning up every ounce of strength and determination she possessed, she breathed a silent prayer for help and opened the shower door. Once she was inside, with the warm water pouring down on her, she began to feel at least slightly human again. A few dabs of makeup later, and she was ready to make a slightly less than grand entrance.

"Grandma!"

Davey spotted her first, his grin lighting up his face as he jumped up from the table and hurried across the room to throw his arms around Carolyn's waist. Though she had to brace herself for his enthusiastic assault, she managed to stay on her feet, smiling down at him the entire time and remembering to keep her breathing slow and steady.

"Hey, sport," she said, ruffling his hair. "How was school?"

"OK," he said, a slight pucker between his eyes. "But Mom said you were tired today. You must have really been tired if you didn't get up until dinnertime."

Carolyn chuckled. "Yes, I suppose I was. But I'm feeling much better now."

"Good," Davey said, taking her hand. "Then come and sit with me while we eat. Mom made hot dogs."

Carolyn resisted the impulse to raise her eyebrows in disapproval. Hot dogs were hardly a healthy choice for a growing boy, though no doubt a popular and easy one. She glanced at the table and confirmed her suspicions: no veggies or salad, just a bag of chips to complement the main course.

She lifted her head and locked eyes with Miriam, quickly determining not to allow her disapproval to show. Instead she smiled. "I love hot dogs," she declared. "Have you got enough for me?"

Miriam returned the smile, her shoulders relaxing in what Carolyn was sure was relief, as Davey assured her there was plenty of food for all of them. Though the thought of eating anything, let alone hot dogs and chips, did not appeal to her in the least, she dutifully and cheerfully took her place at the table between her grandson and daughter, and silently asked God to give her the strength and fortitude to share in this meal.

CHAPTER 12

THE SUN HAD NEARLY SET, LEAVING THE NEIGHBORHOOD IN semidarkness, but still Don Alfredo remained in his favorite chair in front of his *casita*, enjoying the peace of the quiet evening. He had spent the morning in prayer, stopping only long enough to fix himself a light meal slightly after noon. Then he had returned to sit at the feet of *El Señor* and to bask in His presence. It was not until late afternoon that the old man moved from his spot at the kitchen table to sit outside in his front yard and watch the day pass into night.

He was surprised when he saw Don Felipe come out of his house across the street and walk toward him. Though the two had visited occasionally over the years, they did not make a habit of it. Both had lost their wives years earlier, and without the two women to keep the friendship going, they had drifted apart. Now, even as the last rays of daylight gave way to darkness, Don Alfredo could see that his neighbor had something on his mind.

"Don Alfredo," the man greeted him, nodding with respect, "how are you, my friend?"

"I am as well as an old man can be," he answered, smiling as he rose to offer the man his chair. "And you, Don Felipe?"

The younger man waved away the offer. "No, no, Don Alfredo, do not get up, please." His eyes landed on an old crate leaning against the front wall of Don Alfredo's *casita* and pulled it up beside Don Alfredo's chair. "I will sit here, my friend. This will be fine. And I am well, *gracias*."

"That is good to hear," Don Alfredo said, surprised at how pleased he was for the company, however brief it might be. "And your *familia*? They are also well?"

Don Felipe nodded. "*Sí*. They are all well, *gracias a Dios*."

Don Alfredo also nodded. Thanks to God indeed! He knew without question that they owed every breath they took to *El Señor*, the faithful One.

"And yours?" Don Felipe peered at him as he spoke. "Any word from your *familia*, from Isabella and her *esposo*? Did it go well for them? Are they safe and well in the United States?"

An alarm bell rang in Don Alfredo's mind, as he realized how many people knew that his *nieta* and her *esposo* had attempted the crossing. Don Alfredo had told no one and had warned Isabella and Francisco not to divulge their plans to anyone, but others had tried to do the same and still the news seemed to leak out. He supposed he should not be surprised, though he was concerned.

"I have had no word of them," he confessed, distressed at the tears that threatened his otherwise peaceful demeanor. "I pray daily, but . . . nothing yet."

Don Felipe shook his head. "It takes time," he said. "Perhaps it is not so easy to send news back across the border, at least until they are settled."

Don Alfredo had told himself that very thing many times, and with all his heart he prayed that was the case for his loved ones. "*Sí*," he said, unable to speak more.

"Whatever happens, I do not blame them for trying," Don Felipe said. "If I were young again, with a family of my own, I would surely do the same thing. Though opportunities north of the border are less than they were a few years ago, the growing danger here is greater than the risks involved in leaving. It makes me wonder how many young families will remain in our neighborhood if this violence continues."

Don Alfredo raised his eyebrows in surprise. Never before had he heard his neighbor speak so openly about such things. It was a topic on everyone's mind but seldom on their lips. Even those who came to offer their condolences to Don Alfredo when his family was killed did their best to avoid the reason or manner of their deaths.

"I am sorry that I have reminded you of your loss," Don Felipe said, laying his hand on the old man's arm.

Don Alfredo could feel the roughness of the man's calloused hand through the flimsy material of his shirt, and for some reason it forced the tears from his eyes onto his cheeks. "It is a terrible thing," he said, nearly choking on the words.

"*Sí*," Don Felipe said. "And now the Mendez family..."

His words drifted off as Don Alfredo lifted his head and searched his friend's face for an explanation. The Mendez family? The parents with the two young children and the teenage daughter who often walked the neighborhood, minding their own business and enjoying one another's company? He had seen them only a few days earlier. What was Don Felipe saying? Had something happened to them?

Don Felipe frowned. "You...did not know? You have not heard?"

Don Alfredo could not speak. He only shook his head and waited, his heart screaming a loud "no" that echoed in his ears.

"They...they were celebrating their daughter's *quinceañera*, just a couple of days ago. Her mother was afraid to have it at the park because of all the gang activity there, so they held the party at their home. The children were playing games outside when *los malos* came in their car and shot them—all of them! Twelve children, including the girl who had just turned fifteen, gunned down in the yard." He shook his head, dropping his hand from Don Alfredo's arm. "I still cannot believe it. Just a few blocks away." He looked up. "Like your *familia*, my friend. Killed right here in our own neighborhood, in their own home."

Don Alfredo thought his heart would stop. He willed it to do so, for the pain was just too great to bear. But it continued to beat, and he wondered at the irony of it—that two old men would sit in the yard and discuss the deaths of a group of children at a birthday party. And the pain of the parents who were left behind! It was nearly past imagining.

Nearly ... but not quite, for Don Alfredo knew that pain only too well.

Ay, Dios mío! The cry screamed from his heart but would not push past his lips. There were simply no words that could do justice to the evil that had come upon them.

Isabella cried, though she held her sobs inside. Only silent tears trickled down her face as she lay in the cramped corner of the room with Francisco, feeling the rise and fall of his chest as she rested her head on his shoulder. The room was full of night noises—snoring and heavy breathing, an occasional sigh or whimper, and even a whisper or two in the darkness as a couple attempted to share their intimate thoughts and concerns in an environment that otherwise offered them no privacy whatsoever.

But it was not the sounds of this room that made Isabella cry; rather it was what she heard coming from the girls' room. Muffled though the sounds were, she recognized the voice of a young girl begging for mercy, asking to be spared whatever tortures she was being subjected to for the profit of her owners.

For that is exactly what they were, Isabella had decided. Though the ones who oversaw what happened at the house and even those like Alberto who brought in new workers and accompanied the men to their jobs during the day continually referred to themselves as their "benefactors," implying that they were helping rather than harming, Isabella knew better. They were evil, selfish, greedy people who used and abused others to make money. And Isabella did not doubt that not even Alberto or Olivia or their other overseers were the ones who actually owned the house or benefited most from what went on there. Isabella had heard Olivia speak of *"el patrón"* more than once, and she was certain that he was the man who was in charge of the entire operation.

How evil must that man be, she thought. *If El Señor is good, as others say He is, why does He allow such a man to exist? Why does He not answer our prayers and set us all free from this terrible place?*

The questions loomed unanswerable to the heartbroken young woman who knew only that she and Francisco must do whatever was necessary to escape before her first birth pangs came upon her. She was nearly certain that her *esposo* had heard the sounds from the girls' room by now and at least suspected what was going on in there, but she would make certain of it tomorrow. Somehow she would find a way to tell him clearly what those young girls were enduring, and then insist that they leave this place immediately, even if they had to return to the desert and die there. Anything would be better than staying in such a place as this.

And then what?

The question haunted her, not just because she had no idea where she and Francisco would go or what they would do if they managed to get away, but what about those they left behind? Surely they had some responsibility to help them, especially the children. But who would they tell? Who would listen to them or believe them?

Isabella sighed. It would be another long and sleepless night as she wrestled with the unknown. But one thing was certain: She would not allow another day to go by without being certain that Francisco knew what was going on in that house and how necessary it was that they get away from there as quickly as possible.

Once again Miriam sat under the starlit sky, this time with her boot-clad feet propped up on the porch railing, a hot mug of coffee clasped between her hands, and her ever-present ponytail hanging behind her. Blue jeans, a flannel shirt, and a padded ski jacket completed her thrown-together ensemble, keeping her at least relatively comfortable in the cold night air.

Day after tomorrow is Thanksgiving, she thought, directing her unspoken words toward the memory of her late husband. *This time last year we were arguing about how soon to set the turkey out to thaw and how many pumpkin pies to bake.* She clenched her jaws to help push back the tears. *This year I don't care if we have a turkey at all. What's the point?*

Her grip tightened around the mug. Who was she kidding? She knew what the point was; it was to keep things as normal and bearable for Davey as possible. Though he desperately missed his father, he needed a Thanksgiving dinner with all the trimmings. He needed to sit in his pajamas that morning and watch the Macy's Thanksgiving Day parade and then football as the day progressed. That meant a lot of preparing and cooking on Miriam's part, since she was beginning to doubt if her mom would feel up to helping much.

She frowned and took a sip of the still hot, black liquid. Was something wrong with her mother? The woman was only in her early fifties and had always taken care of herself, but that was no guarantee; David's early demise was proof enough of that. And the timing couldn't be worse. Thanksgiving was only the beginning of the holidays. Christmas would be here before they knew it, and Miriam had no idea how she'd hold up under the combined weight of memories and loss. If ever she needed her mom's strength to help her through, it was now—though she was far too stubborn and proud to admit it.

A shooting star caught her eye, and she watched the spot where it had disappeared. Did she dare make a wish? No. It would be too close to praying, and she wasn't about to fall into that trap. How many prayers had she shot up over the years, only to see her hopes and dreams go down in flames! Life was too short to waste on pie-in-the-sky religious nonsense. As weak and helpless as Miriam often felt, she would stand on her own two feet and give whatever was left of her life to raising her son. It was what David would have wanted her to do, and it was the only thing that kept her getting out of bed each day—that and the anger. If she could get her hands on just one of those illegal immigrants sneaking across the border—

No, she couldn't let herself go there. The anger was eating her gut away, but she just didn't know what to do about it. There was a time she believed all those words in the Bible that talked about forgiveness, but that was before the country she loved and the government she trusted had betrayed her and sold them out for people who didn't even have a right to be here. How could she not be angry? The very people who should have protected her husband instead made it nearly impossible for him to do his job. As a result, the finest man who ever lived was gone, even as criminals continued to pour across the border, taking over Americans' land and stealing their children's birthright.

You bet she was angry. But for Davey's sake, she'd do her best to hide it and try to give him a decent Thanksgiving and Christmas—though if her mom wasn't feeling better soon, it was going to be a tough act to pull off.

CHAPTER 13

WHEN DON ALFREDO WALKED OUTSIDE HIS FRONT DOOR THE NEXT morning, he was pleased to see Don Felipe already at work in his little garden. Don Alfredo wondered if he should take the initiative and interrupt his neighbor's work to bid him good morning, or just wait until Don Felipe took a break. As it turned out, he did not have to make the decision, as Don Felipe looked up from his work before Don Alfredo could sit down to watch from a distance.

Don Felipe stopped hoeing and rested his hands on top of the hoe, nodding in acknowledgment toward Don Alfredo, who returned the gesture wordlessly. After a moment, Don Felipe set the hoe down and sauntered across the street, squinting against the morning sun. Don Alfredo, with his ever-present straw hat, was shielded by the brim and therefore better able to view his neighbor's actions and expressions. At the moment, the man's expression was quite serious.

"*Buenos días, Don Alfredo,*" he said, stepping up beside him and once again perching on the old crate that he had used for a seat the day before. "How are you today?"

Don Alfredo nodded. "I am fine, *gracias*. And you, *amigo?*"

"I am well," Don Felipe said, *"gracias a Dios."*

Don Alfredo nodded again, and the two sat quietly in the morning sun, their eyes fixed on the ground in front of them. At last Don Felipe spoke.

"I would like to go and pay my respects," he said, not looking up. "And to offer my condolences to the parents who..." He choked and paused before continuing. "Who lost their children. But I...I do not know if I am strong enough."

He lifted his gaze then, and Don Alfredo was not surprised to see tears glistening in his dark eyes. "I wondered if...Would you accompany me, Don Alfredo?"

Don Alfredo had not expected the invitation, but he was not shocked by it. Such a venture was always easier when made with a companion. Perhaps the two old men could help one another through what would certainly be a very difficult and painful visit.

"It is the right thing to do," Don Alfredo said.

Don Felipe nodded, as the two of them sat very still, listening to the familiar morning sounds of the neighborhood where they had lived for so many years. And then, as if on cue, they stood to their feet and turned their faces toward the street, as they silently took their first steps. Don Alfredo was grateful for the brim of his hat, which hid the tears that were even now beginning to leak from his eyes.

Thanksgiving, Carolyn thought. *How can tomorrow be Thanksgiving— already? Didn't we just do that holiday?*

Memories of Thanksgivings past danced in her head, as she lay in bed, trying to convince herself that she was feeling better today and could help Miriam prepare tomorrow's feast. Just last week she had promised with confidence to bake the pies, but now that the day for baking was upon them, she wondered if she could really summon the strength to follow through.

Already she'd heard Miriam getting Davey ready for school and then driving off in the pickup as they headed down the long driveway to the bus stop. For the next several hours she no doubt had the house to herself—the perfect time for slicing apples and cooking pumpkin filling and rolling out dough. Maybe if she pulled a stool up to the kitchen counter she could manage most of the work sitting down.

"What's wrong with me, Father?" she whispered. "You know this isn't like me at all. I've never been afraid of a day's work in my life, and now suddenly I can barely find the strength to get up and take a shower. Help me, Lord, please. Miriam and Davey need me. There are pies to bake today, and a turkey to stuff and roast tomorrow—"

Rest.

The word floated like dust mites in the morning sun, yet echoed deeply in her heart. Carolyn had walked with God long enough to recognize His voice when she heard it, so she closed her mouth and opened her ears. She knew she had a bad habit of getting so caught up in "doing" that she often forgot that doing wasn't nearly as important as "being." Her late husband used to ask her that question often: What will you choose to "be" today—busy or blessed? And then he would smile and remind her to choose blessed, making time spent with God her priority. The busyness would follow as God purposed.

She smiled, closing her eyes and allowing herself to become immersed in praise and worship, enjoying the very real presence of her Lord without concern for time. When at last she sensed a release to arise and get on with her day, she felt amazingly refreshed, though still physically tired. She sang her way through the shower, and then made her way out to the empty kitchen, determined to do whatever needed doing in order for her family to have a nice Thanksgiving.

What she found was a note from Miriam, waiting for her on the table: "Mom, don't worry about Thanksgiving dinner. I've got it covered—ordered from our favorite restaurant and ready to pick up first thing in the morning. Just relax and rest up today. We want you feeling your best for our big day tomorrow."

Carolyn smiled. Miriam might be angry and heartbroken over David's death, but she still had a tender heart that somehow, someway, would one day be open to a healing touch from the Savior she had once known and loved.

"But how, Lord?" she wondered aloud. "How will it happen? I've tried to talk with her about it, but—"

Rest.

The word she'd heard earlier came back to calm her heart and remind her that God's ways and timing were always perfect. How much easier life would be if she could just hold on to that truth at all times!

Francisco's hand was slightly better today, though it still throbbed as he repeatedly plunged the shovel into the dirt and then threw it over his shoulder. The monotony of his actions was almost worse than the pain and exhaustion. He was glad when it was his turn to maneuver the heavy wheelbarrows away from the digging site and over to the trucks that would haul the dirt away. At least he could change position for a while and move his legs a little before returning to the same routine.

The noonday sun was directly overhead now, shining down with a warmth that surpassed welcome and very nearly achieved miserable. He tried to imagine how much worse it must be in the middle of summer, as he had been told the temperatures could reach twenty or thirty degrees hotter than this time of year. The thought reinforced his determination to escape with Isabella and find something else before their *bebito* was born.

"You!"

The voice repeated just behind him, and Francisco realized someone was speaking to him. He stopped digging and turned around to find Alberto glowering at him. When their eyes met, Alberto nodded toward the overflowing wheelbarrow.

A Christmas Journey Home

"Get it out of here," he ordered. "And be quick about it."

He did not have to tell Francisco twice. Gratefully he laid down the shovel and picked up the wheelbarrow handles, ignoring the shooting pain in his right hand. Sooner or later he was certain his hand would heal, for now he simply had to learn to live with it.

Pushing past the angry glare of the man he had once considered his rescuer but now knew was his guard, Francisco moved quickly along the well-worn path toward the waiting trucks. He was not even sure what it was they were working on, though he had heard it rumored that it was a large industrial complex that would take many months to complete. Under any other circumstances he would have considered that good news because it meant months of employment, but since he had yet to see any of the money he had supposedly earned while doing such backbreaking labor, he realized he was probably trapped until he could find a way to escape when no one was looking. And, of course, it had to be when Isabella was with him, which further complicated the situation.

He skirted a rock and continued to push the wheelbarrow as he focused on the beautiful face of his *esposa*. He should never have agreed to bring her here. Life had been difficult in Mexico, but it was worse here.

Despite the sunshine that beat down on his bare back, he shivered at the memory of what he had heard during the night. How could he not have realized what was going on right there in the house where he lived? Maybe it was because he was gone all day, and when he returned at night he was so tired he did little more than eat some dinner and go to sleep. It was obvious that Isabella was deeply disturbed about something, but no doubt to protect him from unnecessary worry she had not yet told him. But last night he had awakened when even Isabella was finally asleep, and he had heard the whimpers and sobs from the next room. No longer could he convince himself that they were the simple cries of homesick teenagers who did not like being separated from their parents, even by a single wall. They were the cries of children in pain, children who were frightened and begging to be left alone.

Quite obviously their pleas had fallen on deaf ears, for the sobs and whimpers continued.

Francisco dumped his load of dirt and turned around to go back and resume his digging. He had heard of such things as child prostitution and slave labor, but never had he dreamed that he and Isabella would be caught up in the middle of it. Now he knew it was a fact, and not only did he have to find a way to get his wife out of there safely, but he also had to do something to help those they would leave behind.

It was a daunting task for a lone man with no money, no contacts, and only a moderate knowledge of the English language. But he was confident that *El Señor* would provide a way. With that thought as his only assurance, he once again picked up his shovel and plunged it into the merciless ground in front of him.

CHAPTER 14

IT WAS THE FIRST TIME DAVEY COULD REMEMBER NOT SMELLING freshly baked pies when he came home from school on the day before Thanksgiving. But then again, he really couldn't remember many Thanksgivings at all, since he was only six years old. The last Thanksgiving, when his dad was still alive, was the only one he could remember clearly at all, as he pushed through the front door and tossed his backpack on the couch before heading to the kitchen.

"I'm starved," he announced, pleased to see his grandma sitting at the kitchen table with her Bible open in front of her. Maybe she'd fixed something special after all.

Carolyn smiled as she looked up, and Davey noticed her skin seemed gray. He felt confused. Wasn't it just your hair that got gray when you were old? He knew his grandma was getting old, but he'd never noticed that she looked that way before. The thought scared him, and he didn't like it one bit.

"Hi, sport," she said. "How was school?"

Davey shrugged, relieved to hear his mom walk in behind him. He usually enjoyed being alone with his grandma, but today, right now, he was glad that his mom was there.

"OK," he said. "I'm off for four days now."

His grandma nodded. "I know. Isn't that wonderful? We can have a lot of fun in four days."

Davey knew he should smile, but for some reason he just couldn't. All the fun things he was used to doing with his grandma didn't seem like a good idea right then.

"How are you feeling, Mom?"

Miriam's voice interrupted Davey's thoughts, and he turned to see his mom standing directly behind him. He knew she was taller than a lot of his friend's moms, and his dad had been tall too. Everyone told him he'd probably be a basketball player someday just because he was already taller than most of the kids in his classroom, but he doubted it. He really didn't like basketball that much. He'd rather ride horses.

He followed his mother's gaze back to his grandma, whose smile didn't seem quite right. "I'm fine," she said. "I feel rested today." She picked up a piece of paper from the table. "This was very thoughtful of you," she said, her eyes still focused on her daughter, "but you really didn't have to do that. I would have been glad to bake a couple of pies today while the two of you were gone."

"No need," Miriam said, her answer coming more quickly than Davey would have expected. Why was everyone acting and talking so strange? "You know Polly's has the best food anywhere around here, so why not get our pies and turkey dinner from them? Let someone else do the cooking for a change."

Davey's eyes moved back and forth from the two women in his life, and he sensed that the words they were saying weren't the same as what they were thinking and feeling, but he had learned that grownups did that sometimes. He especially noticed it when his dad died. Everyone seemed to want to make him feel better when all he wanted to do was cry, so they said things that didn't always make sense. Still, he somehow understood that it was because they loved him.

Was that what this was all about? Were they getting their Thanksgiving dinner from a restaurant instead of cooking it themselves because they loved him and didn't want him to know what was really going on? The question only increased Davey's confusion, and he wondered just what sort of Thanksgiving they were all going to have if this was the way it was starting out.

The memory of the previous day's visit still weighed heavily on Don Alfredo's heart. The walk with Don Felipe to the house only a few blocks away had seemed to last forever. Finally they had stood in front of the house where bullet holes pockmarked the outside walls. A shattered window attested to the indiscriminate shooting that had gone on just days earlier. Bloodstains on the dirt and porch gave testimony to the lives that had been lost there.

Little lives. Young lives. Children's lives.

Don Alfredo sat at his table, his head in his hands, weeping over the vision that would not go away. He and Don Felipe had nearly had to hold one another up as the reality of the carnage swept over them. Then, before they could move or say a word, the front door had opened and the man who lived there had come outside, carrying a cardboard box. The two old men watched wordlessly as he loaded it into a child's rusted, once-red wagon in front of the house. A couple of sacks of clothes and two other boxes already filled the cart. If the man saw them, he gave no indication before adding the new box to the cart and then turning to go back inside. A moment later he returned, this time with a woman beside him. Don Alfredo knew they were the parents of the slain children, for he had seen them walking through his neighborhood many times.

The man stood in front of the wagon and picked up the handle. With his wife beside him, a heavy knapsack over her shoulders, the two of them began to walk away from the house and toward Don Alfredo and Don Felipe, who still stood near the street, watching the heart-wrenching scenario. The couple stopped just in front of the two old men and nodded in recognition.

"We heard about your *familia*," Don Alfredo forced himself to say. "We came to express our condolences and...and to tell you that we are praying for you."

The man nodded again, as a sob escaped from his wife. Don Alfredo dropped his eyes before speaking again. "We are so very sorry for your loss."

"And I for yours," the man said. "We heard what happened to your *familia* as well."

Don Alfredo looked up, tears blurring his vision, wishing he could speak, though he had no idea what to say next. Don Felipe stepped in and took the lead.

"Where...where are you going?" he asked, nodding toward the overloaded wagon.

"Away from here," the man said, a hint of bitterness tingeing his words. "It has become too violent and dangerous to stay. When your own children cannot—"

He stopped to compose himself, as his wife's sobs intensified. "When children cannot have a birthday party in their own yard, it is too evil a place to stay." He turned his head toward his wife. "Everywhere we look, we are reminded of the pain." He shook his head. "We must go."

Don Alfredo frowned, at last finding his voice. "But where? Where will you go, *señor*?"

The man shrugged. "Away from here," he said again, turning his head for one last glance at the place he had once considered his home. "That is all I know. Just away from here."

And with that he had nodded, moving on with his wife walking just a step behind, still crying as she bore the burden of the heavy knapsack. Don Alfredo had wanted to help, to offer some sort of solace or comfort, but he had nothing to give except a silent promise to lift them daily to the care of *El Señor*.

"What else is there?" he now asked aloud, his head still in his hands as he sat at the table while the sun sank slowly toward the horizon outside. "No safety here, no word from Isabella and

Francisco over there. Only You, *Señor*. Only You, and Your perfect care for us."

Isabella had heard of the American holiday called Thanksgiving, but she had never celebrated it. Even if she had, she could not imagine having anything to be thankful for under their current conditions. But apparently it was of some importance to Alberto, who had informed the workers on Wednesday evening that they would have the next day off. He also announced that he was going to visit his family on Thursday, and in his absence he expected everyone to enjoy the day but to be on their best behavior and obey Olivia's directions even as if he were there himself.

Was it true? Would he really be gone all day, and would she and Francisco be together, possibly even alone so they could talk and plan? Isabella pondered these questions as she tossed and turned throughout the long night. Francisco too seemed restless, and she wondered more than once if he was truly asleep.

How can anyone sleep, she asked herself, *with what we know is going on in the room right next to us? Tomorrow may be a holiday for the* Americanos *and even for Alberto, but nothing has changed for the girls. I saw two men come in and pay money to Olivia just minutes before we went to bed, and then they disappeared into the room. How cruel! How can anyone make money from children's misery?*

The strong jab under her ribs reminded her that they could not wait much longer to escape this place. Their *bebito* would come soon—possibly within the next month or so—and she could not risk still being here when that happened. They must go soon, very soon, if they were going to escape at all.

She nearly cried out when Francisco laid his hand over her mouth. Her eyes widened in the near darkness until her heart calmed and she listened for his voice.

"Tomorrow," he whispered, placing his lips next to her ear so no one else could hear. "Be ready. Watch me. Stay close. By this time tomorrow, we will no longer be in this terrible place."

Her heart raced again, and she nodded. Francisco removed his hand and kissed her softly before lying down and pulling her into his embrace.

Yes, she thought. *Tomorrow! Maybe we will make it, maybe not. But even if we die trying, it is better than staying here another day. After that . . . we will see what happens. Perhaps, if El Señor hears our prayers, He will give us a miracle.*

CHAPTER 15

ISABELLA DETERMINED TO KEEP HER EYES FIXED ON HER *ESPOSO'S* EVERY move, just as he had instructed. She had no idea when or how they were going to escape; she knew only that today was the day. And if they made it, then perhaps she would understand what this Thanksgiving holiday was all about.

Olivia had not come to awaken them before dawn, as she usually did, with a loud knock and a shout. Instead they had awakened on their own, for the first time in weeks for some of them, stirring and daring to speak louder than a whisper as they rose from their makeshift beds on the crowded floor.

Slowly they began to venture out of the room into the kitchen, hoping to find something to eat. To their surprise and delight, stacks of warm tortillas and bowls of *huevos* and *papas fritas* greeted them in the kitchen.

Eggs and fried potatoes, Isabella thought, surprised that she could even consider eating when she was so nervous about what the day might bring. And yet she knew that whatever happened, it would go better for them if they were strong from having a good meal in their stomachs.

"Can you run?" Francisco whispered into her ear, just before they exited the bedroom that morning.

Isabella had turned to eye him questioningly. She realized then that he was not asking her to run at that moment; he only wanted to know if she was able to do so if necessary. Quickly she nodded. "*Sí*," she whispered. "I can...and I will."

Francisco, his face solemn, had nodded.

Now they sat in the backyard, devouring the food they had scooped onto their plate as if it might be their last. And who knew? It might very well be, at least for an indefinite time.

Isabella was surprised that they had been allowed to come outside to eat. Normally they were restricted to the house at mealtimes, but even Olivia seemed festive on this special day. If only she knew how very special it might be!

One other couple sat outside, just across the yard from them. The others had opted to stay inside to avoid the chill in the air. But Francisco and Isabella, as well as the other couple, had wrapped their sleeping blankets around their shoulders and come outside anyway. Isabella sensed that Francisco was watching for the right moment, no doubt wishing the other couple would go back inside. This might be the best chance they would have all day.

As if in answer to an unspoken prayer, the other couple stood to their feet and made their way back toward the house, but instead of going inside, they wandered around to the side near the garden. At least they were out of sight—meaning that Francisco and Isabella were no doubt out of their sight as well.

Isabella raised her eyes to Francisco's. He was already looking down at her. Their eyes locked, and he nodded. They set down their plates and took one last furtive glance in the direction of the house. When they saw no one, they turned and, with Isabella's hand locked tightly inside Francisco's, ran as fast as they could toward the stand of trees where they had waited when they first came to this place with Alberto and the others. Once safely hidden by the branches, they stopped only for a moment to catch their breath, as Francisco pulled Isabella close.

"Are you all right, *mi amor*? Can you keep going, or should I carry you?"

Isabella shook her head. "No, no, I am fine. Truly I am. But we cannot stop. We must keep going."

Francisco nodded. "*Sí*," he said. "You are right. They will miss us before we get far. We can only pray that Olivia will not risk leaving the others to come after us in the truck. But who knows how close Alberto may be? She could call him, and he could be after us in his van in moments."

"Then let us go now, quickly," she urged.

Francisco's head pivoted as he took in the terrain. "That way," he said, pointing in the opposite direction they had come from when Alberto brought them in. "They will assume we have gone back the way we came, so we will go the other way instead."

"Do you know what is there?" she asked.

Francisco looked down at her, his smile weak. "No. But *El Señor* does, and I believe that is the way He is directing us to go."

Isabella swallowed. She would have felt better if Francisco had given her something more definite to hang on to, but for now it was all they had. She closed her eyes and nodded. Just slightly less than a year earlier she had vowed to follow her husband wherever he led. She was not about to break that vow now.

Miriam knew she walked a fine line with both her mother and her son. She did her best to act as if bringing home a boxed Thanksgiving meal from nearby Polly's was a perfectly normal thing to do, but she wasn't kidding herself that any of them believed it.

The sun had risen a bit thinner this morning, intensifying a definite hint of late autumn in the air. As she chugged back up the long driveway home, the box full of turkey and stuffing and pies safely ensconced on the seat beside her, she thought for the first time in years about the Thanksgivings they'd had back East when she was little. The air turned nippy weeks before the big feast day rolled around, and often there was snow on the ground by the time Miriam and her little brother sat down to watch their father carve the turkey while their mother brought in the last of the steaming plates of food from the kitchen. Her mouth watered just thinking about those days, yet her heart ached to think how much life had changed in the interim.

Not only had Miriam's father died of cancer several years earlier, but her brother had also been killed while serving his second tour in Iraq. Now David was gone as well. It seemed the men in their family just didn't live to a ripe old age.

All the more reason to protect Davey, she thought, pushing in the clutch and downshifting as she pulled into the yard. *If anything happened to him—*

Shaking off the morbid thoughts, she parked the truck and got out, going around to the other side to unload the box and carry it into the house. By the time she got to the porch, Davey was already there, beaming as he stood barefoot in his pajamas, holding the door for her.

"It smells great, Mom," he exclaimed, his blue eyes shining. "When do we eat?"

Miriam's laugh exploded from her chest. Only her son could evoke such a reaction when only moments earlier she had been in danger of falling into one of her melancholy moods again. She shook her head as she walked past him. "It's not even noon yet," she said. "Not even close to time to eat yet. And look at you! You're still in your PJs."

"But Mom, it's Thanksgiving! I always watch the parade in my pajamas."

Miriam nodded and set the still warm box on the kitchen table. "That's absolutely true," she admitted. "But you also always get dressed before we have dinner."

She glanced around at the empty kitchen, her eyebrows rising slightly. "So...where's your grandma? Is she up yet?"

Davey was already peeking in the box as he answered. "Sure. She's sitting on the couch in her robe, watching the parade with me."

Miriam felt her shoulders relax. Good. At least she was up. Maybe she really was feeling better after all. Still, Miriam was glad she'd ordered the dinner. There was no sense in any of them spending all day at the stove when they could sit around together and enjoy the day. And despite the fact that missing her husband hung around her neck like a heavy millstone, weighing down her heart with every memory that invaded their day, she was determined to keep smiling and give Davey the best Thanksgiving she could.

Then, tonight, when everyone was asleep, she could let the pain pour out before she had to start another day.

Isabella felt as if she could not take another step—running *or* walking! Francisco's earlier offer to carry her was sounding better all the time, though she knew it would slow them down so she would just have to keep going. How many miles had they come? It seemed like many but was probably not more than a few. They had stayed off the roads as much as possible, willing themselves to be invisible and trying their best to hide each time they heard a vehicle approach from any direction.

If only they had thought to bring some water! In their haste they had left without any provisions. At least they were not hungry—not yet anyway. But what would they do as the afternoon melted into evening and their breakfast no longer satisfied them? Would they soon be back to hunting for *nopalitos*, as they had done before Alberto had found them?

Francisco walked just steps ahead of her, turning every few moments to check on her. This time he stopped when he saw that she was lagging farther behind and came back to walk at her side, putting his arm around her waist to keep her going.

"Do you know yet where we are going?" she asked, not wanting to add to his pressure but desperate for some sort of assurance.

"No," he answered. "But I want to put as much distance between us and that house as we can before nightfall. Then I will look for a place for us to sleep."

"I was thinking of *nopalitos*," she said.

He chuckled. "So was I. We must watch for them. We are far enough outside of the city that we just might find some."

She raised her head and took in the vast horizon, flat and dusty and barren. Did anyone besides Alberto and Olivia and the others at the home they had left behind live out here? She doubted it.

As if reading her thoughts, Francisco said, "I think there are ranches out here, though I do not know if that is a good thing. Some of the people might be friendly and help us, maybe give us some water or food, but most do not want us here."

"What will happen if the ones who do not like us find us? What will they do to us?"

Francisco glanced down at her, even as he continued to move forward and to help her do the same. "Do not worry, *mi querida*. If they do not want us here, they will turn us in to *la policía*, and they will send us back home."

Isabella stopped, forcing Francisco to halt as well. She raised her eyebrows. "They would send us back to Mexico, back to Ensenada and my *abuelo*?"

Shadows of doubt danced on Francisco's face, but at last he nodded. "*Sí, mi amor*. I believe that is what they would do."

She frowned. "But you are not sure."

He dropped his head for a moment before looking back at her. "No," he admitted. "I am not sure."

She sighed and bit her lip, placing her hand over her rounded stomach. "Then we will keep going for now. Perhaps *El Señor* will direct us to safety."

A smile replaced Francisco's look of concern. "That is exactly how I am praying, Isabella. And I know *El Señor* hears and answers."

They turned back in the direction they had been going and continued their journey then, with Isabella's heart only slightly lighter than before they had talked. But in moments Francisco stopped again, turning slowly to look behind them.

"It is as I thought," he said, a hint of resignation and alarm in his voice. "We are being followed."

Isabella gasped and turned to look behind them. There, in the distance, coming up quickly behind them, were two unrecognizable figures. And though she told herself they were just two people out for a walk, in her heart she knew better. They were indeed being followed, and that could not be a good thing.

CHAPTER 16

THE BOXED DINNER HAD BEEN SURPRISINGLY PLEASANT, THOUGH FAR from as tasty as Miriam remembered previous Thanksgiving meals being, particularly the last year's. *No doubt because that was before those stinking illegal immigrants murdered my husband,* she fumed silently, trying not to let her feelings show on her face as the threesome sat around the table, polishing off pumpkin pie and whipped cream.

Miriam was relieved that her mother seemed a bit better today, and she tried to find a point of gratitude in that thought, rather than focusing on her anger and pain over the senseless loss of the man she loved. Though Carolyn had started the day off slowly, watching the parade in her robe and slippers with Davey by her side, she had eventually showered and dressed and even offered to set the table before they ate. Miriam had watched her closely and was pleased to see that she had eaten well. Maybe she'd just had some sort of bug, and now it was gone.

Her gaze shifted to Davey, who seemed to have enjoyed the parade as much as ever and had eaten his turkey leg with gusto. Periodically, though, she saw shadows flitter across his otherwise beaming face, and she knew the boy missed his father every bit as much as she did.

Davey looked up from his pie and caught her watching him. His smile was hesitant, and Miriam hoped it wasn't because he was wary of her. She knew she'd been on edge lately, ready to fly off in anger at the wrong word or gesture. She knew also how wrong that was and how unfair to take out her pain on those she loved most and who were also suffering.

Miriam smiled. "Looks like you did a pretty good job on that pie," she observed. "I was afraid you'd be so full from dinner that you wouldn't have any room."

Davey's smile widened, and his eyes sparkled. "I always have room for pie," he declared.

A chuckle escaped Carolyn's lips, and Miriam joined her. There was nothing like a six-year-old to keep things in perspective! So their Thanksgiving dinner had arrived in a box this year and they were all struggling with their emotions and trying to maintain some semblance of normalcy in the midst of their pain. But at least Davey knew that regardless of what went on around them, there was always room for pie.

"Well, I'm glad to hear that," Miriam said. "And you are absolutely right. In fact, I think there's enough pie left for us each to have another piece before we go to bed—after we watch some football, that is."

Davey shoveled the last bite of pie into his mouth and talked around it. "Yeah, football! Let's go watch it right now."

Miriam swallowed another chuckle. "Don't talk with your mouth full," she reminded him. "Not even on Thanksgiving." She stood to her feet. "But yes, I'm ready to watch football too. Let's take our plates to the kitchen and get them into the dishwasher; then we can turn on the TV."

Before Davey could explode from his chair, Carolyn spoke. "Let me take care of the dishes," she said. "You two go on and watch the game. I'll join you in a few minutes."

Miriam frowned. "No, Mom, you haven't been feeling well. You go sit down and rest. Davey and I can handle the dishes."

Carolyn shook her head. "Not a chance," she said. "I didn't get to cook Thanksgiving dinner for the first time in my adult life; the least I can do is clean up. I'm not an invalid, you know—though I'm sure I seem ancient to *some* people." She grinned, looking more like herself than she had in several days. "Now go on. The game's already started. Go get it turned on, and I'll be in to watch it with you before halftime."

Miriam opened her mouth to offer another argument, but stopped as she realized how much better her mother seemed this afternoon. And besides, she needed to spend as much time with her son as possible. Why not now, when they could enjoy their shared passion for football?

"OK, Mom," she conceded, and then turned to Davey. "Did you hear that? We got a reprieve. Grandma's going to clean up, and you and I are going to curl up on the couch and watch some serious football together."

Davey's yelp of excitement preceded his race to the other room. Miriam considered calling him back and cautioning him against running in the house, but thought better of it when she saw the smile on her mother's face.

"Let him go," Carolyn said. "It's Thanksgiving."

Miriam nodded, returned Carolyn's smile, and then went to join her son.

Late afternoon shadows were already stretching across the barren sands as Francisco and Isabella did their best to hide themselves behind an abandoned, broken-down car that was covered with layers of sand, both inside and out. It was a poor covering at best, but the only one available as far as they could see in any direction. They could only hope and pray that the two figures they had seen walking behind them would pass them by without stopping, though they realized the chances were slim.

"What will you do if they find us?" Isabella whispered, huddled on the ground beside her *esposo*, in back of a tireless wheel.

Francisco hesitated before answering. "I do not know," he whispered back. "I am praying that *El Señor* will either blind their eyes or show me what to say or do if they approach us."

That sounded like a serious prayer to Isabella, and she so hoped her husband had found enough favor with *El Señor* that He would choose to answer. *I know that He can,* she mused. *He can do anything! But why would He do something for us? Is it true that He cares for us, as my parents and my* abuelo *always told me and as my* esposo *believes? I have seen little proof of that lately.*

"Can you see them yet?" she asked, her lips close to his ear.

Francisco shook his head. "Not from here. But I think I can hear their voices, though I do not know what they are saying."

Sweat trickled down Isabella's back as she held as still as possible, straining to hear. A distant crow cawed, its cry echoing in the dry air. And then she heard it—voices. She closed her eyes, trying to block out all but the sound. Yes, a man and a woman! Had they come from the home? She tried to tell herself they had not, but why else would anyone be out there?

"Francisco?"

Fear pierced Isabella's heart as the male voice called her husband's name. No longer was there any doubt where the two had come from and that they were looking for them. But why send two people on foot to find them? Was it because Olivia did not want to leave the others and come looking for them in the truck? Had she been unable to get hold of Alberto to tell him they were gone, or was he just too far away?

So many unanswered questions, the greatest of which was what Francisco would do, now that the man had called his name. Isabella remembered her husband's prayer and held her breath, daring to hope for a miracle.

Francisco slid his arm across her shoulders and squeezed, just as the man's voice rang out again.

"Francisco, surely you are here. Where else could you go? We watched you leave, and we followed you. Please answer us, *amigo*. We are here as your friends. We too wish to escape that terrible place. *Por favor*, Francisco, answer me."

Slowly, Francisco loosened his grip from Isabella's shoulders. To her horror, she realized he was standing to his feet.

"I am here," he said.

Silence nearly smothered Isabella as she waited, the pounding of her heart in her ears the only sound she could hear. She wondered if Francisco and the ones who had followed them could hear it as well.

And then another voice, a woman's, called out, "Isabella? It is I, Lupe. My *esposo* and I have come to join you, to escape with you."

Isabella felt her eyes widen. Lupe? The woman with the sad eyes who seldom spoke? Isabella had been drawn to her from the beginning, sensing that the older woman had experienced much loss of her own and would understand Isabella's as well. And yet they had never spoken to one another except as much as was necessary to complete their duties in the house or garden.

Francisco reached down for Isabella's hand and helped her to her feet. "Isabella is with me," he said, reaching his arm around her waist and waiting as the other couple joined them in the small sliver of shade behind the dilapidated car.

"Ernesto," Francisco said, grasping the man's hand and pulling him into an embrace. "Have you and your *esposa* truly come to join us? You were not sent to bring us back?"

Ernesto shook his head, his full black mustache seeming to affirm him as he spoke. "We watched you from the side of the house and left as soon as we realized what you were doing. We knew we would probably never get another chance. We have wanted to leave for a very long time, but they watch us so closely. Today was like a miracle."

Lupe nodded, showing the first hint of a smile that Isabella had ever seen on her once beautiful face. "*Sí*," she exclaimed. "¡*Un milagro!* A miracle! We have prayed and prayed to *El Señor* to help us escape, and now—"

She interrupted herself as tears sprang into her dark eyes, wetting her long lashes. "If only it had been in time—"

This time it was Ernesto who wordlessly interrupted his wife's speech by laying a hand on her arm. Confused but sensing that the woman needed comfort, Isabella surprised herself by gathering Lupe into an embrace.

"We are glad you have come," she said, wondering if indeed it would be easier or more difficult to have the added company as they traveled. Was it possible Ernesto and Lupe might know of somewhere they could go?

Before she could ask, she saw the smile of approval on Francisco's face, and she knew he was affirming her for offering comfort to Lupe. Her heart warmed, as it always did when her *esposo* was pleased with her. She also realized she should allow him to be the one to ask questions of the new arrivals.

"We brought a few things," Ernesto said. The short, middle-aged man reached toward his wife to remove a few things from the large pockets in her apron. Isabella watched as he pulled out a plastic bottle full of water and a large squash from the garden. Isabella's heart quickened. It was not much, but it was enough to carry them all through at least until morning.

"As soon as we noticed that you might be planning something," Ernesto explained, "we went to the side of the house where the garden is and watched you from there. When you took the opportunity to run, we grabbed what we could find and hurried after you before anyone else noticed you were gone."

"Surely they know by now," Francisco observed.

Ernesto nodded. "Without doubt. But Olivia will not leave the others to come after us, and Alberto will not be home until late. If we can find shelter by nightfall, I believe they will give up and leave us alone."

A tiny ray of hope sparked in Isabella's heart to think that they might not be pursued or forced to return to that place. But where would they go? What shelter could they possibly find out here in the middle of nowhere?

"I heard of a place," Ernesto said, lowering his voice a notch though no one but the four of them could possibly hear. "Just a couple of days ago, I heard a rumor from one of the others that there is a migrant camp nearby—just a few miles from the house and not far from here at all. We cannot see it now, but if we continue to head west, we should find it in a couple of hours...if the rumor is true, of course."

Francisco nodded. "*Sí*. If it is true." He turned to Isabella and raised his eyebrows questioningly.

"What choice do we have?" she asked, her voice soft as she pleaded with her eyes for some assurance.

Her *esposo* seemed to understand. "We will go west," he said, a tone of determination and leadership in his words as he looked toward the sun that was even now making its descent from the vast Arizona sky. "That way," he said, pointing.

Isabella took his hand, and the foursome resumed their journey.

Davey chased away the sad thoughts about his dad that had tried to creep in during the day, especially now as he and his mom watched football. The memory of the three of them, sitting on this very couch and watching the game together, tugged at his heart and caused tears to sting his eyes, but he wiped them away when he thought his mom wasn't looking. He didn't want to upset her, especially when they were getting along so well and having such a good time.

He frowned. Wait a minute. Where was Grandma? She said she'd be in before halftime, and they were already past the two-minute warning. The score was tied, and Davey knew his grandma would want to see the best part of the game so far.

"I'm going to go get Grandma," he announced, jumping to his feet.

"Good idea," he heard his mom say as he headed for the kitchen. She must be nearly done by now because he didn't hear any noise from dishes being rinsed and put in the dishwasher.

He pushed against the kitchen door but it only moved a few inches. That was strange. It was a swinging door, one his dad had added because his mom asked for it, and Davey knew there wasn't anything behind it. He shoved again, but the only response he got was a moan from the other side.

"Grandma?"

Fear shot up his spine and tingled in his scalp. Something was wrong.

"Mom!"

The tears he had successfully avoided earlier now spilled out of his eyes and onto his cheeks. His voice was a scream now: "Mom!"

Miriam grabbed him from behind and moved him aside before pushing against the door. "Call 911," she ordered, finally gaining enough space between the door frame and door to squeeze her tall but lean frame through and out of Davey's sight. Her gasp propelled him back into the other room, where he ignored the announcer's excited voice about an onside kick, snatched the cell phone from its charger, and punched the emergency numbers with trembling hands.

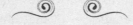

A Christmas Journey Home

CHAPTER 17

DON ALFREDO HAD SPENT THE BETTER PART OF THURSDAY IN PRAYER, not only for his *nieta* and her *esposo*, but for the couple he had seen walking away from what was once their happy home, full of children and laughter and joyous memories. Somehow they had managed to pack up what was left of that life and load it into one knapsack and a child's wagon, and then walk away with no destination other than to escape the painful location where so many young lives had been snuffed out. Don Alfredo prayed they would find a peaceful haven where their hearts would somehow heal until *El Señor* called them home and they could be reunited with their loved ones again.

It had all seemed so surreal, as he and Don Felipe stood together, staring at the bullet-marked house. The blood in the yard and on the porch screamed for justice, but Don Alfredo reckoned there would be none in this world.

"How does anyone go on without the hope of heaven?" he wondered aloud. "If this were all there was, how could we survive the pain of injustice and cruelty?"

Rising from his chair where he had sat for many hours, praying and reading from his *Biblia*, he poured himself a cool cup of water and carried it outside to sit in the chair in front of his *casita* and watch the last dying rays of sunshine fade away into the night. Memories of his own family, so recently killed in a similar incident to the one that had wiped out the children, tore at his heart with the approach of darkness.

Nightfall. Soon it would come for all of them. None could escape it. Life would end, whether in a barrage of bullets or a peaceful last breath, taken while asleep. And then what? How foolish that so many refused to give serious thought to that question—and to make the necessary preparations.

Don Alfredo remembered that day, so many years earlier, when his beloved *esposa* was still alive. It was she who had first introduced him to the real *Jesucristo*—not the corpse hanging on a cross, but the living, risen One who wished to know him personally. It had seemed so impossible when she first told him about it, but watching the way she related to *El Señor*, the way she spoke with Him as if He were her closest and dearest Friend, convinced Don Alfredo that it was indeed possible to have such a relationship. Since he had opened his heart to that possibility, asking for and receiving forgiveness from *Jesus* and inviting the Spirit of *El Señor* to live in his heart, he had never again felt alone. True, he had spent many years living in his little home without human companionship, but never had he been alone—and he knew he never would be.

But what of those who did not know or love *Jesucristo* as he did? What did they have to look forward to, in this life or the next? The fresh revelation of eternity without *El Señor* swept over him, and for the first time that day he was able to pray for those who had fired the bullets that killed not only his *familia*, but also the children who had been celebrating at a birthday party.

Miriam chewed what nails she had, as she paced the corridor outside the waiting room, her boots clunking against the sparkling tile floor. Davey sat slumped in a chair against the wall, his feet crammed into his own boots, as unable as she to stay inside the tiny waiting room but preferring the relative openness of the hallway.

She glanced at her watch. Seven-thirty. The sun had already slipped below the horizon, and still they waited. How much longer?

"Mom?"

Davey's voice quivered, and Miriam stopped midstride to look in his direction. When would she learn to be more patient, more concerned with others and less absorbed in herself? As always she had become preoccupied with her own distress to the exclusion of Davey's. What kind of mother was she? What kind of person?

She stepped to the empty chair beside her son and lowered herself into it, sliding an arm over his shoulders and pulling him close. "What is it, baby?"

A sob shook his frame as he looked up at her, his eyes puffy and his cheeks red. "Is Grandma going to die like Daddy did?"

A jagged bolt of searing lightning seemed to pierce her heart, taking her breath away before she could answer. At last she regrouped and swallowed, kissing his forehead and blinking back her own tears. "No, sweetheart. I don't think she is. I can't tell you that for sure, but I truly don't think so."

Davey sobbed again but said nothing for several minutes. At last he asked, "Do you...do you think it's because we let her do the dishes?"

Miriam thought her heart would break as she fought to suppress a cry. "Oh no, Davey, not at all! It's just some...some sort of bug or something. She'll be fine once the doctor finds out what's wrong." His silence told her he wasn't convinced, so she lifted his chin with her finger and did her best to give him the most self-assured smile she could muster. "Grandma takes good care of herself. She always has. She's healthy and strong, and she's going to be fine." *Please, God!* she begged silently. *Please let that be true!*

"Mrs. Nelson?"

A deep male voice snapped her from her thoughts, and together she and Davey sprang to their feet. "Do you have news about my mother?" she asked, stepping toward the tall middle-aged man in the white coat.

He nodded. "I do," he said. "It's preliminary, and I want to keep her for a couple of days to run some more tests, but her blood pressure is a bit high and I think she may have some heart issues."

Miriam felt her eyes widen and her mouth drop open, but before she could speak, the doctor held up his hand and continued. "That may not be as bad as it sounds," he said. "I really don't want to venture a guess at this early stage of the game, but whatever we discover, I'm relatively confident that we've caught it early on. Right now she's resting comfortably, which is the best thing for her. You can see her briefly, but then you may as well go on home. There's nothing more you can do here tonight. We should know more tomorrow."

Miriam nodded, aware of her son's grip on her hand. She had to remain calm for his sake. And, as the doctor said, there was nothing she could do for her mother tonight. She would take a peek at her and then head home with Davey, doing everything possible to convince him that his grandma was going to be all right.

She took a deep breath and once again breathed a silent plea that it would be so.

It was becoming nearly impossible to continue on in the dark, but Isabella did not want to be the one to ask them to stop. The others seemed determined to try to find the migrant camp before morning, so she held tightly to Francisco's hand and kept putting one foot in front of the other. But even the child within her seemed to sense that it was time to rest. He was agitated, as if he could not sleep until she stopped moving and settled in for the night.

"Just a little further," Lupe urged her, seeming to understand Isabella's need to rest. No doubt she too had experienced pregnancy and childbirth in her earlier years, and Isabella was glad to have an older, more experienced woman with them—just in case.

"Are you sure you do not want me to carry you?" Francisco offered yet again. As tempted as she was, Isabella refused. So long as he held her hand, she would be all right. Surely they would stop soon, even without her asking!

The moon was three-quarters full that night, just enough to see shapes and outlines in the vast expanse of desert that seemed so endless as they trudged westward. When Isabella first saw what appeared to be a slight glow in the distance, she worried that perhaps she was hallucinating, or maybe they were coming into a town or nearing a farmhouse, either of which could prove to be dangerous. But the excited comments from the men gave her hope that they might indeed have stumbled on to the camp.

Within moments, their hopes were realized. Ernesto knew the password to call from a distance in order to obtain safe entrance, and just when Isabella thought her legs would surely give out, they found themselves welcomed into a small camp where a pot of *frijoles* and another of coffee bubbled over a campfire. Collapsing into Francisco's arms at last, she rejoiced that *El Señor* had heard them and answered their prayers. Surely now things would get better at last.

CHAPTER 18

THE HOUSE SEEMED COLDER AND LONELIER THAT MORNING AFTER Thanksgiving, and for the first time since Miriam could remember, she wasn't looking forward to slicing the leftover turkey for sandwiches. In fact, in the midst of waiting for the ambulance and then grabbing Davey to race to the hospital, she'd forgotten all about putting the leftovers away the previous day. She'd salvaged what she could when she got home that evening, using the activity to help unwind so she could eventually get some sleep.

For all the good that did, she thought, measuring out the grounds for a fresh pot of coffee. She still hadn't gotten used to making just enough for herself, though David had been gone for many months now and she knew her mother didn't drink coffee. "Even when she's home," she mumbled aloud, hitting the brew switch, "which today she's not."

The reminder of why she'd been unable to sleep that night had already rolled through her mind many times that morning. She was glad Davey seemed to be sleeping in, since she knew he too had experienced difficulty getting to sleep the previous night.

"Is Grandma going to be all right?" he'd asked her, countless times, as she cajoled him into his pajamas and into bed, then read him a story before finally shutting out the lights.

"I'm sure she is," she'd answered. "The doctor will tell us more tomorrow, but he said they caught the problem early. No doubt with a pill or two and plenty of rest, Grandma will be as good as new."

Davey's expression had been skeptical and more than a little frightened, but Miriam imagined that was normal, particularly for someone so young who had only recently lost his father.

And is it normal for me? she wondered, snagging a mug from the cupboard as she prepared to begin her caffeine-induced day. *Davey's just a little boy, barely six years old. Of course he's frightened! But so am I, and I'm nearly thirty. I should be handling this a lot better.*

Nearly thirty. The implications felt like nuclear shock waves as she took her now steaming full mug of coffee to the kitchen table and plunked down. It didn't seem that long ago that thirty felt ancient to her, and now she was looking it in the eyeball. How was it possible that so many years had flown past so quickly? And yet, to put it all in perspective, thirty was awfully young to already be a widow.

Hot tears pricked her eyelids, but she brushed them away before they could take hold. She might hate the situation she was in, but there wasn't much she could do about it. Her life partner was gone, thanks to lowlife scumbags who made their living crossing the border illegally and then selling their poison to foolish victims who didn't have enough sense not to throw their life away so thoughtlessly. And as much as she despised the ones who had perpetrated the crime that killed her husband, she also resented the government that allowed it to happen. Where were they when David was fighting to protect his country from illegal activities? In their ivory towers, of course, taking taxes from hardworking Americans and then dispensing that money to those who had no right to be here.

Miriam's stomach roiled at the thought, and she very nearly spit out her coffee. Instead she breathed deeply and regathered her composure. She was going to have to get Davey up soon and take him with her to the hospital. Though she preferred not to bring him along, there was no one to care for him while she was gone, so she had no choice.

It was an added complication she didn't even want to consider if her mother didn't get better, but one that could no doubt come into play quite often in the days to come.

The morning sun on Isabella's face woke her with a sense of well-being that she had not experienced since before her parents and siblings were killed. The warm rays were a kiss of promise that she dared believe were a sign of good things to come, though the cold of night still lingered. Even the sandy ground over which their blanket was spread, with another one over the top of them, felt welcoming after the nightmare they had escaped.

Isabella shivered at the memory of what went on in that home, and then rolled to her right, expecting to find her husband lying next to her, but the spot where he had been when they fell asleep the previous night was empty. The first hint of alarm sprang into her heart, and she sat up to get a better view of her surroundings.

Twenty or more people still slept in various spots near the smoldering campfire. Quite obviously someone had stood guard during the night and kept the fire going—several people, no doubt, working in shifts. Knowing that enabled her sense of safety to return.

She spotted him then. Francisco stood with Ernesto and two other men less than twenty yards from where she now lay, close enough that she could hear the slight buzz of their voices but far enough that she could not make out the words. Their expressions were serious, though, and their conversation muffled so as not to disturb the others.

Or to keep us from hearing, she thought, a pinprick of alarm shooting up her spine. Would they never be safe again? Must they always be on guard, watching and running and hoping not to be caught—or worse?

The *bebito* belted a strong good morning against Isabella's ribs, and her hand went immediately to her stomach. All she wanted was to live in peace and security with her *esposo* and their child. They would work long and hard for that chance, if only someone would give it to them.

El Señor. Had he not answered their prayers and helped them escape both the desert and that horrible house where things went on that were too terrible to talk about? Had he not brought them to this camp where they could find out how to get jobs and a place to live? Surely He had—and surely He would not abandon them now. And yet the frown on Francisco's face was not encouraging.

A couple of the older women were stirring now, stoking the fire and preparing to make coffee. Maybe the situation would look brighter on a full stomach. Isabella hefted herself to her feet and took a few hesitant steps toward her *esposo*. When he caught sight of her and smiled, a glimmer of hope returned to her heart.

Carolyn still felt groggy, but her situation was becoming clear. She'd drifted in and out of sleep throughout the night, interrupted in what seemed to be very short intervals as the blood pressure cuff around her arm inflated and deflated, bringing bleeping sounds to the forefront. Despite the fuzziness in her mind, she understood that she was hooked up to various machines and monitors, including an IV that dripped clear liquid into a vein in the back of her hand.

Morning light had displaced the darkness she'd seen out the window over the last few hours, as she watched what must be the new shift nurse check her vitals and jot down notes on what was obviously her own chart.

"Good morning," Carolyn said, her voice coming out in a dry croak.

The short, chubby woman with the no-nonsense salt-and-pepper bun on top of her head jerked her head up, her gray eyes wide. "Well, good morning to you, Mrs. Sinclair," she said, her features relaxing as a smile took over her pleasant face. "I didn't know you were awake."

Carolyn returned the smile. "I probably wasn't when you came in."

The nurse, whose nametag said Marti, chuckled. "No doubt. I have a knack for waking patients from a peaceful sleep with all my poking and prodding."

Carolyn raised her eyebrows. "Does that mean you're about to poke and prod me some more?"

Marti's smile widened. "No. Not right at the moment anyway. But don't be surprised if the lab doesn't send someone in this morning to take more of your blood."

"You mean I have some left? I was certain they got it all last night."

Marti's laugh was unrestrained this time, as she patted Carolyn's arm. "I can see we're going to get along just fine," she said. "But for now, I'm through here. Why don't you try to doze off again until the next person comes in to annoy you?"

"I believe I will," Carolyn said, her heavy eyelids responding well to the suggestion. "But I'm sure I'll see you again before the day's over. Am I right?"

"Count on it!" Marti promised, waving over her shoulder as she exited the room.

CHAPTER 19

DAVEY HATED THE SMELL OF HOSPITALS. HE HADN'T SPENT MUCH time in them in his short lifetime, but the couple of times he had gone there to visit someone, he always thought the place smelled too clean, like somebody was trying to cover up what really happened there.

True, his dad hadn't died in a hospital; he hadn't even lived long enough to ride in an ambulance to one so he could die in a bed with his family nearby. He had died out in the dirt, shot in the head by a drug smuggler from Mexico. Davey knew his mother didn't realize he knew those details, and she was careful not to talk about them when he was around. But he wasn't a baby. He heard things, and he understood more than they realized.

Now he wondered if his mom was trying to hide things from him about his grandma. Was she going to die too? His heart squeezed with pain every time he let himself even think that question. His mom kept telling him his grandma was going to be all right, and he sure hoped that was true.

He walked down the very long, shiny hallway at his mom's side, his hand in hers as they headed for his grandma's room. Davey wondered if she would be awake when they got there. When they peeked at her last night before they left to go home, she'd been sleeping. She had lots of machines by her bed and a tube with a needle at the end poked in her hand. Davey had tried to be brave when he saw her, but his legs felt weak and he had been anxious to leave. He hoped it wouldn't be like that now.

His mom slowed down as they neared a door at the far end of the hallway, and Davey knew they had arrived at his grandmother's room. He took a deep breath and silently asked God to help him be brave.

Miriam kept her grip on Davey's hand as she stepped into her mother's room. It seemed unnecessary to hold him so tightly, but she felt compelled to keep him close and not let him out of her sight. After all, hospitals were large places and people could get lost.

She shook her head. *Stop it*, she scolded herself. *Your mother is going to be fine, and Davey is not going to get lost if you don't have him tied to your side. You're going to scare him if you don't stop acting this way.*

Slowly she loosened her grip, and she sensed her son relax a bit, though he continued to hover only inches away from her. No doubt he was already scared, poor guy.

Miriam turned her attention to the woman in the bed. "Mom?"

Carolyn lay silently on her back, the monitor still bleeping at her side and the clear liquid still dripping into her veins through the IV. Miriam was glad for such medical marvels but recoiled at the need for them. Her mother had always been healthy and strong, watching her weight, exercising regularly, and eating properly. She'd never smoked or drank alcohol, and now here she was, dealing with high blood pressure and who knew what else. It just didn't make sense.

"Mom?" she repeated, a little louder this time.

Carolyn's eyes fluttered. In seconds she was focusing on Miriam and Davey, and a smile spread across her face, making it appear less pale and drawn. "I knew you'd come," she said, her voice hoarse. "I've been waiting for you."

Miriam smiled and stepped closer to the head of her mother's bed, feeling her son following right behind her. "We would have come sooner, but I wanted to give Davey some breakfast first—"

Carolyn raised her free hand, the one without the IV attached, and waved away Miriam's words. "Of course you did," she said. "I wouldn't expect you to do anything else. I just meant that I was looking forward to seeing you and letting you know I'm doing OK. You needn't worry, you know. I'm going to be fine."

Miriam nodded, hoping her mother was right. She'd feel a lot better once she'd talked to the doctor. "I know, Mom," she said, feeling the need to reassure all three of them, but mostly Davey. "But you still have to rest. The doctor I talked to last night said they should know more today. I'm going to try to find him, or someone, and see what I can find out."

"Good morning," a cheerful voice called out, catching their attention as they all turned toward the door. A short, plump nurse with graying hair stood smiling at them. "I'm Marti," she said. "I'm Carolyn's nurse today, and I'm here to check her vitals again. It will only take me a moment, and then I'll get out of your way."

Instinctively Miriam laid her hand on Davey's shoulder and guided him away from the bed as they both stepped back to let Marti in. Would this be the lady who could tell them more about her mother's condition? Even if she could, would she? Miriam knew that hospital personnel were guarded in how much information they disseminated to friends and family members. Miriam might have to wait until she found a doctor to learn everything she wanted to know, but it couldn't hurt to ask—and she certainly intended to do so.

The sun was obscured by thick, gray fog, but Don Alfredo did not mind. He had not made the short trek to the ocean from his *casita* since Esmerelda died, and he certainly had not expected to do so today. But Don Felipe had arrived at his door with the morning light, inviting his neighbor to join him on a little outing.

"My daughter, Yolanda, and her *familia* have the use of a car today, and they have decided to go to the ocean. She has packed a nice lunch and says she has plenty for both of us to come along."

Don Felipe's usual serious look had changed to one of near joy, one Don Alfredo had seldom seen. He had to admit the man appeared twenty years younger.

Don Alfredo had smiled. "*Gracias, amigo.* It is kind of you and your daughter to include me, but I think it would be better if I stay home. You and your *familia* should go and have a good time without me. It has been a long time since this *viejo* has gone to the ocean."

Don Felipe's eyes had twinkled. "All the more reason for one old man to join the other on such an outing! We can keep one another company so my family does not feel obligated to entertain me." He paused, eyeing Don Alfredo closely. "It is because of Esmerelda, *sí?* I remember the two of you would go there every chance you got, riding buses and even walking part of the way. You have never gone back without her, have you?"

Reluctantly, Don Alfredo shook his head. The thought of watching the breaking waves and smelling the salt air without his *esposa* was a challenge he had never been willing to face.

"She would want you to go," Don Felipe said. "It has been far too long. And besides, it is a miracle that my daughter's neighbor loaned them the car for the day. We should not pass up a miracle, eh?"

Don Alfredo chuckled in spite of himself. His friend had a point. And to be able to make the trip by car, rather than on the bus and on foot as he and Esmerelda had done so many times, piqued his curiosity as to how much quicker the trip would go under these rare circumstances. He had heard people say the drive by car took no more than half an hour. Was that truly possible?

And so he had agreed. Now he sat on a sand dune, slightly separated from Don Felipe and his *familia*, watching his friend's grandchildren dig in the sand and even dare to dip their toes into the cold water before squealing and scampering back to their parents' side. The sight of them interacting and enjoying themselves with such abandon tore at his heart, and yet he was glad he had come.

The breeze off the Pacific was damp and cool, but Don Alfredo's wide-brimmed hat sat firmly on his head, as he closed his eyes and wondered what was happening with Isabella and Francisco. Were they still alive? Would he see them or even hear from them again in this lifetime? Or would he have to wait until heaven to learn their fate?

Had he made a terrible mistake encouraging them to leave? On days like this, when even in his violence-torn homeland he found such an oasis of peace, he thought perhaps he had. But then the memory of the murder of his *familia*, as well as the vision of the bullet-marked home where the children had been killed while celebrating a *quinceañera*, shot needles of pain through his heart, and he knew he had done what was necessary. The vision of the heartbroken couple walking away from their home with all their worldly belongings carried in a knapsack and a wagon was the only confirmation he needed. But how much easier it would be to retain the knowledge of that confirmation if he heard from the young couple he had sent to America.

"Don Alfredo?"

The voice of his friend and neighbor interrupted his reverie, and he opened his eyes to look up into the face of Don Felipe.

"We are going to eat now, *amigo*. Will you join us?"

Don Alfredo smiled and nodded. "*Sí*. I will gladly join you and your *familia*. You are all very kind to this *viejo*. *Gracias*."

CHAPTER 20

ISABELLA DID INDEED FEEL BETTER AS THE DAY PROGRESSED. NOW, with the sun directly overhead, she sat in the shade of a rock overhang with Francisco at her side, his left arm around her as she leaned on his shoulder. His right hand rested in his lap, and he had assured her it was feeling better every day. At times like these, it was nearly impossible not to feel at least somewhat hopeful.

"We are going to be all right," she commented, her tone begging for affirmation.

Francisco squeezed her shoulder and pulled her closer. "*Sí, mi amor*. We will be all right—you and I, and our *bebito*."

Isabella smiled. When he spoke like that, she believed him. Still, it would be nice to know some details, to find out if there was some sort of plan.

"Will we...stay here long?" she asked.

This time Francisco did not answer right away. She glanced up to see him staring out into the vast expanse of the Arizona desert, where even with Christmas soon approaching, the sands shimmered in the sun's unrelenting heat.

Just as she found herself wondering if he might not have heard her, he answered. "Only as long as we have to—and I do not know how long that is. I talked with some of the men who have been here awhile, and they say this place is safer than most but never a sure thing. All camps are eventually discovered and raided, but often not for weeks or months. So maybe we can stay here long enough to save a little money and then go off on our own and find somewhere to live—a real house with walls and doors and windows. I do not want you living out here in the desert when our *bebito* is born. The nights are getting colder all the time."

Isabella could not argue the point, as she had shivered through much of the previous night, even with a blanket over her and her *esposo* holding her close. This was indeed no place to have a baby.

"But . . . how will we save money? You must find work first, *sí*?"

Francisco nodded, though he continued to stare into the distance. "*Sí*. The men said that a truck comes most days to take us into town so we can work. They are hoping it will be here tomorrow. And if it comes and we find work, we will get paid the same day." He pulled his gaze from the horizon and looked down at her, his dark eyes serious. "Not like with Alberto. He owed all of us *mucho dinero*, but he would never pay us."

Isabella knew he was right. There were so many things about that house, that place where she had felt trapped in the midst of evil beyond imagining.

Francisco pulled her close and kissed the top of her head. "I know about the girls," he said, his voice husky. "I know what went on there. You knew too, *¿verdad?*"

Isabella could not bring herself to speak, so she nodded.

"We will not forget them," he said, his chin resting on her head. "As soon as we can, we must find a way to report Alberto and Olivia, and rescue the others."

Tears spilled down Isabella's cheeks at the memory of the weeping and whimpering and pleading that seeped through the wall separating the two bedrooms in that terrible place. Yes, they must never forget what went on there. They must never abandon those who had not escaped with them—especially now that

Lupe had told her how her own daughter had been sold to a man who took her from the home and never brought her back again. Somehow, they must find a way to report what went on there to the authorities as soon as possible—even if it meant putting themselves at risk.

She laid a hand on her stomach, and as if in response, her little one hiccupped.

Don Alfredo arrived home that evening feeling exhausted but exhilarated, more so than he had been in a very long time. Though the visit to the familiar stretch of beach had been emotional, bringing back many memories of a more pleasant time in his life, he was glad he had accepted Don Felipe's invitation.

Settling down at his table with a hot cup of coffee, he wrapped his wrinkled hands around it, savoring the warmth and hoping it would seep into his bones and begin to dispel the aching arthritis that had flared up as he sat out in the fog for so many hours. How he had enjoyed watching Don Felipe's children playing, digging in the sand and chasing the waves! The food prepared by Don Felipe's daughter had been delicious, and the fresh air had done him good, though the dampness had taken a toll. He hoped the sun would return tomorrow.

He sipped his coffee and closed his eyes in an attempt to follow its path down his throat and into his body. Living in a climate where sunny days were the norm, he had forgotten how painful it was when an occasional cool day took over and played havoc with his aging joints.

But it had been worth it, he decided, particularly the long walk along the beach that he had taken with Don Felipe. Though they had spoken little as they wrapped their jackets tightly around themselves and meandered down the coastline and back, the camaraderie had soothed his aching heart. His longtime neighbor seemed to realize how wounded the old man was after the loss of his *familia*, and Don Alfredo thought his friend's offer to include him on the family outing and then to spend time with him without insisting on small talk had indeed been one of the greatest gifts he had ever received.

The Lord gives, and the Lord takes away.

The verse from the Book of Job floated through the old man's mind as he continued to sip his coffee, willing the warmth to thaw him a bit. *"Gracias a Dios,"* he whispered. "My *familia* is gone from me now, but You have given me a friend to help ease my pain. You are so good to me, *Señor*—so faithful! Sometimes I wish only to come home, to be with You and with my loved ones once again. But You have left me here for a reason, I know."

Reassurance warmed his heart, more than the coffee had been able to do, and the *viejo* smiled. He knew why he was still here, and he would be faithful to finish the Father's business until at last *El Señor* called him home.

He bowed his head and began to pray—for Francisco and Isabella and the *bebito;* for Don Felipe and his *familia;* and yes, for those who had cruelly and purposely taken the lives of so many innocents. For truly they needed to know *Jesucristo*, even as he did.

Another day and night had come and gone, and Isabella awoke on Saturday to the sound of rumbling, drawing closer with her every breath. Alarmed, she sat up, only to find that Francisco and the other men had jumped up ahead of her and were scrambling to pack up a few personal things, including water and tortillas to get them through the day.

"Que pasa?" she cried. "What is happening, Francisco?"

Her *esposo* stopped to look back at her. "The truck is coming," he said. "We are going to work."

She felt her eyes widen and her pulse race. Francisco would be gone all day, leaving her here at the campground with only a handful of women and children for protection and company. What if he did not return?

Isabella shook her head. She was being foolish. Of course he would return. The men would work long, hard hours, but then they would come back with their day's pay. At last she and Francisco could begin to save up so they could get a *casita* of their own where their little one would make his entrance into this world.

She smiled. "That is wonderful, *mi amor*. I am so grateful that we have found this place and you can now earn the money we need."

Francisco nodded and bent down to kiss her. "Stay warm and safe, *mi querida*." He patted her tummy. "Take care of our little *bebito* until I come back." He kissed her again. "I will miss you."

She nodded, blinking away tears. As hard as their life had become, so long as she knew Francisco would come back to her, she would be all right. With that thought still clutching at her heart, she watched him pile onto the truck with the other men and pull away.

CHAPTER 21

ISABELLA HAD PASSED THE DAY BY VISITING WITH LUPE AND THE OTHER ladies in the camp, but always her ears and heart were tuned to the sounds of the desert, waiting for them to be broken by the telltale rumbling of the large truck that had taken Francisco and the others to work. When at last she heard it, the sun had already disappeared on the horizon and she had begun to imagine that her *esposo* would never return. Though she had prayed to *El Señor* throughout the day, as so many in her life had taught her, she had nearly given up on an answer.

But now he was here, leaping from the back of the truck with a smile on his face. He ran to her and scooped her up into his arms, holding her as close as he dared with the *bebito* in the middle. "I worked today," he declared, kissing her lips and her cheeks and then her lips again. "We all did! We worked, and look." He let her go and dug in his pocket to pull out a handful of bills. "Look, *mi amor*, we got paid!"

Isabella noticed he was holding the money with his right hand, meaning he was no longer favoring it. She thought her heart would burst from joy. At last, they were making progress toward the new life they had dreamed about, the new life that had caused them to leave everything near and dear to them behind and begin a very dangerous journey into the unknown. For the first time since they were abandoned and robbed by the *coyote*, she dared to allow herself to feel vindicated in their decision. Perhaps they had not been wrong after all. Perhaps it was the right thing to do to take her *abuelo's* money and leave their homeland for another country. Oh, how she prayed it was true! They had given up so much, suffered so much, and now she saw at least a small hint that it would all be worth it.

Gracias, Señor, she prayed silently, surprised that her words came from her heart.

With her husband's arm once again around her shoulder, they walked together to the campfire to join the others as they ate a simple meal of *frijoles* and *tortillas*. But Isabella thought she had never tasted anything else half as good as the meal they now shared under the muted light of the Arizona moon. With the fire to warm her and her husband's strength and presence beside her, she willed the next day to be even better.

Soon, she thought. *Very, very soon my* esposo *and I will have a* casita *of our own, where we can raise this* bebito—*and many more.*

Though a wave of sadness washed over her to think that her *familia* would not be there to share this new life with them, she was also grateful to think that they would be able to send word to her *abuelo* that all was well and that he had indeed made the right decision to give them his money and send them away.

Two days had come and gone since Thanksgiving, and at last Davey's grandma had come home. He was glad he had another full day before he had to return to school because he planned to spend it right next to Grandma Carolyn, getting her anything she needed and making sure that she rested and got all better again.

He sat on the chair next to her bed, exactly where he'd been since he and his mom brought Carolyn home from the hospital a few hours earlier. For the past thirty minutes or so, since they finished dinner, he had watched her doze. He'd had a hard time eating himself, though he thought Carolyn should have eaten more. However, his mom had explained that it took a while to get your appetite back when you'd been sick. But at least she didn't look so pale anymore. Davey didn't like it when his grandma's skin looked grayer than her hair.

Her eyes fluttered then, and he sat up straighter in his chair. He didn't want her to think he wasn't paying attention when she woke up. He leaned forward and waited for her to spot him sitting there.

It didn't take long. "Hey, sport," she mumbled as soon as her green eyes connected with his. Davey realized that though her eyes were the same color as his mother's, they weren't nearly as dark or bright. Did the color in your eyes fade away like the color of hair when you got old? He suppressed a sigh, not pleased by his conclusion.

"Hi, Grandma," he said. "I've been watching you."

Carolyn's laugh was weak but warm, and Davey smiled as she answered him. "I can see that," she said. "But it's really not necessary, you know. The doctor says I'm going to be just fine, so that means you can go do something fun instead of just sitting here next to my bed and waiting for me to wake up."

Davey shook his head, letting his smile fade to serious again. "Nope. I'm not going anywhere until you're all better. When you can sit outside on the porch with me, then I'll go outside again."

His grandma looked like she was going to say something, but then Davey thought she changed her mind. "You are turning into quite the young man, aren't you?" Tears flickered in her eyes, intensifying the green momentarily. "I am very proud of you, you know."

Davey smiled, feeling compelled to nod despite his embarrassment at her words. Deep down he loved it when his mom or grandma said they were proud of him, but it also scared him just a little.

"So what's your mom up to?" Carolyn asked.

Davey shrugged. "Cleaning up the kitchen, I think."

"Ah, of course." Carolyn smiled again. "I noticed you had chicken. Did your mom make it from scratch?"

"Nope." Davey shook his head, resisting an urge to grin and say something like, "That'll be the day!" Maybe his mom had made fried chicken from scratch at some time in the history of the world, but Davey sure couldn't remember it. If chicken didn't come in a bucket or a box, it didn't end up on their table. "She's probably just putting everything in the fridge and throwing away napkins and stuff."

Carolyn nodded. "More than likely." She took his hand and squeezed it. "You know you're going to have to leave that chair sooner or later and go to bed, don't you?"

Davey knew nothing of the kind. He had already thought about it and planned to sleep right where he was, but he knew it wouldn't do any good to say that to his grandma, so he just smiled and changed the subject.

"Will you be able to take me to church tomorrow?" he asked, hopeful of a positive response but not really expecting one.

Carolyn's smile seemed sad. "I don't believe so, sweetheart. Not this week anyway. But next Sunday for sure." She paused before continuing. "What about your mom? Have you thought about asking her if she'll take you?"

Davey's heart sank. No way was his mom going to do that! She'd use the excuse that someone needed to stay here with Grandma Carolyn—which was probably true—but Davey knew the real reason was that his mom was mad at God.

When he didn't respond, Carolyn squeezed his hand again. "Soon," she said. "In a week or two. We'll all go then, when I'm feeling better."

Davey nodded. He was encouraged that his grandma thought she'd be well enough to take him then, but he knew his mom would find some other excuse not to go. The thought made him very sad, especially when he reminded himself that heaven is where his dad was now.

The campfire burned a little brighter that evening, as a happy group gathered around to rejoice over the day's work and wages. The driver of the truck had promised to return on Monday and indicated that he believed they would have work for several weeks to come. Isabella certainly hoped he was right.

Even sitting on the outskirts of the fire, she could feel its warmth reaching out to her, coaxing a smile from her heart, which had experienced so much heaviness lately. The *bebito* within her was lively tonight, as if he could feel the soft music from the guitar, strummed by one of the men in the group. But even as she sat there, leaning back against her *esposo*, who sat directly behind her, some in the group began to call for a celebration, encouraging the guitarist to liven things up a bit.

It did not take long for him to respond. Soon the joy on his face seemed to emanate from the strings of his instrument. The other men in the group jumped to their feet and began to dance in a circle around the fire, as the women clapped their hands and joined in with singing. Isabella thought she could not remember the last time she and Francisco had been able to enjoy themselves so freely.

And then the memory returned to her. It had been on their wedding day, just a couple of hours after the church ceremony, with family and friends present to witness the happy occasion. After that they had gone to the courtyard where a mariachi band waited to welcome them with music. Watching her husband and the other men now, as they danced and celebrated together, she remembered the dance she had shared with both her *padre* and her *abuelo*, before dancing with her *esposo*. The image of her father and grandfather in their white suits, their hands clasped behind their back as they faced her and moved their feet to the music, brought fresh tears to her eyes.

Who would have dreamed, she thought, *that in less than one year I would be separated from both of them—one by death and the other...*

Her musings were cut short as the tempo slowed slightly, and the men invited the women to join them. Isabella felt heavy and awkward as Francisco lifted her to her feet, but she was not about to pass up the opportunity to dance in her *esposo's* arms under the desert moon. Despite the sadness of her recent past, she must focus on the bright future that now lay ahead of them.

CHAPTER 22

DON ALFREDO WAS ONE OF THE FIRST TO FIND A SEAT IN ONE OF the pews toward the front of the sanctuary that early Sunday morning. The simple altar, with its mounted wooden cross, called to him as little else could. It was in this very church, after years of praying by his wife and wooing by the Holy Spirit, that he had at last yielded his heart to the Savior, beginning a passionate relationship with *El Señor* that had enabled him to keep going despite anything the world might throw at him.

The death of three infant sons had been one of those trials that had driven him to his knees—and to a deeper dependence on *El Señor*. But at least he'd had his *esposa* at his side throughout those long, dark nights. When Esmerelda too had been taken from him, he had begun to feel like Job, being tested beyond human endurance until only the faithfulness of *Dios* Himself could carry him through.

Now his only surviving child and her *familia* had been killed, leaving Isabella as his only living relative. Had he been foolish to convince her and Francisco to escape the violence and poverty of

Mexico and flee to America? His eyes fixed on the cross before him, he prayed he had not made a terrible mistake. Was it wrong to try to save a life when doing so involved breaking the law? It was a question not easily answered.

Others were beginning to drift into the church as he prayed, settling into the seats around him. He nodded in recognition to some, smiled wistfully at others who came in with their families still intact. He was glad for them, but he could not help feeling a certain amount of sadness that he no longer had anyone to come to church with him.

I am here. I will always be here. Is that not enough, My son?

The words came as light as a feather on the wind but as sure as the blood that had flowed from a cross so much like the one Don Alfredo turned toward now. *"Sí, Señor,"* he whispered softly. "You are more than enough. Forgive me for not being grateful for all You have done for me. May I never forget it."

Miriam had spent the day catching up on things around the house, trying to ignore all that needed to be done outside. Still, she felt she must stay close by in case her mom needed her. Davey told her he'd watch his grandma, and Miriam didn't doubt that he would. But he was six years old. How much could he do in an emergency?

The thought nearly overwhelmed Miriam as she transferred wet clothes from the washer to the dryer and considered how much had changed in the past few days. Though her life had already changed drastically when David died, her mother had come almost immediately to help out and had been there ever since. As a result, Miriam had hoped she would be able to maintain the farm, despite all the work required, so Davey could continue to live in the only home he had ever known, the place where his only memories were. But now . . .

She shook her head. As hard as she tried not to dwell on the negative, she continually felt herself being sucked into it. True, the doctor had said her mother was going to be all right, that they had discovered her congestive heart failure in the very earliest of stages when it could easily be treated with medicine and a slightly tweaked lifestyle. But even those slight tweaks might mean that more of Davey's care, as well as the housework and cooking, would fall directly on Miriam's shoulders. She hadn't realized how much she had depended on her mother to carry that part of the load, freeing her to take care of the many things that needed to be done outside. What would happen now? Though the doctor had assured her that Carolyn would regain her strength and resume a relatively normal life, Miriam couldn't help but think that things would never be quite as they were before.

She pressed the start button on the dryer and turned toward the kitchen, wondering what to do with the last of the leftover turkey. Whatever she decided on, that would be their Sunday dinner. After that, she'd have to come up with something else to cook simply and quickly, while still maintaining at least the very basics of outdoor chores, particularly feeding and caring for the animals.

If only Davey were a little older...

She stopped as she stepped into the kitchen, stomping her foot in frustration. "Well, he's not," she said aloud. "So deal with it! There are only so many hours in the day, so do what you can and...and figure it out from there."

Blinking away tears, she yanked open the refrigerator door and stared at the Thanksgiving leftovers that seemed to mock her anything but thankful attitude. *And just what do I have to be thankful for,* she fumed. *If I can't find a way to keep things going around here, I'll have to sell this place and move to town, whether Davey likes it or not.*

She pulled the platters and bowls from the refrigerator and set them on the sink, willing herself to come up with something tasty and practical that would last them for a couple of days. Nothing came to mind, and it was all she could do not to sit down at the table, lay her head on her arms, and let the tears have their way.

Sunday evenings had always tugged at Isabella's heart, but more so now. As a child she had started Sundays at church with her family in the morning, and then ended them at the same place at the end of the day. Though she had not shared her parents' or siblings' personal passion for *El Señor*, she did relate the day to a special family time. Always her *madre* had prepared a simple meal in the afternoon, and they all sat around together, just enjoying each other's company. And, of course, her *abuelo* had joined them each Sunday, making the day even more special.

No more, she thought, lying in the crook of her *esposo's* arm as they curled up together in a blanket under the pristine night sky. *They are all gone now—dead, except for* Abuelo. *But will I ever see him again?* She hoped so, but he was a *viejo* now, an old man of many years. Would he live long enough to one day see the *bebito* who, even now, tumbled about in Isabella's stomach?

Tears trickled down her cheeks, but she quickly wiped them away. She did not want to risk waking Francisco. He needed his sleep, for he would be up very early to ride the truck back into town. How grateful she was that they had found this camp and that her *esposo* now had work that paid! It was the reason they had left their home behind, coming to this strange land to make a new life for themselves and their little one. It is what her *abuelo* had wanted, and in her heart she hoped it was the right thing. But there were times when she was not so sure.

Francisco moved in his sleep, and she lifted her head to let him turn toward her on his side. His arm went over her automatically, and she sighed with relief. At least she had Francisco! So long as he was with her, she could handle anything, for she knew he would never abandon her or their child. *El Señor* had given her a good *esposo*, and for that, if nothing else, she would always be grateful.

CHAPTER 23

MONDAY BEGAN THE FIRST OF SEVERAL WEEKS OF SAMENESS FOR Isabella. She arose early each morning to kiss her *esposo* good-bye and wish him well for the day. Then she did what she could to pass the time with the other women and a handful of children, each longing for the time when the breadwinner in their *familia* would have earned enough money so they could venture out and find a home of their own. By evening, they were all anxiously listening for the first signs of the returning truck, bringing their loved ones back to them. It was a rugged and tedious existence, Isabella decided, but a promising one.

On a Thursday night a couple of weeks after they arrived at the camp, as Isabella took her turn watching and listening not only for the truck but for any other possible intruders, she shivered under the seemingly endless heavens, sprinkled with shining stars but little moonlight. Even wrapped in a blanket as she sat on her perch atop a small rock outcropping where her field of vision was only slightly expanded, she felt the early chill of darkness as it deepened its hold over the desert. As cold as it had been when she and Francisco were first lost in its merciless barrenness, it was obvious the temperatures were still dropping as the calendar edged ever closer toward Christmas. Even the daylight hours, when the sun nearly always shone, were no longer as warm as they had been just a week or so earlier. The wind blew harder and more frigid than she had ever experienced in her temperate coastland city of Ensenada. The desert was indeed a dangerous and unwelcoming place.

A nearby howl sent an unexpected shudder up her spine. Coyotes and even wolves, as well as an occasional mountain lion and countless insects, snakes, and scorpions, were their constant companions in this lonely desert world, and she was grateful for the continual campfire that kept at least the larger ones at bay. Still, she would be relieved when she heard the first rumblings of the truck in the distance.

Even as the thought danced through her mind, her ears perked up. Was that it? She strained to hear, until she was certain and could finally relax. Francisco and the others were returning at last, and if all had gone well, they now had slightly more than half of the money they would need to strike out on their own. Hope teased her heartstrings, even as her *bebito* turned inside her.

She laid her hand on her bulging stomach. "Your *papa* is coming home," she whispered. "And soon we will be able to get our very own *casita*, so you will not have to be born out here in this terrible place. Rest, *mijito*, my little one. Things are going to get better very soon. Your *papa* will see to it."

Two full weeks, Carolyn thought, as she sat on the edge of Davey's bed, taking her turn at tucking him in. *Fourteen days since Thanksgiving, since I ended up in the hospital. The doctor was right. I am definitely feeling better than I was a week ago, but certainly not as strong as I'd like to be.*

"Grandma?"

Her mind flitted back to the task at hand. How grateful she was to be back to at least of few of her former duties, particularly caring for Davey. Though she and Miriam had agreed that she wouldn't be able to do as much as she once had, she would do what she could. And helping to get her only grandchild to bed each evening was right up there at the top of her list of favorites.

She smiled and smoothed a sandy brown curl from his forehead. "What is it, sport?"

His blue eyes lit up, and she imagined that even the smattering of freckles across his nose glowed. "You're feeling better, aren't you?"

Carolyn nodded. "I sure am. A little rest and a small amount of medicine, and I'm nearly as good as new."

"Does that mean you can start walking me to the bus again every morning—and picking me up in the afternoon?"

She hesitated only slightly. "I don't see why not, but maybe I should ask the doctor first. I have to see him tomorrow while you're at school. Your mom's going to take me."

Davey nodded, the shine in his eyes dimmed only slightly. "Cool. I'm going to pray that the doctor says you're all better again and can do whatever you want."

Carolyn chuckled. "That's a good prayer, Davey. And I'm really glad to know that you're doing that—praying, I mean."

"I pray every day," Davey answered, but his smile faded. "But I missed going to church the last two weeks. Mom wouldn't take me."

Carolyn chewed the inside of her lip before answering. "I'm sure it was because she didn't want to leave me alone, since I'd just come home from the hospital."

Davey sighed and nodded again. "Yeah. That's what she said. But . . . I think it's because she's mad at God."

Out of the mouth of babes! Carolyn flinched at the bold truth in her grandson's words. How could she argue with him? She couldn't. But she could certainly pray with him.

She took his hands in hers. "You're probably right," she admitted, speaking softly. "And it concerns me. But God is big enough to handle it, and He loves your mom too much to leave her that way. He's going to do something to change all that." She smiled reassuringly. "Would you like to pray with me about that very thing?"

Davey grinned. "I sure would. And can you please pray that we'll get to go to church this Sunday too? I really want to see my friends."

Carolyn squeezed Davey's hands and bowed her head. Just before she closed her own eyes, she noticed that Davey was one step ahead of her. Eyes shut and heart wide open, he lay on his back, waiting for his grandma to pray and for God to answer. Oh, for the simple faith of a child—the sort of faith that Miriam had once had and, Carolyn believed, would one day have again.

Miriam awoke early on Sunday morning, the first thought popping into her mind that she was going to have to break down and go to church—or at least take her mother and son. But she couldn't very well just drop them off and then pick them up a couple of hours later. She was stuck, whether she liked it or not.

She climbed out of bed and headed straight for the shower, reminding herself that she did not like her "stuck" situation one bit. True, she had attended church regularly all her life, not only as a child but also as a teen and then as David's wife. She had even told herself it was important for Davey's sake to go regularly as a family, though her once avid faith had long since waned and she worshipped God and prayed more from habit than from passion.

Is that why You took him from me? she questioned silently, turning on the shower and waiting for the water to warm. *If I'd been more spontaneous in my worship or faithful in my Bible reading, would You have protected David?* She shook her head and tested the water. Just right.

Climbing inside, she stepped under the warm, steady stream and immediately felt the tension begin to melt away. *Why do I just not believe that You let David die because I wasn't a very good Christian? I mean, David was faithful, and isn't that what counts? He loved You, he never missed church, he read his Bible every day, he gave tithes and offerings and—*

"No!" She nearly screamed the word, forcefully interrupting her own thoughts. It made no sense to say that God was good and then to believe He punished one faithful person because he or she happened to be related to an unfaithful one. She knew that in her mind, but her heart still dragged with a dark sense of guilt. Either she had to blame herself, or she had to blame God. Which would it be?

Then, of course, there were the illegal immigrants. Isn't that where the true blame belonged? Not just for David's death but for the death of so many, as well as for the many unemployed Americans whose jobs had been taken by foreigners who had no legal right to be here.

The more she thought about those people and their flagrant flaunting of the law, the angrier she became. Even her previous pleasure at the warm water flowing over her faded from her thoughts as she focused only on those who had stolen her happiness and so drastically changed her life. If she ever had a chance to make one of them pay, she decided, then God forgive her but she would take it, gladly. It was a vow that drove her onward as she continued to prepare to drive her mother and son to church, where they would worship a God whom she struggled even to acknowledge, let alone love or trust.

CHAPTER 24

ANOTHER WEEK LAY ON THE HORIZON, AND AS FRANCISCO BOUNCED toward town in the back of the truck, packed in with more than a dozen other men, each with his own dream, he was hopeful that in another week or so he would have the money he needed to begin looking for a home for his little *familia*. He had been nearly too excited to sleep the night before, wondering what Monday morning would bring and praying that the truck would truly show up to take them to work.

I pray that every night, he mused. *And so far, each morning it has arrived on schedule. One more week, Señor. Por favor, a couple more weeks of steady work and money at the end of the day so we will have enough to at least rent a little room somewhere, and possibly even a tiny casita of our own. How I want to be sure Isabella is safe somewhere before our bebito enters this world! Please, Lord...*

The work he and the others had found was backbreaking at times and had few comforts or perks, but he was grateful for any labor that would pay him and enable him to provide for his family. Francisco knew the others felt the same, though he was the only one among them with the added urgency to get settled somewhere before his *esposa* gave birth under the harsh conditions of the Arizona desert.

He smiled as the first faint light of dawn began to streak the distant sky, remembering how Isabella had reminded him not only of their need to find a home so their child could have a real roof over his head, but also of their need to report what went on at the house they had so recently escaped. Francisco had been touched by his wife's tenderness and her sense of responsibility toward the others. Her unselfishness was one of the traits that had first attracted him to her, and though he knew she did not share his deep level of faith in *El Señor*, he also knew she had been taught the truth as a child and would soon make a commitment to equal his own.

It is because You are faithful that I can believe such a thing, he prayed silently. *My own faith is so weak, but Your faithfulness is so strong. Por favor, Señor, reveal Your amazing love to Isabella in such a way that she can no longer doubt or resist the truth. Our child will need her to be strong in You, Father. May it always be so!*

A single ray of bright sunlight sparked the eastern sky, and Francisco bowed his head. *"Gracias a Dios,"* he whispered. And a dozen male voices echoed his words.

Miriam battled with mixed emotions as Monday progressed, wanting to believe the doctor's assessment that Carolyn could now resume most of her usual routine, including walking Davey to and from the bus each day, but unsure that she was comfortable with letting her do that. As a compromise they had picked up a disposable cell phone for Carolyn to carry with her at all times. All she had to do was press one button to be in immediate contact with Miriam, though Carolyn assured her it wasn't necessary.

"I've gotten by all these years without a cell phone," she'd argued. "I really don't see why I need one now. It just doesn't seem right, carrying a phone around with you all the time. It's not like

I'm going to be leaving the property without letting you know. All I'm going to be doing is hanging around the house and walking down the driveway with Davey."

"That driveway is nearly a mile long," Miriam had argued. "If you want to start walking Davey again, you're going to keep this cell phone with you, period. End of discussion."

Reluctantly Carolyn had agreed, and yet still Miriam worried. Sure, the doctor said they'd caught the problem early and Carolyn was responding well to the medication. But what if she passed out again, as she had on Thanksgiving? What if—?

Wiping the dipstick as she checked the oil in her truck before heading out to inspect the fence line, she shook her head as if to dispel the questions. After all, what could she do about it? What choice did she really have? She simply couldn't do it all herself. So long as her mother was willing and able to help, she should let her do so as best she could. But she had to admit it would all be so much easier if they lived in town, in a nice quiet, tree-lined neighborhood, like normal people. Was she being foolish and stubborn to try to maintain this place for Davey's sake?

Undoubtedly, yes. She sighed. But again, what was the alternative? She could try to sell the home and land her son loved—no doubt at a substantial loss—and uproot him from everything familiar to go live in suburbia. Though she knew it could become a necessity if her mother took a turn for the worse, she so hoped they could all hold out until Davey got older and could not only take care of himself but help her with the maintenance of the home he so loved.

She sighed again. The oil was low. She turned toward the barn where she kept a couple of cases of motor oil, along with other emergency supplies, and trudged across the yard to the double doors, yanking them open with one strong pull. Another week had begun, and she could only hope it would prove to be a better one than the last couple had been, though the cold wind that whistled through the cracks and chinks in the barn walls did not leave her feeling optimistic.

Isabella shivered, even as she sat near the fire, a blanket over her shoulders and tucked beneath her folded legs. Nearly another week had come and gone, and it seemed she could not get warm anymore, even when Francisco held her close during the night. The desert had passed from its merciless summer heat to its bone-chilling winter cold. How she missed the moderate temperatures of her coastland hometown, where temperatures seldom dipped below the fifties, even at night, or above the eighties during the days. The memory of the bright red and purple bougainvillea plants that crawled over trestles and bloomed so many months out of the year tugged at her heart, though not nearly as much as the memory of her *abuelo's* weathered face and hearty laugh. What she would not give to be there now—or to at least know that she would one day see him again! Her heart broke to think that she had not even been able to send him a letter to let them know they were all right. How he must agonize over their welfare! She promised herself that once her *esposo* had found them a *casita* of their own, she would immediately write to him to let him know they had arrived safely—though she would never tell him of the horrors they had seen along the way.

The vision of the so-called safe house, with its room full of young girls and the evil faces of Olivia and Alberto, threatened to dissolve her into tears, but Lupe came to join her just before she lost control.

"How are you this afternoon?" Lupe asked, smiling from her kind brown eyes as much as with her lips. "Are you and the *bebito* well?"

Isabella could not help but return the smile. She nodded. "*Sí*, Lupe. *Gracias*. We are well—just cold."

"*Sí*. The wind never stops blowing out here, and it is always too hot or too cold." She laid a hand on the blanket that covered Isabella's arm. "It will not be long now," she said, her voice soothing.

"The men are working very hard, and soon we will have shelter. Very soon, I believe. Before Christmas, ¿*verdad*?"

Isabella's smile widened. "*Sí*. Before Christmas." She patted her round, hard stomach, doing her best to ignore her doubts and fears. "Before the *bebito* comes."

It was Lupe's turn to nod, and the knowing experience reflected in her expression eased the uncertainty in Isabella's heart. "Before the *bebito* comes, *sí! El Señor* will provide a home for your little one by Christmas, Isabella. I am sure of it."

Isabella swallowed and breathed a silent prayer that the woman who had seen at least twice as many years as she was indeed speaking the truth. To be without a home at Christmas, especially with the little one being due so near that time, would be a very hard thing indeed.

CHAPTER 25

CAROLYN WAS RELIEVED, THOUGH SHE WOULD NEVER ADMIT THE reason for it to anyone. She had willingly and even joyfully resumed her duties of escorting her grandson to and from the school bus for the past week, but now that Saturday had arrived, she grudgingly admitted to herself that she had been nearly as concerned as Miriam.

She leaned forward, narrowed her eyes, and examined herself in the bathroom mirror. OK, so she had some gray hair sprinkled in among her short, golden-red locks and her green eyes weren't as wide or bright as they once were, but she was far from ancient. She really should stop behaving that way...shouldn't she?

She sighed and stepped back from the mirror. For years she'd heard the statement that "today's fifty is yesterday's forty" and laughingly repeated it, clinging to its fragile truth. Without doubt people lived longer these days and were often quite active even into their seventies and eighties...and beyond. Carolyn had naively believed she would be among them; now she wasn't so sure.

Not that it mattered, she reminded herself, taking one last swipe with her brush at her unruly hair. It seemed the more gray hairs that inserted themselves among the coppery ones, the more unmanageable her "do" became, regardless of how short she kept it. But did that matter either? Not really. The only reason the age and health thing bothered her was because she had been so sure that God had sent her to help Miriam with Davey. The last thing she wanted to do to her daughter was to become a liability, rather than an asset. So long as she was able, she would gladly devote whatever was left of her life on earth to caring for her grandson, but if she could no longer do that, then what?

She shook her head and headed back to her room to find her shoes and then make her way into the kitchen to get some breakfast started. Miriam had been doing that for Davey ever since Carolyn's trip to the hospital, but Carolyn knew her daughter's breakfasts were limited to juice and cereal. Today Davey was going to get his favorite breakfast of pancakes and bacon, and Carolyn was going to be the one to cook it. Even her own mouth watered at the thought, and she smiled in spite of herself. There was nothing like a lazy Saturday morning and a nice big country breakfast to start the weekend off right.

"Forgive me, Lord," she whispered as she slipped on her shoes. "How can I let myself waste my time and energy feeling sorry for myself and worrying about what might happen—or not—when You've blessed me so much? My life is in Your hands, Father, for however many days You've purposed for me to be here. And when those days are over—or maybe not over, but just changed somehow—I know You'll provide an answer for Miriam and Davey in some other way."

And with that thought energizing her, she pulled open her bedroom door and headed for the still empty kitchen.

Isabella had been disappointed when the truck came again on Saturday morning and took the men back to work. She had so hoped Francisco would stay with her today, as the daylight hours seemed to stretch on forever without him. And yet she knew how selfish she was to think in such a way. They needed the money so they could leave this desolate place behind and get into a place of shelter and warmth before the *bebito* was born. She should be rejoicing that Francisco was earning additional wages today, but she dreaded another day alone with Lupe and the other women.

The children helped. Lately she had begun spending a couple of hours each day telling some of her *abuelo's* stories to those little ones who were old enough to pay attention. Her mother had always told her she had a natural, God-given ability to teach children and to care for them; she imagined that was so, as she truly enjoyed doing such things. But the memory of her mother's words and the way she had spent countless hours teaching and entertaining her younger siblings nearly crushed the joy of doing so right from her heart.

As the midmorning sun offered up its thin, wintry dance, nearly obscured by the freezing wind, Isabella pulled her ever-present blanket more tightly around her shoulders and shivered as she laid her hand on her rolling stomach and edged closer to the fire. "You are growing more and more restless, aren't you, *mijito?*" she whispered. "Soon you will not be content to remain where you are. And though I long to see your sweet face and hold you in my arms, I also want you to stay where you are just a little while longer—just until your *papa* earns a bit more *dinero* and finds us a *casita* where you can be born in safety and comfort. *Por favor*, little one, just a little longer."

The half-dozen children who had become accustomed to Isabella's prelunch stories had begun to approach her, their eyes wide with eager anticipation. Doing her best to ignore the biting wind and the tumbling in her stomach, she smiled at them in welcome and motioned for them to sit down around her where they could all benefit from the warm fire. And then she began to spin her tales, based in truth but embellished with fantasy and adventure, of life as it had once been in a beautiful country called Mexico, before *los malos* brought so much pain and ruination to so many.

Even for their nearly perfect coastal city, Don Alfredo could not remember a more flawless day. The sun had risen that Saturday morning with a glorious shine and promise, driving out the remnants of cool night air and ushering in the sounds of birds chirping their welcome. Despite his lingering sadness at the loss of all who were dear to him, the old man rejoiced in the day *El Señor* had given him.

He had passed the morning in communion with Him, reading from the Holy Scriptures and praying for Francisco and Isabella and their baby, as well as for the couple who had walked away from their bullet-ridden home with all their earthly belongings, with no destination except to escape the reminder of their pain. By afternoon he had succumbed to his satisfied tummy, full of *patas* and *frijoles*, and headed for his chair in front of the house to enjoy what was left of the day's sunshine.

So, patas, he thought. *Always a treat for me, but something Isabella would not even consider.*

"I will not eat pig's feet," she had declared each time he tried to coax her into trying them. "No matter how hungry I get, I will never do that!"

Don Alfredo smiled at the memory. He could hear the fire in her voice, something quite unusual for a little girl who was usually so docile and obedient. How he wished he could hear her voice now, for he missed her more even than those who had gone on ahead through the doorway of death.

He shivered, even in the warm afternoon sun, praying that his beloved *nieta* and her *esposo* and *bebito* had not tragically joined the others. For surely, if what was left of his *familia* had died in their attempt to escape Mexico and start a new life north of the border, it would be his fault for persuading them to do so.

Once again the question of breaking a law to save a life pecked at him like an annoying insect. How did he, as one who claimed

　A Christmas Journey Home

to follow *El Señor* and His Son, *Jesucristo*, reconcile such a decision? And yet, he reminded himself, there were verses in the Bible that indicated it was right to obey God's Word rather than man's law when the two were in conflict.

But were they? Or was he twisting the Scriptures to justify what he had done?

With the questions niggling at him, he at last allowed the toasty afternoon sun to lull him to sleep, though visions of Isabella as a child danced through his dreams. And then, even his dreams were interrupted by the moaning and chanting. Slowly his mind pulled away from the wispy shadows of sleep and came to focus on the reality of his usually quiet neighborhood street, which was at once no longer quiet.

The old man peered out from under his wide-brimmed hat and squinted against the sun, which was just beginning to sink toward the western horizon and shine into his face, causing him to wonder at the sight in front of him. But as he stood to his feet and stepped closer to the street, he realized the sun was not playing tricks on his rheumy old eyes after all.

A funeral procession, consisting of about fifty mourners, moved on foot past his home. Some wept aloud, while others sobbed softly or looked stoically ahead, as four pallbearers transported a tiny white coffin in the middle of the crowd. A child had died, and Don Alfredo's heart felt as if it would bleed with the wrongness of it, particularly when he saw the signs carried by a few of the marchers, bearing the words that declared the little one's death had been due to another senseless shooting by *los malos*.

Will it ever end? he wondered, immediately answering his own question with the reminder that no, it would not—at least, not in this sin-filled, broken world. Only in the next would justice be done and hearts mended, and then only because justice was covered by mercy.

"*Gracias a Dios,*" Don Alfredo whispered, quietly so no one in the passing crowd could hear him. He did not want them to mistake his thanks to God as reflecting his feelings about an innocent child's death. But beholding the depth of sin's tragedy reflected in the tiny coffin, the old man could do nothing but appeal to God's great mercy—for all of them.

A Christmas Journey Home

CHAPTER 26

Francisco was glad that another long week was nearly over. He was physically exhausted, though grateful that his right hand had at last healed up completely. He was also quite encouraged that he had nearly enough money to begin looking for a home, though he would need Ernesto's advice about how best to go about it. He certainly could not simply walk up to homes or apartments with For Rent signs in front and ask about getting a place. He had no papers, no identification, nothing—all had been taken from them by the *coyote* who also took their money without delivering what he had promised. Now it was up to Francisco to use the money he had earned wisely—and quickly—to make sure his family was safe and out of the desert as soon as possible.

As the noisy, jam-packed truck bumped and screeched its way back to the campground, Francisco thought of what he had heard earlier that day. Some of the workers from another camp had not showed up to work that morning, and when Francisco asked Ernesto what he thought might have happened, the older man had frowned and shook his head.

"I do not know for certain," he had answered, "but I heard some of the men saying their camp had been raided."

Francisco's eyebrows had shot up, as had his heart rate. If the other camp could be discovered and raided, certainly theirs could as well. "Who was it that raided them?" he asked, trying to hold his voice low and steady. "Do you think the workers and their *familias* were deported?"

Ernesto shrugged. "I do not know any details," he said. "Only rumors. But if they were deported, it is better than being raided by *bandidos*, who take everything...even, at times, the lives of those who try to stop them."

The image of such a thing happening at the campground where Isabella now waited, defenseless and nearly ready to give birth, had haunted him throughout the day. Even now it caused his muscles to tense and his heart to thump against his ribs, silently urging the driver to hurry and get them back to their families before it was too late. Leaving the women and children alone in the desert while they worked was a burden that lay heavily on each man's shoulders, but one they had no choice but to bear. It was also the purpose that drove them to long hours of labor and saving nearly every penny they earned so they could take their loved ones from the camp and away to a safer place.

Tomorrow, Francisco thought. *It is Sunday, and we will not go to work. Surely I have enough money saved by now that Isabella and I can at last find a little house of our own. I will speak to Ernesto before we go to sleep tonight. And then tomorrow, I will do whatever is necessary to get my* esposa *out of that desert and all its dangers. All I ask, El Señor, is a safe, warm shelter for Isabella and our little one.*

Angry clouds had moved in during the night. Relentless wind swirled the desert dirt and sliced through their clothing and blankets. It had become a full-time job just keeping the campfire from burning out. If the heavy clouds unleashed a torrent of freezing rain, the fire would be extinguished and they would have nothing to keep them warm or dry. Isabella could see that Francisco was as restless as she, possibly more so.

She watched him now, as he huddled with Ernesto and spoke in hushed tones. What were they planning? Was it time to leave the camp and look for a home of their own? Francisco had told her they had enough money now that they might be able to do that, if they could just figure out where to go and how to convince someone to rent to them, even if it was just a small room—anything, so long as it was warm and dry.

Isabella's teeth chattered in the Sunday morning windstorm. She pulled her blanket nearly closed over the top of her head in an effort to keep the sand from blowing into her eyes. Her skin felt grimy, and she longed for a warm shower, but what could Francisco do? It was a long walk to town, and she would slow him down whether she walked at his side or allowed him to carry her. But if they did not try, how would they survive the coming storm that seemed more inevitable with every passing moment?

"Help us, *Señor*," she whispered, peering through the tiny opening she had left in her blanket, her eyes fixed on her *esposo* and his *amigo*. "Show us what to do. Should we leave here and try to find a place to live, even if it takes us the entire day to get there? Or should we wait until the storm passes?"

The thought of remaining out in the open during the approaching storm did not sound like a good choice, but the alternative sounded nearly as impossible. If only there were a cave or at least a larger outcropping where they could all huddle together for warmth and safety! Even then, she doubted they would be safe, as she had heard terrible stories of flash floods in the desert, washing everything away in a matter of minutes. If the sky poured out even half of what she imagined the clouds held, they might all be killed before the day was through.

"It is Sunday, *Señor*," she prayed. "I know my *abuelo* is at church, praying for us. Oh, please hear him—even if You do not wish to hear or answer me. He is a good man, a faithful one who prays to You every day—like my *esposo*. Please listen to them and help us. Bring an answer quickly, *por favor!*"

The wind's eerie whistle intensified, but no other answer found its way into her heart, as Isabella gave in to the tears that burned heavy in her eyes.

Davey was excited to be back at Sunday school with his friends, though the class seemed smaller than usual today. Even the parking lot hadn't been as full when they pulled in. His mom had grumbled that it was because most people had enough sense to stay home in such awful weather, with a storm ready to explode on them at any moment. But Davey had heard his grandmother working hard at trying to convince his mother that the storm would surely hold off until they got back, and that they'd all feel better if they went to church before it hit. Davey was glad his grandma had apparently won the argument because here they were, all three of them in their separate classes, though he'd noticed his mom watching the sky closely as they hurried from the parking lot to the building.

"Does anyone have anything you'd like the class to pray about today?"

Mrs. Mortenson, the Sunday school teacher who always made Davey think of Mary Poppins, stood in front of the room, looking out over the fifteen or so five- and six-year-olds, smiling as she waited. He wondered what she'd look like carrying a big black umbrella. Would she go sailing off into the sky like Mary Poppins? He almost giggled at the thought.

"Did you have something, Davey?"

Her question yanked him back from his imaginings, and he blinked in response. Did he have something? What did she mean?

Mary Poppins Mortenson smiled wider, and Davey wondered how that was possible. "Did you have a prayer request for us, Davey?"

Davey's mind was blank except for the image of his teacher floating away under an umbrella. A prayer request? No, he didn't have one...did he? Somehow he knew he should, though. What kind of person didn't have at least one thing to pray about?

"My grandma," he said, feeling his cheeks flame. "She went to the hospital."

The teacher nodded. "Yes, I heard that. And I heard she's home and feeling better. We're so glad, aren't we, class?"

A hum of agreement and nodding heads joined in, as Davey suddenly wished his mom had won instead of Grandma, and that they'd all stayed home after all.

"We will certainly pray that your grandma will continue to get better," the teacher said. "Anyone else?"

Davey's shoulders eased slightly, as he felt the attention turn toward a girl in the front row who was saying something about her dog being lost. Mrs. Mortenson assured her they would pray for her lost dog, and Davey's mind drifted away once again, this time to the ever-darkening sky outside the classroom window. His mom had said it was cold enough to snow. The thought made him smile. It almost never snowed in Arizona, but if it did today, he knew what he was going to be doing once they got home from church.

CHAPTER 27

THE WEATHER IS JUST TOO BAD," FRANCISCO WHISPERED, WRAPPED in the blanket now with Isabella as they sat just far enough from the fire so the others could not overhear them but still close enough to gain at least a little warmth. "We cannot leave now. It is too far, *mi amor*. You would never make it, not now with the *bebito* so close to coming. Ernesto says he believes it will snow before nightfall, but that is better than rain. At least we will not be flooded out."

"But what will we do?" Isabella asked, her chin pressed against her husband's chest as she bent her neck and peered up at him. She knew she should not add to his concern, but the vision of the two of them freezing to death in the desert was becoming a very real possibility in her mind. "It is already so cold! What will happen if it really does snow?"

He kissed her forehead and smiled. "I will dig a spot in the sand," he said. "Over there, under the outcropping, just big enough for the two of us to squeeze in. I will line it with a blanket for you, and then I will lie right beside you to keep you warm. We will be all right, Isabella."

"But...the others. What about them? The spot is not big enough for all of us."

Francisco nodded as his brows drew together. "*Sí.* You are right. But I have already spoken to Ernesto and the others, and they agree that you need the most protection because of the little one. The others will do their best to huddle together and to keep the fire going. We brought lots of wood back with us last night, so the fire should burn through the night." He smiled. "¿You see, *mi querida? El Señor* has blessed us with these cold temperatures so it would snow and not rain. That will make it a little easier to keep the fire burning."

Isabella marveled at the way her *esposo* could find something to be thankful for, even in the worst situations—and this one was surely the worst. Would they have been better off staying at that house with Olivia and Alberto, despite the evil that took place there? At least they would have been warm and her *bebito* would not be in danger of being born outside.

She shook her head. No. They had been right to leave there, and she had not forgotten her responsibility to report what went on in that place—and she would do so as soon as possible. If only *El Señor* would get them out of this desert safely, then she would find a way to tell the authorities. For now she knew only that they had been right to flee that house.

But was it right to leave Ensenada? Was Abuelo *right to give us the money and beg us to go?*

The questions swirled in her mind like the maddening desert wind. Was there even a right or wrong answer to the questions that tormented her?

Francisco kissed her again. "Stay here," he said. "I will go and dig that hole so you can be safe and warm when the snow comes."

Isabella watched him walk toward the outcropping, as she pulled the blanket tighter and realized he had not said *if* the snow comes, but *when*.

Miriam was nearly faint with relief by the time she finally parked her mother's five-year-old Toyota Avalon in front of the house. She was so much more comfortable driving the old truck, but she couldn't very well squeeze her mother and son into that uncomfortable seat and chug them all the way down the road to church. Besides, the tires on the Avalon were better, and today had been no day to take chances on the road.

She pushed open the door and climbed out, but Davey beat her to the front porch. "It's going to snow," he called back over his shoulder. "I'm going to find my sled!"

Miriam heard her mother's chuckle behind her and turned back, smiling in spite of herself. "We haven't even had a single snowflake yet, and already he's looking for his sled."

"I was thinking the exact same thing," Carolyn said, grinning as she caught up with her daughter, linking her arm through Miriam's. "Well, I for one hope he gets his snow—plenty of it so he can use that sled that hangs on the porch and almost never sees the light of day. And if he does, I plan to bundle up and sit on the porch and watch him. There may not be any hills to slide on anywhere near, but I imagine old Rocky will be more than happy to pull him around in it."

"No doubt," Miriam agreed, although she made a mental note to convince her mother to watch through the picture window from inside, rather than sitting out in the cold.

By the time the two women were in the house and had removed their various wrappings, Davey had managed to get the sled down from its hanging peg and lug it into the entryway. "Here it is," he announced, his blue eyes shining.

Miriam shook her head and ruffled his hair. "Don't you think we should eat lunch first—and maybe wait for the snow to start before taking that thing out there?"

Davey's shoulders slumped, though the sparkle in his eyes dimmed only slightly. "I guess," he said. "But can't I at least put it out on the porch so it'll be ready when the snow comes?"

Miriam bent down and kissed the top of his head. "Sure. Why not?"

Davey's grin was back, as he spun around and headed for the door, his sled in hand and Rocky following close behind, his tail swinging wildly in the air.

Miriam watched them disappear out the front door and then turned to head for the kitchen to start making lunch. Carolyn stood just feet from her, tears in her eyes and a smile on her face. "There's nothing I like better than seeing the two of you getting along like that," she said.

Miriam bit back the tears that threatened to burst out of her own eyes, and nodded. "Me too," she mumbled, afraid to say anything more.

Davey thought the snow would never come. He had waited as patiently as he was able while they ate grilled cheese sandwiches and talked about the low attendance at Sunday School and church. He listened to his mother and grandmother talk about how unusual but certainly not unheard of it was to have snow in the Arizona desert. And he kept his eyes glued to the kitchen window, watching for that first flake to announce the arrival of what he hoped would be the biggest snowstorm this desert had ever seen.

Big enough to close school for tomorrow, he mused. Or maybe even the whole week, which meant he wouldn't have to go back to school until after the holidays since their vacation would start this Friday. Whoa, that would really be cool—no school for three weeks and tons of snow! He glanced down at Rocky, who lay silently at his feet. Davey knew that playing in the snow would be a lot more fun with his dad, just because everything was more fun with his dad. But even without him, Davey had the best dog in the whole world, and his grandma was feeling better, and even his mom hadn't seemed quite so mad lately. All he needed to make everything absolutely perfect was a great big snowstorm that would shut down the school and let him play on his sled clear through Christmas and beyond.

As if on cue, the first white flake caught his eye as it drifted past the window. He felt his eyes widen. Had he really seen it, or was he just imagining it because he wanted it so badly? And then he saw the next one... and the next. Snow! It was here! It was really, truly snowing!

"Snow!" he cried, jumping up from his chair and rocketing his golden lab to life in the process. As the boy *yipped* around the room and Rocky barked his excitement by proxy, the snow intensified, and Davey thought life was just about as good as it could get. Now if he just knew how long it took for those little flakes to build up enough for him to go sledding in the yard.

CHAPTER 28

Don Alfredo's heart felt as heavy as a stone, yet jagged with red-hot pain. Something was terribly wrong, and only God knew what it was. All the weeping old man could do was sprawl on the floor and plead with the Savior for mercy, as he had been doing for several hours now.

It had begun in the earliest of morning hours, long before the sun had sent out even its first rays of light to brighten the eastern sky. Don Alfredo had been awakened from a deep sleep by the sensation of being strangled. Gasping for breath, he had jerked himself from the comfort of his blankets and sat up straight on the side of the bed.

"¿Que pasa, Señor?" he had whispered, begging God to show him what was happening that required such a violent awakening. The call to prayer was unmistakable, but the purpose hidden. Surely it had to do with Isabella and Francisco.

And the *bebito*? Could it be time for the little one's birth? Truly it was close now and could even happen this very night. And yet the trembling *viejo* sensed it was so much more than that.

"Por favor," he whispered, sliding from the bed to his knees, already weeping from the pain and urgency. "Please, *Señor*, show me how to pray. Lead me. Guide me. Help me! I can do nothing without You."

The certainty that Isabella and Francisco were indeed in imminent danger flooded his aching heart, and he quickly began to pray for their safety and protection, asking God to send angels to surround and cover them. But even resting on his knees did not seem humble or desperate enough as he prayed. Without missing a word or a tear, he spread himself on the cold, hard floor and continued to pray for what little was left of his beloved *familia*. Though he did not know the nature of their danger, God did, and Don Alfredo was confident that He alone could save them.

Miriam pulled her still damp hair back into a ponytail and clipped it tight. She peered into the mirror and grimaced at the shadows under her green eyes, making her appear older than her twenty-nine years. Makeup might help, but why bother? Who was going to see it? Her mother? Her son? The animals?

She shook her head and exited the bathroom, stopping in her room long enough to slide on her boots. There was work to do today, despite several inches of snow that would no doubt hinder her progress. A quick cup of coffee and she'd be on her way, leaving her mom and Davey asleep since there would quite obviously be no school that day, or possibly for the rest of the week.

Flipping the switch on the coffeepot, which she'd prepared before going to bed the night before, she smiled as she remembered how joyous Davey had been at the end of the day. His cheeks and nose were bright red and his hands nearly frozen, even through his mittens, but he had declared it to be "the best day ever." Miriam nearly laughed aloud at his youthful exuberance.

As the hot liquid dripped into the glass carafe and the aroma of brewing coffee teased her nostrils, she stepped into the hallway to turn up the thermostat so the house would be nice and toasty. She would have to settle for a warm coat and the less than adequate warmth of the barn as she went about her chores.

By the time she got her thermal mug filled and had donned her jacket and mittens and headed for the front door, she was surprised to find Rocky already waiting for her. The old dog was faithful, but she could handle what needed to be done without him. Better that he stay here and take care of Davey.

"You're in charge, old boy," she said, smiling down at him as she patted his head. "Stay inside and take care of things, you hear?"

Rocky thumped his tail as if he understood. Despite his unfailing loyalty, which would no doubt send him tromping through the snow after her, she imagined he would be relieved to remain indoors. The thought that, if she didn't have this farm to take care of and they lived in town like normal people, she could stay inside too crossed her mind. But she pushed it out as fast as it had come. There was work to be done, and no one else to do it. Best get started.

She opened the front door, sucked in her breath at the blast of cold air that assaulted her, and stepped out onto the slippery porch.

Francisco had kept his arms wrapped around his pregnant wife all night, wondering more than once if they would be frozen solid in the morning. Despite the blankets and shared body heat, he knew that both of them were in danger of not making it through the night. He could not even let himself think of how the others must be faring out in the open.

At least the wind was not as bad as I expected, he thought, hopeful that the flakes had finally stopped falling and perhaps the storm was at last over. Was it possible the fire had kept burning all night? Did he dare move to find out?

Isabella still shivered from time to time, even in her sleep, and Francisco no longer felt the baby rolling in her stomach, even though his arm rested on her side. The little one had been active earlier; Francisco prayed he was now sleeping, along with Isabella.

He turned his head to look over his shoulder, but realized he was going to have to get up to see the others, whom he had left huddled together around the fire when he and Isabella retired to their shelter. At least his precious *esposa* had been sheltered from the brunt of the storm, but he was anxious now to get her up and over to the fire—if indeed it had survived the night.

Slowly he moved his arm from her side and began to pull back so he could stand without disturbing her. Once he was assured that the fire still burned, he would wake her and carry her to it. He raised himself to his feet and turned toward the campfire, the faint spark of hope in his heart reviving when he saw the flickering flames. Ernesto and the others were even now adding wood to bring it back to a roar. How good it would feel to warm themselves around it!

Francisco smiled and bent down to awaken his still sleeping wife. The sooner he could get her to the fire, the better. But as he reached to touch her shoulder, a faint rumbling sound in the distance caught his attention. He stopped and turned toward it, though he could see nothing. Others were also gazing toward the sound, so he knew he had not imagined it. What could it be? Surely the truck was not coming to take them to work on a day such as this! Though Francisco did not want to miss a day's wages, he would never be able to leave Isabella behind in these freezing conditions.

"What is it, *mi amor?*"

His wife's voice pulled his attention back to her side. She sat up slowly, her long hair disheveled as she rubbed her swollen abdomen.

"What is that noise?" she asked, her brows drawing together. "Is it the truck, coming to take you to work?"

Francisco shook his head, anxious to reassure himself, as well as her. "No, Isabella. I am sure it is not. But even if it is, I will not go today. I will not leave you here in this cold." An idea flitted around the edges of his mind, and he paused. Was it possible?

He smiled. "If it is indeed the truck, coming to take us to work, I will ask if you can ride with us into town. I have enough money for you to spend a day in a room somewhere, and I have seen many little motels near where we work. You could stay warm and safe there while I work, and then I can try to find us a more permanent place. What do you think, ¿mi querida? Would you like that?"

Isabella's nod was tentative, as if she could not imagine such luxury falling into their lap. How long had it been since his poor wife had been safe and warm and content? How long since even the dream of a place of their own had been an actual possibility?

Too long, Francisco thought. *I must make it come true quickly, before another night comes upon us.*

He put out his hand. "Come. We will stand by the fire and warm ourselves until we see if the truck is coming for us. If it is, then we will say good-bye to this camp and go to town—together."

Isabella hesitated. "What if it is not the work truck? What if...it is someone else?"

Her words triggered a surge of adrenaline, along with the memory of the men from the other camp who had not shown up for work last week. The general consensus was that they had either been deported...or worse. Was it possible the approaching noise brought more tragedy into their already dismal situation?

Murmurs from the others began to escalate, and Francisco realized that they too were beginning to consider the possible danger that might very well be barreling down on them as they stood, defenseless in its approach. He had to do something to protect Isabella and the *bebito*, and from the growing sound of the approaching rumble, he did not have long to do it.

"Lie back down," he ordered, shushing Isabella's protests as he covered her with dirt from the hole he had dug the night before, leaving only her face exposed so she could see and breathe. Then he scrambled to gather loose twigs and even a couple of tumbleweeds to spread out in front of the entrance to the rock overhang. Satisfied that the camouflage looked natural, as if it had blown and landed there during the snowstorm, he quickly began to cover his tracks in the snow as he backed away from Isabella's hiding place.

"Francisco!" Her voice was frantic. "Where are you going? Do not leave me here alone!"

His heart constricted. "I will be back," he promised, wondering if it was a promise he would be able to keep. "Do not move, and do not speak until I return," he ordered.

"But—"

"Do it for me," he called. "And for our *bebito. Por favor, mi amor.* Do not argue with me. We do not have time. Just stay quiet... and pray that *El Señor* will protect us."

May it be so, he begged silently, and then turned to join the others as they awaited their fate.

CHAPTER 29

ISABELLA LAY PERFECTLY STILL, NOT SO MUCH BECAUSE SHE WANTED TO obey her husband's directive but because the dirt piled on top of her offered little choice. The need for restraint came in not crying out when the rumbling sound came so close that the ground beneath her shook, as if sharing her terror. This was not the sound of the work truck, rolling into camp to pick up the men for their daily trek to town. Isabella was certain that at least two vehicles had arrived, undoubtedly large ones carrying several occupants, for many loud, gruff voices filled the air with commands and curse words, all in Spanish.

Coyotes, she thought. Maybe even Alberto and the others looking for them since their escape. But though she strained to distinguish the various voices, she did not recognize Alberto's among them. She did, however, hear Ernesto's, as he attempted to insert reason into the growing chaos of shouts from the intruders and cries from the women and children.

"*Que quieres?*" he asked, his usual gentle tone raised to be heard above the others. "What do you want? We are just poor men, trying to feed our *familias*. We have nothing of any value here."

Isabella heard the laughter of several men, and it was obvious it came in response to Ernesto's words.

"That you are poor men we can see," declared one voice, "but that you have nothing of value?" The pause was filled with an evil Isabella could almost feel. "That I do not believe," the man said. "We are looking for workers—of many kinds—and I see many among you who would qualify."

He laughed again, and Isabella held her breath. She wanted desperately to believe this was just another group of men looking for day laborers, but her heart knew better.

Ernesto's voice lowered only a notch as he answered. "*Sí*, we are workers. But we already have jobs, working in town. The truck did not come to get us today because of the snow, but we will be back at work tomorrow."

This time the laugh came only from the one who had spoken earlier, and it came out more as a snort. "I do not think so, *amigo*. For when the truck returns for you tomorrow, you and the others will no longer be here. You will be working for us."

Isabella felt her eyes widen, as both her heart and her *bebito* pounded against her ribs. It was only her thought of the little one that kept her from crying out for Francisco.

And then she heard his voice. Francisco. She could picture him, stepping up to address the man who was apparently the leader of this invading group.

"I am sorry, *señor*," he said, his voice humble but firm. "We would like very much to work for you if we could, but we have already promised our time to the man in town. He will be expecting us. We cannot accept your invitation, *señor*."

Laughter once again erupted among the men whom Isabella could imagine surrounded the group, including her *esposo*. ¡*No!* she cried silently. *Do not hurt him! Help him*, Señor! ¡Por favor!

"I do not remember inviting anybody to do anything," the voice growled, silencing the laughter. "Especially you. But since you and your *amigo* are the ones who speak for the others, you can be the first to get into the truck."

A brief silence tore the breath from Isabella's lungs as she waited. When Francisco spoke again, she bit her tongue to keep from screaming.

"We will not go," he said, and then the words were repeated by Ernesto.

Again another silence swept through the camp.

"Fine," the man said, and Isabella's heart leapt. Had Francisco and Ernesto succeeded in forcing the man to back down?

And then she heard the gunshots—for surely that is what they were. Mercifully her throat constricted at the noise, or she would surely have screamed. But others were screaming by then—the women and children—as men shouted and cursed. Isabella wanted desperately to peer through the makeshift barrier that stood between her and Francisco, but it would take too long to push away the covering of sand that temporarily held her captive.

That's why he did it, she realized. *He knew there might be trouble and I would try to go to him. Francisco wanted to keep me and our* bebito *here, safe as long as possible. But how can I remain hidden when my* esposo *is out there with those awful men? What is happening to him, and to the others?*

The little one within her kicked and rolled wildly, as if aware that something was wrong. The reminder of the need to protect him above all else kept her silent, even as tears rolled down her cheeks and into the dirt where she lay. How long would she be forced to stay here, and what would she find when she finally came out?

Don Alfredo was exhausted. The morning sun was in full display by the time he arose from the floor, his ancient bones complaining all the way.

After working out the kinks and massaging some life back into his cold feet, he hobbled to the kitchen area to reheat yesterday's coffee, though he had no desire for food. He felt as if he had been in a very long battle—and he was not yet sure if he had won or lost. But he had long ago learned that even if he lost an occasional battle, *El Señor* had already won the war.

A steaming cup of stale but strong coffee in his hand, he stepped to the front door and pulled it open, sensing the need for fresh air. His own sweat had a fearful edge to it that morning, and he somehow realized that the battle was not over. He would strengthen himself during this brief respite, and then he would be called back into service.

What is it, mijita? he wondered, the vision of his *nieta* as he had last seen her just before she and Francisco left for the States taunting him with possibilities. Was she in labor? In some sort of danger? Could it be a spiritual crisis? Don Alfredo knew Isabella's faith was not as it should be, and he had long prayed about the situation, believing that only *El Señor* Himself could remedy it.

Whatever it was, the circumstances were serious. The old man took a last deep breath of outside air and then turned back to the table where he had spent so many hours reading and studying the tattered *Biblia* that Esmerelda had given him so very many years ago.

He sat down with his coffee and opened the book that was his source of truth and strength. He would continue reading until *El Señor* called him back to intercession.

The eerie quiet of the desert alarmed Isabella more than the screaming and shouting she had heard earlier. It seemed forever that she had waited in her hiding place for Francisco to return, telling herself that surely he would at any moment. But her body ached from the cold and not moving, though her heart ached much worse. The only thing holding her back now was fear of what she might find when she did.

A distant caw of a crow startled her into moving at last. With minimal effort she was able to dislodge herself from the layer of dirt that covered her. She crawled a couple of feet to the loosely piled branches and slowly, painfully, moved them aside until she could see the smoldering embers of the campfire. Two figures lay near it; neither moved. One, she knew, was Francisco.

They have hurt him, she told herself, pushing through the opening and lifting herself to her feet before forcing one foot in front of the other as she hurried to his side. *He is injured, but he will be all right.* El Señor *has surely protected him.*

From the corner of her eye she saw that the other figure lying near Francisco was Ernesto. She was not surprised. The two had apparently assumed leadership in the confrontation and had been injured because of it. She prayed Ernesto would be all right, but first she must check on Francisco. He needed her, and she would not let him down.

Falling to her knees beside his motionless body, she gasped at the blank look in his open eyes. Gathering her courage, she stroked his cheek, horrified at how cold it was.

Of course he is cold, she scolded herself. *What did you expect? He has been out here in the snow, with no blanket to keep him warm.*

"I will keep you warm now, *mi amor*," she whispered, leaning down to press her face against his. As she brushed the dark hair from his forehead, her eyes widened at the dried blood that started at his hairline and spread backward.

"Oh, Francisco, I knew you were hurt, but I did not realize how badly. I am so sorry that I took so long to come to you, but...but you told me to stay there, to wait for you, and..." Tears erupted from her eyes as she threw herself down on the chest that no longer moved with the breath of life. How could she help him now? What could she do to make him better? He was so cold, so still...

That was it. She would take him back to the overhang and cover him with the blankets that had been left behind by the others. Surely if she kept him warm and dry, away from the snow and wind, then he would be all right. He had to get better because this was the week they were going to get their *casita*, where their little one would be born. It was up to her to see that Francisco got well so that could happen.

Though it took her nearly an hour, she pulled and tugged and pushed until she got Francisco under the outcropping and into the shallow pit where she herself had lain not long before. Then she set about gathering blankets and anything else she could find, including scraps of food and water, to take inside the little dwelling that would be their shelter until her *esposo* was well and strong again and could take them to town as he had promised. Surely the truck that picked the workers up each morning would return tomorrow, and by then Francisco would be better. Until then, she would stay at her husband's side and keep him warm, as he had done for her so many times before.

CHAPTER 30

MIRIAM WAS RELIEVED THAT THE SNOW HAD NOT RETURNED ON Monday, and much of it had melted away by Tuesday morning. School was back in session, at least until Friday when they got out for the two-week break that would carry them into the New Year. It would be a lot easier to tackle the myriad of things that needed to be done with Davey in class and little or no snow to hinder her throughout the day. Though she'd accomplished the absolute necessities on Monday, she couldn't imagine how people in the Midwest and other places who dealt with snowstorms on a regular basis ever kept up with their normal tasks, let alone all the extra responsibilities that came with bad weather.

She had insisted on driving Davey to the bus again this morning, even though her mother was up and had offered to walk with him. Miriam had argued that the weather was still far too cold for either of them to be walking, which Davey contested didn't make sense because he'd been out in the cold all day Sunday and most of Monday, playing in the snow. She supposed he was right, but it was really her mother she was most concerned about.

It had been easier to drive him in the truck and kiss him good-bye as the yellow bus pulled up, and then go about her day without worrying about her mother.

Funny, she thought, bouncing along the dirt road toward home, *how snow is so beautiful and white when it first falls, but it sure looks awful when it starts melting. Doesn't do much for these roads either.*

Jerking over potholes that she made a mental note needed to be fixed as soon as possible, she headed for home. There were animals waiting to be fed, and that took priority over bumpy roads. And then she'd better pop inside the house and check on her mom. Though Carolyn seemed to be doing better, Miriam no longer had the confidence that she'd once had in her mother's abilities. She knew Carolyn would do everything possible to help out with Davey and the house, but Miriam also realized that many of those responsibilities could soon fall on her own already overburdened shoulders. If that should happen, a move to town might quickly become inevitable.

Though Don Alfredo had spent another restless night, he had at least gotten some much needed sleep. Tuesday morning dawned bright and warm, and after some coffee and a light breakfast of *huevos* and *frijoles*, he had taken a second cup of coffee outside, where he now sat in his usual spot in front of his house. He smiled in welcome when he saw Don Felipe heading across the street in his direction.

"Buenos dias," he called to the slightly younger man. "How are you this morning, *amigo?"*

Don Felipe nodded in greeting and pulled up the crate next to Don Alfredo's chair. Once settled in, he leaned back against the wall and gazed up into the sky. "I am well, Don Alfredo. *Y usted?"*

"I too am well," he answered.

The two men sat quietly for a moment, until at last Don Felipe asked, "And your *familia? Any word yet from Isabella?"*

The old man's heart grew cold, as if someone had thrown ice water on it. He shook his head. "No. No word yet." Tears stung his eyes. "I have spent much time in prayer about it, but nothing. *Nada.*"

Don Felipe nodded. "It is very difficult, *¿verdad?* We pray and we wait...and we pray some more. Always it is like that."

Don Alfredo knew his friend's words were true. He appreciated that his neighbor had come to sit with him...to help him in the waiting.

"I too have prayed for your *nieta,*" Don Felipe said. "I think of her and her *esposo* often, especially at night when I cannot sleep, and I pray for them."

"*Gracias,*" Don Alfredo said, his heart warmed slightly to know that not only was his friend waiting with him, but he was praying with him as well.

Isabella had slept little, as she spent the night next to her cold, unmoving husband. Why was he not responding to her warmth? She had covered him with many blankets, had wrapped her body around his, and had prayed to *El Señor* throughout the night. Now it was Tuesday; the snow was nearly gone but no truck had come with the sunrise to take the men to work—or to take her and Francisco to town so they could find a place to live. Had the employer heard of the raid on their camp? Surely he had, or he would have sent the truck to get them.

She knew by now, of course, that her *esposo* no longer had the money to get a *casita* for them, even if the truck did come. His boots had not been on his feet when she found him lying by the dying campfire, and that is where he had kept their money. Even when she spotted the discarded boots nearby, she knew before she checked them that they would be empty.

The sun was overhead now—nearly noon. Needing to relieve herself, she ventured out from the little spot where she had shivered through the night with a lifeless Francisco. But though her husband did not move, her *bebito* continued to do so. How much longer until he decided to be born? What would she do then? Oh, if only Francisco would get better! Or if Lupe were here, or at least one of the other women, someone who already had children and knew what to expect, maybe then she would not feel quite so frightened and alone.

"You have failed us, *Señor*," Isabella said as she finished her task and dared one quick glance at Ernesto, who had not moved from the spot where she saw him the previous day. "We prayed to You, but You have not answered. What are we to do now?"

Her feet feeling nearly as heavy as her heart, she trudged back to her tiny shelter and crawled inside. Maybe *El Señor* meant for her and her *bebito* to die after all. If that was so, then it would happen next to Francisco, for she truly had no place else to go.

"What should I do, *mi amor*?" she whispered, lying down beside her *esposo*. "You told me to protect our *bebito*, and I want to do that, but...but I am not strong enough. I have no money and very little food. Where can I go? Who will help me?"

Sobs shook her body as she fell onto his, weeping and calling his name. Her heart knew the truth, but her mind refused to accept it. She would not believe that Francisco had left her alone. He had promised to come back for her, to take care of her and their baby. It was not possible that he would desert her like this! Was *El Señor* truly so cruel that He would take Francisco from her and then leave her and the child to die alone?

"It is not fair," she sobbed, praying in spite of her anger and grief. "You have proved to me that I cannot trust You...and yet You have left me with no other choice. *Ay, Dios mío*, what am I to do? How can I go on? *¡Ayúdame, Señor!* Help me, *por favor!*"

CHAPTER 31

ISABELLA STRUGGLED THROUGH TWO MORE NIGHTS IN THE COLD, cavelike shelter, where her husband's stiff, cold body did nothing to warm her as it had for so many nights before. She was alone, except for the howling wind outside, a squirming baby inside, and a God who seemed not to care if she lived or died. By Thursday morning she knew she had no choice but to leave this place behind and try to find shelter before the *bebito* was born.

"Please wait, *mijito*," she whispered, cupping her swollen belly in her palm. "Just a little longer, *por favor*. We will leave today and try to find a place that is warm and safe before you enter this cruel world."

Tears stung her eyes as she spoke, knowing that she had to leave Francisco's body behind, as well as Ernesto's. But first she would drag the older man into the shelter so at least the two friends could be together until she could somehow return to give them a proper burial.

"I will come back, *mi amor*," she whispered into her husband's unresponsive ear. "I do not know how or when, but I will return for you. I promise."

Jagged pain sliced her heart as she thought of Francisco's promise to return for her, and she could only hope that she would be able to fulfill her word to the man she loved.

Wrapping as many blankets around her as she could and still walk, while carrying the few remaining scraps of food and two plastic bottles of water in a makeshift satchel over her shoulder, she kissed her beloved good-bye and stepped from the shelter into a frigid wind that mocked her with its cries.

You will die out here, it seemed to say. *You do not even know where you are going. Just stay here and die beside Francisco. Why waste the steps to go into the desert, when the end will be the same?*

But she pressed on, remembering Francisco's last words to her about taking care of their *bebito*. What else did she have to live for? Only the little one—Francisco's child. He was all she had left. She would do what she could for him. Maybe she would make it. Maybe she would find help in time. If not, she decided, then it must be the will of *El Señor*.

Miriam's back ached, but she was down to just a half-dozen more bales of hay to stack and she'd be done for the day. David had always told her that cows were practical but horses were for love.

"If you don't love them, you shouldn't have them because they'll eat you out of house and home," he'd say, time and again. Then he'd grin and say, "That's why I have them—because I love them."

She knew that was true, and he had instilled that same love in Davey, who continually nagged her to let him ride more often. At his age, though, the only way he could do that was if she went with him, and that was not her idea of a good time. She was much more at home in the pickup, or even her mom's Toyota.

Horses were just too unpredictable for her. She didn't want to rest her entire body weight on something that had a mind of its own.

"Hi, Mom."

Davey's voice cut into her thoughts as she managed to load the last bale onto her pile. It was bad enough to have animals that didn't earn their keep, but to have them out in the desert where the range was stripped bare and scarcely produced enough to keep the lizards alive was just plain foolish.

She wiped her brow with her sleeve and turned toward her son. His blue eyes shone wide and bright.

"What are you doing?" he asked.

Miriam chuckled, unable to bite back the obvious response. "What does it look like?"

Davey shrugged, his quilted jacket straining at his shoulders. "I don't know. Stacking hay, I guess."

"Good guess." She smiled and tousled his brown curls. "And what about you? What are you doing?"

He shrugged again. "Looking for you. Grandma got tired of playing checkers with me and went to take a nap."

An alarm bell clanged in Miriam's head. "Is she all right? Did she say anything about not feeling well?"

Davey shook his head. "Nope. Just said she was tired."

Miriam nodded. She supposed that could be the case. Still . . .

"Tell you what," she said, laying her hand on her son's shoulder. "I'm done out here, so why don't we go in the house and check on Grandma, and then I'll see if I can find something to heat up for dinner."

Davey grinned. "I was hoping you'd say that. I'm kinda hungry, but Grandma said no cookies before dinner."

"Grandma's right. So let's go see what's hiding out in the fridge. Bound to be something we both like."

"Hot dogs, maybe?"

Miriam feigned shock and positioned her hands on her hips. "You'd eat hot dogs every day if I let you, wouldn't you?"

Davey nodded. "Yep. I love hot dogs!"

She laughed, and he joined in as the two of them exited the barn's double doors and headed for the house. It was one of the few times that Miriam didn't make it a point to stop and lock those double doors before heading inside for the night.

The wind had picked up, and the sky was clear and the temperature dropping as the western sky, ablaze with purple and pink streaks, bade farewell to the day. Isabella was certain she could not walk another step, but she knew she could not spend the night out in the open. Surely there was a rock or a cave or tree or ... something.

And then she saw it. Not just one building, but two—one no doubt a large house, the other an even larger barn. Did she dare take the chance? Surely she would not be welcome in the house, but maybe she could find a way to get inside the barn and sleep there for the night. It would not be as warm as a real house, but at least she would be out of the wind and away from any wild animals that might be roaming nearby. She would rest there for a few hours and then leave, very early before anyone discovered her. The very idea of breaking into someone's barn caused her heart to race, but what choice did she have? She needed to find shelter for the night. She would deal with the morning when it got here.

Darkness covered her by the time she reached the two buildings. As she had suspected, one was indeed a house, with a large front porch and warm lights shining through the windows. How she longed to knock on the door and beg for a chance to come inside! But she knew better. She had heard how the Arizona farmers and ranchers hated her kind—the "illegals," they called them—and she knew she would not be welcome there. But maybe she could hide in their barn for just a little while, if she could just find a way to get inside.

Not expecting to succeed, she tried the double doors and was joyous when they pulled open. Slowly, and as quietly as possible, she opened them enough to squeeze inside and then closed them behind her. The soft sound of horses stomping and neighing alerted her to the fact that she was not alone. She waited until her eyes had adjusted to the near darkness, and then spotted a huge stack of hay bales in one corner. Beside them was a pile of loose hay, which she imagined might work well as a bed for the night.

Going around to the back of the pile, she fashioned a simple nest from the hay and settled down with her blankets on top of her. The hay was scratchy and made her nose itch, but it was warmer than it had been in her rock overhang shelter back at the camp.

The thought of Francisco and Ernesto, lying there stiff and cold, waiting for her to return and bury them, brought tears to her eyes. *"Por favor, Señor,"* she whispered, "do not let the wild animals find them. Please keep their bodies safe until I can find a way to go back and have them buried." She swiped at the tears that trickled down her face and then wriggled a bit in an attempt to get comfortable. Before she closed her eyes for the night, she whispered, *"Gracias, Señor,* for bringing us here. Please keep me and my *bebito* safe this night. I am so very, very tired."

In moments she was asleep, dreaming of the warm beach town of Ensenada and the *casita* where she and Francisco had lived together as newlyweds and where they had been so very happy together, even if only for a short while.

CHAPTER 32

ISABELLA SLEPT LATER THAN SHE HAD MEANT TO, AND THE SUN WAS already peeking through the slats in the barn walls when she opened her eyes. The sound of a rooster's crowing had awakened her before daylight, but she had rolled over and gone back to sleep. Now she shook her head in an attempt to clear it from the fuzziness of slumber and identify her surroundings. When she remembered the lonely trek across the desert and slipping into the barn after dark, her heart ached at the connection to Francisco and all she had lost. But time did not allow for mourning or tears. She would have to sneak out before the farm owners caught her.

Distant voices and the sound of a truck pulling away helped her relax, hoping the owners of the barn where she had slept were leaving for the day. She groaned as she stood to her feet. The baby was growing heavier by the day; it would not be long now until he pushed himself from the safety of her stomach into the cold and dangerous world that awaited him. How would she find shelter for him in time? If only she could stay here, but of course, that was not possible.

She picked up the sack with her meager rations and decided to eat a cold tortilla. It was not much, but it would keep her going for a little while. She washed it down with a couple of sips of water, and then gathered her belongings and prepared to make her exit back into the desert, making sure to straighten the hay so no one would know she had been there.

As she moved out from behind the hay and headed for the doors, she noticed a waist-high gate in the corner, next to the horse stalls. Curious, she decided to risk a couple of extra minutes to peek behind the gate. The horse in the stall nearest her whinnied as she passed by, and she stopped to pat its nose. She had always loved horses, and though she seldom had a chance to ride them, her memories of the few times her *papa* had taken her riding along the beach were among her favorites. Her *papa* had always said she was a natural with horses; she loved them, and they sensed that. She smiled and spoke to the sorrel with the beautiful, light-colored mane, and it tossed its head in response. Then she moved on to the gate.

Peering behind it, she was surprised to find an area the size of a large closet, though open except for the small gate at its entrance. She raised her eyebrows. Did she dare?

Unlatching the gate, she stepped inside. A few loose pieces of hay lay scattered across the floor, but otherwise the area seemed unused.

Her heart was racing now. Was it possible that *El Señor* had not abandoned her after all? Maybe this was His answer for a place of shelter, somewhere she could hide for a little while until the baby came. The thought that she would be discovered caused her mouth to go dry, but she shoved the concern away. What choice did she have? Where else could she go? Unless someone came to the gate and peered over the top, as she had done, no one would see her. And since the spot seemed deserted, there was a chance that she just might be able to stay here for a few days—at least until her food and water ran out. She would deal with that when the time came.

Moving quickly, she placed her belongings inside the gated area and brought just enough hay from the pile to make a small pallet, where she would sleep and wait for her *bebito* to come. She finished readying her little nest just as she heard the returning vehicle approaching her hiding place. Isabella froze, as the engine stopped, a door slammed, and boots crunched on cold, hard ground outside, headed in her direction. Silently, she pulled the gate shut behind her and lay down to wait...and to pray that *El Señor* would make her invisible for as long as she needed to be. She did not doubt that He could do so; the question was, would He?

Miriam let herself into the barn, berating herself for not getting an earlier start.

Not that she'd had much choice. It was either take Davey to the bus before starting her chores or let her mom take him. Though Carolyn was up and claimed to be ready, willing, and able to walk him down the long driveway, Miriam had convinced her to wait until the weather warmed up a bit more.

"Even with your cell phone, I'm just not comfortable with you walking in such cold weather," Miriam said, trying to sound more confident than she felt. "As soon as it warms up a bit, we'll get back to our old routine. Meanwhile, I don't mind driving Davey to the bus in the morning."

The ploy had worked for the time being, but Miriam knew she'd have to face it again when it came time for the bus to bring him home and the weather was better. Until then, one step at a time.

She sighed and headed for the first stall. Best get the horses taken care of and then go check on the rest of the animals. Thank goodness none of their cattle were dairy cows; she couldn't imagine having to milk them each day. It was enough just to keep the entire menagerie fed and watered.

The sorrel nudged her as she came close, and Miriam flinched. David used to say that was how the horses showed affection, but she wasn't interested in an emotional relationship with the animals; she just wanted to get them fed and move on to the next chore that needed to be done. Part of her wished she could be more like David or Davey, who seemed to be able to communicate not only with the horses but with the rest of the animals too. Maybe it was because she'd never really cared enough to try.

A multicolored flash caught her eye, and she swerved to identify it. Calico, named for her coloring, sauntered by, her tail twitching as she meowed her good morning. "Silly cat," she muttered, irritated with herself for being so jumpy. "You nearly scared me to death. You might have nine lives, but I only have one, so give me a little warning before you show up next time, will you?"

She wondered briefly where the other cat, Purr-Ball—aptly named by Davey for his never-ending purring and rubbing against anything that stood still—might be but dismissed the thought and moved on with the task at hand. One nice thing about barn cats, they fended for themselves and kept the mice population down in the process.

"Not like you, Milky Way," she said to the sorrel as she avoided its swishing tail. "You horses don't do anything to earn your keep around here. You just eat us out of house and home."

The light, reddish-brown steed shook its head and whinnied, as if in self-defense. Wasn't it enough to be beautiful and majestic and to carry its riders around on its back? For David, it had been, and for Davey as well. For Miriam? Definitely not. Every time she looked at any of the three horses that David had bought just a couple of years earlier—named Milky Way, Snickers, and Licorice by Davey—all she saw was dollar signs. But just about when she'd convince herself it was time to get rid of them, she'd catch Davey staring at them with such admiration that her heart would break inside her, and she knew she couldn't do it.

It's ridiculous, she thought. *Now that David's gone, these horses hardly ever get ridden anymore. But maybe, when Davey's older…*

She shook her head, much as Milky Way had done minutes earlier. Time to quit thinking and get busy working. There was just way too much to do, and not enough time to get it all done.

Isabella waited, scarcely breathing, until she was certain the woman had gone. How grateful she was to realize that the cold, hard ground outside crunched underfoot when someone was approaching! That meant she could venture out of her little spot and move around the barn a bit, so long as she paid close attention and scurried back to her hiding place if she heard anyone coming.

Gently she approached the first stall where the sorrel stood, munching its hay while keeping one eye fixed on the intruder. Isabella held out her hand as she opened the gate and stepped up to the magnificent animal, gently but firmly patting its thick neck, marveling at the strength she felt under her fingers.

"So your name is Milky Way," she said. "I am not sure what that means, but it is a very nice name."

The animal nodded its head and snorted, continuing to eat.

"My name is Isabella," she said, drawing closer to the horse's torso and allowing herself to make contact as she leaned in against the powerful body. The horse twitched but did not pull away. Isabella knew she had made a friend.

"I am glad to meet you, Milky Way," she said. "I hope you do not mind if I share your home for a little while." With one hand still on the horse's neck, she laid the other hand across her stomach. "I will have a *bebito* soon. Maybe you will be the first one to greet him when he comes into this world."

A soft nicker from the next stall caught her attention, and she moved from Milky Way's side, closing the gate behind her. Though she had been aware of the animals the night before, it had been too dark to see many details. Now she realized this dark brown horse in the middle was smaller than the other two, while the black one on the far end was the largest of all.

I wonder if there are three people living here, she wondered. *Maybe a man and woman and a child. The smaller horse in the middle would be just right for a little boy to ride.*

She smiled at the memory of her first horse ride with her *papa*. She had been no more than five, and her *madre* had been hesitant to let her go, thinking Isabella was too young and would be afraid of the huge animals. But Isabella had felt at home from the moment she saw them, gleaming under the Mexican sun. Sitting astride the old swaybacked nag had seemed the most natural thing in the world, and she had never missed a chance to ride again, however rare the occasions might have been.

"I am glad I am no longer alone," she said in a hushed tone, watched by three sets of eyes. "Thank you for allowing me to join you."

When she returned to her spot behind the gate, she was surprised to find an orange tabby licking itself as it lay on the hay. It eyed her warily as she sat down beside it, but the minute Isabella reached out to stroke its soft fur, the curious feline revved up its motor and purred. Isabella had found yet another friend.

CHAPTER 33

SCHOOL WAS OUT FOR TWO WEEKS, AND DAVEY COULDN'T BE happier. Even though the public school he attended referred to the annual vacation as "winter break," his grandma had told him that it used to be called "Christmas vacation," and he had decided that was exactly how he would think about it. Though he didn't believe in Santa Claus, since his parents had always told him the jolly man dressed in red was just a legend based on a man who once lived, he did believe in Jesus, whose birthday much of the world observed on this annual holiday. What could be more special than that?

Only six more days! Davey's Christmas countdown was in full swing. He always started it the day after Thanksgiving, and even though things had been a lot different this year with his grandma in the hospital, he hadn't forgotten to start marking the calendar. Now the big day was one week away, though he didn't count today since it was nearly over. Six more days seemed like forever, but the important thing was to get the decorating done before it got any closer.

"Mom?"

He hated it when his voice squeaked like a girl's, but he was nervous about bringing up the topic that he'd already mentioned several times. Before his dad died, they always decorated on Thanksgiving weekend. He understood why they hadn't this year, but he really thought they should have done so before this. He took a deep breath and tried again.

"Mom," he said, a bit louder this time as he stood in the doorway to her room, watching her sit at her desk, her head bent over a pile of papers. "The last time I asked you about decorating for Christmas, you said we could do it soon. Can we do it now?"

Miriam raised her head, her reddish-gold ponytail moving only slightly against her back and shoulders. Davey watched as her green eyes seemed to struggle to come into focus.

"I'm sorry, Davey," she said, her smile thin. "What did you say?"

The thought that she was probably paying bills and he hadn't picked a good time to talk to her crossed his mind, but he'd already interrupted her, so he might as well finish. "I...asked about decorating for Christmas. You said we could do it soon, and...Christmas is almost here."

A flash of irritation flitted across her face, and Davey cringed but stood his ground. He'd learned that his mother's temper was closer to the surface these days, but deep down she really loved him. He just needed to be patient, but it was getting harder to do that with each hour that ticked toward Christmas.

"This really isn't a good time," she said. "I'm in the middle of something right now."

Davey nodded. "I know, Mom. I didn't mean tonight. I was thinking...tomorrow? It's Saturday and..."

His voice trailed off, as tears threatened his eyes. Why did he have to be such a baby? He'd promised himself he wouldn't cry, and now he was right on the edge.

Miriam's smile widened then, pulling him back. "You're right," she said, standing from her chair and walking toward him. "We absolutely need to get those Christmas decorations up before another day goes by." She knelt in front of him and put her hands on his shoulders. "As soon as the animals are fed in the morning, we'll get right to work—inside and out. We'll even take a run over to the uncut place down the road and bring a tree home. What do you say?"

Davey's heart felt as if it would burst. "I say, great! I'll even help you feed the animals."

Miriam laughed. "Sounds like a good deal to me. We'll surprise Grandma and make breakfast before we get started."

She pulled him close and planted a kiss on his forehead, making Davey's insides feel warm and his toes tingly. He threw his arms around her neck. "I love you, Mom," he whispered.

"I love you, too, son."

Isabella had managed to keep herself hidden while the woman and child, whom she'd figured out by listening carefully was her son, fed and cared for the horses. She overheard them talking about feeding the chickens and cows too, all of which she had grown used to hearing by now, especially the rooster, which crowed each morning and woke her before daylight. Even her feline friend had left her to go out and greet the mother and child as they worked in the barn.

But now they were gone, chattering about something to do with Christmas decorations and plans, as best Isabella could understand. Christmas. *Navidad.* How would she face that special day all alone, with no one for company but a cat and some horses? She had spotted another cat roaming the barn but had been unable to coax it to come near her.

Worse than the loneliness, Isabella was running out of food and water. What would she do when there was none left? She rationed it carefully, but at best it would last no more than a few days. The hay-strewn corner of the barn was not much, but it was the only shelter she had right now, and she hesitated to leave. Where would she go? How would she keep up her strength so she could feed her *bebito* when he arrived, which would surely be any day now?

Voices caught her attention, and she crawled to a crack in the wall that she had discovered gave her a clear view of the house. There on the porch stood the woman and child who had come in earlier to care for the horses. An older woman sat bundled in a blanket on a rocking chair on the porch, eyeing the other two. What were they doing?

As Isabella watched, unable to distinguish their words at such a distance, their occasional bursts of laughter pierced her heart. How was it that some people went through life without experiencing any serious loss or pain, while others—like herself— lost everything? She had found herself praying to *El Señor* a lot lately, mostly out of necessity rather than choice, but she still could not understand why such a powerful God who was supposed to be so loving seemed not to care for her at all. Had she really been so bad a person? And what about her parents and siblings...and Francisco? Had they not all loved and worshipped Him? And yet He had allowed them to die. How could that be? Though she was afraid to say the words out loud, she often thought that if she were God, she would be much kinder.

Folding her legs beneath her, she leaned sideways against the barn wall and watched the house become a lighted display of tinsel and colored lights, with even a manger scene in front of the porch.

The holy familia, she thought. *They are revered in my country. Joseph, Mary, and Jesus.* The thought that the little family had nowhere to go when it was time for Jesus to be born, that they ended up in a place much like where she sat even now, struck her as quite sad.

"But at least Mary had Joseph," she whispered, as tears stung her eyes. "I no longer have my *esposo*. I am all alone, with no one to help me. What am I to do, *¿Señor?*"

A familiar hum started up beside her, at the same time she felt the soft fur against her hand. Absently petting the orange cat, she continued to watch the happy threesome as they put the finishing touches on their decorations, even taking a few extra moments to string a few lights around the barn doors. Though Isabella could not see those particular lights from her vantage point, their soft glow slipped through the barn's cracks and lent a muted hue to her surroundings.

Finished at last, the family gathered together in the yard to stand with their arms around each other, inspecting their handiwork. Isabella thought she had never in all her life felt so very alone.

Don Alfredo's heart was heavy. Isabella and Francisco had been gone nearly a month and a half now, and still he had no word from them. He dared not let himself dwell on the worst possibilities, telling himself they were just busy getting settled and had not been able to get a letter out to him yet. Still, he knew his *nieta* would not want him to worry and would do everything possible to let him know when they had arrived safely.

Tales of unscrupulous *coyotes* danced in his head, but he shoved them away, as he sat in front of his house, basking in the afternoon sun. Distant voices and even an occasional burst of laughter invaded his privacy, but not nearly enough to suit him. There was a time, not that long ago, when the air had been filled with the sound of children playing and families visiting back and forth. Now, terror filled the streets, and parents were afraid to let their little ones go outside to enjoy the fresh air. Such sadness grieved the old man nearly as much as the lack of news about Isabella and Francisco.

The bebito *will be coming soon*, he thought, *if he has not done so already. Was I a foolish* viejo *to send my* familia *away when I could have kept them here and held my* nieta's *little one in my arms? Is it possible that I sent them from a bad place to one that is even worse?*

How he prayed that it was not so! And yet, had he not prayed before giving them the money and sending them away? He had been so sure that *El Señor* had heard and answered, and that He would protect his loved ones as they fled the violence of the Mexican streets. What if he had been wrong? What if *El Señor* would not honor the old man's prayers because he had convinced Isabella and Francisco to break the law?

Doubts assailed Don Alfredo, but he continued to push them away to try to recapture the peace that came only when his mind was focused on *El Señor* and His faithfulness. What other hope did he have?

A familiar figure caught his eye then. Don Felipe had come out of his house and was making his way across the street, heading straight for the old man who wrestled with demons. How grateful he was to have a neighbor and friend who understood his need.

Wordlessly, Don Felipe nodded in greeting and pulled the crate over beside Don Alfredo's chair, where together they leaned against the wall and opened their hearts to the warm afternoon sun.

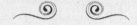

CHAPTER 34

WHEN DAVEY WOKE UP ON SUNDAY MORNING, HE HAD RACED outside before he even got dressed, just to see the decorations once again. His mom had called him right back into the house, but his heart had felt warm in spite of the cold air, just looking at the lights and tinsel, and especially the plastic baby Jesus in the manger.

Now they were back from church and had finished lunch. With his mom back in her room, saying she needed to finish paying the bills, and his grandma taking a nap, Davey was bored. Lying on his bed with Rocky at his feet, he stared at the ceiling, counting the familiar cracks and wondering what to do for the rest of the afternoon. He sure wished his dad was still around. He knew what they'd be doing right now if he were! They'd be out saddling up Snickers and Licorice for a ride around their twenty acres. Mom might even have come along on Milky Way.

Davey's heart burned as he remembered the few times the three of them had ridden together. The memory tugged at him until at last he sat up and announced, "Come on, Rocky. We can't go riding by ourselves, but we can at least go out to the barn and visit the horses. I haven't spent much time with Snickers lately, and I'll bet he's lonely."

Rocky, immediately alert, thumped his tail in agreement, and then quickly jumped off the bed and followed his master out of the bedroom door. Stopping just long enough to grab some apples from the fridge and his jacket from the hook near the front door, Davey called out, "Me and Rocky are going out to the barn to play for a while."

"All right," his mom called back. "But don't forget your jacket, and don't go anywhere else without letting me know. And stay out of those horse stalls! They'll stomp you if you get under their feet."

Davey sighed. "OK, Mom. I have my jacket."

He slammed the door behind him and ran toward the barn, with Rocky right beside him. He was no sooner inside than all three horses neighed their greeting, assuring him that he'd done the right thing to come and visit them. He might have to stay out of their stalls, but he could at least climb the gates and pet their noses. They liked that, almost as much as they loved eating apples.

Since Snickers was Davey's horse, he went to him first, climbing up on the second rung of the gate and petting the animal he so longed to ride. "Hey, boy," he said. "I've missed you." The horse nodded his head, and Davey was sure he had understood. Digging in his jacket pocket, he pulled out an apple and offered it to him. Snickers took it immediately, tickling Davey's hand in the process.

After a few moments the boy climbed down to go see the other horses, but noticed that he couldn't see his dog anywhere.

"Rocky, where are you?" he called, glancing around.

A sharp bark caught his attention then, and he followed its sound, spotting his faithful golden lab standing near the gate to an old storage area against the side wall near the front of the barn. His feathery tail was swishing back and forth, as he sniffed around the bottom of the gate, turning briefly to look at Davey as if inviting his master to join him, and then returning to his activity.

"What are you doing, you silly dog?" Davey asked, abandoning the horses momentarily and walking toward Rocky. "There's nothing back there. Come on. Come over here with me."

But the dog ignored him, whining now as he snuffled against the base of the gate and looking as if he were trying to find a way to squish himself underneath it.

"Rocky, stop it," Davey said, coming up beside him. "I told you, there's nothing back there..."

His voice drifted off, and he felt his eyes widen as he glanced between the slats of the old wooden gate and saw a large bundle of rags against the back wall. Lying next to the bundle was Purr-Ball.

"So that's what you're barking at!" He grinned. Rocky and the cats had long ago declared a truce, but they had never become what Davey considered actual friends. So Purr-Ball had found a new place to sleep. Well, why not? It looked like a nice private spot—warm, too, from the looks of those rags.

Wait a minute! Rags don't move, and the bundle he was staring at just did. He jumped backward, wondering if he'd imagined it, then stepped back up to the gate and peered inside. Focusing his eyes and checking the bundle more closely this time, he gasped. Someone was staring back at him!

Davey's first instinct was to run and get his mom, but the eyes seemed more frightened than he felt. He stopped and took a deep breath.

"Who...are you?" he asked, his hand on the gate's latch. Should he open it?

"I am...Isabella," came the answer, the voice shaking and so heavily accented that Davey had a hard time understanding.

He swallowed and made a decision. Pulling on the latch, he opened the gate and stepped inside. Sure enough, a lady with dark hair was huddled in the corner against the wall, with Purr-Ball snuggled up beside her. No wonder Rocky was trying to get inside!

The dog danced around his master's feet now, obviously itching to sniff out this intruder, but Davey held him back. "Sit," he commanded, hoping that for once the stubborn old dog would pay attention. Miraculously, he did.

"I'm Davey," he said. "What are you doing in our barn?"

The woman frowned. *"No entiendo,"* she said. "I . . . do not understand."

She speaks Spanish, Davey thought. *I wonder if she's one of those illegal immigrants they're always talking about on the news—like the ones that killed my dad. But she must understand some English, or she wouldn't have answered me like she did.*

He stepped closer and checked her out carefully. He might be only six years old, but he knew when a woman was going to have a baby, and this lady looked ready. She sure didn't look like a criminal.

What do I do now, he wondered. *If I tell Mom . . .*

All sorts of possible scenarios ran through his head, most involving the police and jail. How could he be part of putting a lady in jail when she was about to have a baby? But if he didn't tell his mother . . .

Suddenly he remembered the remaining two apples in his jacket pockets and pulled out one to offer to her. Her dark eyes widened, and her hand shook as she reached to take it from him. He watched as she devoured it, eating even the core. Had he ever been that hungry? He didn't think so.

"Wait here," he said, holding out his hand to try to show what he meant. "I'll be right back. I'm going to get you something else to eat."

Shutting the gate behind him, he and Rocky raced for the front porch, right past the baby Jesus and Mary and Joseph. He didn't even stop to admire the Christmas tree in the living room as he made a beeline to the kitchen. For once he was glad that both his mom and grandma were busy in their rooms. This was a situation he was going to have to think about a lot before he decided what to do. For now all he knew was that there was a very hungry lady in their barn, and he was going to feed her.

"It's been nice having Davey home from school these last few days, hasn't it?"

Carolyn smiled as she made the comment, wondering how her daughter would respond. Carolyn didn't doubt that Miriam loved her son, and she had seen signs of closeness between them lately, but she also knew that Miriam was driven and felt she could accomplish so much more when Davey was away at school all day.

"I suppose," Miriam answered, holding a head of lettuce under the faucet while Carolyn sliced tomatoes and carrots and cucumbers. Glancing up, she added almost defensively, "Of course it has. It's always nice having him here."

Carolyn nodded. She hadn't meant the comment as an attack or even a criticism, but she knew that Miriam often took things that way, regardless of how innocent the statement. Carolyn decided to ignore the innuendos and continue with what had so far been a pleasant Tuesday. "The day after tomorrow is Christmas Eve," she observed. "It's hard to believe, isn't it? Davey is so excited."

This time Miriam's response seemed genuine, as she chuckled a bit before answering. "Excited is an understatement," she said. "I was actually dreading this holiday season, thinking it would be really hard on him."

Carolyn detected a slight choke in her daughter's words before she continued, but she knew better than to mention it. "Occasionally I see a faraway look in his eyes, and even a hint of tears," Miriam said, her composure regained. "But overall, he seems to be looking forward to Christmas nearly as much as he did when his father was still alive."

The words hung in the air between them for only a second too long before Carolyn cleared her throat and jumped in. "Well, I'm about done with these veggies. You want to pass that lettuce over here and I'll finish the salad, or would you rather I work on the potatoes?"

Without looking up, Miriam handed the lettuce to her mother, and Carolyn knew her daughter was once again blinking back tears. Resuming her chopping for the salad, she waited while Miriam snagged the peeler and got to work on the spuds.

"Where is Davey anyway?" Carolyn asked after a few moments. "He's usually in here pestering us for dinner by now. I haven't seen him since lunchtime. Of course, I may have missed him when I was in my room, taking a nap."

"He's out in the barn again, with Rocky—eating. The two of them have been out there nearly nonstop these last few days, taking snacks for what he calls 'barn picnics' with the animals. He says he likes to hang out with Rocky and the cats and horses, and I suppose there's nothing wrong with that. It isn't like he has any other kids around here to play with."

Carolyn laughed. "That's true—just a couple of old ladies!" She glanced up at her daughter, hoping Miriam had taken the comment as lightly as she'd meant it. Apparently she had because she was smiling back at her.

"I imagine that's exactly how he thinks of us," Miriam said, working her peeler as she talked and dropping the peels into one bowl, while the denuded potatoes went into another. "And after all, I am going to be thirty before you know it."

Carolyn shook her head. "I can't believe that. It seems just yesterday that you were running around like Davey, enjoying your vacation from school and counting the days until Christmas. How did the years fly by so quickly? We certainly never know what time will bring, do we?"

Miriam's smile faded, and Carolyn realized she had inadvertently reminded her daughter of how young a widow she was and how lonely her life had become. Though the two of them continued with their chores, the air felt heavier than it had been just moments earlier.

Carolyn chewed her lip and prayed that God would somehow touch Miriam's heart, but before she could utter a silent "amen," she heard the front door open. Seconds later, Davey burst into the kitchen.

"I'm starved!" he announced.

Carolyn laughed and was pleased to hear Miriam do the same.

"How can you be starved?" Miriam asked. "You just had lunch a few hours ago, and you even took an extra sandwich and fruit out to the barn for a picnic." She shook her head. "You need to go straighten your room and then wash up before dinner. It'll be ready in less than an hour."

"Aw, Mom, I want to go back out to the barn. I just came in for a snack—"

"No more snacks," Miriam insisted. "You'll ruin your dinner. Now go do as you're told, and we'll eat in a little while."

Like a deflated balloon, Davey dragged from the kitchen with his faithful mascot at his side, headed for his room as if he'd been sentenced to thirty lashes. Carolyn watched him go and smiled at the memory of how many times she'd seen Miriam do the same thing. Life sure had a funny way of coming full-circle at times, she thought, and then turned back to the task at hand.

Christmas Eve day dawned cold and windy, with frigid air whistling through the cracks in the barn wall. But Isabella could not complain. Her new friend, Davey, had somehow managed to bring her extra blankets and even a pillow, not to mention food and water. She was beginning to feel at home in her little nest, with the cats and horses for company.

She smiled at the thought of the little boy with the brown curls and sprinkling of freckles across his nose. How she enjoyed their visits together, despite the language difference. The child learned quickly, as they exchanged English and Spanish words and filled in the blanks with hand gestures. Even the child's dog had come to accept her. But what would happen when the two women who lived in the house, Davey's *madre* and *abuela*, learned that a very pregnant Mexican woman was living in their barn? Isabella could foresee nothing but trouble when that occurred, though

Davey continued to assure her that everything was going to be all right.

"It's almost Christmas," he'd told her on his last visit the evening before. "I asked God for a special present this year—not for me, but for you. And I know He's going to give it to us."

The boy's blue eyes had sparkled when he made the announcement, and she hoped he was right, though she had not yet had the nerve to ask what the special present might be. For now she was content to have a warm, dry place to rest, out of the wind and away from the many dangers of the desert. She left the confines of the barn only at night or during the day when she was certain everyone was gone, and then only long enough to relieve herself. Isabella was especially grateful for the food the child brought her and the company he shared with her. But at night, when Davey and his *perro*, Rocky, went back into the house and left her alone with only the *bebito* inside her, the memory of Francisco's body, lying cold and helpless next to his friend Ernesto, brought fresh tears gushing from her eyes, as she once again sobbed herself to sleep. Even Purr-Ball's presence could not ease her pain then.

This morning, however, she peeked through the chink in the wall at the Christmas decorations in front of the house. Was it possible that *El Señor* would listen to the boy's prayers and grant her some special present? The little one inside her had been quiet throughout the night, as an aching in her back had increased. She would rest this morning and wait for Davey to come with her promised breakfast. Then they would see what this Christmas Eve would bring.

CHAPTER 35

DAVEY WAS PLEASED. HE'D MANAGED TO HIDE TWO BANANAS AND A cinnamon roll under his jacket before heading back out to the barn. He could hardly believe tonight was Christmas Eve! He and his mom and grandma were all going to church that evening, and then they'd come home and make hot chocolate and talk about the Christmas story. He just wished Isabella could join them. It didn't seem right for her to spend Christmas in the barn.

The big door creaked only slightly as he pulled it open just enough for him and Rocky to squeeze inside. Then he shut it tightly behind him and headed straight for the gate where he knew his friend was waiting.

"Good morning, Davey," Isabella said, her English beginning to come more readily as she used it more.

Before Davey could answer, Rocky bounded toward her and buried his big head in her embrace. Davey smiled when Isabella giggled and spoke to the dog in Spanish, who seemed to understand that just as well as English and wagged his tail furiously in response. Purr-Ball guarded his position at Isabella's side, and even Calico sauntered over to check out all the commotion.

Davey plopped down on the ground close to Isabella and the animals, pulling the food from his jacket and shooing away the four-legged moochers before handing his smuggled provisions to his friend.

She smiled and took it from him. *"Gracias,"* she said, her voice soft as she sprinkled her English with Spanish. "I am not too hungry this morning, but I will save it for later."

Davey nodded. He had understood enough to know she was grateful, as she always was. He liked that about her. In many ways he knew she was an adult, especially because she was going to have a baby soon, but sometimes he felt as if she weren't all that much older than him. Maybe it was because she didn't make him feel like a baby.

She rubbed the small of her back as they eyed one another, and Davey found himself wondering what had happened to her husband. Did he dare ask? He swallowed and took a deep breath.

"Your...husband," he said, his voice cracking despite his best efforts not to let that happen. "Where...is he?"

Tears immediately pooled in Isabella's dark eyes, and Davey knew she had understood his question. He hoped he hadn't been out of line, but they were friends after all. He waited.

"Mi esposo," she began. "My husband...he is...dead. *Muerto.*"

Davey nearly cried out from the pain he felt in her words, though he had somehow expected the answer. Why else would she be hiding in their barn when she was going to have a baby? Something terrible must have happened, but he wasn't about to ask any more questions. It was enough just knowing what she'd already told him.

"I'm...sorry," he said, wishing there were some way to make her understand that he really, truly meant it. And then he knew how to make that happen. "My dad is...dead too," he said, nearly choking on the words.

This time the tears in her eyes spilled over onto her cheeks. *"Pobrecito,"* she whispered, holding out her arms.

Poor little one. He knew what that word meant, and he knew she understood. Without another thought, he fell into her extended arms and allowed her to rock him while he sobbed out the story of his father's death. Though he'd already shed many tears since losing his father, something had always prevented him from crying as he did right now. This time he held nothing back, letting the tears come from deep inside, and he wondered if he would ever be able to stop.

Isabella never did get around to eating the food Davey had brought that morning. Her stomach just was not up to it, and her backache was getting worse. She had not wanted to worry her little friend, especially now that she knew how very much he missed his *papa*. Oh, how Isabella could relate! She missed her own parents and siblings, her *abuelo*—and most of all, her beloved *esposo*. Though Davey had kept her company for much of the early part of the day, he had later returned to the house to get ready to go to the Christmas Eve service with his mother and grandmother. Now it was just Isabella and the animals once again.

And You, Señor, she thought, lying back on the straw with blankets on top of her and the faithful Purr-Ball curled up beside her, periodically reminding her of his presence with his buzz-saw hum. As the ache in her back had intensified throughout the day, beginning now to extend into her abdomen, tightening it into a hard ball every fifteen minutes or so, her mind had turned more and more to the God she felt had abandoned her and yet was her only hope.

"Are You there, *¿Señor?*" she whispered, her hand across her belly as another band of fire interrupted her rest. "I cannot do this by myself. *Por favor,* if You are there, if You can hear me, please show me." Tears filled her eyes as the pain ebbed. "I am frightened," she cried softly. "Where are You?"

I will never leave you or forsake you.

The words floated on the air around her, as lightly as a feather but more real even than the pain that rolled and ebbed around and through her. *Gracias a Dios!* He was here, even as her *abuelo* had told her so many times. And as surely as He was with her, she knew at that moment that He loved her as well.

As her stomach relaxed between pains, her tears flowed. "Hold me, *Señor*," she begged. "I need You. *¡Ayúdame!* Help me! Bring my *bebito* safely into this world...and then show me how to care for him. *Por favor, Señor. Por favor!*"

One of the horses neighed, and the cat purred in reply, but no other sound penetrated Isabella's heart. And yet she knew she was not alone. She understood that the pain would continue—and even get much worse—but *El Señor* was with her, and He would get her through. That was all she knew at that moment, but it was enough.

Davey sat three rows back from the front, his mother on one side and his grandmother on the other. Though he was concerned for his friend, his heart felt lighter since he'd let himself cry while she held him. Christmas would never be the same without his dad and he would never stop missing him, but somehow he knew he was going to be all right. Now if he could just be as sure about Isabella.

The choir had opened the service with many of his favorite Christmas carols, and he'd sung right along with them. Now, he listened as the pastor gave a short but familiar message, beginning with a reading from the Scriptures.

"And she brought forth her firstborn Son," the pastor read, his balding head bowed over his open Bible, "and wrapped Him in swaddling cloths, and laid Him in a manger, because there was no room for them in the inn."

A picture of Isabella popped into his head. Would his friend have her baby in a barn, like Mary had Jesus? Davey's heart rate increased at the thought. It wasn't right that she should be out there in the cold, or that her baby would be born in such a cold, lonely place when they had a perfectly warm house with plenty of room. But how would he convince his mom to let her come inside? How would he even tell her about Isabella? He knew how his mom felt about the Mexicans who came across the border illegally, and even though Isabella hadn't told him that's what happened, he was pretty sure it had.

What am I going to do?

Davey wasn't sure if the words he'd just heard in his mind were a random thought or a prayer, but he decided he'd better make them a prayer because he sure didn't have any ideas of his own. And he already knew that when he got home, he was going to have to tell his mom and grandma what was going on. He just couldn't leave his friend out there in that barn for another night— especially not on Christmas!

That decided, he settled in to wait and see if God would help him figure out what to do next.

CHAPTER 36

THE PAINS WERE COMING CLOSER NOW, LASTING LONGER AND cutting deeper. Each time Isabella thought she could not endure another moment, the fire in her belly intensified until she finally stuffed the corner of a blanket in her mouth to muffle her screams.

¡Ay, Señor, ayúdame!

Though her pleas were silent, her groans were not. She was glad she had seen the car drive away earlier, no doubt carrying the house's three residents to their church's Christmas Eve service in town. How she wished she could be in such a place, rather than here, suffering as she was. If only Francisco were here to help her through it!

I am here.

The voice returned, silent as a breath but real as the pain that took her breath away each time it attacked. And with each reminder of *El Señor's* presence, her guilt intensified. Why had she ignored Him for so long? Why had she blamed Him for her problems when all He had ever done was love her? And why was it that she suddenly understood that so clearly?

Maybe it is because I have never been so alone with You as I am now, Señor, she thought in one of her rare pain-free moments. *I have no one but You to help me, and now I know that You are here with me and that You love me.* She brushed away a tear. *But I also know I am guilty for not coming to You sooner. I am so sorry,* Señor, *for all the years I doubted You and left You out of my life. Is it too late? Will You forgive me now, and let me be Your child,* as my familia *always told me You wanted me to be?*

A rush of warmth flooded her body, dispelling any lingering doubts that God loved and accepted her. But even as the joy of the moment washed over her, a burning sword of pain sliced through her abdomen. She bit down on the corner of the blanket, still stuffed into her mouth, and felt a gush of water burst from between her legs onto the ground below her. Though she knew very little about what to expect as her *bebito* came into the world, she had little doubt that this signaled the time was near.

¡Ayúdame, Señor! ¡Ayúdame, por favor!

Her silent prayer continued as she imagined this is what it must be felt like to be torn in half. If God did not answer her prayer to help her, she knew she would surely not live to see her baby born.

By the time the three of them returned from church, Carolyn was exhausted. She didn't want to say anything to cause Miriam to worry, but she had to admit that she just didn't seem to have the strength she'd had just a few weeks earlier. Still, with rest and medication, the doctor had said she should be fine for many years to come. She would force herself to sit up and enjoy a couple of hours of quality family time with her daughter and grandson, and then head off to bed for some much needed sleep.

"Hot chocolate, coming up!" Miriam called from the kitchen. "Davey, turn on the Christmas tree lights, and we'll all sit and watch them while we have our drinks."

Carolyn watched Davey's reaction. Something wasn't quite right. He'd sat through church and had seemed to pay attention to the service, and yet it was obvious that his heart just wasn't in the celebration. Carolyn imagined that he was thinking of his father, but she couldn't help but wonder if there was something else going on as well.

"You OK, sport?" she asked, standing a few feet from the tree and waiting for Davey to respond to his mother's instruction.

Davey, still wearing his jacket, had been staring past the tree and out through the picture window toward the barn. At the sound of her voice, he seemed to jerk himself back from some faraway place. He looked up at her and blinked.

"Grandma? Did you say something?"

Carolyn smiled, stepping closer to her grandson and laying her hand on his shoulder. "I asked if you were okay." She paused. "Are you?"

Davey nodded, but Carolyn noticed his cheeks took on a reddish hue. "I'm fine," he answered. "Why?"

"Oh, I don't know," she answered with a shrug. "You seem a bit distracted. Something on your mind?"

Davey's blue eyes widened. "No, nothing. Just...Christmas, I guess."

Carolyn decided not to push him and instead reminded him of his mother's instructions to plug in the tree lights so they could have their hot chocolate together.

"Oh, yeah," he stammered. "OK. I just..." His head turned away as he once again glanced out the window before turning back to face Carolyn. "I...have to do something first. I'll be right back."

Before Carolyn could say another word, Davey had spun around and raced for the front door, with Rocky only a step behind. The door slammed shut behind them just as Miriam came into the room, carrying a tray with three steaming mugs of cocoa. The frown on her face deepened as she looked at Carolyn.

"What's going on with that boy?" Miriam asked.

Carolyn shook her head. "I have no idea. He just said he had something he had to do and that he'd be right back."

Miriam set the tray on the coffee table in front of the couch. "Well, I'm not going to wait until he gets back to find out what's going on. I'm going out there to see for myself."

Carolyn watched her daughter head for the front door, and then grabbed her jacket from the chair where she'd set it only minutes earlier. If everyone else was going outside, she might as well go along too.

Isabella held the squirming, tightly wrapped bundle next to her chest, relieved that the pain had finally ended and her son had arrived safely. When she heard the familiar squeak of the barn door, she prayed the child would not cry and give them away.

"Isabella?"

The baby fussed but did not cry out, and Isabella relaxed. Davey had come to check on her. Now she could introduce her *bebito* to her friend.

"Come in, Davey," she whispered, determined to answer in English. "I have . . . a surprise for you."

Davey stepped inside the gate and knelt beside her, wide-eyed as he stared at the tiny face, barely visible within the blanket folds.

"This is my son," Isabella said.

Davey nodded and looked up at her. "You had the baby while we were gone?"

She smiled and nodded. *"El Señor*—God—helped me."

"What . . . what's his name?" Davey asked.

Isabella opened her mouth to tell him, but the barn door squeaked again, and she sucked in her breath. How had she not heard the approaching footsteps? In her excitement of introducing her son and her friend, she had apparently not been paying attention. Until now she had been able to hide from Davey's mother, but the boy had left the gate to her hiding place open. Surely the woman would find them now.

"Davey?"

Davey's eyes widened, but he did not move.

"Davey, where are you? What's going on out here?"

And then she was there, a tall woman with a reddish-gold ponytail, staring down at them, her mouth a large O of surprise. Before any of them could speak, an older woman joined them, stepping up behind Davey's mother and also registering her silent surprise as she stared down at the startled child, the weary young mother, the sleeping infant, two cats, and a dog, all of whom waited without a sound.

"What . . . what is going on in here?" the boy's mother repeated at last, directing her questions to her son. "Who is this woman, and what is she doing in our barn?"

Davey jumped to his feet, placing himself in front of Isabella and the baby. "This is my friend Isabella," he said. "And her baby."

His voice trailed off and he turned to look down at Isabella. "What did you say his name is?"

Isabella swallowed, took a deep breath, and spoke her child's name for the very first time. "His name is David Francisco Alcántara."

Davey's eyes grew wide once again. "David?" he whispered, his eyes locking with hers.

She nodded. "Sí. David. For your *papa*. And Francisco for his *papa*. Two very . . . how you say . . . brave men, who are now in *el cielo* with *El Señor*."

Isabella saw Davey's tears, but she saw his smile, too, as he turned to face his mother and grandmother, and no doubt to see what would happen next.

CHAPTER 37

DON ALFREDO SIGHED. IT HAD BEEN A LONG DAY, THOUGH IT HAD ended on a sweet note, as he attended the midnight service in honor of *Navidad*. Christmas was celebrated with great joy in his country, as it should be, but the old man also thought it should be remembered with great dignity and respect. It was no light thing to honor the birth of the One who was both fully man and fully God.

But now he had come back home, having walked to and from the church with his *amigo*, Don Felipe. A good friend indeed, Don Alfredo thought as he prepared for bed. He was grateful to *El Señor* for sending such a companion for his last days—for surely that is what they were. Don Alfredo had sensed it for more than a week now. His time on earth would soon be over. He was saddened that he had not heard from Isabella and Francisco, but *El Señor* knew where they were, and Don Alfredo would have to leave them in God's hands and heart. It was the only safe place to be.

"I am weary, *Señor*," he whispered as he climbed into the familiar bed that had seen so many nights and heard so many prayers. "And I am yearning to see Your face."

And I, yours, came the response.

Don Alfredo smiled. *El Señor* was always close by, as near as his own breath, more faithful than any earthly friend. They had been through much together—joys and sorrows, laughter and tears, blessings and losses—but never had the old man had to walk through any of them alone.

The thought flooded him with warmth and contentment as his eyes fluttered shut and he drifted into dreams of his younger days, when he was yet so foolish as to think that he still had strength of his own.

Carolyn felt as if she'd been hit in the chest with a sledgehammer, but she knew it had nothing to do with her congestive heart failure. This was a lot bigger than that—and a lot more serious. David Francisco Alcántara. The name said it all, and everything they had wrestled with over the last months seemed to come into conflict in the fateful combination.

What were they going to do now? More specifically, what was her daughter going to do? For even as Carolyn stood rooted to the ground, her mouth hanging open as she stared at the surreal scene in front of her, she knew that ultimately the next move would be Miriam's call—and that call would depend a lot on just how deeply her hatred of her husband's murderer ran, and whether or not she could still hear the pleading whisper of God's voice.

As Carolyn had suspected, it was Miriam who broke the stunned silence and responded first to Davey's pronouncement. "How dare you," she began, the venom in her words amplified by their controlled delivery. "How dare you give my husband's name to your child? You didn't even know him . . . and none of us knows you!"

"I do," Davey said, his response pulling his mother's eyes from the woman huddled against the wall. "I told you, Mom. Isabella is my friend."

Miriam's green eyes appeared wider than Carolyn had ever seen them. *Help us, Lord,* Carolyn prayed silently. *Only You can diffuse this situation, Father!*

"That woman is not your friend," Miriam hissed, the veins in her neck standing out against the reddish hue of her skin. "She no doubt snuck across the border illegally just to have that baby on American soil. You're too young to understand that, Davey, but it happens all the time." She took a step closer toward her son and leaned over slightly as she continued. "But there's one thing you need to know about that woman." Without removing her focus from Davey, she extended an arm and pointed in Isabella's direction. "She is part of the same bunch that killed your father. Do you hear what I'm saying, Davey? It's people like her that killed your dad. If it weren't for her and her kind, who pay no attention to laws or borders, your father would still be alive today!"

Carolyn saw Davey blanch at his mother's words, as the woman named Isabella shrunk back farther against the wall, pressing her baby more tightly into her chest, as even Rocky and both cats drew closer to the terrified Mexican woman. Things were not going well at all, and Carolyn knew that if God didn't intervene soon, the situation would go from bad to worse.

"Miriam," she said, moving toward her daughter and reaching out to lay a hand on Miriam's arm. "Please, calm down. It's Christmas Eve, and this lady has just had a baby—"

Before she could say another word, Miriam whirled on her mother, jerking her arm upward and shaking off Carolyn's touch as she did so. "Mom, stay out of this—and don't you dare tell me to calm down. I will not calm down! Why should I? This woman has broken our law, and now she has the nerve to hide out in our barn, on our property, and have her baby here. I will not tolerate it. Do you understand? I will not be a part of this, in any way."

She spun back toward Davey, her finger waggling in his face now. "And neither will you, young man. Is that clear? I'm going into the house now to call the authorities so they can take her back where she belongs." Her eyes moved from Davey to Carolyn and back again. "And don't either one of you try to stop me."

Without another glance at Isabella or the baby, she turned on her heel and nearly ran for the barn door, pulling it open with a jerk and slamming it shut behind her. The baby's startled wail was the only sound that followed her into the night.

Miriam half-ran, half-stumbled toward the house, wanting only to put the scene of the Mexican woman and her baby behind her. If only she could outrun the plaintive cry that had started when she slammed the barn door! How could she be expected to tolerate such a bitterly ironic development? Surely God would not require her to show compassion to someone who had illegally crossed the border and trespassed on her property—a woman who might have walked across the very piece of border land where her beloved David had been murdered!

David. It was bad enough the woman had picked their barn to hide in, but to give birth to her son there and then name him after a man of honor, one who had given his life to uphold the law. It was just more than Miriam could fathom or tolerate.

With tears stinging her eyes, she raced blindly ahead, not seeing the unexpected obstruction in her path until she'd slammed her foot against it and tumbled headlong onto the dirt beside it. A sharp stone bit into her palm as she tried to stop herself, barely avoiding landing with her face on the ground. Tears of frustration increased as she raised herself to her knees under the heavens and turned to see what had taken her down. That it was the plastic manger with the ever-smiling baby Jesus in it unleashed the last vestige of her reserve, and she crumpled with her face in her hands, leaning on her bent knees in the dirt and nearly wailing with pain.

Daughter...

The word danced on the night air, swirling around her and penetrating the sound of her own sobs. Why now? Why would God come to her now, after months of hiding His face?

I have been here all along.

The crack in her heart split wider, as the truth she'd known all along imploded within her. It wasn't God who had hid His face from her, but she who had abandoned Him. The anger she'd held back for so long rolled out of her in waves, and she railed at the One she had once called Father—the One she had been so sure had let her down.

"Why?" she whispered, her teeth clenched. "Why didn't You protect David? It would have been such a simple thing for You, but You didn't. You let him die. Why, when You knew how much I loved him and needed him?"

I am your Husband now.

That was not the answer Miriam had wanted, and yet she immediately realized that it was the only one she was going to get. God would take care of her and Davey, but that didn't change the fact that she was furious with Him for the way things had happened.

"I'm so angry at You," she said. "I know it's wrong, but . . . I can't help it. I don't know if I can ever get past that."

I will carry you.

The word *carry* jolted her head up. God hadn't said He would hold her hand or even help her walk; He had said He would carry her. At that moment she knew that was the only way she would ever make it.

The sight of the plastic manger, leaning on its side in the dirt, tugged at her heart. She was having a lot of trouble reconciling her opinion of God with a loving Father at the moment, but the baby Jesus was another matter. Tenderly she reached out and righted the manger. She still had a long way to go and she wasn't sure she'd ever get to where she needed to be, but at least it was a start.

"Jesus," she whispered, the memory of the tiny bundle in the woman's arms coming back into focus as the sound of his crying reentered her consciousness. "You came as a baby," she said, touching the plastic face.

And there was no room for Me in the inn.

Once again tears sprang to Miriam's eyes. Not only had God sent His Son as a helpless baby, but that baby had been born in a structure quite possibly like the one behind her. She swallowed at the thought. Was she really any different from those who turned away Joseph and Mary on that long-ago night in Bethlehem?

The barn door creaked behind her, and she pulled herself to her feet, turning to see who had dared follow after her. There, in the barn's open door, illuminated by a lonely strand of Christmas lights, stood Davey, watching her. Wiping the tears from her cheeks, Miriam walked toward him, her arms outstretched. He was in them before she made it back to the barn.

CHAPTER 38

ISABELLA THOUGHT HER HEART WOULD STOP WHEN THE WOMAN returned to the barn with Davey. The older woman had remained behind with Isabella, but they hadn't yet spoken, and Isabella had no idea if she dared hope the woman who was obviously Davey's *abuela* might also be her ally.

Tonight was the first time Isabella had seen Davey's mother up close. Before this she had only peered at her through cracks in the gate, watching as the tall, red-haired woman fed the horses or cleaned their stalls. Even with her limited observation of the woman called Miriam, Isabella could tell she was not comfortable with the big animals. The horses sensed it too. Several times Isabella had found herself wishing she could offer her help, but she realized that was not possible. Her plan had been to stay hidden until the baby was born, and then as soon as she was strong enough, to strike out on her own and pray that *El Señor* would lead her to wherever He wanted her to be. Now that plan had been changed, and Isabella had no idea what would happen next. Had Miriam already called the *policía*? Would she be returning to Mexico with her *bebito* but without her *esposo*? The thought tore at her heart, though there was little comfort in the idea of staying in America without Francisco. What did it matter where she was? She was a widow now, with a baby to feed and protect. Perhaps it would be better to return to Mexico after all. At least there she would have her *abuelo*, though she knew it would grieve his heart—and Francisco's—if she went back.

Isabella sucked in her breath and held it, as Miriam passed by her mother and, with Davey following just a step behind, entered through the gate and knelt down beside her. The woman with the tear-stained face appeared different than she had moments earlier—tender, as she stared down into the tiny face of little David Francisco Alcántara. Isabella pulled back the blanket that surrounded the little one's features, revealing thick, black hair that curled in tiny ringlets. Her heart swelled at the sight of him. Surely he looked just like his *papa*! How grateful Isabella was at that moment for the gift she had received from *El Señor*.

"He's beautiful," Miriam said, her voice cracking as she reached to touch his cheek. "May I?" she asked, glancing up at the child's mother.

Isabella nodded. "*Sí*," she said, correcting herself and determining to speak as much English as she was able. "Yes. Please."

Miriam had no sooner laid her index finger against the child's skin than the boy reached from under the blanket and grasped the finger in his fist. The woman appeared startled but pleased, as the hint of a smile crossed her lips.

"David Francisco," Miriam crooned. "A perfect name for such a strong little boy."

Swallowing the lump that had formed in her throat, Isabella nodded again. It was a perfect name indeed.

Isabella could still not believe that she was lying in a real bed, with clean sheets and a soft pillow. It had been nearly two months since she last slept in a bed, and that had been beside her *esposo*, in their humble *casita* in Ensenada. The memory nearly jarred another round of tears from her heart to her eyes, but she blinked them back before they could escape. At least for now, on this Christmas Eve night, she and her *bebito* were warm and safe.

She peered down at his precious face, which she'd nearly memorized already, and smiled. He looked so fresh and clean now, dressed in a pair of Davey's newborn pajamas and wrapped in a soft blue blanket. Would she ever tire of staring at the Christmas gift *El Señor* had given her? She was sure she would not, and she saw no reason to turn off the bedside lamp when all she wanted to do was watch her little one sleep.

A light tap on the door broke her concentration, and she lifted her head. She had thought everyone in the household had gone to bed, and for just a moment a prickle of fear touched her skin. Had Davey's mother changed her mind about letting her stay in the guest room?

She swallowed. No, Miriam had not only offered the room, much to everyone's surprise, but she had personally escorted Isabella and David Francisco inside. She had even given Isabella a clean nightgown and allowed her to take a shower before coming to bed. Miriam and Carolyn had taken turns holding the baby, while Davey looked on, his eyes wide with wonder. Isabella knew then that *El Señor* was at work in the hearts of all present, and she could not imagine that Miriam would now turn her away, at least not before morning.

"Entre, por favor," Isabella called softly, wanting to extend a polite invitation while not waking her *bebito*.

The door opened just enough for Miriam to slip inside. "I hope I didn't wake you," she said, "but I noticed your light was still on, so I thought it would be all right to come in."

Isabella nodded, understanding enough to be amazed that the woman who owned this house would ask her permission to enter. *"Sí,"* she said, continuing to keep her voice soft. "I did not turn out the light because I want to see his face."

Miriam smiled as she crossed the room and lowered herself carefully onto the side of the bed. "That's why I came too. I wanted to see him one more time before I went to sleep."

Isabella's heart swelled with gratitude. What a miracle *El Señor* had done here tonight! A woman who once despised the sight of her now wanted to gaze at her sleeping baby. Once again Isabella blinked away tears, as together the two women focused on the sleeping infant.

"It seems like just yesterday that Davey was that small," Miriam said, a wistful lilt to her voice. "I'll never forget that night. We thought we had plenty of time to get to the hospital, but Davey was in a hurry, and we barely made it." She laughed. "My husband had to drive like crazy to get us there."

Isabella glanced up at Miriam's face. Just as she had suspected, the woman's laugh had scarcely touched her expression before the sadness returned. Isabella reached out and laid her hand on Miriam's arm. "*Yo entiendo*," she said, and then switched to English, her voice cracking in the process. "I understand. Davey told me what happened to your *esposo*. It is a terrible thing. I too miss my husband so very much."

Miriam lifted her head, and through Isabella's tears she saw her friend's green eyes glisten. To think of this woman as her friend was yet another miracle, she realized, but she knew without doubt that God had joined their hearts.

"Yes, I believe you do," Miriam whispered. She paused before continuing. "I'm not surprised that Davey told you what happened to his father. But . . . do you mind telling me what happened to your husband?"

Burning pain seared Isabella's gut at the thought of telling the story, but she knew she must. She owed it to this woman who had shown her such kindness, and she knew she would have to tell it sooner or later anyway, if ever she was to reclaim the bodies of her *esposo* and his friend, Ernesto.

Haltingly, she began, starting with her marriage to Francisco and the horrible massacre that had taken the lives of her *familia*, bringing Miriam's tears from her eyes onto her cheeks. Isabella spared no details, telling Miriam of how her *abuelo* had given her his life savings and encouraged her and Francisco to find a *coyote* to take them across the border to escape the violence and to try to find a better life for themselves and their *bebito*. She related the difficult trip through the desert and their discovery by Alberto, who took them to a house where terrible things happened and where, even now, people suffered.

Indignation replaced sadness on Miriam's face as she listened. "We must help those people," she said. "We'll report them to the authorities as soon as possible. Do you think you can remember how to direct them to this house?"

Isabella hesitated and then nodded. "I can try," she said, trembling at the thought.

Miriam squeezed Isabella's hand. "I didn't mean to interrupt you," she said. "Tell me what happened next."

And then Isabella told it all—the escape from the house, how they were joined by Lupe and Ernesto, how they came to the camp and the men found work... and how she had believed that at last they were about to realize their dream.

"And then it snowed," she said, "and everything changed."

By the time Isabella had completed the story of dragging Francisco's and Ernesto's bodies into the tiny shelter and doing her best to protect them from predators before striking out on her own, both women were weeping openly. When Isabella came to the part about stumbling onto their farm and finding the door open to the barn, Miriam leaned down and gathered her into her arms.

"Oh, thank God," she sobbed. "I'm so glad God brought you here. What would have happened to you and the baby out there?"

With her free arm, Isabella returned Miriam's embrace, being careful of the *bebito* sleeping soundly in her other arm. What would happen tomorrow or where she and little David Francisco would go when they left here, Isabella had no idea, but somehow she felt as if she had finally come home.

It was nearly midnight when Miriam closed the guest room door behind her and started down the hall toward her own bedroom. She stopped midway as she passed the front room that looked out onto the barn. Had she forgotten to turn off the Christmas tree lights? She frowned, sure she had unplugged them before going to talk with Isabella.

Moving from the hallway toward the blinking lights of the tree, she realized she was right—she had turned them off after all. Davey had obviously plugged them back in, for there he sat, on the floor in front of a handful of gaily wrapped packages, staring at the old wooden crèche Miriam's grandfather had carved so many years earlier and passed down to the family.

Without a word Miriam sat down next to her son and waited. She didn't want to intrude on his time, but she needed to be near him just now.

After a few moments he broke the silence. "It's a miracle, isn't it?" he said, more as a statement than a question. "Jesus being born and sleeping in a manger, I mean."

Miriam was only partially clear on what Davey meant, but she didn't prod. He would explain himself in time.

He glanced up at her. "He was a baby, but He was still God."

Miriam nodded. Her six-year-old's thoughts ran a lot deeper than she sometimes realized.

"If people knew who He was, they would have given Him a better place to sleep."

Tears stung Miriam's eyes, as Davey laid a hand on her arm. "Thanks, Mom...for letting Isabella and the baby sleep in the guest room."

Miriam nodded again. She didn't trust herself to speak.

"What are we going to do tomorrow?"

She swallowed, not sure how to answer the question that had been rolling around in her own heart for the past few hours. It was obvious something had to be done—two dead bodies reclaimed and buried, a houseful of prisoners and their captors reported, not to mention what to do about Isabella and her baby, who were as much victims of Mexico's violence and corruption as Miriam and her family.

Before she could answer, a voice behind them said, "Tomorrow is Christmas."

Miriam and Davey raised their heads to Carolyn's smiling face. She was wrapped in a fuzzy blue robe and wearing her scruffy pink slippers. For a moment Miriam found herself thinking that the older her mother got, the more beautiful she became.

Carolyn leaned a hand on Miriam's shoulder and one on Davey's, lowering herself to sit cross-legged with them. "Christmas is for celebrating," she said. "It's for remembering the greatest Gift ever given, and for recommitting ourselves to spreading the news of that Gift anywhere and everywhere possible—and for sharing it with anyone God brings across our path."

Miriam took her mother's hand and squeezed it. "You're right, Mom. Tomorrow we will all celebrate together. But... then what? What do we do after that?"

"God will show us," Carolyn said. "We just need to be open and listen."

"Maybe God wants Isabella and her baby to live here." The simplicity of Davey's declaration jarred Miriam's peace, challenging her more deeply than she wanted to admit. And yet, hadn't that very thought crossed her own mind?

"Maybe," Miriam said. "But it's not that easy, Davey. There are laws. Isabella came here illegally, you know."

Davey bowed his head, and his shoulders sagged. Miriam wished she could say something to encourage him, but it was best that he face the facts. Even if they were to consider doing something so dramatic as offering Isabella and her baby a place to live, there would be a lot of red tape to jump through to make it happen.

"You'd think there'd be a way," Carolyn said. "I mean, she's all alone, and her baby was born here..."

Miriam's head snapped up and she stared at her mother. Of course! David had told her several times that there were certain laws that pertained to people from other countries who had been victims of crime while in America. She couldn't remember the details, but she was certain it had to do with offering those victims medical and psychological assistance, as well as a fast track to citizenship if they were interested. Did it include immigrants who came illegally? She didn't know, but she'd make it a point to find out as soon as their Christmas celebration was over.

"Isabella could help us," Davey said, looking from Miriam to Carolyn and back again. "She told me she's a good cook and likes to clean and take care of kids and...and she loves horses. Don't you think she could stay and help take care of me? I'd really like to have a little brother." His face brightened. "I could even give him my cowboy boots someday!"

Miriam smiled. Davey's words made sense, but she didn't want to offer false hope. "All of that is certainly a possibility to consider," she said. "Including the boots. But let's don't run ahead of God on all this. It's important to wait and see what He has in mind, don't you think?"

This time it was Carolyn's turn to squeeze her daughter's hand. When Miriam looked into her mother's eyes, she knew the tears she saw there were joyous ones. She nodded and squeezed Carolyn's hand in return.

"It's good to be home again," she whispered, knowing her mother knew exactly what she meant.

"It really is a Christmas miracle," Davey said, reaching out to touch the baby in the manger.

EPILOGUE

WHEN CHRISTMAS MORNING DAWNED OVER THE LITTLE *CASITA* IN Ensenada, Don Alfredo was even wearier than when he had crawled into bed the night before.

"*Buenos días, Señor,*" he whispered, lying on his back as he stared past the familiar ceiling toward the heavens beyond. "*Gracias, Señor,* for sending Your Son to save us. *Gracias* for *la Navidad.*"

The response was a wordless flow of warmth, wrapping the old man in a sense of peace that nearly burst his heart with joy. If only he knew his *nieta* and her *esposo* and *bebito* were safe, he would ask nothing more, for his life would be as perfect as any man's can be on this earth.

Your loved ones are fine, came the silent voice. *Each is in My care, and each is exactly where I have purposed them to be at this moment. You do not need to be concerned for them any longer. You can lay your burden down now. You have fought the good fight; you have finished the race; you have kept the faith.*

"Then all is well," Don Alfredo said. "I need nothing else— only You, *Señor.* Only You."

Yes, that is true. It is time to come home, My son.

Don Alfredo nodded. He knew it was so. And with an expectant smile on his face and his wide-brimmed straw hat on the little table beside his bed, he closed his eyes for the very last time.

The End

A Christmas Journey Home

New Hope® Publishers is a division of WMU®, an international organization that challenges Christian believers to understand and be radically involved in God's mission. For more information about WMU, go to www.wmu.com. More information about New Hope books may be found at www.newhopedigital.com. New Hope books may be purchased at your local bookstore.

Use the QR reader on your
smartphone to visit us online at
www.newhopedigital.com

If you've been blessed by this book, we would like to hear your story. The publisher and author welcome your comments and suggestions at: newhopereader@wmu.org.

Additional Titles by Kathi Macias

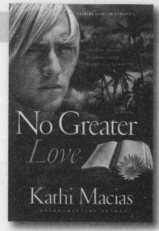

No Greater Love
ISBN-13: 978-1-59669-277-0 • $14.99

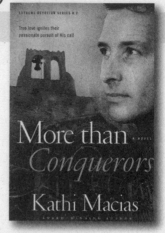

More than Conquerors
ISBN-13: 978-1-59669-283-1 • $14.99

Red Ink
ISBN-13: 978-1-59669-279-4 • $14.99

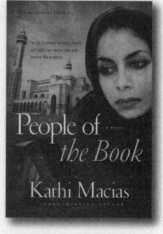

People of the Book
ISBN-13: 978-1-59669-282-4 • $14.99

Act 1, Scene 1:
Prolonging the Magic

I was sitting on the front porch of my rented trailer watching the wind blow leaves out of a nearby tree when I realized that I was living a perfect moment. Inside, "It's a Free World, Baby" by REM played while I sat, barefoot, wearing jeans and a flannel shirt in August, enjoying the breeze. *Not bad for a Florida girl,* I thought. It occurred to me that I needed to remember the moment for future times when I would be stressed out, when I got back home and realized that I needed to start a career. Thankfully, those stressful times seemed far away.

I had taken this job to catch up on some bills I had accrued in college. I could have gone anywhere, but the thought of moving somewhere cool and quiet was too tempting to pass up. After four and a half frenzied years of classes, working, and socializing, living down the street from a major hospital and hearing sirens at all hours, it was great to hear nothing. It was great to see no signs of civilization and hear just the crunch of rocks and leaves beneath my hiking boots. I could read, sleep, get high, and just relax. Indeed, seasonal resort employment is like summer vacation for grown-ups. The 40 hours a week we had to work were quickly forgotten the rest of the time,

when we hiked and just hung out in our digs or at the two local watering holes.

I arrived in Anchorage three days after my graduation, and a few days after that I caught sight of a map of North America in a bar. Unlike the usual U.S. maps with Alaska and Hawaii just kind of stuck off to the side, I actually saw the whole North American continent. Suddenly, it made sense that my plane trip from Tampa to Seattle took as much time as my flight from Seattle to Anchorage. I was far from home, as they say. So I looked at that map and decided that I'd better not get into any serious trouble up there– no broken legs or anything. I was all alone, but I was free.

My roommates were at work, and I was enjoying the time alone. Although we worked at a resort, our accommodations were not glamorous, to say the least. We lived down the hill and seven miles from the places where we worked among the rich tourists. But we had come to Alaska for adventure, not glamour, so we did just fine.

A familiar figure made its way down the tree-lined road and waved to me as it got closer. It was Caleb, the third and final (and best) boyfriend of the summer. Since there was a four-to-one male-to-female ratio up in Denali Park, I had enjoyed unprecedented popularity there.

I hadn't expected him, but since we didn't have telephones or anything, it was perfectly normal to have unexpected visitors turn up.

"Hey, Gina," he said quietly.

"Hey, what's going on?"

"I saw some moose down the street, toward the river. Do you want to see them?"

"I have to put on my shoes," I said. The rocky terrain was no match for my delicate dogs.

He turned around and offered me his back. "Hop on," he said. And so we were off, into the woods to see the moose. It turned out that it was a mom and two young ones.

"Check it out, baby," I said, "mooslings."

He laughed and we quietly made our way back to the trailer. Caleb wasn't much taller than I was, about five foot nine I'd guess,

and I could feel the strain he was experiencing, carrying me around. Although I was used to being thin, the constant stream of available food from the cafeteria that summer had caused me to put on a few pounds, which had appeared on my thighs, naturally. I had first hoped that it might bump me into a bigger bra size, but no such luck. That's usually the skinny girl's lament. I realize that a lot of people think that skinny girls are not entitled to laments, but I have to disagree.

Back at the trailer, I asked him about his future plans. He was leaving for Texas to go back to school the following week.

"I'm going to live there and finish my degree, and after that I don't know. Might come back here to work next year, if I'm done with school."

"Do you know where you will live and all that?"

"Yeah, my parents have a house in Amarillo. I'll live there."

"Wow, do they make you pay rent?"

"Actually, no," he said, looking sheepish.

"Well, it must be nice," I started off, and I'm sure my speech that followed sounded something like when somebody's parents tell them how they had to walk barefoot in the snow to school back in their day. But it really wasn't fair. Caleb's father was a doctor, and while he wasn't spoiled, he certainly had it easier than I did. There was a little nagging voice in the back of my mind that seemed to think that I would descend into madness, or at least poverty, the instant I got back home.

With the leaves swishing around overhead and an attractive blond man next to me, it was not the time to be darning my own luck or worrying about the future beyond the next month. And so we spent the next few days together, and off he went to Texas. Four weeks after his departure, I returned to sunny Florida to officially start my post-college life.

Act 1, Scene 2:
Revisiting Reality

It didn't go so well.

If the dizzying Tampa heat wasn't bad enough, living below the poverty line was unbearable. I'd lived in Florida my whole life so I was used to the heat, but I had operated under the assumption in college that when I got to be a year out in the world, I would be making decent money. My job in Alaska had paid off most of my debts, but when I returned and looked for a job, I found myself back in the red rather quickly.

The frustrations were endless. I hopped from job to job with no direction, hoping the next one would be better. Unfortunately, I had a habit of quitting one job without having a better one lined up, so I'd end up taking whatever I could get. Typically, these were not improvements. I scoffed at the idea of taking some stable job at some solid company because that would interfere with my artistic vision; that wasn't "me." Well, *working* wasn't really me, but I knew that unless I inherited vast wealth, I had to somehow afford my diva palace, chariot, trousseau, toys, Target shopping sprees, trips to the spa, and so on and so forth. I had to work to get this money from somewhere, so that my non-working life could be all I wanted it to be.

For a while, I worked in retail and spent my time on my feet from dawn to dusk. It was an easy way to stay thin, and I slept deeply at night since I was tired from actually standing around and moving all day long. But the money and the hours were bad, and this type of work was a crushing blow to me. All the time I'd been in Alaska, if some disgruntled baby boomer vacationer asked me why I was working there, or if it was the best job I could find, I'd shrug and look out at the mountains. It didn't matter that I had a crummy job there, because I was being adventurous and living life. But back home, it was different.

One of my notable post-college jobs was for a chain of bridal shops. Now, I know what you're thinking. You're thinking, *Gina, don't do it. If you work in a bridal shop, you'll chase away every possible man who might be interested in you simply by virtue of working there*. But I needed the money, so for eleven months, I got to stack shoes in the back room, haul really heavy dresses back and forth from the floor to the dressing rooms, deal with tearful moms and spotlight-hogging brides, and live a completely man-free life. The occasional sale brought a frenzy of women in to the store, which could get very ugly.

The people who worked at the shop were more like the cast of a soap opera than just normal people. Someone was always getting engaged, getting a boob job, or getting into a snit about something. One notable character was always talking about love and Jesus, but if you turned your back on a customer for a second, she would be escorting her up to the register to take credit for (and claim the commission on) your $600 sale.

To add to the fun of working there, my manager would wait until the last possible second to give me and the other employees our schedules for the following week, so scheduling job interviews was quite a challenge. If you had a serious need to be away for a day or part of the day, she would make sure that your work schedule directly conflicted with what you'd requested. It got to the point where I had to stand up and say, "I am going to the gynecologist on Wednesday afternoon, and you can't stop me!"

As a student I had interned at radio and TV stations and worked as a temp for one of the daily newspapers and two entertainment magazines, but when I went back to those places that could have offered me a job that would have been close to cool, there was never anything available. Two places asked me to come back and work for free, though. It's great to be wanted, but it's much better to get paid for it.

Even when I was just a kid, I always knew that I'd be a career woman. I pictured myself with a newspaper byline or with a microphone in my hand, getting blown around by the wind as I reported on the latest hurricane from some beach in Louisiana. I had honed my writing skills in high school and college, thinking that it would be easy enough to get a job eventually. It never occurred to me that finding a job in television or journalism would be so tough. With only that in my base of experience, besides having spent the past ten years as an amateur actor, what would I be qualified to do?

How was it possible that I had worked so hard for a career that might not ever materialize? It sounded whiny to think so, but it just wasn't fair. Now I understood what the people from the College of Arts and Sciences who'd graduated the year before, or the year before that, were all whining about. Apparently, it's a jungle out there!

The only beacon of hope that came along in my few years out of college was the announcement that some of my old actor acquaintances had started up a nonprofit theatre group in the area. They were soliciting for original plays and performance pieces that would eventually be performed in a festival, a year and a half in the future. It was a chance to do acting and creative writing– for fun! It was so up my alley it wasn't even funny. I vowed to write something and perform it, but what?

I had a while to think about it before I sat down and started writing, because my friend Anne and I had decided to quit our jobs and go to Europe for a month.

Act 1, Scene 3:
Footloose and Fancy-Free

We had $420 plane tickets going from Tampa to Amsterdam and Paris to Tampa, and 30 days in between with no real agenda. Whatever would we do to fill up the days?

I will let the journal speak for the trip.

First Stop: Amsterdam. I guess I didn't really research the place enough, but apparently the smell of urine wouldn't come through just pictures in a magazine or online anyway. We are in College Boy's Paradise. You can pee in the streets, enjoy a hooker for $20, and get high wherever you want. It's a little scary for two skinny girls at night, so of course we made friends with about five guys from Miami, and they are now our escorts whenever we go out. Excellent.

Anne keeps telling people we're staying at the Sheltering Pig, which isn't true— it's called the Flying Pig, and it's a youth hostel. I think it has something to do with what we smoked last night, that she keeps forgetting the real name and fully inventing something else. So we went to the Van Gogh museum and the Anne Frank museum, which was thoroughly depressing but very educational. It's been a few hours since we left, and I am still nauseous. Oh well, I fit in here in the land of excess. Everyone feels physically ill over something they did today, or they will soon enough.

There was some big-deal soccer game last night, and eventually all the Spanish people were dancing around getting drunk while the Italians looked pretty glum. I guess Spain won. In any case, I never knew what a big deal it was. They call it football here, and it's as big as our football back home.

Next Stop: Munich. We went on a bike tour through some park and the scruffy tour guide took us on a detour so that we wouldn't meet up with this huge skateboarder convention. Anyway, we're pedaling along and suddenly there are a bunch of naked men, laying on blankets in the sun. Now, it would seem like this would be an ideal thing for two single gals like us to stumble upon, but as with most nudist parks and beaches, the people who tend to get the most naked are the ones who really have no business doing so. Besides, since there were no females to be found, we could only guess that we were surrounded by gay naked men, the most naked of which being the most unsightly. So we pedaled and stared straight ahead until we got to some great beer garden, where we drank away the memory. All Anne has to do is whisper "flabby white cheeks" to me now and I wince.

Anne and I got to know some good-looking boys from one of the Dakotas on the tour. I can't remember all of their names, but they were all brothers and cousins and stuff, and they were all cute. One walked us home, but then was so drunk that he didn't know where he was. Hope he found his people at some point. Poor guy.

Bella Italia: Before we got there, I must record for posterity that the border guards in Austria have some big guns. It was a little scary, but A was laughing at me about it. She said, "Of course they have big guns, they are guarding a *border.*" We saw the hills that are alive with the sound of music from the train and finally crossed into Italy, which is even better than I imagined. I can't believe people live here, it is such a beautiful place.

We went to Venice and got a "room" (if you can call it that– there was a clothesline with a bedspread hung from it that served as our door, and there was a row of beds in what looked like someone's attic that made up our hostel for the night) and proceeded to share a bed

(called *il matrimonio*, as in a marriage bed where two people sleep), wearing our money belts, clutching our camera bags as we slept, and enjoying not a bit of privacy because A was too polite to the owner's son, Nicolo, when we checked in, so he wanted to hang out with us. The good news is that I met an Australian boy named Roger and he took me out on a little date, drinking red wine by the canals while A avoided Nicolo's advances. I swear, my friends back home may all be engaged or married and so blissfully happy, but how many of them got to hang out and drink wine with a cute Australian boy in Venice recently?

The next day we went to see Juliet of "Romeo and Juliet" fame's tomb in Verona, and I stood at the balcony and thought of my own star-crossed love, Evan Dando, whom I met once when he was on tour with the Lemonheads. I thought of the beauty of Evan and the joy that the jangly guitar sound that the Lemonheads are known for brings to me, and I felt love on the balcony. Then I saw some people feeling the breasts on the statue of Juliet and got really annoyed. Apparently that is the thing to do in Verona. When we left through an alleyway, I got annoyed again because lovers are supposed to write their names on the wall there and I had no one to write about. I guess I could have written about Roger from Venice, now that I think about it. He was awfully cute.

Firenza: It's not just a brand of clothing that you could buy at The Limited 15 years ago. Ah, the art, the cuties, the statue of David, the cute young guy who hit on us at McDonald's– Florence was great. We even stayed at this hostel where the guy running it demanded that we leave our laundry there for him to wash. What a guy. If I had any money to spare, I would tip him. We came back to find our clothes happily dancing in the wind on the balcony. Funny. I was worried that someone might try to steal my pajamas, which are flannel and have cute little ice-skating bunnies on them, but A said I was crazy. Then I made up a song about them, which goes, "Bunny pajamas, bunny pajamas, everybody wishes they had bunny pajamas," and I sang it over and over. I was punchy and couldn't stop. I can still see her writing in her journal, recording what a lunatic I am.

Rome wasn't built in a day, but we got sick of their damn heat wave in about that same amount of time. The only thing that saved this stop on our tour was the fact that we met five guys from Canada and Anne had a one-day romance with some guy named Morgan, while I hung out with his cute Australian friend, Anthony. They took us on the midnight tour of Rome, and we saw the Trevi Fountain and the Spanish Steps by moonlight. Much better than during the heat of the day, if you ask me, even though people on motorcycles apparently clog the streets of Rome at every hour. Also we went on a walking tour of the Roman Forum without the boys during the day, which was cool. I've been drinking a lot of bubbly water these days.

After two people tried to pick my pocket there, we decided to have a gelato and then hop the train to the south to visit Sorrento, the most beautiful place on earth. There, after I'd eaten my 27th (and best so far) Insalate Caprese for breakfast, we went down to the water to dip our toes in a new and exciting body of water. I have decided that when they teach English to Italians in school, they teach the boys to say, "I get off of work at nine, let's meet up here if you like," because that is what all the waiters say to us when we go out to eat. We haven't been too tempted to take anyone up on it yet.

We stayed in a converted apartment, and it had this beautiful furniture and a garden– it was so beautiful. Also, we had dinner outside one night, and it was delish. They are known for their wines and lemon liquors and that is probably why I had some trouble walking home. When I noticed the sidewalk moving, I fell over. Anne was laughing at me all night long. Apparently she can handle her liquor better. Good thing we didn't have to walk far!

More fun at the beach in Cinque Terre, in the northern part of Italy near France. Oh, yes. More gelato, more Insalate Caprese, the best gorgonzola pizza ever, beautiful views. Everything is so picturesque, so why are we leaving to go to France? Anne wants to go. Oh, it's OK. We've been in Italy for two weeks. Let's go.

Nice is nice. Marc Chagall has a museum here. He really liked to paint chickens. It is kind of funny! Anne is a big fan of his, she must be chicken crazy too. Also, the beach at Cannes is great. We dreamed

of walking arm-in-arm with whatever star of the day will be big when we're the queens of Hollywood as we strolled along. Anne tried to lay claim to George Clooney, but I guess I don't mind. There are plenty of other hot eligible men in that world. Plus, I could always cross over to music. Something tells me that Mark McGrath of Sugar Ray will never settle down, for one.

First run-in with a rude Frenchman took place when I had absentmindedly placed my bag next to me on a bench. Some poor tired-looking man, who was probably really tired of serving cocktails to Americans like me all day long, was looking at me and acting kind of frantic. I asked him what was wrong and he said– no, shouted, "I want to put my *ass* where your bag is!" Geez, buddy, you could have just asked. I didn't have any problem moving my bag so he could sit down. Anne and I had quite a laugh about it. We ended up making friends with the guy by explaining that we were from Florida and had our own issues with being overrun by tourists.

Oh yes, and we can't forget the seven lovely men from Canada who showed us around, also providing a late-night tour of the marina and casino in Nice. They were, as they say, fantastique!

The rain in Spain is mainly in the plains. Anne found out that the town of Figueres, which is just over the border from France, is where Salvador Dali is from. Of course, we went to his museum. It was covered with giant eggs. And we'd be letting everyone down if we didn't stay out all night and party like it's 1999 here in Barcelona. The food is good, we saw an Elvis impersonator on the street, and this is fun. Luckily our trip will be over soon, since we are running very low on money.

To wind down our tour, let me just say that I love Paris in the springtime. We had 24 hours to see the Louvre, go to the Eiffel Tower, check out a World Cup game featuring Scotland— there were Scotsmen in the street wearing kilts, excuse me as I swoon!— and eat some of the pastries that France is famous for. Then we had to leave.

I didn't realize how much I'd missed being home. When I got to New York, I heard a Sicilian woman speaking English in an airport

bathroom and just about cried. It was so nice to know that I'd get to go home and lock the door behind me– not listen to the huge bald guy sleeping in the bunk above mine and snoring like a chainsaw, but be alone. Not be separated by other travelers by a bedspread or a thin wall, but really be in my own bed. Really go home!

Act 1, Scene 4:
Selling Out

After weeks of fruitless searches among my former places of internship and so on, my friend and roommate Christine agreed to help me get a job at her uptight corporate employer, which serviced credit card accounts.

It was the acting role of a lifetime. First, I had to act like I wanted a job taking phone calls all day long. After I was hired, I received the costume requirements: I was to dress up at least as much as the local newscasters, so that I could sit in a cubicle where nobody could see me and answer questions all day long while wearing a headset that pushed my earrings into my head. I'd hoped that they'd come down a notch for me since I was really just voice talent at that point, and luckily the rules were relaxed early on in my employment. And so, Business Casual Gina was born, although I couldn't bring myself to wear anything like polo shirts.

What was striking about the work environment at first was that it was like school. Not college, high school. If you were out sick for more than three days, you needed to produce a doctor's note. This was ironic because the recirculated air, which was kept at a frigid 65 degrees, acted as a breeding opportunity for all kinds of germs. People were always sick.

There were the principals, who strolled around and wondered what kind of work you were actually doing. Their jobs were to make all the phone monkeys be motivated and happy. They'd always harp on the company benefits, as if to say, "You have such great health care, vision and dental, 401(k) match, and vacation time– you'd be crazy to leave!" Ironically, with the type of work we did I quickly developed a digestive disorder and my eyesight worsened. Good thing I had those great benefits, but not really when you realize that the job caused the problems to begin with. They also liked to look important by making charts and spreadsheets, but their real purpose was to squeeze more work out of the underlings who made $24,000 a year.

After a few months, I decided to give up and accept my lot for the time being. I took vacations, put in my 40 hours and went home, took advantage of the benefits, and saved my money. I knew that this would pass eventually, but in the meantime it inspired the first monologue of my show:

Work to live, or live to work? For me, it's always been work to live. There's something about work that is intrinsically not fun. That's why we get paid to do it.

A lot of people say that we should enjoy our jobs, since we spend so much time on the job. To this I say, I'll enjoy my work as soon as I find some type of enjoyable work, and the act of trying to find work that I find meaningful and fulfilling has taken up the last ten years of my life already, so I don't know when the search will end at this point.

Since I've been dating and working for the same amount of time, since about age 15 or 16, I've come to realize certain truths that apply to both of these things. They are:

Number One: Grunt work is necessary, and you might not ever get what you want. If you do get what you want, you will then have to guard it against others who will want to take it away from you.

Think about it– when we date, we essentially break in the guys we date. We teach them how to put the toilet seat down, not to leave the hand towels in a heap on the bathroom floor, and how to give a

decent backrub. The list goes on and on. Then, when the relationship falls apart, off he goes to date some other woman who will reap the rewards of the work that we've already put in.

With work, we start off doing all the crap that no one else wants to do, and usually get paid very little for it too. If it becomes apparent that maybe there isn't anywhere to go with the job, or there's no position worth our time with that particular employer, it's as if our efforts were wasted entirely.

But it wasn't a waste. We have accrued money and karma points too. When we move onto the next level, whether it's securing a promotion or getting upgraded to "girlfriend," it is well deserved. And it may not have anything to do with where we started out.

Similarity Number Two: The audition process is demeaning.

Let's contrast first dates with interviews. Both involve clothes we don't usually wear, questions we aren't used to asking or answering, and a general feeling of discomfort overall. There is a point when one party says that he or she will call, and this may or may not happen, depending on the other options. The other is left to wait and wonder. Either party can follow up the meeting with a phone call, card, or e-mail, but that is not a guarantee of winning the job or second date.

The new concept of speed dating has revolutionized this process for single people. Instead of wondering if one guy will call, you can wonder if several will call instead. I find that it has also increased the number of men I would date and the number of men who would date me, but unfortunately those two types of men rarely coincide.

Similarity Number Three: The more desirable it seems to the outside world, the more high-maintenance it is for you.

Think about what it would be like to date a major celebrity. Let's call him George Clooney, for example. You and George are dating, and it looks like a picnic. He's got all the money in the world to show you a good time, and you get to go to all these exciting and glamorous parties with him. But think again... If you get to be a size eight or higher, the tabloids will have a field day with you and tell the

whole world how pudgy you are, photographers and reporters would be constantly stalking your man, and his job would take up so much of his time. Think of the pressure– he can't pick a bad role, he can't gain weight or look old. All these Hollywood rules will make him crazy after a while.

Highly regarded jobs are the same. I am sure that the leaders of the free world would love to put in 40 hours a week and go home, but they can't. Actors have to stay thin, models have to be really thin… the pressure is on, I'm telling you.

Similarity Number Four: Breakups or layoffs can leave you anywhere from confused to depressed, which makes it difficult to move on.

Once in a while you'll meet someone, like my friend Norma Jean, who can take something as huge as a layoff in stride. I met her when I lived in Alaska, and she had lost her job that spring. So she made a few phone calls, moved to Denali Park, worked 40 hours a week as a customer service rep, flirted with boys, hiked, ran around and even took a side trip to Hawaii. When she got back home in the fall, she got a new real job, with a summer in Alaska etched in her mind as a four-month working vacation.

But most of us aren't so good with rejection. Instead of realizing that new opportunities will open up, we might wallow for a while.

It's the same with love. Lots of women swear that the man they're in love with at age 17, 20, 25 or 30 is "the one," that they'll be together forever, and that everything will be as glamorous as it looks on their favorite TV show for the rest of their natural lives. When reality sets in and he makes some decision or looks in a direction that wasn't on your life itinerary, things can get trying. If an agreement is not reached, which is common at the beginning of careers and adult life, the couple breaks up and the two separate parties are left to improvise separately and figure things out for themselves.

Similarity Number Five: They stress teamwork and partnership, but they can suck you dry if they're not right for you.

22

Here's a rule for life: if you need a pep talk every few days to deal with it, it's not right for you. If you spend hours on the phone with your friends and family complaining about it, and it's making you depressed, you need to move on.

People stay with jobs that don't suit them for all kinds of reasons: they think they're indispensable, that they don't have enough experience to do something else, that they hate looking for jobs, and so on. People stay living in the land of "we should break up but not just yet," because they're afraid of being alone or disappointing the other person.

When the comfort zone isn't even comfortable, it's still hard to leave. But you have to move on at some point. Otherwise, you're not being true to yourself.

Similarity Number Six: Learning from the past can give you clues as to what to look for in the future when you make a new selection.

After you've acquired the karma of training all of your exes to behave, you might find that you are attracting new people who are better trained. Observing the behavior of your nearest and dearest can help you formulate a shopping list of things that will serve you well in your future searches. Doing the same works for jobs as well. A job can be just a paycheck or a step in a sequence of moves to establish a career, but it has to somehow apply to your development as a person.

Being a smarter shopper can benefit you in innumerable ways. Trust me.

Final Similarity Number Seven: When you find your perfect match, your joy knows no end. As time goes on, there are ups and downs, but if you're on the right track, you stick with it. And all of your friends who are not so blessed are desperately jealous.

There is nothing better than being satisfied and knowing that you are content, for one, and looking forward to whatever happens too. You get to be happy. You went out and looked for something, found

it, and now you have it. Hooray!

This doesn't happen all the time, so when it does, prepare to be humble and thankful. This invites more good karma into your life and keeps the jealousy of others at bay.

Act 1, Scene 5:
The Sisterhood

Christine's two "work friends" had become my favorite gal pals as I settled into the role of a lifetime at the call center.

Julie was tall and cute but almost always dateless; she was observing the universal truth that if one guy likes you, they all do, but if you can't get one to like you, then none of them will. She had wavy auburn hair (she spent a lot of money on it, and it looked fabulous) and couldn't wait to go to her ten-year reunion because she was much more a swan at 28 than she'd been in high school. Every day, she ate a salad for lunch in hopes of becoming a size six before the big reunion weekend.

At age 33, Tara was the oldest of the group; she'd been engaged once but had never married. She had that caustic, Miranda from "Sex and the City" air about her. Her sarcasm was fueled by the fact that the man who had caused her to temporarily drop her cynicism and fall in love had just relocated to Fargo, North Dakota. He had broken up with her a few weeks before he moved, and we were relieved, because Tara was a Florida girl and had no business moving to some landlocked Dakota anyway. Since the breakup, she'd chopped her long brown hair to her chin and dyed it blonde. It looked really good, especially since she was usually tan.

Still, she was devastated. We tried to get her to go out a lot, otherwise, she might stay home alone and look at all the things that Bill had left behind in her apartment.

Finally, Christine and I had met in school, many moons before our foray into the glamorous call-center world. She was infinitely patient with everyone and very relaxed. At home, she would pull out a bottle of wine at the first sign of trouble or stress. We both were wanna-be redheads and had monthly henna sessions at the apartment, but my hair was darker so hers picked up more of the red tones. Also, her hair was naturally wavy. I was so jealous.

I tried to decorate and maintain our apartment according to the laws of feng shui, but her love affair with clutter kept winning out. She said to me, "That book talks about how if you want to meet a man to date, you need to have pairs of stuff all over your house. Well, when all my shoes are out in the living room, don't you see that I'm helping us? That way, there's pairs of *shoes*... everywhere!"

Staying mad at someone like that is nearly impossible, almost as hard as actually getting mad at her. Especially when she keeps the wine handy and pours it liberally.

The four of us would get together for lunches, usually over at our apartment, and talk about tons of stuff, but usually the conversation would swivel around to men: when was the last time one opened a door for you, when was your last date, and so on. It became apparent that we were too comfortable with just hanging out with each other and talking about men when I received the dreaded telephone call.

I always know it's trouble when a girlfriend who isn't usually involved with my life socially gets in touch. It means one of two things: she is getting married or she is pregnant. Either way, I have to stretch my budget to buy someone a present every time I get one of those calls. Then, I am obliged to attend a party in which someone else, who has apparently made better life choices than I have, is showered with gifts for her new life ahead. And then I go home to my wine-filled apartment and smoke a clove cigarette on the porch while I ponder the fact that I wouldn't be ready for the major life change that I just bought a gift for my friend to celebrate.

Anne of the famed European tour sounded very happy.

"Can you meet me out?" she asked.

"Sure, where do you want to go?"

"I'm hungry, can you meet me at the sandwich shop?" There was a place between our apartments where we always met. She could never remember its name.

"Good thing I'm hungry, I'll be there in about 15. OK?"

"Yep, see you there."

She looked like she was about to burst and lifted her left hand up to me to show off her new sparkler. I had to smile; she just looked so happy. And her guy, James, was really nice. Much better than anyone she'd dated whom I had met, and I had known her for about ten years. She'd just met him the previous Halloween, and he gave her a silver love knot ring from Tiffany's as a promise ring by Christmas. Amazing.

So then the big question came: "Will you be my bridesmaid?"

Of course I would. But I had to bargain with her.

"Please don't pick a dress that is too expensive or ugly. And for God's sake, please let me and the other girls wear normal shoes. I have a strict, anti-dyeable shoes agenda."

Luckily, it was prom season, and Target was well-stocked with slinky black tea-length gowns. They were $20. When the other girls and I bought the dresses, I told her, "Not only are you the woman of James' dreams, you are the bride of my dreams as well."

She gave us rhinestone accessories to wear and fantastic bouquets of hot pink roses to carry. We looked as good as I've ever seen bridesmaids look, and this was a pleasant surprise. Until I discovered the Cinderella Project, which takes new and "gently-worn" evening gowns and matches them up with underprivileged young women so that they can attend the prom, I had accumulated quite the menagerie of off-the-shoulder taffeta numbers and such. It was such a relief to whisk them out of my closet and bask in my charitable donation at the same time when I had located the nearest gown drop-off location earlier that year. And in keeping with the guidelines of feng shui, it made room for something better to come into my life (and closet),

such as a $20 black dress that I might actually wear again.

Anne looked smashing in her empire-waist wedding dress with beaded top and simple veil. If I'd been the bride, I would have had a Priscilla Presley-style multi-layered fountain veil, but perhaps that's just me.

I was so busy smiling for pictures and visiting with her family and friends that I didn't realize that I was attending the event man-free until well into the reception. The disc jockey asked all of the couples to join Anne and James on the dance floor, so therefore every man in the room was occupied. I sat alone at my table and watched the groomsman I'd been paired with dance with his girlfriend. I sat there for a while, and then I wondered how long had it been since I'd had a man in my life.

The answer was: months and months. Since most relationships start with actual dates and mutate into nights on sofas watching movies, the amount of time that had gone by since I'd had a date was difficult to calculate. I'd have to check the journal at home. I only wrote in it when I was really happy or really upset.

October 8. Went to Casey Burke's going away party at Tahiti Joe's last night and met fabulous tall blonde, Steve. He stuck by my side all night and swore he'd call me to take me out soon but I'm still waiting.

It's been several months since this entry, so I guess I am still waiting.

In keeping with how you're only popular with one guy if the whole gender is interested in you, I met someone else, Tony, who is in some branch of the armed service, and we're supposed to go out soon. Hmmm... I gave him my number too. It was a red-letter night. I had to escape and come home early to ensure that I wouldn't screw anything up and remain desirable on both counts.

OK, so it had been seven months since my first few dates with Tony, which degenerated into couch/pizza sessions and trips to see manly war movies that gave me nightmares. Good thing he got transferred to Germany.

But it occurred to me that I needed to use this empty feeling, this

crushed ego, this existence of being the lone bridesmaid in a sea of couples, for my show. My high school acting teacher used to ask us what was going on in our lives and tell us to apply it to our performances. "Use it," she'd say. How could I be writing *The Independent Woman's Guide to Life*, which was the working title of the show, if I didn't include observations on life as a bridesmaid?

Hi. My name is Gina and I am a career bridesmaid. In my life as a bridesmaid, I have worn velvet, satin, crepe, and a few other unidentifiable fabrics.

A lot of people think that bridesmaids are a bunch of bitter, jealous hags, but let me tell you that this just isn't true. Let me address the "hag" portion of this theory first. It's a given that every bride wants to be the most beautiful person at her wedding. Since we stand right next to her, we have to look especially bad. This is why most bridesmaid dresses unfairly accent the hips and come in such an unflattering array of colors. It's a conspiracy throughout the bridal fashion industry.

As far as the bitter part goes, that may be true of some, but that isn't true of all of us. When we're standing up in front of everyone, holding our flowers and smiling, the last thing we're thinking is, "I wish I was the bride." Mostly, we're thinking either, "My feet are killing me," or, "That groomsman is kind of cute." We're not dreaming of true love, we're wondering how we're going to pay for the ugly $150 dress we're wearing. And most of all, we're not taking mental notes about what we'll do when it's "our turn." We're looking forward to the open bar at the reception, and a chance to sit down.

Act 1, Scene 6:
The Parade of Suitors Begins

"Do you really think it's time?" Christine asked me.

"We might as well get back into dating," I responded. "I know I'll need something to do while the rest of my friends are busy being madly in love. Plus, it's summertime and there's nothing to do."

"Good points," she agreed.

We, and by that I mean Christine, Tara, Julie, and I, signed up for speed dating in the hopes that if we encountered the same old crap in the dating world, at least it would be over with faster. Also, naturally, we hoped to beat the odds and actually find someone who we'd want to keep, and who'd want to keep us. Finally, we knew that if we didn't take advantage of this trend, we might not have any good dating stories for our paired-off friends.

Our following adventures, while entertaining in themselves, also inspired "The Seven Stages of Dating" for my show. I stole the introduction from William Shakespeare:

All the world's a stage, and the men and women merely players. We have our exits and our entrances, and one man in his time plays many parts. His stages of life are the seven ages of modern man.

At first the player, flirting with the ladies, drinking way too much, and puking in the nearest latrine; and then the charming boyfriend, bearing flowers and sentimental poetry; and then the lover, with charm and romance to spare; and then the career man, with his conquest and money foremost in his mind; then he's the successful man about town, showering all with his knowledge and expertise.

The sixth age shifts into the time when he slows down and goes fishing more often, when he starts spending all that money he worked so hard for when he was younger. Finally, he is an old man, oblivious to the things he has and hasn't done, content for once to mellow out.

What I notice about this story is that at the beginning, he's got time for the ladies, but once he gets out into the outer world, we gals are all but forgotten. So that inspired me to write The Seven Ages of Modern Woman:

First of all, if all the world's a stage, then she'll be needing better costumes, and more costume changes as well.

At first she is the little lady, whose days are filled with ladybugs and butterflies; and then the student, when note passing and hormones hopefully do not interfere with higher learning; and then she's the bachelorette, partying with players who may or may not hold her hair back if she pukes; and then the woman in love, wondering if she should hang her hopes on her man; and then the working woman, going out to make a dent in the world; and then the juggler, who tries to manage a career, man, and life the best she can. Finally, she wears purple and spends time gardening, writes letters and sends cards, and winds down her life at last.

We went to a cheesy dance club over the bridge in the Feather Sound district of St. Pete for our rendezvous with destiny. We wore the uniform of the modern confident woman: semi-dressy Capri pants, cute shoes with heels, and sleeveless or short-sleeved blouses. The four of us were a sight to behold, very *Sex and the City* with a tropical twist.

31

A woman about our age, who was holding a clipboard and smiling, greeted us as we stepped into the darkness of the club. I had parked my Mazda just outside the entrance in case we needed to make a quick getaway.

"Hi there," she said, and started to hand out name tags to us.

"I'm Gina Malone," I said, to get started. She checked off my name and assigned a number to me.

"Tara Davis," Tara said and tried to squeak out a smile. She was already nervous, and her hands shook when she reached out for her official score card and name tag.

"Remember, it's just window-shopping today. Just browsing. We'll be fine. It's just reintroducing ourselves to the dating pool." I was explaining this to myself as much as I was saying it to her.

"Christine Leone and Julie Berdin," Christine said, taking over for Julie, who was staring into space. The disco balls were already spinning, and Julie had had too much to drink the night before, so she was easily distracted. The smiling woman helped them with the official rules of the game as well as their name tags.

The rules were as follows. Admittedly, we made some of them up ourselves.

1) Have a refreshing alcoholic drink and eat a light but substantial meal before attempting the speed-dating process. (For Julie, this helped with the hangover.)

2) You have six minutes to determine if a guy is date worthy, then the smiling lady rings an annoying bell and off he goes to the next woman.

3) Stand up and stretch legs between introductions to determine if a prospective beau is too short for your liking.

4) Keep expectations low to allow room for pleasant surprises.

5) Ask interesting questions such as, "Who is your favorite Beatle?" and "If there were a movie made about your life, who would play you?"

6) Take excellent notes for the post-game wrap-up with fellow shoppers.

7) Be nice and don't ramble on about stupid things, if possible.

It was a tall order, but we were up for the challenge. Well, Julie really wasn't, but she would make a great listener in her hung-over state. When the starting bell rang, I was sitting at my assigned table with a cold glass of water next to me, ready for action.

Bachelor number one was a car salesman who looked way too old for me. He was nice, though, and well-traveled, so I asked him questions about where he'd been. And then, ding, he was gone.

Bachelor number two was a hot doctor with a great sense of humor. He was tall, thin, and very distinguished looking, in a Mark Darcy sort of way. He made me laugh in a real way, and I hadn't run across a guy who'd done that in a long time. I checked yes for him. And then, ding.

Bachelor number three was a computer engineer or something, very nice but not very interesting. I asked him about his outside interests and then he droned on about something sports-related. And then, ding, he was gone.

Bachelor number four was clearly the party guy of the bunch. He reminded me of the cool guys in college who always had female admirers, but he was of course older and had a real job. Interesting guy, and very nice. He had a kid and an ex-wife. Ding.

Bachelor number five was another computer engineer, but he was tan and pretty cute. Something about him reminded me of one of my high school crushes. He was very nice too, but I wasn't overwhelmed with a feeling of magic. Ding.

Bachelor number six was new to the area and looking to meet people. We didn't have a damn thing in common. It was kind of comical actually, even though it was a bit of a strain to find stuff to talk about. It kind of went, "Oh, you like going to the theatre? I like watching Nascar." Nice guy, though. Ding.

Bachelor number seven set off my gaydar. Now, I know that's not fair, but a gut feeling is a gut feeling. Not surprisingly, I had a great time talking to him. Mostly we talked about work and made fun of our jobs. He had interviewed with my employer and walked away with a pretty uptight view of the place. Ding.

Finally, bachelor number eight was sweet and friendly and looked like he was too young to date my little sister. He turned out to be four years younger than me. Sorry, but no. Ding.

So, just being in the mood for getting my feet wet and nothing more, I put down "yes" for the doctor and the tan computer engineer and left the rest blank. I spent a few minutes with Christine talking with the car salesman and the tan man afterward, but then I noticed that Julie and Tara had relocated outside. So, we excused ourselves and went to meet them.

Julie clearly needed to lie down, as the drink that had temporarily uplifted her was now letting her down. And Tara was a wee bit shaken.

"Do you mind if we get the hell out of here?" she whispered to me.

"Not at all. OK, girls, into the car!"

And so we returned to my apartment. I made up the couch so that Julie could snooze all night long, and the rest of us sat around my retro chrome-and-white table and compared cheat sheets.

"First of all, let me just say that I am not ready to date again," Tara said. "But I am glad I went, and I'm glad that you were all with me. So, being in that not ready place, I didn't put down a yes for anyone."

"Not even the hot doctor?" Christine asked. She couldn't believe it.

"Not even him, although I'll admit that he'll have no problem finding someone. He was awfully cute. Too young for me though."

"I liked the tan guy and the doctor," I said. "I picked both of them."

"You liked the tan guy? I never would have guessed," said Tara. "But he was cute too."

"I picked Bachelor Number Four," said Julie from the couch.

"The ex-wife and kid didn't scare you off?" I asked.

She sat up and looked at me, all crazy-eyed. "He has a kid?"

"Yep."

"Oh, man!" she said, and lay down again.

The three of us had all picked the doctor. Other than that, of course Tara picked no one, and Christine picked Bachelor Number Six, and Julie also picked Bachelor Number Eight. He was close to her age, after all.

Act 1, Scene 7:
Crash Landing

The next time I checked my e-mail, I noticed a message from the dating service.

"Dear Ms. Malone:

Thank you for participating in our event last week. We hope you enjoyed your time with us and the speed-dating process. Unfortunately, none of the matches that you picked also picked you. However, please be assured that some of the other men did choose you as a possible match.

We hope you enjoyed our service and will contact us again.

Sincerely,

People Matches Inc."

Oh my God. It *is* just like being out there, only it's over more quickly. This way, I found two guys I liked who didn't call at the same time, and more who liked me that I didn't find attractive. At this rate, I will definitely be engaged by age 33.

But in keeping with the tradition— the tradition that is, that if your love life is going well, then your career or health is bad, and vice versa, with at least one of the three being amiss—I was approached

by my general manager. He wanted me to apply for a promotion to a department that I'd never heard of. One huge distinction that the department held was that nobody took telephone calls. They wrote e-mail correspondence instead.

My first thought was, that's a promotion? How strange, in a place where no one wants to take telephone calls, that not taking calls would be a promotion. But why would I argue with that, when it would amount to a raise for me? So I called the girls together for a powwow before the big interview. I needed to see how their dating lives were too. We met at Denny's around 10 p.m.

"I hope none of you have my disease," I said. "My bachelors didn't pick me."

"That hot doctor didn't pick any of us," said Julie. "How rude!"

"He was hanging out with that blonde chippy," observed Tara. "Typical. She's probably a natural blonde too. How obnoxious! You have no idea how expensive it is to keep up with my roots."

"You need to join the henna club with me and Gina," Christine said. "It doesn't leave roots, and you can be a redhead. As you all know, redheads have the most fun anyway. This blonde stuff is overrated. At least it didn't work for me."

"It's something to think about," said Tara. "It would make hair maintenance more enjoyable, that's for sure.

"I went on a date with that party guy, but he wasn't really what I remembered. So I don't think we hit it off," said Julie.

"You needed to drink more, then you would have fun," Christine laughed.

"True. Fair enough," Julie answered.

"So the reason I've called you all here today," I said, trying to be serious for a second, "is because my big boss told me about a job at work and I'm interviewing for it. I need your help with the interview questions."

"Are you high maintenance or low maintenance?" asked Tara. "That is my favorite interview question. And of course they always want you to say you're low-maintenance. But it's better if you mean it."

"Think of all those scenarios that they like to bring up, such as 'give an example of you going above and beyond a customer's expectations' or 'tell us about a problem that you identified and solved within your current job.' Stuff like that," Christine added. "Also, the fortune-telling questions, like 'where do you see yourself in five years?' Now, I feel sorry for anyone who can honestly plan that far ahead, but maybe you should have some kind of answer made up for that. It doesn't have to come true, you know."

"You're going to get a raise if you get this job?" asked Julie. "That is cool! You'll be one of the people who actually does a job that she prepared for in college!"

I had majored in journalism in college. If I got this job, I would write about boring things all day long. Oh, the professional bliss!

One of the managers in my department, who was probably too nice for his own good, took me "out of routing" and away from my usual phone monkey job for an hour to help me out with the interview. He ran all of the usual stodgy questions by me and scanned my resume to find good examples that I could use in the interview to "impress the judges." Christine and I went into our closets and assessed my wardrobe options. After a few hours and a few glasses of wine, we made up the winning ensemble. It was a black skirt and jacket, a lime-green knit top, Christine's peridot earrings, and chunky black shoes.

The interview was one of the more interesting auditions I'd been to in my life. Apparently, in some effort to appear hip and with-it, the interviewers asked some pretty off-the-wall questions. (Maybe some pop-psychologist had invaded their corporate Human Resources Department, we'll never know.) They wanted to know what kind of activities I enjoyed in high school and stuff like that. Of course, I had to search my brain for acceptable activities and omit the details about skipping last period to drink daiquiris by my friend Laurie's pool while we worked on our prom tans.

Apparently, my responses were either amusing enough or just led them to believe that I was a good candidate. In any case, I was offered the job a week later. I could hang up my phone monkey headset

forever and have a real job, finally, and I'd make over $30,000 a year. It was a wonderful feeling: out with the old, in with the new. I recycled most of my current paper-strewn desk on my last day with the phone monkeys since I wouldn't be needing that information anymore. I was dateless as usual, but at least I had a new job to learn, and a whole new floor of the building to meet.

Christine had similar luck not long after my promotion. She became a presenter and went to work "in the field," which was all over the state of Florida, to promote the company and provide information about credit counseling. She had a little office in our building, but she wasn't there much, so I mostly saw her at home. Our household income increased substantially, so we went out and bought some furniture and electronics. We both ended up with new computers, and I sprung for a new television set while she bought a new couch. Our neighbors became accustomed to seeing our discarded furniture with signs that said "Free to a Good Home" taped on them, and nothing lingered for long outside our door. While the Diva Palace was never showroom quality, we very much enjoyed our new surroundings.

My new-found interest in feng shui, gleaned mostly from magazines of course, had provided me with a new insight into my surroundings. One basic idea was to get rid of the things that reminded you of being poor, so with each piece of furniture that we placed outside our door and every bag of clothes that I donated to Goodwill, I really did feel more free. I was making room for bigger and better things to enter my life.

Act 1, Scene 8:
Giving of Myself
and Meeting a Cute Boy

The promotion yielded more unexpected fun. Namely, people valued my opinions and came to me for help. It was crazy, because at age 28, this was the first time in my life that my job provided me with any kind of authority or prestige. I attended training sessions and wrote all day long now. I could wear headphones and enjoy the melodic sounds of the Mavericks as I worked. For work in a cube farm, it was a huge step up.

Over the first few weeks after my promotion, I realized to my ultimate relief that it was a decent job after all. I wouldn't have to scour the classifieds every Sunday and constantly ask everyone I knew if they knew about any cool job openings. I could park there for a few years, learn the job, and get on with my life.

The transition was unexpected but welcome. Making a living as a 20-something single woman hadn't turned out to be as glamorous as I'd pictured as a kid—I wasn't on television after all—but it wasn't so bad either.

It was nice to have a tolerable job at last because in the back of my mind I knew that I had to keep working on the one-woman show. There was no cohesive group or meetings to attend, so I was in charge

of my own progress. Closer to the time of the show, I'd get in touch with them to find a director who would work with me and make suggestions about the script. But the best I could do, at first, was learn my day job and go home exhausted.

During a meeting with my new supervisor, she asked me if I had any interest in volunteer work. I told her that of course I did; I had spent the last three Oscar nights sashaying around in an evening gown, tiara, and gloves entertaining the guests of Oscar Night America at the Tampa Theatre. What was fun about this event was that ordinary people could get dressed to the nines, walk up the red carpet at the theatre, go inside to enjoy some drinks and food, and watch the Oscars on the big screen. Tampa Theatre was a beautiful venue, with Mediterranean architecture inside, tiled floors and walls in the lobby, and a dusky ceiling with twinkle-light stars inside the theatre. Since the place was built in 1926, it even had resident ghosts. They showed art films, foreign films, and classic films on Sunday afternoons, and hosted live musical and comedy acts. It even had an enormous marquee that lit up in the old-school style. The theatre was such a cool place!

So in answering that question enthusiastically, I was nominated to work on a volunteer committee that organized volunteer events for the employees in our office. I would have to get in touch with the aspect of volunteering that involved less glamour and more sweat, but it seemed like an appropriate thing for me to do. For the first time in my life, I was taking home more money than I absolutely needed, so it was a good time to give something back.

One of the first events I attended took place in a sweaty warehouse in Ybor City, which is an old area of Tampa where many Italian, Spanish, and Cuban immigrants lived years ago. Through the years it fell into disrepair and then was resurrected as a miniature version of Bourbon Street in New Orleans. Crowds fill the streets every weekend night, and gaggles of bachelors and bachelorettes stumble from bar to bar. Once in a while you'll see some idiot couple pushing a baby stroller down Seventh Avenue at 10 o'clock at night. Very classy.

My group and I met in the low-rent area of Ybor City, several blocks away from the main drag, to work for a food bank. We wore plastic gloves and bagged onions for about three hours one weeknight. The men in the group were responsible for hauling big bags of onions back and forth from the pallet, and one in particular started kidding around with me. His name was Paul and he was pretty cute. Tall, brown hair, green eyes, kind of a Ewan MacGregor look to him. Sigh!

Later on, over drinks at a nearby watering hole, I found out that he met my boyfriend criteria: he was close to my age (a tad older, actually), liked Elvis and the Beatles, and he was very, very unattached. Not on the rebound, simply single. That last trait is very important, because if his last breakup was too recent, then a potential boyfriend may simply attach himself to whatever woman comes along first because he's lonely. Plus, then you have to deal with someone else's relationship leftovers. Ideally, they should be free of the past when they take on something new. Like I was. I could barely remember my most recent relationship at that point.

When we ended the night with no telephone numbers exchanged, I had to wonder: did I even want to date someone from work? He seemed nice enough, but you never know. What had attracted him to me that night? Was it the smears of dirt on my t-shirt that made me seem approachable? Men seem to love it when you're not trying to impress them; then you're a challenge or something. You can be carefree or apathetic, or even just sweaty. It doesn't matter, they always go for it. One thing was clear: I'd have to put out some pretty apathetic and unthreatening signals to get a date with him.

Too bad we couldn't just exchange dating resumes to better check each other out. On them, he and I would provide our signs of the zodiac, favorite foods, and important interests. Also, crucial questions, such as those named below, would be addressed:

How long has it been since your last relationship ended?
Are you in a relationship now?
Do you have a job? If so, what is it? If not, why?

Have you been married before?
Do you have children?
Have you spent any time in prison? If so, why?
Do you like to debate politics and religion? (If so, please date
    someone else!)
Do you hope to marry someone someday?

Think of the time we could save if people could just be up-front about these things!

The next month I went to the volunteer event again, and he was there too. This time, we bagged potatoes. Over drinks, he made a reference to taking me out "some time." I provided him with my telephone number. And then, the waiting game began.

"Why hasn't he called me yet?" I asked Christine one Saturday while we were watering the plants on our porch.

"The best answer to that question is another question, Gina. Who cares? Your job is to only deal with the guys who call, not the ones that say they will. He could have a wife that no one knows about. He could be a serial killer. You shouldn't spent your time thinking about it— it's a waste of time!"

"What you and I need is a male prostitute," Julie interjected later over margaritas at a nearby Mexican restaurant. "Not even to sleep with, mind you. I just miss having a man around. And I figure, if I'm paying him, he'd have to be sensitive. You know, cook for me, wash the dishes, provide intellectual conversation, rub my feet, rub my back, watch a great movie with me and snuggle on the sofa."

"He'd probably go home after a night like that and cry in the shower. He'd be saying, 'I feel so *used!*'" I interjected.

"Only if he was like a woman," added Tara, and we laughed.

I was a little shy about bringing it up, but eventually I spilled my news:

"I've been spending some time with Paul Eastman lately."

"He has our number, but he hasn't called her yet," added Christine.

"I didn't know he was your type," joked Tara. "I mean, he's not

some sweet young thing or anything."

"I told you I gave up dating younger men," I responded. "Too much like babysitting."

"Ah, that is what became of Bachelor #8, ladies," said Julie. "He was 25. It was just too much for me, even though that's just a little bit younger than I am. He just kept testing my limits like a two-year-old. Finally I told him to bugger off. But about Paul, I didn't know you didn't know him. I see him all the time at work."

"He was one of those hundred or so people at work that I say hi to but don't know the names of," I explained.

"I think he seems nice," said Tara. "A bit career-obsessed, but nice."

"I always get a kick out of people who work with us who really bust their ass to get noticed. I didn't know he was like that."

"Yes, you might want to think about that," said Christine. "You don't want to trade boyfriends who are obsessed with action films and sports for boyfriends who are obsessed with money and work. Although, it seems that no matter what kind of guy you meet, he is going to be obsessed with something."

"And if they're obsessed with *you*, we're moving into stalker territory, which is also scary," I added.

"I'd make all the healthy, normal men meet up in one convenient location at the same time, if I could," said Tara. "But as it is, we're on our own. And it's scary to think that you can be with someone for a couple of years and that they can pick up and move out of your life, just like that."

"Better luck next time," I said, "and that goes for all of us."

Act 1, Scene 9:
The Audition

The striking parallel between interviewing for a new job and interviewing for a new boyfriend became apparent in the following weeks. After I ran into him at restaurant near work one night to celebrate one of our co-workers' last day with the company, we actually set up a date for that weekend.

We went to a Mexican restaurant around 8 p.m. on a Friday night. As Christine helped me get ready, I had worked myself into such a nervous frenzy that I forgot to have a snack. I had worn black Capri pants and a black blouse, along with basic accessories: diamond studs, ring with enormous blue topaz, no necklace. I figured that my flamboyant personality could stand alone against a blank canvas of wardrobe, if you will.

The hostess had promised us a reservation for 8:15, but naturally they had lost the reservation. Not to worry, as they gave us an excellent spot minutes later. I had to compliment Paul on how gracious he had been when they told him that they didn't have his reservation.

"I always try to be nice," he said to me and winked. "It's how I usually get what I want anyway."

Cute, I thought.

We discussed misadventures of youth and college at dinner, and kept each other laughing. The sangria that we started to drink before our appetizers arrived clashed with my churning stomach, but I kept a smile on my face anyway. It hardly seemed the time to recount to him that I was reliving my adventures with the digestive disorder.

He seemed to be quite a dear. He had an older sister and two younger brothers, and they had grown up in Maryland. I couldn't find much wrong with him.

"OK, where is the last place you went on vacation?" I asked.

"Rhode Island, to visit my friend Eddie. You?"

"A week on the beach with my best friends, before our high school reunion."

"What beach?"

"Longboat Key."

"Nice."

"What's your next vacation?" I asked.

"Not planned yet. Although I'd love to go to… Graceland."

Oh my God, if he wasn't Mr. Right, then he was definitely Mr. Right Now. I'd wanted to go to Graceland for years. I hadn't had any luck at all convincing my girlfriends that Memphis was the vacation destination of choice.

"Very cool. I've wanted to go there too. And Vegas. I still haven't been to Vegas. But, there is always hope for the future."

Soon the food arrived, and we ate in a comfortable silence. Paul seemed to breathe a sigh of relief when he asked me if I was a vegetarian (I'd ordered cheese quesadillas) and I said no. That is a great first-date question, now that I think about it. Otherwise, think about what Thanksgiving might be like? Or even Taco Night at Mom and Dad's. Great question, indeed.

Ever the gentleman, he walked me to my door, kissed me on the cheek, and was gone in a flash. I let myself in, kicked off my shoes, and watched "Blind Date" and the news in anticipation of Christine's return to the apartment. I rehashed my earlier musings and penned a few thoughts for the show, too:

When meeting someone new, it would be helpful to know some important information at the start. Of course, through basic conversation, you can nail down the basics: general areas of interest, sign of the zodiac, work situation, and so on. But what I want to know eventually, what we as consumers want to know is stuff like:

How long has it been since your last relationship ended? Why did it end?

Are you in a relationship now? Do you have or want to have children? Do you know if you have children already?

Are you the kind of guy who dates a woman for two or three years before getting jitters and running in the opposite direction? Or do you run away early on in the relationship?

Do you have a job? If so, what is it? If not, why?

Have you spent any time in prison? If so, why?

Do you hope to marry someone someday?

The search and application process is an integral part of being single. Just as you scrutinize potential dates, you are scrutinized as well. This generally sends the majority of the consumers (especially the vegetarians in my case, since I love tacos) scurrying in the other direction. But alas, this is part of the game, the revolving door of love, the turnstile experience. The more frogs we kiss, the more we can edit our shopping list. And as time goes by, our shopping savvy is increased.

After Christine and I rehashed the night's events, it was soon forgotten with the silence of the telephone for the next two weeks. Paul was still shopping, apparently, and not ready to make a purchase. My routine returned to normal overall.

On my way home from work one day, a driver coming from the other direction lost control of his car and seemed to be headed straight for me. My brain's automatic pilot kicked in and I maintained my speed in the hopes that he would miss my car entirely. Time slowed down as I turned to watch his car miss mine by three or four inches.

He hit the car behind me head-on. The passengers managed to get

of the car, which was totaled. I drove to the next block, parked my car, and ran back to the site of the accident with my cell phone. Fortunately, the cops came quickly and all was settled; they didn't need me as a witness. So I sniveled as I drove home.

Christine was outside when I drove up, and her face fell when she saw my expression.

"Honey, it was *one* date!" she yelled. "You barely *know* the guy! He's not worth this!"

"But there was a car, as old as we are... and it came straight at me, and then it totaled the car behind me... missed me by this much," I said, motioning with my hands to indicate about four inches. "The driver lost control... I am just so glad that I wasn't hit, that all the teeth weren't knocked out of my head."

She started laughing as soon as I figured out what she was talking about.

"Oh, my God. Well, it's understandable that you're upset about *that*. Come inside and I'll pour you some wine. You had me really worried there for a minute."

"Christine, I haven't been 17 for a while now. I don't drive around crying about boys anymore!"

"Yes, and thank God for that," she added.

This incident made me realize something: I wasn't going to let a good-looking chap like Paul get away from me on our second date, if we had one, without giving me a real kiss. But, he would definitely need to call me to make any of that happen.

Act 1, Scene 10:
Romantic Bliss

Eventually, he did call– the next day, in fact. After he won the bid to be my next boyfriend, we were off on an exciting new adventure.

What can be said for that fun time when you're getting to know a new love? You leave your regular shopping habits for a while and venture into strange terrain where you are a part of a couple. Suddenly, old routines are abandoned in favor of new and exciting outings. Dirty clothes don't get washed, career initiative takes a back seat, and you have a date to take to your cousin's wedding. You meet his family, he meets yours, and your fantasies are filled with pictures of you and him living in a Craftsman-style bungalow with a baby in your arms.

There is a down side to this, of course. Like I said, your clothes stay dirty, the refrigerator eventually empties out, and you don't see your girlfriends as much. The last is probably the worst thing for me when a new man arrives on the scene.

I knew stronger, better women who balance things better, but I frankly didn't know how to add a man to an already-full life. In my sane moments, I knew that every woman needs time with her sisters and friends to get to speak her native language, for one. She needs her

alone time, or she and the rest of the world will suffer her PMS. And most importantly, the most pitiful type of newly-single woman out there is the one who forgot about all her friends and devoted all her time to her man before he turned tail and ran.

In the event that he should exit, she is left bewildered and alone. Friends are like an insurance policy that women maintain, since real friends can be called upon in an emergency situation for assistance.

But I wasn't planning for contingencies in the first few months. Instead, I was soaking up the couples culture.

Our first out-of-town trip went well. We rented a room at the beach and then invited some friends to join us. Christine was away on business, but Julie and Tara came and drank margaritas with me on the tiki deck of the nearby resort. Some of Paul's friends came too, and they tried to form love connections with Julie and Tara, who weren't having that at all. So that provided us with some real-life drama too.

We went to my cousin's wedding in Orlando, too. He met the extended family and danced with me most of the night. We had some moments of displeasure when he insisted that I dance with him immediately after dinner, when I was stuffed full of Chicken Cordon Bleu. The evening ended with me enjoying a glass of Alka-Seltzer instead of tripping the light fantastic with my boyfriend. I was not pleased.

As a treat, we went to Memphis for a long weekend. We arrived early in the day so that we could spend some time at Beale Street and then retire back to the hotel. The next day was spent strictly at Graceland and Sun Studios, and the following day we departed for home. I've never seen so many gold records and jewel-studded costumes with capes in all my life. Elvis lives!

When it came time to exchange birthday gifts, the girls and I spent a day at the Safety Harbor Spa and called it even. We bobbed around in the pool and soaked our newly-massaged bodies in the spring, nearly passed out in the sauna, and even nagged ourselves into joining a yoga class. Finally, Paul and I went off to Longboat Key for a relaxed weekend on the beach. We were up with the sun and tooling

around in the sea kayak all day long. We also checked out a nearby aquarium, went on a boat tour around the islands, and ate ice cream like an old couple after dinner both nights.

We were probably very annoying in our always-together, usually-happy way of being there for a while. Naturally, we stressed each other out sometimes, but for the time that we could be, we were happy. I'd cook dinner for him at night, and we'd sit—in candlelight— and talk about something mellow while we ate.

There were the intangible, priceless things that I loved about our courtship. The way, when he walked into the room, that I could feel his beautiful eyes (that were sometimes blue, sometimes green, depending on what he wore) cast their gaze upon me. I felt almost arrogant about how happy we were, and got into a phase— albeit brief— in which I wanted everyone to know just how great it was to be with someone I loved that much. The feelings were overwhelming. Sitting on the couch watching football became a lot more fun with my man by my side. Our friends tolerated each other, I had met his family, and he had met mine. It seemed that we were on our way… to something or somewhere. I felt excitement in the pit of my stomach when he appeared at my door or at my desk. Yes, by the ripe old age of 28, I was in love.

Act 1, Scene 11:
Resuming Normal Life
with Boyfriend in Tow

Christine had been single for all intents and purposes since she'd had a whirlwind romance with a Romanian guy a few years back because no one she'd met had come close to having his worldly air and sophistication. And so, I can only imagine how strange it must have been for her to have a man around the house again. Paul was over at the apartment often, acting princely for the most part. For example, he gallantly brought us a bouquet of flowers after he managed to pass on a bad case of the flu to both of us.

When Christine was out of town for work, Paul and I would play house. This was by far the most fun when he brought over his George Forman Grill and a couple of steaks. I would get to work cooking or preparing the "nonessentials" that Paul wasn't a fan of, such as mixed vegetables or salad, while he'd do the grilling.

"What is it that you are doing?" he would ask me with mischief in his eyes. "Chopping some type of green bunny food?"

"I am making salad, and you are going to help me eat it!"

"But that will disrupt my whole system! I haven't had lettuce since taco night, and the grease and taco meat canceled out the lettuce and tomato. My body might go into shock if I ingested *salad*!"

"You will eat it, and you will like it!" I threatened, laughing at him.

When the steaks were cooked and the veggies steamed, we'd sit down to eat a balanced meal, just like a couple of grown-ups. It was very civilized.

After dinner, we'd usually watch TV or go out to meet friends. Once in a while, my neighbor friends would stop by and we'd have an impromptu gathering.

Christine and I didn't have as much time to have the girls over for our fun weekend luncheons once Paul entered the picture. It was hard to plan anything at the apartment, since one of us was always gone. It seemed like everything happened on the spur of the moment anymore.

One such thing happened on a Thursday night: Julie showed up unannounced just as we had started to wash our dinner dishes. She looked distressed.

"I'll do the dishes," Paul said to me quietly.

"Thanks so much," I answered as I steered her into my bedroom and shut the door.

"What is wrong?" I asked her.

"My high school reunion is tomorrow night, and I am about to shit a brick."

"Why?" I asked, and then I remembered my own ten-year reunion. The thrill of walking into a room and confronting all of my adolescent issues at once. Arriving without a man on my arm. Feeling that my weight/car/career would never measure up. Worrying that I would be embarrassed by my own inadequacy, until I had a few drinks and realized that everyone else was just as nervous as I was. And hey, at least I was brave enough to show up. I knew of more than a few people who lived in town and didn't go to the reunion.

"Do you know anyone who is going?" I asked. "It's easier if you can go with someone, or at least know that someone will be there when you arrive."

"I know a few couples," she said. "Couples! It's so obnoxious. I

haven't had a date since the youngster and I haven't had a real boyfriend for two years. I have to show up at my class reunion alone."

"It's OK, I did that, and I haven't needed counseling since. Are these people you know married classmates, or is one person in the couple not from your school?"

"They all married guys they met later on, so the men aren't from school."

"And you know them?"

"Yes."

"You'll be fine! You'll have the guys to talk to when you're too nervous to go get reacquainted with your classmates. They'll be glad you're there, too, to explain who used to be fat and skinny and popular or whatever."

"Oh," she said, and seemed to calm down a little bit.

"Hold on, I'm going to go get Paul. He went to his reunion all by himself, too."

I went out to the living room and found him in front of the TV.

"Can you come hang out with us?" I asked. "Julie is paranoid about going to her class reunion tomorrow."

"Are you sure you want me around?" he asked.

"Of course!"

Back in my room, Julie was sprawled out on my bed, half asleep. She sat up when I opened my squeaky door.

"Tell me more about your reunions," she asked us.

"When I went to mine up north, I was one of about ten people who didn't bring a date. My graduating class wasn't huge and only half of us showed up, so it was a pretty small gathering."

"Did you have fun?" she asked him.

"Yeah, I'm really glad I went. I had a great time. I hadn't seen most of those people since graduation."

"I think it might be easier to not take a date," I added. "A lot of people I know didn't bring their significant others to the reunion."

"The wives and husbands usually don't know anyone except their spouse," Paul said. "So that's why they might not go."

"Plus, there's always the chance that you'll hook up with some

hottie from your class. You wouldn't want to bring a date and miss out on that, would you?"

"That's true!" said Julie. "I hadn't thought about that!"

"See if you can get together with at least one of the couples before the party and drive there with them," I offered.

"Good idea," she said. "I'm supposed to call my friend Cherie before I leave tomorrow. We can just meet up then, for moral support and all. Since I have the day off and she's here on vacation, we might even catch a movie beforehand."

After the three of us had talked for a while, I glanced at the clock and realized it was way past my bedtime. Julie must have noticed this too, because she got up to leave around 11 p.m. Paul and I sawed logs until the alarm went off at 6:30 a.m. Then, it was a mad rush to get dressed and drive to work.

Act 1, Scene 12:
Questions Arise

Several months in, when it seemed like he wouldn't be going anywhere, I decided that hormonal birth control was for me. Only, it wasn't. The first prescription, which was about three times stronger than it needed to be, turned me into a raving psychopath. I wanted to quit my job, dump Paul and move to the wilderness. I was crazy.

The next prescription calmed me down to the point where I would fall asleep at 7 p.m. each night. That lasted about two weeks, and I threw out the rest of the pack.

Finally, thanks to the miracle of modern science, I found a cute little electronic device that would predict my ovulation. The drug store sold it to people who were trying to conceive, but it worked pretty well for the opposite goal as well. I could tell that even if my romance didn't work out, my relationship with the electronic ovulation detector was the beginning of a beautiful friendship.

The months that it took for me to decide on a way that I could avoid pregnancy definitely affected my relationship with the only person who had a chance of getting me pregnant. Paul seemed impatient and exhausted with me. My mood swings were pretty bad, but I tried to tell him that what I needed was some time alone to figure

out what moods were genuine and what moods were induced by synthetic hormones.

Some things were really starting to bother me. First off, I was upset by the way Paul thought he could resume an enthusiastic relationship with drinking after our honeymoon period wound down. It probably wouldn't have been so bad if he had had the body of a 21-year-old when he decided to drink like one, but since those days were gone, it took a serious toll on his body– and personality. He liked to arrive at my house late on a work night, or turn to me on the barstool next to him at his favorite dive and start political debates. First, he would go red in the face talking about family values and how the lack of family values was causing America to go straight down the toilet. Then he would move on to scintillating topics like gun control and how the Environmental Protection Agency was out to undermine our constitutional rights. It was like dating an angry political commentator from the Fox Network.

The idea of "family values" with the modern pop culture definition always made me laugh. I remember an old boyfriend of Anne's practically preaching it one night over chicken wings at Hooters, which was already a contradiction in itself. He was giving off the impression that he was a stand-up, old-fashioned guy with a ton to offer her; his attitude implied that she would be "taken care of " if they ended up staying together. He thought that opening doors and always picking up the check were absolute proof that he was a gentleman. However, with all that self-imposed grandeur, his sense of decency must have been lost in the shuffle. Apparently, his idea of "family values" meant that he could have a nice, sweet girlfriend like Anne and a secret out-of-town girlfriend in another city he frequented because of his job. It was as if he was rehearsing for the one day when he'd have a wife and a mistress. His "family values" made sure that he was always in charge of every situation and accountable to no one. He got to be the king, because he was lucky enough to be born male.

Anne found out about the "other woman" and gave him the heave-ho, but in the control-freak style that is popular with young male

family values enthusiasts, he kept on coming around, trying to wear her down so that she'd take him back. The last time I saw him was when I attended her college graduation, and it surprises me that he didn't bleed from the look I gave him. Eventually, he gave up on her and got lost.

The overall idea of family values is positive, but the spin it has received has given it an almost condescending tone. It's as if the American politicians and talk show hosts want to reminisce about how great things were when women had little or no economic or political power. No one comes out and says that; it's just implied. I'm sure it was great for men when they held every possible public office, made all the money, and had all of the decision-making power in America, but that doesn't mean it was ever right. When a young man from a modern generation finds this appealing, it's a big red flag.

The first time Paul called the apartment in a drunken haze, it was funny. But as time went on, we relished his slurred voice on the answering machine less and less. Frankly, I was embarrassed.

Over time I saw a change in the way he perceived me. While at first my differing opinions and independent thinking had proved to hold his attention, now they were a detriment. In time it seemed that, according to him, it was time for me to cast everything aside and just take on his opinions as my own. It seemed like "family values" were undermining our relationship. Well, that was crap altogether. I knew, at least on some level, that something would have to give.

I noticed a change in Christine whenever Paul was mentioned or in the room. Having listened to my endless ranting through the hormonal testing phase and witnessed the drunken messages on the answering machine, she was not so impressed with him anymore. After the bliss period had ended, I felt frustrated at the same time I felt loved, and I felt guilty for not being the perfect woman, which was what Paul (and to be fair, every guy) seemed to want. The problem was that the criteria for his idea of perfection seemed to change on an hourly basis and included mutually exclusive qualities that I didn't necessarily want to embody or possess. It was family values at work again! And, horror of horrors, his eating habits, which

I now sometimes enjoyed, had pushed me through to a bigger size than I had ever worn. I wondered if I could love any man enough to rationalize having to buy a larger wardrobe unless I was carrying his child.

He had this bar that he loved, and as time went on, he wanted to share his love of this place with me. It was not the sort of dive I would have chosen on my own. Instead, it was a place where bikini-clad waitresses impressed patrons with their surgically-enhanced cleavage and served cheap American beer. It became less of a novelty when I found myself dragged there week after week. My independent-thinking, self-respecting female friends wouldn't go there, so I'd get to spend the evenings talking to Paul's buddies while they drooled and leered or played Golden Tee for hours on end. It doesn't do much for a woman's confidence to frequent a public place where girls who looked better than she does in a bathing suit parade around her boyfriend. This problem affects many women in the Tampa Bay area, which is the birthplace of Hooters and home of the world-famous strip club, Mons Venus.

My mind would drift while I'd be stuck at the stupid bikini bar, and I'd fantasize about being back at my apartment, paying bills or doing laundry, or better yet, drinking wine with Christine. Maybe I'd be out at the grocery store, stocking up on good food that wouldn't raise my cholesterol and poundage like the meals Paul preferred. Not the stuff of usual fantasies, but stuff of mine at that time, since I felt so disconnected from my friends and my life. The only fantasy I had about the bikini bar was stopping Paul in mid-ogle of his favorite waitress and asking him how he'd feel if his sister took a job there.

I didn't go to the theatre any more, and I was totally frustrated. Where was my time going? As time moved on and I inhaled about three tons of secondhand smoke in my boyfriend's favorite bars, the answer to that question seemed to be: down the drain. It didn't matter that he had once been a charmer. I wanted out.

Luckily, this angst fueled some new and very colorful writing for the show:

Forget what I said about being a happy bridesmaid. You're only enjoying it for the free meals and handsome groomsmen when you're happy and free. When you're subjected to wedding after wedding as your latest love affair falls apart, let me tell you, it ain't pretty. Everywhere you go, everyone is just so damn happy. And you want to escape, but then you realize that this is the path that your friends, except for those who are divorced, have taken. It's like your party life dries up one day.

It's at this point that you realize that people don't get married necessarily because they're in love. They get married because they don't want to end up like you: bitter, cynical, tired, wishing for a life that is now extinct, in which you aren't the fifth stupid wheel all the damn time.

Worse yet is when you've been dating your boyfriend for the same amount of time that the bride and groom have been together. Here they are, happy and together, while you and he are plotting ways to drive the other insane. Ways you can jam each other into roles that the other doesn't want to play. So when you see these happy people, you want to be like them. The only way you have a fighting chance to do that is to ditch your current man.

When you share these thoughts with friends, sisters, et cetera, there's always some delusional optimist out there who says something like, "God is preparing someone for you." With delusional energy, they do not stop to think of what if God isn't, or what if God wants me to be single? Other people live this way and don't kill themselves. Apparently it isn't the end of the world to live as a single woman. In fact, I have noticed several ways in which it is much preferable over the alternative. But the paired-off others in your life don't like to hear that, just like you don't like to hear that when you're happily paired off.

I prefer the saying, "The man for you is stuck in traffic." Because that is what this mess feels like: a huge traffic jam.

Act 1, Scene 13:
Beginning of the End

Christine, Julie, Tara, and I were enjoying happy hour at a nearby watering hole with Paul and about 10 of our co-workers one Friday night when Paul announced that he was applying for a job in Charlotte. It was the first time I'd heard anything solid about it.

"Oh, you know, I thought I mentioned something about it to you," he said to me.

"Hmmm... I guess I must have said that it would be rather, uh, inconvenient."

"Yeah, but it's a great opportunity for me. And I won't be that far away. Just a quick plane ride."

Yes, it would be a great opportunity for him. Too bad I couldn't transfer to that office too without being the chippy who followed him there. And too bad that the country was in a recession, making it hard for mere mortals like me to keep their jobs, let alone upgrade.

This wasn't the first time I'd chased a man far away. I could boast of three ex-boyfriends on the other side of the Mississippi River by the age of 26.

Julie's jaw had dropped to the floor when the announcement was made, and she still couldn't close her mouth. She propelled me

outside to a porch, where we sat down on a bench. I must have been in shock.

"If he gets this job, and even if he doesn't since there will always be something lurking out there, what will you do?" she asked.

"Hell, I don't know. The first thing that crossed my mind was what a break it would be to *not* be dragged to that disgusting bikini bar week after week. And then the second thing I thought of was, I can be selfish again and do what I want when he's gone. Stop trying to make him happy and just make me happy for a change. It's ironic, but I do love that guy. I just don't know if I have the patience for this relationship crap."

"Guys like to test their boundaries– like toddlers."

"Yes, and you know what? He can have it, if that's the life he wants. He's driving me crazy with this family values crap anyways."

Tara had found us, and she sat down next to me and actually held my hand.

"This is a great opportunity for you to decide if you want to keep him. I wish I'd had the choice, because, you know what? I would have totally broken up with Bill when he transferred his job out to the frozen West. It was such a shock to me when he left me and picked up and moved out of town. But in the long run, it was a great thing for me. For one thing, I found out just how long I could go around with a huge chip on my shoulder." She looked at her watch, as if to read the time. "Eleven months and counting!" she added.

This was the most she'd ever shared, so I was curious.

"Why would you have dumped him?" I asked.

I must have seemed low, because she went on to explain herself. Tara was usually so private about things.

"Most of the time I was with him, I was trying to make him happy. I started forgetting about what made me happy on my own, and concentrating on him. Of course, it wasn't like that at first, and that's when we got along better, and that's why all my relationships are better in the first few months. You each have your own interests, you're not haunted by the ghost of each other's exes yet. You want to be together. But then, the insecurity sets in. That's why he and I were

always together: mutual paranoia and insecurity. At least, that's how it seemed at the end. We were utterly dependent on each other. And, although I didn't want to admit it to myself and kept pushing the thought away, I hated to be like that. It felt very wrong, having my life revolve around one relationship, one which even turned out to be a precarious arrangement, as we found out when he hauled ass out of town.

"I mean, the thought of me, Florida girl, Bucs season ticket holder since 1995, dating a man who would go to a place where everyone has to *drive an all-wheel-drive truck through the snow for half the year* is just ridiculous anyway," she added.

"So, should I feel guilty for suddenly noticing hot guys in the bar?" I said. It seemed that I'd awakened from a mild coma in the past few minutes.

"No, you should be noticing them. The head bartender is absolutely gorgeous–like Eric Stolz in *Some Kind of Wonderful*," Julie added.

"I was lucky to know Julie so well, and then meet you and Christine, after Bill left," Tara said. "It was wonderful for me, in the middle of all that crap. My mom is convinced that you all have some great cosmic role in my life right now, considering how I met you all when everything was falling apart, and you just included me like it was no big deal. I didn't have to be alone or worry about catty girlfriends talking behind my back at work either. It was by far the easiest thing I've been involved with in the past year."

"And we'll be around for you too, whatever you decide," Julie added. "I'll be there to remind you when you've forgotten to ogle your share of hot men when we're out, for example. I'll get you all to go speed dating again."

"I'll make sure you drink enough wine," added Christine, who had just found us. "And then some."

"Oh, my God, can we please talk about something else?" I asked. "Julie, tell us about your reunion. Was it as traumatic as you thought it might be?"

"No, I had a great time," she said. "Most of the people there were

really nice! And honestly, it seemed like I was meeting most of them for the first time, and that we all just happened to be the same age and go to the same high school."

"That's really cool," I told her. "I'm glad you went, since you had such a good time."

"Were there any cute boys there?" asked Christine.

Julie blushed.

"All right!" said Tara.

"Any love connection?" I asked.

"Sort of," she said. "He's now an e-mail buddy."

"Hopefully he'll get the nerve to ask you out before Christmas," I said.

Act 1, Scene 14:
The Oldest Trick in the Book

Christine wanted to throw a party, and that was about all the reason we needed to clean up the apartment, stock up on toilet paper, purchase several bottles of soda and fruit juice, and visit the neighborhood liquor store, where we purchased several types of our favorite hard liquor: rum.

"I've gotta tell you, this is a great distraction," I said as we set up for the party. She set up a smoking area on the balcony while I chopped vegetables and made dip.

We had invited everyone we knew, and in our usual disorganized fashion, we had no idea who was actually attending. With parties, especially as we got older, we accepted the fact that fewer people would be able to come, and even less alcohol would be consumed. It seemed a cruel trick of fate, since we didn't have the money to entertain when we were young and unencumbered and all of our friends were free to stay out all night and drink every drop of rum. There were a few Saturday night parties Christine and I hosted in college in which our older friends, who were out in the working world, would actually schedule the following Monday as a vacation day so that they could thoroughly enjoy the event. Now, with careers

and babies and spouses, our friends didn't party like before, but perhaps that was a good thing.

Paul called late that afternoon and we chatted briefly. I didn't sense anything amiss. Hours later, with 20 people crowded into my apartment, I started to panic when I was asked, "Hey, Gina, where's your boyfriend?" for the fifth time.

I called his cellular phone and he answered, but the noise in the background was deafening, and he just shouted into his phone, "I'll call you back later, sorry."

"Where is he?" Julie asked me when she saw me hang up the phone.

"He's out somewhere where it's really loud and apparently in no hurry to leave," I answered. "Maybe Mons Venus?"

"Nice," she said. "What are you doing to do?"

"No idea," I said.

"Do you want some advice?" she asked.

"Sure, fire away."

"I'd dump his sorry ass," she told me. "You deserve better."

"I know this. You are right," I told her. "But the question is, how? Other guys I've dated I could scare away with a mean look. He's not like that. He even likes to argue."

"You'll think of something," she said. "It's getting to the point where he's even driving me crazy."

Act 1, Scene 15:
The Post-Game Wrap-Up

It was time to have a tough talk with Paul. He was about to make a dramatic exit, and I wanted to have my say.

First, there was the denial. He claimed that he hadn't changed, but I had changed. The guy who brought me flowers and serenaded me while playing guitar was the same sloppy drunk who liked to debate political issues. He thought that both sides were equally loveable. It was my fault for not seeing that and adjusting my expectations accordingly.

That was an interesting theory, but I wasn't going for it. We had dated for months. I had to be thinking of making a purchase at some point in the future, but how could I do that when our core relationship was going sour? I was mad at him for not remaining the charming serenader who'd first won my heart, while he was mad at me for not morphing into an apron-wearing, family-values-loving waif who would defer to my man for every decision that I had to make. It was time to stop being mad at each other, and just let it be.

My efforts were met with much resistance and denial at first, but once he latched onto the idea of breaking up and claimed it as his own, there was no stopping it. (I have found, in studying Scarlett

O'Hara in *Gone with the Wind* and also from observing my modern life, that a woman can get a man to do just about anything, as long as she makes him think it's his idea.)

When he got the promotion that he had applied for, I dropped off his random belongings that had accumulated at my apartment just in time for the movers to come and take them away to his new place in North Carolina. We tried to part on good terms, but as you can expect, the office was stirred up in a fury of controversy over our breakup and his move. Just like when Bill moved away from Tara.

Thank God I had my friends to help me out. They made sure I ate, slept, and got to work for the following weeks when I just didn't give a damn. Tara even got me out of the apartment and took me to a Tampa Bay Buccaneers football game, where we ogled all the hot players (especially Joe Jurevicius) and cheered the team to victory.

When the storm finally died down, and it was just me alone, typing at my computer, I came up with one of the best parts of the show.

What can I say about the breakup of a relationship? You know it's coming along when a little tiny clock inside your head starts ticking. It says to you, it's time to wrap this thing up. You have this much time, and after that, all hell will break loose. Your subconscious gives you a deadline. It's just that easy. And whether you take it as a hint or just some vague thing floating out there, you know the jig is up.

Dating an alcoholic, or just a twenty or thirty-something man who is careening down the path to full-blown alcoholism, is like a really unrewarding babysitting job. There is crying, throwing up, tantrums, and no parents to save you from further torment at the end of the night. Your mental clock is ticking down the time when he will be out of your life, and you know it's just a matter of time because you've gotta take care of #1.

He's always been right about everything else, and damn it, it's his right to drink himself into a stupor whenever he wants and not take care of himself. And soon that's all there is: the argument. Arguments all the time. Arguments that occur because the man

you've chosen to date hasn't evolved into a civilized enough creature for you to move forward with. You've gotta leave him behind.

So now that we've visited the seven stages of modern man and woman, we can explore the six stages of heartbreak. I mean, dating has taught me many things, but mostly it's taught me that I'm better off single. The journey back to living life as a singleton is a tough road. You can go to Steak and Shake and have to hold back tears when you realize that you are not only eating the Original Single, but you are the Original Single, too.

So let's see the six stages. The first one, naturally, is denial. Always a favorite. You say to yourself, he'll change, he'll grow up, he'll suddenly get over this obsession with frequenting seedy bars and ogling bikini-clad waitresses. Yes, like that will happen.

Then there's depression, another popular favorite. Depression sets in because you know that, while most men are basically wild boys at heart, one might straighten up and fly right if he's convinced that you are the woman for him and that he can't imagine life without you. So you've obviously failed this test. Enter depression.

This is when lifting your head off the pillow is enough to exhaust you for the whole day. The alarm goes off about six hours too early every day, since you're up half the night worrying over things you can't help. Minute problems seem huge, and bursting into tears is a constant activity. Often accompanied by food consumption, especially chocolate.

Anger directed at others characterizes the next step on the path to Fabulousness for One. It's when you sit back and look at other people and wish you could curse them for being so damn happy. No one has problems compared to you, so what do they have to complain about? Have you ever been this annoyed in your entire life, anyway?

Anger directed at yourself is the next step. Why did you waste your time with that guy? Couldn't you figure that he wasn't right for you sooner? And then there's always the classic question: What was I thinking? How did I miss that he was a mamma's boy/druggie/control freak/ jerk/ insert appropriate label here? Because if you'd known this earlier, you'd be through all the first

four stages of heartbreak by now.

But at some point you'll have to make peace with yourself, and that is the fifth step. That's when you say: Hey, I had a man to be with for a while; I even got to take a date to a wedding once when we were together; I got to fulfill my lifelong dream of going to Graceland. He was pretty cool most of the time. We enjoyed our time together, some of it, before it all went south. Let it be, it's all good.

And then comes the sixth stage, which is my personal favorite: completely selfish behavior. And oh yes, this stage can last as long as you want it to. That means, no relationships with men, unless they revolve around men simply admiring your goddesslike beauty or clamoring to buy you a free dinner or drink. That's right, it's all about you, Miss Thing. It's all about you. You get to do all those things that he used to get in the way of before: watch Friends *instead of wrestling on Thursday nights, see a movie that you're interested in that doesn't involve wars or kung fu, take up all the room in the bed and not listen to snoring- the possibilities are endless. No breakup is complete without a list of "Things I do not miss about the Ex." That is an important list to make and share.*

It was during one of these phases, right after I'd attended a good friend's wedding, that I decided to buy myself a ring. For years, I had watched friend after friend get engaged and acquire some fabulous gems along the way. Since the Three Fates, in their infinite wisdom, had not thrown a fabulously compatible guy across my path, I had to take matters into my own hands. There was simply no need to be penalized in the jewelry department because I was single.

That is why I went out and bought myself a six-carat emerald-cut garnet in a silver setting. Some say it's ridiculous, others say it's fabulous, but the only thing that matters is that I love it. As I adjusted to the weight of this bauble on my hand, I realized that five or six carats of a pretty gem on my ring finger made the absence of a man in my life seem much less tragic than some would have me believe.

Rings symbolize a lot of things. If you win the Super Bowl, you get a huge diamond ring that symbolizes that you were a part of the best football team in the world. If you get a class ring, it confirms that you

attended high school, for one, and also shows the world your official birthstone and extracurricular activities. For women, the status that the engagement ring brings is overwhelming. It says to the world, "Someone has promised to love me forever."

But my ring says, to me at least, that no matter what happens with the men in my life, I'll always have me. And if need be, that will be enough.

II.
Intermission

Act 2, Scene 1:
The Show Must Go On

Paul moved away the week after Christmas and I took a few mental health days off of work. Naturally, I was depressed and angry. Fortunately, this was the fuel I needed to get through writing and performing the show.

I got a preliminary schedule of the performance festival, which was taking place in late March, and a mysterious e-mail from someone named Sean, who was supposed to be my director. Excellent. Because if there's anything that a gal who's just dumped a man needs, it's a major distraction.

After a kiss-free New Year's Eve came and went, I had just under three months to pull the whole thing together. I gathered my notes, which ranged from pathetic to hilarious, and met my mystery man at the Village Inn near my apartment one Wednesday night for our introduction and brainstorming session.

"You are more lovely than I imagined," Sean gushed as soon as I walked into the restaurant. He reached out for my hand and then kissed it.

"So are you!" I answered. Sean was gorgeous. Black hair, blue eyes, light skin. Absolutely beautiful, and absolutely gay. What a crying shame!

This is one major peril of acting: it's hard to meet straight men in theatre. But when you think of the cool makeup, the crazy costumes, the singing, the dancing, the curtain calls, and the laughter and applause, it's a decent tradeoff. I wonder how many thousands of dollars that could have been spent on counseling are saved through the theatre. Personally, I've gone out to auditions whenever my life has needed improvement for one reason or another, and the universe hasn't let me down. I get cast in a show whenever I have needed the fun, the distraction, and the applause. Getting dressed up and flitting around on a stage is much more therapeutic than picking apart one's childhood on a sofa. It's more fun altogether.

We were seated right away, and he started rifling through my notes as soon as his coffee and my seltzer water with lime had been ordered.

"What is your theme, or title?" he asked.

"Independent Woman's Guide to Life," I answered.

"Sounds great! The only thing I'd have to suggest, right off the bat, is that you need to truly concentrate on the lifestyle and such. You shouldn't bash men too much, although sometimes it's absolutely unavoidable!"

"Got it," I said.

"Have you given any thought to costumes?"

"I was thinking, I had to wear a bridesmaid dress at some point. Independent women always get stuck being bridesmaids. People think that because you don't have kids to spend money on that you're dying to go out and spend $150 on an ugly dress," I answered.

"Life is cruel, isn't it?" he asked. What a guy!

Of course we totally hit it off. And somewhere in the midst of our meeting, he came up with a rough outline, which he called the Seven Stages of an Independent Woman's Life: Student, Bridesmaid, Girlfriend, Ex-girlfriend, Worker Bee, Gal Pal, and Vacationing Goddess. I'd write a monologue for each role and come up with a costume for some of the roles. I could wear Capri pants, black slides, and a basic (cleavage-enhancing) tank top as my core costume and add accessories, such as a travel bag for the vacationing goddess or

a book bag for the student. In addition, my lovely tea-length purple taffeta bridesmaid dress, which had somehow escaped my donation to the Cinderella Project the year before, could simply be worn over my basic costume for the bridesmaid monologue. After about two hours of brainstorming, we both had a much better picture of what the show would be like.

"Is the dress awful?" he asked. " I want you to look like Little Bo Peep. Like Rachel Green at Barry and Mindy's wedding. We really need to play this bridesmaid thing up!"

"I'll let you see it and we can decide then," I told him. "If it isn't bad enough, we'll go to Goodwill and see what we can find!"

"I'm thinking teal and black with sequins," he said, "but maybe that's too prom and not very bridesmaid."

"Darling, that would be fabulous!" I laughed.

"What music should we have going on during the scene changes?" he asked.

"God, I don't know. Something subtle like *I am Woman, Hear Me Roar*?" I joked.

"I'll go online and see what I can download. I'll look for something instrumental. Maybe some nice catchy jazz. That way, the audience doesn't have to listen to any lyrics. The words will all come from you."

"Good idea," I said.

Sean had tons of great ideas. Did I get lucky or what? He worked as a waiter at the very restaurant that Paul and I had gone to for our first date, so he made good money. Sure, he wouldn't be available most weekends when I'd be writing or practicing my lines, but he'd be there for me in spirit.

"Wait until you meet the crew," he told me after we'd paid the bill and were making our way outside. "You will love them. They're mostly family, of course."

"Awesome," I answered. "I just chucked a straight man, and so now my punishment is to hang out with a bunch of hot gay men!"

"Oh, honey, they're not all hot," he told me, "but you will love them anyway."

Act 2, Scene 2:
Resume Acting Job at Work

As it got closer to my deadline, I was consumed with writing the show wherever and whenever I could. Since I spent so much time at work, it became the main location of my covert operation.

It was hard to pretend to be interested in my day job, but since it was the very thing that my income depended on, I had to keep showing up and turning out work. Many times, I'd pretend to be working on something productive when I'd actually be gathering my thoughts on paper for the show. I'd send e-mails to myself full of ideas for the show. I'd print out these secret messages to myself and then rush over to the printer so that they wouldn't be intercepted by someone who might then announce, "What is this essay on modern dating doing on the printer?"

Probably what was most fun was bringing my secret documents to work so that I could peruse them on company time, such as the time that all of the employees had to gather and listen to the old men who ran the company drone on and on about providing top-quality customer service. Julie sat in the back of the room next to me and wrote down well-received comments in the margins of my pages to help with the show and make fun of the old men. My favorite comment was a cartoon she drew of a big bald guy with a word cloud

that said, "Provide better customer service so that I can end up with $3 million dollars in stock options this year instead of a measly $2 million like last year. And your year-end bonus might increase about $40!"

My secret documents were held in a binder that was innocently labeled "Quality Team Initiatives."

It was a great feeling to have everyone fooled. While most people steal office supplies from work, I was stealing the most precious thing of all: time.

Eventually, however, news of my upcoming show leaked out to the office. This was probably a result of my asking my boss for five vacation days at the end of March. I told her why I needed the time off, and then she told her cohorts, and after that just about everyone knew. At first I was annoyed, and then it occurred to me that this might really help my ticket sales. In time, I was glad about the questions people started to ask me. After my show became known by my colleagues, I had to cut way back on the at-work musings.

Sometime in late February, I got a most unexpected interoffice instant message from Paul Eastman, star analyst of the Charlotte office:

I heard your show is coming up soon. How is that going?
Things are a little crazy. It's hard to concentrate on work with the show a month away.
Well, I am sure it will be a great show. You really seemed inspired about it when we were dating.
Yes, you inspired several parts.
Really?
Yes and no.
Should I be worried?
Yes and no. Just kidding.
When is the show?
End of March. March 24-29 actually.
I'll be down then, for a meeting. Do you mind if I come see the show?

*No, come if you want to see it. I don't make fun of you or my
other exes that much in the show anyway.*

How nice. So how is life treating you?

*Pretty well, I can't complain. It's been really busy lately, and it
will be up until the show is done. But I am definitely not
complaining about that. How about you?*

Doing well here. I haven't met that many people yet, since this
office is small, but it's nice up here. Closer to the parents, which is
good. The job is keeping me busy so I don't go out as much as I used
to.

Aw, poor Paul. I thought. *He doesn't have a trashy bikini bar
anymore, or a girlfriend to drag to the nasty bikini bar. His life must
be so empty.*

*I'm sure you're enjoying that raise ;) Hey, I have to go to a
meeting in a few minutes. Have a good one.*

You too.

After the meeting, I put down some of my thoughts on Paul's
post-breakup persona:

*Isn't it funny that as soon as you give up and break up with a guy
because it seems like his vices will never go away, he seems to turn
back into the man you fell in love with? Suddenly, he's Mr. Nice Guy
again, not drinking himself into a stupor like before. He's normal,
supportive, and nice, not the person who makes you dependent on
Alka-Seltzer because he upsets you and your stomach so much all the
time. It makes you wonder if the Mr. Asshole persona he took on in
the last few months of your relationship was just a ploy to get you to
dump him.*

*Once I give up on a guy, my angst is over. At that point, I don't feel
the need to look at the man while he is praying to the porcelain
goddess and wonder how I can mold him into husband material.
Once the pressure is off, I am sure I am much easier to be around too.
He can ruin his health, call me when he's drunk off his ass at a strip
bar and totally screw up his professional or personal life, and I am*

no longer that concerned. The ex-boyfriend becomes relegated to some category for acquaintances who I just care about on a casual level. As long as they don't kill themselves driving home drunk, I am not that concerned about their welfare.

Men are funny. Like my friend Julie has said, they test your limits like two-year-olds. Maybe it's my perception, or maybe this really happens, but when they're done dating a girl but don't want to break up with her, the Id comes out. In terms of man logic, this means that several months of bad behavior that would cause them to be dumped is more worth the effort than one mature discussion about the relationship. It makes me wonder if it's more fun for them to behave badly and have someone to answer to than behave badly as bachelors and not have anyone around to witness it.

I am guessing that they want an audience for their antisocial antics, and on some level I can understand that. After all, I am an actress.

Act 2, Scene 3:
Catching up with the Gals

Since I was spending so much time away from work alone in my room, I decided it was time to host a soiree. I'd been sitting in front of my computer or pacing back and forth spewing out partial monologues to an audience of zero (or one if you count Christine in the next room) most nights, and I needed to be around people. By having people over, I could re-join society in the comfort of my own home.

I asked Anne to come over first since we never had the time to get together. She helped me make a chicken salad and a green salad for the event while we chatted.

"So how is married life treating you?" I asked.

"Great," she answered. "Kind of surreal, actually. It's weird to remember that I have a husband sometimes. And I changed my name, so I'm a missus. That's different. And sometimes I forget to write my new name on things. That part is strange, too."

"James is a good guy," I told her. "I like him much better than your other boyfriends."

"Yeah, me too," she said, and we laughed.

"What about you? Giving the old man the heave-ho?"

"Yeah, well we were driving each other crazy. I'm not sure how else to handle that," I answered.

"I'm sure he misses you," she said sympathetically.

"Well, what can you do? I need to be happy, too."

"Of course. And toward the end there, before he even mentioned moving, you were starting to look a little..."

"Frazzled? Yeah, I was. It was hard to balance what I wanted out of life along with dating someone. I've always had that problem. It gets to the point where I can't wait to be single again! I start making all of these fun man-free plans, like going with the girls to see Sugar Ray in concert and ogling Mark McGrath."

"Yeah, I know that all too well. Wouldn't it be great if we could be carefree and relaxed like we were in Europe?"

"And run into scores of men who'd take us out on the town every night? You're not kidding, honey, that would be nice. Once in a while, I'll read my travel journal to cheer myself up."

"Me too. I think of Spain every time I hear that obnoxious song *Mmm Bop* too."

"Oh God, they played it at the hostel in Barcelona. Remember that cute boy who was trying to check out when we got there?"

"You should have flirted with him more."

"I know! Him and the *Braveheart* Guy." The *Braveheart* Guy had taken on legendary status. We'd been at a Halloween party in St. Pete about six years before and there he was, the man of my dreams: kilt, blue face paint, long wavy hair, and everything. I sigh just thinking about him now. But despite Anne's encouragement to "Drink more, think less, and just go talk to him," I was paralyzed with fear and therefore unable to do so. Regrets, I've had a few... We never figured out who he was in real life, and thus the legend was born.

Christine emerged from her bedroom, and in mere minutes the rest of the gals had arrived. We commenced the eating of the potluck bounty and only slowed down when Tara unveiled that afternoon's entertainment: *Chocolat.*

"This is a wonderful movie, girls," she told us. "There's chocolate in just about every scene, and when there isn't chocolate,

you'll most likely get to ogle Johnny Depp. One could say it is the perfect movie!"

And so we watched the movie on my fabulous new television set, sprawled out on Christine's beautiful new couch and loveseat.

It was early evening when Anne had to leave and meet her husband for a date. We all sighed at her fortunate engagement and walked her out. Then, Christine had an idea.

"Grab your script and all your notes. We're going to help you with your show!"

"Huh?" I asked.

"Just get in the car!"

And we were off to Clearwater Beach, where Christine, Julie, and Tara performed the show for me. (Naturally, we took a brief pause to watch— and applaud— the sun going down.) I was able to see and hear what I'd been working on instead of mutter it to my walls, thanks to my friends. We found a little ice cream shop and enjoyed some dessert as well. It was lovely.

Act 2, Scene 4:
A Visit to the Venue

Before I walked through the theatre doors leading into the playhouse, I could hear an unfamiliar woman's voice onstage.

"We have to hang up all those lights because of the fact that we're doing six shows— six shows, people—and all of the lighting has to be in place for when we're switching back and forth based on who's performing that night."

"Hello?" I said into the cavernous theatre.

"Hi there," said Sean, who was up on the stage.

As my eyes adjusted to the darkness, I saw a few people milling around the area. I dropped off my updated script and bag in a seat toward the end of the second row and climbed onstage.

A tall, heavy-set woman walked out to me and held out her hand. "I'm Nora, the stage manager. Are you with one of the shows for the festival?"

"Yes, I'm the independent woman."

She smiled approvingly. "I'm an independent woman too. Very good. So I take it you're the one-woman show?"

"That's me! And you'll be happy to know that all I'll need you guys to do is dim and raise the lights for my show. Nothing fancy."

"Except I want you to bring out that shimmer in that lovely taffeta gown she wears!" added Sean, who had just walked up to join us. "Maybe with some blue lights?"

The State Theatre was an older theatre in downtown St. Pete, which is across the bay from Tampa. The entire festival, which was made up of six shows, would take place there. It had elements of the old, such as the beautifully tiled floors and the time-ravaged bathrooms, which made no secret of the fact that the theatre had been hosting some rocking concerts as of late. A well-worn marquee, which had stood up to at least a half-century of hurricanes, still announced its presence along the street. The usual fare at the theatre included tons of local musicians, an occasional national act, and local film festivals. It was the only place in twenty-first century America where patrons could watch a movie and smoke at the same time. Before the festival setup began, The Reverend Horton Heat had lit up the stage for a night.

Well-worn maroon carpeting coated the floors on the inside of the theatre, and all the walls were painted black. Up in the balcony, a myriad of chairs were jumbled together. Eventually, the crew would get everything set up so that it would be like a real theatre. For the time being, however, they were airing out the post-Horton event.

"Get up here and push a broom!" yelled Sean.

"You know, that's like making your bed every day. It makes about as much sense. You sweep, and then people track in more dirt. It never ends!"

"Even so, honey, we are trying to make this place ship-shape. So what do you think of the space?"

"It's great! All I want is a simple curtain as the backdrop, and all my stuff onstage."

"Where will you put it? A treasure chest?"

"Maybe. Or maybe a hat rack. Also, I'll get one of those room divider curtain things to dress behind."

"You mean like those things that are always in old Doris Day movies?"

"Exactly. For the Bridesmaid Monologue."

"Of course, darling. You in that purple shimmering dream of a dress. You'll need to put it on behind the curtain and then make a grand entrance."

"Oh, I can't wait! I am sure that will get a few laughs."

After I was done pushing the broom and surveying the space, we went off to a coffee shop to once again go over my script.

"How's Vacationing Goddess? I would think that would be the easiest one to write."

"It will be as soon as I get around to it. My life is so not like a vacation now. I need to throw back a few Coronas and write that one. I have some ideas, though."

"What is done for the most part?"

"The monologues about being a student, about being a bridesmaid, and about being the girlfriend and ex-girlfriend. Trying to brainstorm about career woman and the vacationing thing."

"They're not able to give us much stage time before the show," Sean said, waving his hand in the general direction of the theatre. "So we'll have to be creative with our rehearsal space. We can meet at my house if you like, or at your place. We're really only here for a few days before your opening night."

Act 2, Scene 5:
A Jimmy Buffett State of Mind

Summoning the spirit of the vacation goddess wasn't so hard the next Wednesday, when I took a few hours off work in the afternoon and headed to the beach. Armed with an umbrella, sunscreen, a notebook, a pen, a towel, and a smashing Kathy Ireland tankini from K-Mart, I was ready for action out on Clearwater Beach. I set up camp just south of the Adam's Mark Hotel, which boasted a Jacuzzi and a clean women's bathroom in the air-conditioned cavern of their lobby.

So... to meditate on travel. Driving down the road at age 20 with one of my gal pals singing, "Lord, I was born an ramblin' woman," immediately came to mind. We weren't armed with cell phones or anything– just a couple of $20 bills and a whole lot of attitude. We drove to everywhere we wanted to go, and everything turned out all right, no car troubles or blown tires. For some karmic reason, "Ramblin' Man" by the Allman Brothers would inevitably play on the radio sometime in our journeys too. Then I remembered visiting my high school friends up in Tallahassee, when an unseasonable cold snap had me wearing a full-length flannel robe while I pumped gas to stave off the chilling wind. I must have been quite a sight.

Then, a stray moment from Ireland came to mind. Ireland, after all, was where Christine and I first got to be friends. The Irish Gaelic word for fun is craic, which is pronounced just like the modern street drug crack, and they call their boats "hookers." One of the girls on the tour turned to the rest of us and said something like, "We're having lots of crack on this hooker!" and we were all giggling hysterically for a while as we rode on the hooker to an island called Innisheer, where we met cute boys named Dermot. Actually, there are cute boys named Dermot all over Ireland, and we tried to meet them all.

Plus, living in Florida had given me and my friends complete license to run off to the beach and get away, just as I had done to get inspired. But our day jobs got in the way these days. What is glamorous about living 30 minutes away from the Gulf of Mexico if you work five days a week and then have to devote the rest of your time to mundane pursuits, like washing your clothes so that you don't run out of clean underwear all the time?

It is a given that when you're young, you'll have time and no money and when you're older, you'll have money but no time to do anything. This is an occasion in which lowering your expectations will get you far. If you're truly interested in going somewhere, you won't mind sleeping on a couch for a few days once you get there. Honestly, if you wait until you can afford a hotel to go some place, your life will be half over by then.

Do you know that more women than men travel abroad to study? Did you ever wonder why? I'll give you a hint: they have names like Antonio. If you can get school credit for exploring a foreign land, I say do it. You'll learn tons more than you would in a classroom, and the memories will last a lifetime. Being an American woman overseas is like being a celebrity. Your waiters can't stop asking you out, and you're popular no matter where you go. It is a wonderful life, and it is a darn shame when your money runs out and you have to go back home. But you'll always have Paris, Dublin, or wherever you've gone.

Traveling is another big confidence booster. Once you make your

way through a foreign land, you feel pretty savvy. And the separation makes you realize what things in your life are important, and which things you're better off without. Being away gives you time to think, and time to just be.

Then, I remembered that I'd fibbed about having the student monologue ready, so I wrote it too.

If you've ever suspected that life isn't fair, that men have hundreds of advantages over women, do yourself a favor and take a women's studies class in college. If you do that, you get to find out actual factual information that shows how much more money they take home, how the work they do is more highly valued, how the world revolves around all things male. You'll learn fun facts too, like how the happiest people are single women and married men, and you can theorize why that might be.

I wonder what the world would be like if women weren't supposed to be so obsessed with appearances. Would modern businesses run as efficiently if men wore stomach-squashing pantyhose and had to worry about having stubble-free legs and made-up faces every day? Of course, they do wear nooses around their necks– you know, neck ties. But I don't think that makes them even with women, as far as the degree of discomfort in shoes or clothes and the endless pursuit of beauty. It makes you wonder, too, what the world would be like if we were free of these expectations. Would more work get done, would more businesses be successful, would more people be rich if women were free of the constant beauty contest going out there in the world? Would men be more sensitive to all that we do if they were required to endure just one eyebrow waxing treatment?

But back to being a Career Woman. Having a degree, whether it's from a high school, college, or trade school is desirable. You don't have to have one to get by, but my goodness, doesn't it help? Just like if you're a blonde chick with big boobs, doesn't that help you get a date? And when you get out there to try to carve out a life for yourself, you need all the help you can get! There's a curious new demographic that's come along in the last 15 years or so— I don't

know if you've noticed— but there are a ton of single women out there who live alone or with roommates, who work and save their money, buy houses, go on vacation and have absolutely no idea where they can meet a decent guy. These women benefit from being educated since that can increase their earnings, because gals like that are out there going it alone. It's like Attack of the Bridget Jones clones. I don't know if sociological conditions should be blamed or praised for this recent development.

As I wrapped up writing the last of the student/career monologue, I was contemplating whether or not I should go get my feet wet in the surf when my cell phone rang.

"Where are you?" Christine asked me.

"I'm at the beach, dahling, finishing up some monologues. You?"

"We need you to come back to town now, babe. Tara's having a bad time today. She just found out that Bill is engaged."

"What? You are kidding. No! Where are we meeting?"

"Tara's place. She's not in the mood to go anywhere."

"What should I bring?"

"Fizzy water if you can get some. She's getting addicted to it."

"OK, done. I'll be on the road in five minutes."

I had to at least put my feet in the water, so I ran down to the water and took in the scene. The sky was painted with pink and purple clouds as the orange sun sunk lower into the horizon.

It looked like it was probably 6 o'clock. My watch was hidden far into my bag, as I had sought to avoid getting a "watch tan," which is an unfortunate condition. It means that your arm is a nice tan shade while your watch has left its mark on your wrist, leaving the skin beneath it lily-white.

Driving back to town, I ran into a Publix and picked up some flavored seltzer water, which had become the drink of choice among my friends. It had no calories yet was fizzy, which was more interesting than regular water. Not knowing which flavor would be popular and also being in a rush, I chose the lemon flavor as well as the cranberry lime.

When I got to Tara's condo, I gathered the bottles of fizzy water as well as my bag containing my change of clothes, purse, and phone, and headed inside.

Weeks before, in a private moment, Tara had told me that she finally felt free from Bill and their history.

"For the first time in a while, I wake up and think I need to find something better for me out there. I don't know what: a job, a new man, something. I just think I might be ready for something new, ready to stop wondering what went wrong with him."

But it was clear that her resolve had been shaken by this harrowing news. She had dated the guy for two and a half years; he'd only been gone for one year. And in that time, he'd met and dated someone who he now planned to spend his life with while she had hung out with the girls and nursed a big grudge.

"Hello, gals, kisses," I said as I walked into her main room. "I come bearing fizzy water."

Christine sat in a purple overstuffed chair while Tara laid on her red couch. Colorful throw pillows, which were usually so decoratively arranged, were strewn all over the floor and her cats, Lance and Gwen, were playing among them. It was eerily quiet.

"I just have to run and change," I said. "I'll be back in a second."

I could hear their muffled voices through the door, and when I emerged in sweat pants and my Mavericks t-shirt, Christine was chopping up pieces of cheese and arranging crackers on a dish. I went straight to the kitchen and popped a frozen pizza into the oven. If we were going to have this powwow, we needed to do it right.

Breakups are tough, but post-breakup updates are the worst. Poor Julie heard from some co-worker that her ex was seen going out (or rather, going home) with Miss Nude Tampa after they broke up. On top of missing the guy who used to be significant in her life, she had to deal with the embarrassment that this caused. Miss Nude Tampa. Good God.

So now it was Tara's turn, and I suppose it was more frustration she felt than anything else. Here she had invested over two years of her life in someone who went out and married the first girl he met in North Dakota.

"You've earned tons of karma points with Bill," I told her. "You broke him in for somebody. That means somebody else out there is breaking in your guy as we speak."

"And your guy will love Buccaneer football," Christine told her. "He'll be rich and own a beautiful house, and he'll love your cats."

"I am getting too old for this!" Tara said. "When does this bullshit stop? And why do people have the need to update me on the goings-on in Bill's life? I am trying to start a new life without him! Even though the thought of dating someone makes me completely nauseous right now."

"That might continue for a while, just make yourself happy," I told her. "People tell you his business because they associate you with him, I don't think they're trying to be mean. People tell me Paul's business all the time. I think they get a vicarious thrill from it. I've just had the show to keep me busy, but if I didn't, it would probably bother me too."

"I can't imagine being more busy than I already am," she said. "I'd like to be so busy that this doesn't bother me, that I don't have time to think about it, but you know, my brain is making time to think about it. And that is really pissing me off!"

By this time, the acid in my stomach was churning and it was giving me a headache. While the night wasn't about me, it was making me wonder when I would get this kind of news. However doomed the romance with Paul may have been, he was still my close friend when we broke up. I located an ice pack and filled it with cubes, then alternated it between my head and my belly. It's an old holistic remedy.

"What are you doing?" asked Tara. Christine knew the situation well.

"It helps me feel better. I get a stomach ache sometimes, and then inevitably I get a headache. It's what 15 years of dating has done for me. I get new stress-related health problems every time I go back out into the dating world. Tonight, I'm just living vicariously through you."

"Tell me about it!" Tara responded.

Julie let herself in and walked over to Tara to give her a hug. "There is only one way to deal with a crisis like this," she told her. "As soon as Gina's show is done, we are going on a road trip! Where do you want to go? St. Augustine, the Keys, you name it. I'll even consent to go camping if you want. It's up to you."

Tara smiled and said, "Let's find out where the best H&M in the southeast is, and go there. That would be marvelous!"

H&M was a clothing store that boasted of classic cuts and reasonable prices. We'd read about it in our various magazines and such. Tampa Bay had not been blessed with an H&M store, so we figured that the closest one would be in Atlanta or Miami. And if not, a shopping trip to Manhattan would have to do.

Act 2, Scene 6:
Getting Back to Work

Houseplants, hand washables, and personal relationships took a back seat in the "home stretch" of the show's creation. The weekday schedule went something like this for about three weeks:

6:30 a.m. Alarm rings.

6:55 a.m. Get out of bed.

8 a.m.: Arrive at work, log in to computer, and consume that day's breakfast (usually a Tupperware jar full of cottage cheese and fruit, a Slim Fast meal replacement bar, or something from the downstairs cafeteria) while typing.

12:30 p.m.: Go over lines while eating lunch, which was usually a cup o' noodles.

5 p.m.: Log off computer, drive to apartment.

5:15- 6 p.m.: Watch TV, eat homemade dinner if Christine was in the mood to cook, eat one of my own signature dishes if not: tuna casserole, pasta salad, or chicken breast with instant mashed potatoes and green beans.

7 p.m.: Arrive at theatre or rehearsal space, meet up with attractive gay director, go over show details with stage manager Nora, and revise script and stage blocking as needed.

10 p.m.: Drink down well-deserved cider with Sean at nearby Irish Pub and ogle men.

Weekends were another story. Since we never scheduled rehearsal for Friday nights, a very strange pattern emerged.

Friday, after work: Ask all friends if they have change for a dollar.

6:15 p.m. at apartment: Go through dish of coins and hoard quarters as if they were bullion. Count bullion to determine how many loads of laundry are possible.

6:30 p.m.: Separate whites, colors, darks, and delicates. Determine that delicates are too much trouble and can wait another month to get washed, and place them back into laundry basket. Load laundry bag, put on sandals, procure detergent, and carefully place bullion in pocket of shorts. Make way to laundry facility and scout the location. Proceed with all three loads at once if possible.

6:55 p.m.: Return to apartment, greet Christine if she is there, undress, step into shower, and have Calgon moment.

7:05 p.m.: Put on pajamas.

The rest of the night: Move clothes from washers to dryers and from dryers back to apartment, fold clothes, and lounge.

Socializing on Friday nights became a matter of convenience. Specifically, if someone came over, then I would be able to socialize. If not, I could spend quality time with Ewan MacGregor and John Leguizamo by watching *Moulin Rouge*, or I'd catch something on prime time if it was good.

As luck would have it, I got most of my great ideas either driving around or in the shower: two places where it was nearly impossible to write anything down. One day, as I lathered up a washcloth with a bar of classic Dial, I realized that I could capitalize on Sean's good looks and lack of a lisp to play the boyfriend and ex-boyfriend and perhaps throw out a few one-liners as a groomsman, classmate, co-worker, and sexy traveler in a foreign land.

That meant that he would sit at the side of the stage and talk to the audience about my character. In addition, sometimes he would interact with me during my monologues. It was a brilliant idea, but one that required more organization.

So now it was time to go through the script and keep some, dump

some, and add more so that Sean could be a beloved addition to the story. Editing the show was like operating on my own little newborn: a bit traumatic at times. I'd think to myself, *But I love that part*, as I drew a big red X through it.

I figured out a great way to counteract my student of women's studies monologue with Sean.

Man, you haven't had the urge to run away so fast as you will if you dare set foot in a women's studies class. All these women are having a powwow to figure out all the ways that you are The Enemy. Men are evil, they make more money, they don't value us and our work, they think they're better than us, et cetera, et cetera. Even if some of it, well, most of it, is true in some ways, it's still pretty scary to be sitting in a room with a whole bunch of women who are all pissed off at you and what you represent at the same time.

I took a class on women in popular culture to satisfy a sociology requirement. I never dreamed that I would have to endure lectures stuff like on menstruation. I didn't make it through that lecture. I did stick around long enough to learn that in most Native American cultures, women were excused from all household duties and responsibilities when they were having their moon time, as they call it. I think if we did that in modern America- you know, just told women to take a few days off at their most volatile times- the world would be a better place. I bet they'd like it, too.

Since I was on a roll, I figured it wouldn't hurt to try for another.

Well, I can definitely see her point about the open bar at the reception. That's what I'm waiting for too, when I get roped into usher or groomsman duty and have to rent a monkey suit. I think I can sort of identify with her angst about the ugly dress she has to wear since I've also had to wear some pretty awful ties and cummerbunds in my day. The worst was this turquoise shiny material. So, I feel for her there. At least I get to give it back after the event.

Going to wedding after wedding affects us guys too. For me, it's usually a reminder of how glad I am to be unmarried. I don't know if I love any woman enough to wear a monkey suit and walk down an aisle that is swallowed up in carnations. If I ever do that, everyone will know that I have lost every shred of my manly decency, at least for a day.

And another:

You know what guys love? Girls on vacation. They don't worry if you'll call them or ask them out on a real date. They are happy to get in the conga line and have various liquors poured down their throats at some bar in the Bahamas. They don't give a crap, and they are out for fun.

The rest of the time, they, and I, if I'm in town, are less enthusiastic. Let's face it, it's hard to go out and let it all hang out every weekend when you're thinking about mowing the lawn and washing your car the following morning, before it gets too hot outside. That goes for them maybe more than it does for us. Women keep their stuff cleaner and in better shape overall.

And finally:

In the career department, as with most other things, guys are in competition: with themselves, with each other. Our job is what defines our place in the world. If you take away that, where do we go from there? I think most of us assume that we'll settle down and be family men eventually, but we never talk about it. We want to be firemen or business tycoons when we grow up, drink lots of beer, and hang out in hot tubs full of hot chicks in bikinis. Everything else is incidental.

Saturdays were writing days, and Sundays were rest days. There was a lot of sleeping involved. All the while, I was torn between being glad to be busy, which meant that I could put off any post-Paul meltdowns for at least a few weeks, and wondering what life would be like if I could be my usual lazy self.

Act 2, Scene 7:
Tech Week

There comes a time in every actor's life when everything he or she has to put into a show must come out. This is commonly known as Tech Week, which immediately precedes the opening night and subsequent performances.

Since I had the performance days and the day after the last show off from work, I would get to pretend that I was a real actor after opening night. However, all of my technical rehearsals were done after a full day of work.

As they say in the world of theatre, "Bad rehearsal, good opening night." Happily, there were several bad rehearsals that week. When he was able to come, Sean had a tendency to improvise his lines since he hadn't had time to learn them, and that would throw me off. I tend to memorize the last few words of another actor's lines in relation to the first few words of my own lines, so when he made up some lines that I hadn't anticipated, I managed to get several monologues out of order. This caused havoc with Nora, who didn't know what stage cues to request from the lighting guys up in the fly loft, and then we all ended up standing around looking confused onstage. Sean had managed to get a beautiful blue light set up so it could shine on me in

all my purple taffeta glory for the bridesmaid scene, however. So, in some ways, things were coming together. I knew that, as was the case with every other section of life, somehow this would fall together at the last minute and be all right. It just had to.

The crew had become a new little circle of friends for me. Sean was right; everyone except for Nora was a gay man. Sean's good looks caused him to be frequently ogled by the guys, while my friends were happy to check him out until they realized he was my gay director. As Julie said one night over hoagies after I had introduced them, "Why, God, why?"

Yes, it wasn't fair. The prop manager, Keith, took an interest in Sean the instant they were introduced. Keith was a print model who worked in local theatre to satisfy his artistic cravings. I recognized him from the Sunday paper, where his picture in a polo shirt and action slacks had graced a full-page advertisement.

When it became obvious that they were interested in each other, I was filled with mixed emotions. It was like watching Keanu Reeves and River Phoenix flirt with each other in whatever movie they made together back in the 80's. A little alarm goes off in my head, saying, "Two hot guys and not a woman in sight– not fair!"

After a particularly flawed rehearsal, which took place the night before opening night, I took Sean and Keith out for a beer at the nearby Irish pub so they could flirt with each other and I could survey the local talent. Since my trip to Ireland I couldn't stay far from the pubs, and it had been no coincidence at all that Paul had resembled Scottish hottie Ewan MacGregor. Vacations and relationships with men had taken on the same kind of status, really; they were just something I got around to once in a while. Special and mostly fun, but fleeting. I either ran out of money, patience, or both, a few weeks or months into it, and had to eventually return to my natural state as the Original Single, back home and without a man. It was an interesting parallel: The Original Single with a side order of fruit at the pub, as it were.

Halfway through my cider, it occurred to me that the vast majority of my friends were going to watch me perform my show in less than

24 hours. Even some members of my family would be there. All my work, all my observations, would be subject to criticism and even ridicule. People would hear my words and make judgments about me, even though half of the stuff in the show was either sarcastic or put in for comic relief. Everyone sees things differently, and some would take me and my statements seriously. Good gravy.

As if on cue, the shepherd's pie that I had just eaten started to congeal. Then I remembered that the "shitting a brick" phase is integral to any stage performance. It would be a cozy night at home, hugging a pillow and alternating the ice pack between my belly and head. People have been known to say that theatre is a cruel mistress, and most of the time, that's not true. Rehearsing can be fun, and writing the show had been a great outlet for me. But on the night before the opening, when the only other actor in the show couldn't remember his lines, it became apparent that they might have a point.

Act 2, Scene 8:
Opening Day

Christine and I are dressed to the nines, looking through the crowd to find our friends. We find Julie, wearing a trapeze-style mini dress, and Tara, who is surrounded by three really attractive guys, posing for a picture on the stairs of a cruise ship. Tara runs over to me after the picture is snapped and says, "As soon as we get done with the receiving line, we're invited to the jacuzzi with those groomsmen." She pauses to smile and wave at one of them, who is a tall, young version of George Clooney.

"I am *so* glad Bill is in the frozen west," Tara adds, as Julie catches my gaze and subtly points out yet another groomsman who is headed our way. He looks like Sean but he is clearly interested in meeting us ladies.

"Score!" Christine whispers to me as we check him out.

"Who is getting married?" I ask.

"Some people on the ship," Christine replies. "They did all their wedding stuff on formal night, and they want to meet everyone on the ship. So we're expected to go through the receiving line."

A million things are racing through my mind. Weren't receiving lines outlawed in the 1980s? What kind of higher power intervened

so that Julie, Tara, Christine, and I would get to schedule the same vacation days? When did we book this cruise? Was that hot guy who looks like a straight Sean checking *me* out? Where did I get this fabulous evening gown?

Things become even more muddled when I met the bride and groom. The groom says, "It's always good luck when the bride kisses you," and the bride plants a peck on my left cheek, leaving a magenta mark on my face.

"Thanks," I say, a little surprised.

"Hey, have a great time on the ship," the bride says, as if she owns it and knows me at all.

The girls are waiting on me when I pass by the newlyweds.

"OK, let's go get changed and order some fruity drinks," Julie says. And so, I follow them back to our cabins. The rest is a blur.

Upon waking a few minutes later, I grabbed my dream interpretation book and tried to read about my dream symbols in the semi-darkness. It said, "a dream of attending a wedding means you will soon experience an occasion or event that will cause you bitterness and delayed success. Can also symbolize a new beginning or transition or reflect the dreamer's issues about commitment and independence."

Issues about commitment and independence were self-explanatory, but did they have to mention bitterness or delayed success? That is not the type of thing I wanted to think about after a week's worth of bad rehearsals and a show opening in less than 12 hours.

"To see a ship in your dream means that you are exploring your unconscious mind. A cruise ship augurs for a pleasant state of mind."

Well, at least there was that.

"Don't stress about the dream, I'm sure it's not as bad as all that," said Sean when I called him. "For one thing, there's a ton of people coming to the show tonight. Friendly people. And I have this habit of knowing my lines when it's really important, so don't worry about me. Finally, if you think about it, your dream was just about the show. Traveling, out with your friends, not missing ex-boyfriends,

meeting new boyfriends. It was about your life as the independent woman."

"What if people really don't like it?" I asked him.

"They'll let you know, don't worry about that. Keith is wild about your show, and he's doing the props for all of them. So I don't think you have anything to worry about for the festival. Sure, we're just a couple of gay guys, but who else is going to come to the festival? We're your target audience!"

I laughed in spite of myself.

"Do you want to meet me for lunch?" I asked Sean. "I need some food before I go to get a manicure and a pedicure this afternoon. It's all I can think of to do, to relax."

After a few hours of girl talk and pampering, I was ready to go home and get ready. Christine was there when I got there, and she helped me go over the lines as I applied my stage makeup at our dining room table. The lighting backstage just wasn't sufficient.

I had packed my car pre-manicure, so I floated to my car and began the strange journey to the theatre. People in the cars beside me in traffic were going on with their lives without rehearsal, and here I was, running off to a place where I sought to escape from life by accurately depicting it. The knots in my stomach started to dance as I realized the thought I have for every opening night: If I didn't think to do it before now or I didn't learn it well enough, it's too late now.

The tableau of Nora, Sean, and Keith greeted me as I walked into the dark theatre. The chairs had been arranged in uniform lines throughout the house, and the fresh scent of Pine-Sol mixed with the stale smoke that clung to the walls.

"The fly loft guys are loving you," Nora told me. "Your show is a lot easier than most of the others."

"I'm glad to hear that," I told her. "Now, if me and Sean can just remember our lines, we'll all know what's going on up there, and we won't screw up any more cues."

I was supposed to hide backstage or eavesdrop from the wings for the other two shows that night. My show was second of the three.

With makeup done, props placed neatly next to the stage for Sean

and Keith, and a group of fly loft guys loving the lack of cues that my show required, I didn't know what to do with myself. It would have been convenient, at that moment, to be a smoker. Smokers smoke to relieve stress, or help it along, I don't know. Either way, a smoke break is a great way to kill time before a show.

Sean and Keith were smoke-free, as was I. So I studied my lines instead.

The first show went off with only a few hitches; it was a trio of guys that had come up with their own comedy formula after studying everyone from the Marx Brothers to Bill and Ted. A few lines were skewered along the way, but by the end, this just added to the overall success of the show. The audience was very responsive and at one point absolutely roared in laughter.

There was no intermission between their show and mine, because both of our shows were relatively short. I had been informed by Christine to keep my schedule clear after intermission so that we could all get together, so I didn't plan to see the third show. There would be time for that throughout the week, with our subsequent performances.

As the applause died down and Keith and Sean set up my simple set, I took several deep breaths and waited. When it came time for me to take my place onstage, I willed myself not to look out into the audience.

Act 2, Scene 9:
After Much Ado, the Performance

The lights came up as I said my first lines:
All the world's a stage, and the women merely players. We have our exits and our entrances, and one woman in her time plays many parts. Her stages of life are the seven ages of modern life.

(Aside) *But if all the world's a stage, then she'll be needing better costumes, and more costume changes as well. A large budget for shoes is advisable.*

Already, I could hear some giggles in the audience. Some familiar, some not. It was comforting. In some ways, I wanted to know that there was an audience out there, and in other ways I wanted to block them out.

At first she is the little lady, whose days are filled with ladybugs and butterflies; and then the student, when note passing and hormones hopefully do not interfere with higher learning; and then she's the bachelorette, partying with players who may or may not hold her hair back if she pukes; and then the woman in love, wondering if she should hang her hopes on her man; and then the

working woman, going out to make a dent in the world; and then the juggler, who tries to manage a career, life and maybe a man as well as she can. Finally, she wears purple and spends time gardening, writes letters and sends card, and winds down her life at last.

Tonight's show will focus on most of these stages. So that we don't overwhelm you with the feminine perspective, our own Sean will be available to offer his own two cents every now and then.

Sean gave the audience a sexy wave from his chair, which was placed stage left of where I stood.

His first observation will revolve around the fertile topic of higher education in the modern world.

I went behind the screen to put on a raggedy flannel shirt over my black tank top and Capri pants and grab my first prop of the night, which was a book bag, while he charmed the crowd. My goal was to look like a poor college student.

Sean: Man, you haven't had the urge to run away so fast as you will if you dare set foot in a women's studies class. All these women are having a powwow to figure out all the ways that you are The Enemy. Men are evil, they make more money, they don't value us and our work, they think they're better than us, et cetera, et cetera. Even if some of it, well, most of it, is true in some ways, it's still pretty scary to be sitting in a room with a whole bunch of women who are all pissed off at you and what you represent at the same time.

I took a class on women in popular culture to satisfy a sociology requirement. I never dreamed that I would have to endure lectures stuff like on menstruation. I didn't make it through that lecture. I did stick around long enough to learn that in most Native American cultures, women were excused from all household duties and responsibilities when they were having their moon time, as they call it. I think if we did that in modern America- you know, just told women to take a few days off at their most volatile times- the world

would be a better place. I bet they'd like it too.

Hopefully looking the part of a serious student with no money, I emerged from behind the screen and began my observations:

If you ever suspected that life isn't fair, that men have hundreds of advantages over women, do yourself a favor and take a women's studies class in college. If you do that, you get to find out actual factual information that shows how much more money they take home, how the work they do is more highly valued, how the world revolves around all things male. You'll learn fun facts too, like how the happiest people are single women and married men, and get to theorize why that might be.

I wonder what the world would be like if women weren't supposed to be so obsessed with appearances. Would modern businesses run as efficiently if men wore stomach-squashing pantyhose and had to worry about having stubble-free legs and made-up faces every day? Of course, they do wear nooses around their necks— you know, neck ties. But I don't think that makes them even with women, as far as the degree of discomfort in shoes or clothes and the endless pursuit of beauty. It makes you wonder, too, what the world would be like if we were free of these expectations. Would more work get done, would more businesses be successful, would more people be rich if women were free of the constant beauty contest going out there in the world? Would people whose livelihoods depended on selling overpriced beauty products be first in line at the unemployment office? Would men be more sensitive to all that we do if they were required to endure just one eyebrow waxing treatment?

But back to being a Career Woman. Having a degree, whether it's from a high school, college or trade school is desirable. You don't have to have one to get by, but my goodness, doesn't it help? Just like if you're a blonde chick with big boobs, doesn't that help you get a date? And when you get out there to try to carve out a life for yourself, you need all the help you can get! There's a curious new demographic that's come along in the last 15 years or so— I don't

know if you've noticed- but there are a ton of single women ou who live alone or with roommates, who work and save their mon buy houses, go on vacation and have absolutely no idea where they can meet a decent guy. These women benefit from being educated since that can increase their earnings, because gals like that, like us, are out there going it alone. It's like Attack of the Bridget Jones clones. I don't know if sociological conditions should be blamed or praised for this recent development.

A lot of the women in the audience laughed at the end of this monologue. I retreated behind the screen to ditch the flannel and put on a gray and black blazer for the next monologue as Sean provided the next bit of entertainment.

Sean: *In the career department, as with most other things, guys are in competition: with themselves, with each other. Our job is what defines our place in the world. If you take away that, where do we go from there? I think most of us assume that we'll settle down and be family men eventually, but we never talk about it. We want to be firemen or business tycoons when we grow up, drink lots of beer, and hang out in hot tubs full of hot chicks in bikinis. Everything else is incidental.*

Stepping out from behind the screen in what Sean and I could only guess was in the manner of a successful business person, I began my next monologue:

Work to live, or live to work? For me, it's always been work to live. There's something about work that is intrinsically not fun. It's why we get paid to do it.
A lot of people say that we should enjoy our jobs, since we spend so much time on the job. To this I say, I'll enjoy my work as soon as I find some type of enjoyable work, and the act of trying to find work that I find meaningful and fulfilling has taken up the last ten years of my life already, so I don't know when the search will end at this point.

more familiar with being on the stage, I
o the audience and saw not only the gals but
. This was very comforting.

and working for the same amount of time,
6, I've come to realize certain truths that
apply to both of these things. They are:

Number One: Grunt work is necessary, and you might not ever
get what you want. If you do get what you want, you will then have to
guard it against others who will want to take it away from you.

Think about it— when we date, we essentially break in the guys we
date. We teach them how to put the toilet seat down, not to leave the
hand towels in a heap on the bathroom floor and how to give a decent
backrub. The list goes on and on. Then, when the relationship falls
apart, off he goes to date some other woman, who will reap the
rewards of the work that we've already put in.

With work, we start off doing all the crap that no one else wants
to do, and get paid very little for it, too. If it becomes apparent that
maybe there isn't anywhere to go with the job, or there's no position
worth our time with that particular employer, it's as if our efforts
were wasted entirely.

But it wasn't a waste. We have accrued money and karma points
too. When we move onto the next level, whether it's securing a
promotion or getting upgraded to "girlfriend," it is well deserved.
And it may not have anything to do with where we started out.

Similarity Number Two: The audition process is demeaning.

Let's contrast first dates with interviews. Both involve clothes we
don't usually wear, questions we aren't used to asking or answering,
and a general feeling of discomfort overall. There is a point when
one party says that he or she will call, and this may or may not
happen, depending on the other options. The other is left to wait and
wonder. Either party can follow up the meeting with a phone call,
card, or e-mail, but that is not a guarantee of winning the job or
second date.

The new concept of speed dating has revolutionized this process for single people. Instead of wondering if one guy will call, you can wonder if several will call instead. I find that it's also increased the number of men I'd date and the number of men who would date me, but unfortunately those two types of men rarely coincide.

Similarity Number Three: The more desirable it seems to the outside world, the more high-maintenance it is for you.

Think about what it would be like to date a major celebrity. Let's call him George Clooney, for example. You and George are dating, and it looks like a picnic. He's got all the money in the world to show you a good time, and you get to go to all these exciting and glamorous parties with him. But think again... If you get to be a size 8 or higher, the tabloids will have a field day with you and tell the whole world how pudgy you are... photographers and reporters would be constantly stalking your man... and his job would take up so much of his time...

Highly regarded jobs are the same. I am sure that the leaders of the free world would love to put in 40 hours a week and go home, but they can't.

Similarity Number Four: Breakups or layoffs can leave you anywhere from confused to depressed, which makes it difficult to move on.

Once in a while you'll meet someone, like my friend Norma Jean, who can take something as huge as a layoff in stride. I met her when I lived in Alaska, and she had lost real job that spring. So she made a few phone calls, moved to Denali Park, worked 40 hours a week as a customer service rep, flirted with boys, hiked, ran around, and even took a side trip to Hawaii. When she got back home in the fall, she got a new real job, with a summer in Alaska etched in her mind as a four-month working vacation.

But most of us aren't so good with rejection. Instead of realizing that new opportunities will open up, we might wallow for a while.

It's the same with love. Lots of women swear that the man they're in love with at age 17, 20, 25 or 30 is "The One," and that they'll be

together forever, and that everything will be as glamorous as it looks on their favorite TV show for the rest of their natural lives. When reality sets in and he makes some decision or looks in a direction that wasn't on your life itinerary, things can get trying. If an agreement is not reached, which is common at the beginning of careers and adult life, the couple breaks up, and the two separate parties are left to improvise separately and figure things out for themselves.

Similarity Number Five: They stress teamwork and partnership, but they can suck you dry if they're not right for you.
Here's a rule for life: If you need a pep talk every few days to deal with it, it's not right for you. If you spend hours on the phone with your friends and family complaining about it and it's making you depressed, you need to move on.
People stay with jobs that don't suit them for all kinds of reasons: they think they're indispensable, that they don't have enough experience to do something else, that they hate looking for jobs, and so on. People stay living in the land of "we should break up but not just yet," because they're afraid of being alone or disappointing the other person.
When the comfort zone isn't even comfortable, it's still hard to leave. But you have to move on at some point. Otherwise, you're not being true to yourself.

Similarity Number Six: Learning from the past can give you clues as to what to look for in the future, when you make a new selection.
After you've acquired the karma of training all of your exes to behave, you might find that you are attracting new people who are better trained. Observing the behavior of your nearest and dearest can help you formulate a shopping list of things that will serve you well in your future searches. Doing the same works for jobs as well. A job can be just a paycheck or a step in a sequence of moves to establish a career, but it has to somehow apply to your development as a person.
Being a smarter shopper can benefit you in innumerable ways. Trust me.

Final Similarity Number Seven: When you find your perfect match, your joy knows no end. As time goes on, there are ups and downs, but if you're on the right track, you stick with it. And all of your friends who are not so blessed are desperately jealous.

There is nothing better than being satisfied and knowing that you are content, for one, and looking forward to whatever happens too. You get to be happy. You went out and looked for something, found it, and now you have it. Hooray!

This doesn't happen all the time, so when it does, prepare to be humble and thankful. This invites more good karma into your life and keeps the jealousy of others at bay.

I'd noticed a few chuckles from the audience with this last monologue, but had to concentrate fully on my next costume change, since it was the most complicated. From the side of the stage, Keith had been ever-so-sweetly hanging up my discarded costume changes. This time he waited for me with a hanger in one hand and my purple taffeta bridesmaid dress in the other. Once my blazer was off and placed on the hanger, the bridesmaid dress went over my head in one smooth motion. A quick zip, and I was ready to bound out onstage to the applause of every ex-bridesmaid out there.

Sean: Once we all have a steady paycheck and a bunch of friends, another twenty-something duty is bound to rear its head. It happens to us guys, too, but I understand that it might be a little bit more traumatic for the ladies.

I'm talking about weddings. Weddings every month. Buying someone a new a wedding present every time you go to Target. It happens to all of us in our 20's, at some point. Gina will tell you her feelings on the subject in a moment.

As I emerged from behind the screen, I heard applause from the back of the house. The eggplant-colored monstrosity was a hit!

Hi. My name is Gina and I am a career bridesmaid. In my life as a bridesmaid, I have worn velvet, satin, crepe and a few other unidentifiable fabrics.

A lot of people think that bridesmaids are a bunch of bitter, jealous hags, but let me tell you, that just isn't true. Let me address the "hag" portion of this theory first. It's a given that every bride wants to be the most beautiful person at her wedding. Since we stand right next to her, we have to look especially bad. This is why most bridesmaid dresses unfairly accent the hips and come in such an unflattering array of colors. It's a conspiracy throughout the bridal fashion industry.

As far as the bitter part goes, that may be true of some, but that isn't true of all of us. When we're standing up in front of everyone, holding our flowers and smiling, the last thing we're thinking is, "I wish I was the bride." Mostly, we're thinking either, "My feet are killing me," or, "That groomsman is kind of cute." We're not dreaming of true love, we're wondering how we're going to pay for the ugly $150 dress we're wearing. And most of all, we're not taking mental notes about what we'll do when it's "our turn." We're looking forward to the open bar at the reception and a chance to sit down.

I'd find in the days to come that this monologue would receive the most laughter and applause. *Next time*, I thought, *I'll just write the bridesmaid show.* Once I was behind the screen, I pulled the dress over my head and threw it to Keith.

Sean: Well, I can definitely see her point about the open bar at the reception. That's what I'm waiting for, too, when I get roped into usher or groomsman duty and have to rent a monkey suit. I think I can sort of identify with her angst about the ugly dress she has to wear since I've also had to wear some pretty awful ties and cummerbunds in my day. The worst was this turquoise shiny material. So, I feel for her there. At least I get to give it back after the event.

Going to wedding after wedding affects us guys too. For me, it's usually a reminder of how glad I am to be unmarried. I don't know if I love any woman enough to wear a monkey suit and walk down an aisle that is swallowed up in carnations. If I ever do that, everyone will know that I have lost ever shred of my manly decency, at least for a day.

All this wedding activity makes us, and by that I mean women and men, judge and analyze our own lives. It makes us single people wonder why we haven't met the man or woman of our dreams yet.

I emerged with a clipboard and a meaningful look on my face to deliver the next monologue.

When meeting someone new, it would be helpful to know some important information at the start. Of course, through casual conversation, you can nail down the basics: general areas of interest; sign of the zodiac; work situation; and so on. But what I want to know, what we as consumers want to know is stuff like:

How long has it been since your last relationship ended? Why did it end?

Are you in a relationship now? Do you have children? Do you know if you have children? Do you want to have children someday?

Are you the kind of guy who dates a woman for two or three years before getting jitters and running in the opposite direction? Or do you run away early on in the relationship?

Do you have a job? If so, what is it? If not, why?

Have you spent any time in prison? If so, why?

Do you hope to marry someone someday?

The search and application process is an integral part of being single. Just as you scrutinize potential dates, you are scrutinized as well. This generally sends the majority of the consumers (especially the vegetarians in my case, since I love tacos) scurrying in the other direction. But alas, this is part of the game, the revolving door of love, the turnstile experience. The more frogs we kiss, the more we can edit our shopping list. And as time goes by, our shopping savvy is increased.

There's not very much interesting to say about being blissfully in love. It's like when you watch the news; they don't report on the good things happening in the community or country; no, it's the disasters and crises that get our attention. And while being in love might be great, falling out of love is extraordinarily interesting to the everyday observer.

I set down the clipboard so that it would not hinder my movement for the breakup monologue.

What can I say about the breakup of a relationship? You know it's coming along when a little tiny clock inside your head starts ticking. It says to you, it's time to wrap this thing up. You have this much time, and after that, all hell will break loose. Your subconscious gives you a deadline. It's just that easy. And whether you take it as a hint or just some vague thing floating out there, you know the jig is up.

Men are funny. Like my friend Julie has said, they test your limits like two-year-olds. Maybe it's my perception, or maybe this really happens, but when they're done dating a girl but don't want to break up with her, the Id comes out. In terms of man logic, this means that several months of bad behavior that would cause them to be dumped is more worth the effort than one mature discussion about the relationship. It makes me wonder if it's more fun for them to behave badly and have someone to answer to than behave badly as bachelors and not have anyone around to witness it.

I am guessing that they want an audience for their antisocial antics, and on some level I can understand that. After all, I am an actress.

But a breakup wouldn't be complete without some delusional optimist, like a friend whose been married for 10 years, your sister, somebody- telling you some lame crap about how you just haven't met the right one yet. They like to say something like, "God is preparing someone for you." With insane energy, they do not stop to think of what if God isn't- what if God wants me to be single? Other people live this way and don't kill themselves. Apparently it isn't the

end of the world to live as a single woman. In fact, I have noticed several ways in which it is much preferred over the alternative.

So now that we've visited the seven stages of modern woman, we can explore the six stages of heartbreak. I mean, dating has taught me many things, but mostly it's taught me that I'm better off single. The journey back to living life as a singleton is a tough road. You can go to Steak and Shake and have to hold back tears when you realize that you are not only eating the Original Single, but you are the Original Single too.

So, let's see, the six stages. The first one, naturally, is denial. Always a favorite. You say to yourself, he'll change, he'll grow up, he'll suddenly get over this obsession with frequenting seedy bars and ogling bikini-clad waitresses. Yes, like that will happen.

Then there's depression, another popular favorite. Depression sets in because you know that, while most men are basically wild boys at heart, one might straighten up and fly right if he's convinced that you are the woman for him and that he can't imagine life without you. So you've obviously failed this test. Enter depression.

This is when lifting your head off the pillow is enough to exhaust you for the whole day. The alarm goes off about six hours too early every day, since you're up half the night worrying over things you can't help. Minute problems seem huge and bursting into tears is a constant activity. Often accompanied by food consumption, especially chocolate.

Anger directed at others characterizes the next step in the path to Fabulousness for One. It's when you sit back and look at other people and wish you could curse them for being so damn happy. No one has problems compared to you, so what do they have to complain about? Have you ever been this annoyed in your entire life, anyway?

Anger directed at yourself is the next step. Why did you waste your time with that guy? Couldn't you figure that he wasn't right for you sooner? And then there's always the classic question: What was I thinking? How did I miss that he was a mama's boy/druggie/control freak/jerk/insert appropriate label here? Because if you'd known this earlier, you'd be through all the first four stages of heartbreak by now.

But at some point you'll have to make peace with yourself, and that is the fifth step. That's when you say, Hey, I had a man to be with for a while; I even got to take a date to a wedding once when we were together; I got to fulfill my lifelong dream of going to Graceland. He was pretty cool most of the time. We enjoyed our time together, some of it, before it all went south. Let it be, it's all good.

And then comes the sixth stage, which is my personal favorite: completely selfish behavior. And oh yes, this stage can last as long as you want it to. That means, no relationships with men, unless they revolve around men simply admiring your goddesslike beauty or clamoring to buy you a free dinner or drink. That's right, it's all about you, Miss Thing. It's all about you. You get to do all those things that he used to get in the way of before: watch "Friends" instead of wrestling on Thursday nights, see a movie that you're interested in that doesn't involve wars or kung fu, take up all the room in the bed and not listen to snoring- the possibilities are endless. No breakup is complete without a list of "Things I do not miss about the Ex." That is an important list to make and share.

It was during one of these phases, right after I'd attended a good friend's wedding, that I decided to buy myself a ring. For years, I had watched friend after friend get engaged and acquire some fabulous gems along the way. Since the Three Fates, in their infinite wisdom, had not thrown a fabulously compatible guy across my path, I had to take matters into my own hands. There was simply no need to be penalized in the jewelry department because I was single.

That is why I went out and bought myself a six-carat emerald-cut garnet in a silver setting. Some say it's ridiculous, others say it's fabulous, but the only thing that matters is that I love it.

I held up my left hand and gestured meaningfully to the audience. *"Can everyone in the back row see my ring?"* I asked. The rowdy back row, which contained several of my girlfriends and work colleagues, roared for a minute. I went back to the monologue after most of the noise died down.

As I adjusted to the weight of this bauble on my hand, I realized that five or six carats of a pretty gem on my ring finger made the absence of a man in my life seem much less tragic than some would have me believe.

I had to pause for their applause again.

Rings symbolize a lot of things. If you win the Super Bowl, you get a huge diamond ring that symbolizes that you were a part of the best football team in the world. If you get a class ring, it confirms that you attended high school, for one, and also shows the world your official birthstone and extracurricular activities. For women, the status that the engagement ring brings is overwhelming. It says to the world, "Someone has promised to love me forever."

But my ring says, to me at least, that no matter what happens with the men in my life, I'll always have me. And if need be, that will be enough.

There was a pause for more applause as I went behind the screen and put on a plastic Hawaiian lei.

Sean: Well at this point, our heroine is in the midst of repairing her broken heart and moving on with her life. Whatever should she do? You know what I think? She should get a few friends together and get out of town.

Why do I say this? Because do you know what guys love? Girls on vacation. They don't worry if you'll call them or ask them out on a real date. They are happy to get in the conga line and have various liquors poured down their throats at some bar in the Bahamas. They don't give a crap, and they are out for fun.

I emerged from behind the curtain to deliver the last monologue.

It is a given that when you're young, you'll have time and no money and when you're older, you'll have money but no time. This is

an occasion in which lowering your expectations will get you far. If you're truly interested in going somewhere, you won't mind sleeping on a couch for a few days once you get there. Honestly, if you wait until you can afford a hotel to go some place, your life will be half over by then.

Do you know that more women than men travel abroad to study? Did you ever wonder why? I'll give you a hint: they have names like Antonio. If you can get school credit for exploring a foreign land, I say do it. You'll learn tons more than you would in a classroom, and the memories will last a lifetime. Being an American woman overseas is like being a celebrity. Your waiters can't stop asking you out, and you're popular no matter where you go. It is a wonderful life, and it is a darn shame when your money runs out and you have to go back home. But you'll always have Paris, Dublin, or wherever you've gone.

Traveling is another big confidence booster. Once you make your way through a foreign land, you feel pretty savvy. And the separation makes you realize what things in your life are important, and which things you're better off without. Being away gives you time to think, and time to just be.

Finally, Sean joined me in the middle of the stage for the ending.

Sean: In winding down the show, the independent woman and I would like to thank you for coming.

I closed the show by saying:

I don't know if how I've presented the lives of independent women like myself as if they're something to be feared, admired, envied or what. All I know is that this is the way we are: bound to nothing but the people we love and the adventures we choose for our own lives.

With the help of the guys in the fly loft, who immediately dimmed the lights, the audience figured out that the show was over and began

to applaud. I clasped Sean's hand and we bowed in unison. When we came up from the bow, I noticed a rose on the stage. Sean squealed, "Please, stop throwing roses," and I started laughing hysterically. Keith had thrown the rose up on the stage, for both of us, but I told Sean to keep it.

III.
Encore

With just me backstage, it was still a frenzy. I was trying to remove my stage makeup, apply something less frightening to my face, get the props together to be loaded into my car, reign in all of the costumes and clothes that were strewn around the room, and figure out who had sent me the flowers on the make-up table. I couldn't find the card until the makeup had been rounded up and placed back into my purple tackle box. The card read, "Best wishes to you, Sean and the crew." How sweet!

The gals came in and brought their nervous energy along with them.

"Fabulous show, darling. Your performance left me wondering whatever would you do next?" Julie said.

I had been thinking about this. "Well, this is the year I'm turning 30. And we're going on a road trip to shop at the nearest H&M. When do we leave?"

"I don't even want to know how much money we're all going to part with once we set foot inside the store," observed Christine. "Imagine if they sell shoes too!"

"Indeed," agreed Tara, who was generously packing up the props. "Give us the props and the costumes, honey. Christine and I will load her car while Julie whisks you away to the cast party."

"Did you see Paul out there in the audience?" Julie asked. "I know I saw him out there."

"There is no telling how many ex-boyfriends are going to hear about the content of this show. Hopefully, none of them will take credit for being all of my inspiration. They were all instrumental, you know, working together to make sure I'd learn how to be a happy single woman."

"I'm glad to hear that," said Paul from the doorway. Christine jumped and almost dropped her bag full of costumes and makeup. The girls scattered to the winds to give me and Paul some privacy.

"It's water under the bridge, darling," I said, smiling at him. "How are you doing?"

"Pretty well, thanks. I didn't know you'd be so busy with this show. It must have taken a lot of work, and I'm really proud of you."

'Thanks," I said. "I might not ever earn what you earn out there, but for tonight, I get to be queen of the night in here," I added, motioning to the stage.

"People think I'm so much more interesting when I tell them that I know someone who's doing a one-woman show. Everyone up in the office wants to see your picture and hear about the show. It's really funny, actually," he said, as he wrapped his arms around me and gave me a big bear hug.

I could feel the color creep into my face while we stood there, and he must have noticed too. He said to me, "Well, I guess I'd better get the hell out of here before we start to drive each other crazy again." I nodded, but stopped him as he walked past me.

"I'm glad I dated you," I told him.

"I'm glad I dated you too," he responded.

"Graceland was awesome," I added. "And dating you helped me write the show. I guess I owe you."

He laughed and gave me a gentlemanly kiss on the cheek.

"Should I be glad about that?" he asked, then disappeared into the hallway. I could hear his footsteps fading away as I checked my purse for the essentials: money, drivers license, keys, and lip gloss.

Quite strangely, dating Paul had gotten me a lot closer to coming up with a final shopping list than I could even believe. And his drinking binges and political debates, while painful to endure at the

time, were somewhat entertaining now that I had distance and perspective, and could allude to them in front of a live audience. It's just how I've said before: theatre is much better than therapy.

Julie popped her head into the dressing room long enough to say, "Are you ready to hit the town?"

I grabbed the last of my things and left to go to the cast party, where we would toast each other and Sean and the crew. I hadn't invited Paul to come along, because that night seemed like a new beginning for me. No need to invite along any ghosts of the past.

I flipped off the light switch and prayed that the rest of the shows would go as well. I didn't have to be back until 4 p.m. the following day, so it seemed that a wild night on the town was in the works.

Somewhere in the recesses of my mind, I knew that I'd wake up in about a week and the show would be over. I'd realize then that I probably should do something with my career, invest in real estate, or find my soul mate. But with my friends surrounding me and a night of frolic and fun ahead, it was hardly the time to worry about that.

I would like to thank all of my English teachers and writing instructors for the support and guidance that they gave to me. I'd also like to thank the staff of PublishAmerica for editing and publishing this book.

Saving the best for last, I'd like to acknowledge that this story wouldn't be what it has become without the help of my extremely talented friend, Lisa Pelamati Creswell. Not only has she helped me "research" the book since 1995, but she also showed me how to turn my ideas into my first book.

Enjoy! ♥ Gabi Lovino

To my family, friends, and the people I've known in school and through all the jobs and extracurricular interests I've held over the years. Special thanks to my ex-boyfriends too. If it hadn't been for those doomed relationships, what would I have to write about now?

Most of all, this book is dedicated to all the independent women out there—goddesses and ya-yas in great particular.

First printing

ISBN: 1-4137-2309-8
PUBLISHED BY PUBLISHAMERICA, LLLP
www.publishamerica.com
Baltimore

Printed in the United States of America

Independent Woman's Guide to Life

By
Gabi Lorino

PublishAmerica
Baltimore

ACKNOWLEDGMENTS

This book is the product of an entire community of investing enthusiasts, supporters, and volunteers, in both the virtual and the physical world.

Many thanks go to the original Armchair Millionaire supporters. Without a doubt John Bowen and Robert Levitan top that list. Many professionals lent much more than their expertise, including Dan Ambrose, Geoffrey Menin, Jim Safka, Pamela Saunders, and Richard Laermer.

Some of the folks that helped us bring ArmchairMillionaire.com to life: Walston Bobb-Semple, Jr., Amit Gupta, Barry Hoggard, Alex Knowlton, Amanda Meffert, Tony Morelli, Matt Potosnak, Michael Slattery, Jill Schwartz, Katie Soden, David Wagenheim, Gary Wiebke, and Nic Wolff.

Agent Bob Levine and Pocket Books president Judith Curr believed in this book . . . twice! Thanks and thanks again.

Jimmy Fitzgerald, Bill Karsh, and Craig Goldberg, you've given much more than you've gotten in return (so far).

Two important people deserve special acknowledgment for their contributions to *The Armchair Millionaire:* Kate Hanley, whose voice has joined ours on every page of this book, giving it life and energy throughout; and Gary Hallgren, illustrator and creator of

"Rich," whose devilish figure can be spotted at the opening of each chapter.

From Lewis:

Thank you to the influential people who said "yes" at just the right time: Randy Jones of *Worth* for allowing me to put his magazine online even before I knew what I was doing; and Scott Cook, founder of Intuit, for letting me put ArmchairMillionaire.com on Quicken.com when it was just an idea.

Our biggest thanks must go to the members of the Armchair Millionaire community, who are the real heroes of our story. They make every day a day closer to financial freedom for themselves and for each other.

CONTENTS

INTRODUCTION

LEWIS SCHIFF

Investing is a lot like buying a car. As a consumer, you've got many choices, but there's no such thing as the "best" choice for everyone, only the one that's right for you. Some folks are looking for speed. Others want safety. Still others don't care what they drive, so long as it gets them there.

There are so many choices in the car market, with not a great deal of difference between them, that the manufacturers and marketers rely on hype to convince prospective customers of the superiority of one model over another. It's gotten so bad that even if one of these companies actually managed to create a truly great product, it would be difficult for car buyers to know.

Once you've decided you want a minivan rather than an SUV, you're still faced with a bewildering choice of vehicles. In reality, a minivan is a minivan is a minivan. One model isn't all that different from another. This is where marketers come in, filling magazines, newspapers, and airwaves with so much hoopla that you don't know what to believe anymore.

In the face of all that, you will eventually make a car choice because a car, for most of us, is an essential tool for living. Unfortunately, beginning your investing plan often doesn't have the same

priority. Given what you have to go through to start an investing program, I completely understand why.

With all that noise—experts offering conflicting advice on what
to do, stock markets and interest rates going up and down, new
economy stocks replacing old blue chips, and thousands of mutual
funds and brokers to choose from—investing can seem like a risky
proposition. That's too bad, because a solid investment strategy is
every bit as crucial as a car. And it will certainly get you farther than
a car ever could.

I was lucky. I was a nerd who was drawn to investing at an early
age—not because I come from a family of savers or investors and
not because I am in love with numbers. What drew me to investing
was that, like a puzzle, it seemed so complicated on the surface that
I had to get inside and figure it out.

My interest in investing dates back to my very first job. As a
fourteen-year-old, I worked on Wall Street one summer as a messenger for an international investment bank. My grandfather got me the
job (he was a messenger, too). As I sped from tower to tower, delivering packages, I sensed that there was less to Wall Street than met
the eye.

About a decade later, I ended up working at a financial magazine—not as a reporter, but as a computer consultant. My job was to
use technology to make magazine production more cost effective. I
had been bitten by the investing bug a few years earlier, and now I
wanted to get inside the industry to see how it worked. My upbring-
ing as a skeptic led me not to Wall Street this time but to a magazine, where I imagined I'd find out how investing and stock markets
really worked, not how "the Street" said they worked.

What I learned at the magazine was very disappointing. It was no
different than other parts of the financial industry. Investing professionals, whether they are journalists or stockbrokers, are paid to act
as interpreters for their readers or customers. In that sense, the
more you know, the less you need them. So they rely on a constant
river of complex ideas and alluring possibilities to keep you coming

back—from biotechnology stocks to investment trusts to mortgage-backed securities.

The World Wide Web changed all that. The interactive nature of the Web allows investors to "talk" to each other in a way that they never could have before. This directly challenges the broker-client relationship. In tiny virtual communities, people share the ideas that have really worked for them—ideas that are making them wealthy, ideas that are not very difficult to understand. In fact, they make a lot of common sense.

I began the Armchair Millionaire Web site because I knew—along with a great many other people—that investing intelligently doesn't have to be complicated. Thus the world's first commonsense savings and investing community was born.

There are at least tens of thousands of Armchair Millionaires, and probably a whole lot more than that. We have ordinary incomes, but our portfolios have done extraordinarily well. We don't have super-computers in our homes to analyze data, and we don't eat cat food in order to save money to invest. We lead normal lives.

Well, we may stand out in a few ways. We are patient and we are disciplined. We understand the dangers of easy credit—too often from experience. We found out how to invest successfully on our own because we are "do-it-yourselfer" types who need to know how and why things work before we jump into them. We are skeptics, but not cynics. Our goal is financial independence but our expectations are realistic. Most important, we are all either millionaires or on our way to becoming millionaires.

How simple is it? Well, I don't want to exaggerate. There are a few new ideas that are going to sound foreign at first. There's also new terminology that you will need to learn.

And then there's the financial services industry.

They are not crazy about simple, commonsense investing strategies. There is a prevailing wisdom out there, whether you hear it at a cocktail party or from your uncle, the stockbroker, that investing is a macho game in which you are judged not by how well you do for yourself, but by how much better you do compared to those around you. These folks tell you that you need to be in the "top performing" fund or that they've found the next Microsoft—"Get in while you can!"

The fact is, the successful investors who make up the Armchair Millionaire community are more interested in reaching their long-term goals than in attracting a crowd at a cocktail party. They also know that there are several factors that affect your long-term portfolio's performance—and the increase in value of your investments is just one of them. Spending as little as possible on fees and commissions is another.

And so, the tools you need to implement this commonsense investing strategy—we call it the Armchair Millionaire's Five Steps to Financial Freedom—are not available at every bank or brokerage. But they are available at the some of the biggest firms (we'll tell you which in Chapter 8, "Use the Armchair Investing Strategy"). More and more companies are realizing the value of the long-term investor each day. In fact, there's been something of a revolution in the past decade, wherein the investor on Main Street has gained access to the kinds of investing tools and information that used to be available only to the super-wealthy and to institutional investors. We'll show you how to benefit from that revolution and navigate through the brokerage world to get the most services while spending the least in fees.

Of course, there's much more to becoming an Armchair Millionaire than just implementing the Five Steps to Financial Freedom. While the steps are simple in and of themselves—we've laid out each step for you in this book—they require a certain degree of emotional intelligence, too. Patience and discipline are an Armchair Millionaire's key to realizing investing success and financial independence.

The books on investing that line shelf after shelf at your local bookstore will try to tell you that successful investing is complicated. Armchair Millionaires realize that these books may make for interesting reading, but they aren't required to build a sophisticated portfolio.

That's what makes this book different from all those other books—
Armchair Millionaires say that investing isn't about complicated formulas, or anything else that's complicated. This book will show you,
step by step, how to invest successfully. It includes simple, clear,
straightforward investing advice for people in every stage of life. We
will show you which investments to buy, how much, and when.

In these pages you'll hear investing wisdom from a wide variety
of people—from the most prominent investing giants in history to
individual investors who may be a lot like you. They'll describe their
enthusiasm for these very simple concepts. Shutting off the noise
and relying on common sense is the thread that runs through their
stories. They will share their own investing experiences with you in
this book as they do on the Armchair Millionaire Web site each day
in our forums, bulletin boards, surveys, and other community events.

Listen to these folks. You'll find out that there is a "best" way to
invest for most people. It's simple, easy to implement, and powerful
enough to help most of us achieve financial independence.

So, whether you are deep in debt, a nincompoop about money,
or hopelessly pressed for time, don't despair. You'll find someone in
this book with a similar predicament. The only difference between
them and you is that they have put these five commonsense investing steps into action, and now they've accomplished what they previously believed was near impossible. Think of them as the "after"
and yourself as the "before."

Best of all, their wisdom and support are available to you twenty-
four hours a day for no charge (except for the cost of hooking up to
the Internet). At the Armchair Millionaire's online community,
you've got a sounding board, a research tool, a place to get inspiration, and a whole group of friends who share a very important priority—financial freedom.

Please let me know how you fare on your own journey to financial independence. I'm at lewis@armchairmillionaire.com and I'd
love to welcome you to our commonsense investing community.

Part I

Getting Ready
for the Journey

CHAPTER 1

What Is an Armchair Millionaire?

"You don't need a million bucks to be an Armchair Millionaire!"

When you visit Armchair Millionaire on the Web (www.armchairmillionaire. com), you'll see this phrase scattered throughout our site. It means that being an Armchair Millionaire is not about having a million dollars, but having the attitude that will get you there. It is a state of mind, rather than a number in a bank account. When you are an Armchair Millionaire, you are mindful of the future, walking on a path toward an attainable goal of financial freedom.

You'll discover as you read this book and meet actual members of our community that Armchair Millionaires come from all sorts of backgrounds. They are in different stages of life, and their portfolios are of widely varying sizes.

But there are some distinct characteristics that all Armchair Millionaires share. Once you understand these traits and begin to adopt them for yourself, you too will become an Armchair Millionaire. Even those of you who are terrified to start digging around in your personal finances. And those of you who don't think you have enough time to actually maintain an investing plan. And all the folks who dare to dream of being financially secure but don't have the first idea how to go about it—especially you!

An Armchair Millionaire Is...

Someone with a Goal

The basic goal for every Armchair Millionaire is financial security. Even though there are an infinite number of ways to define "security," we can probably all agree on this basic definition: Security is having more than you need to survive; not living paycheck to paycheck; and not lying in bed at night worrying what would happen if you lost your job or got sick.

On the other hand, having more than you need to survive doesn't necessarily mean having the best of everything—such as shaved mink coats and multiple luxury cars and adorable little six-bedroom summer cottages. If your goal is to live extravagantly, you're missing the Armchair Millionaire mantra. Money is our friend, but it's not our savior. And the less we spend, the more we'll have. Even fabulously wealthy people can spend themselves into the poorhouse. An Armchair Millionaire is too smart to do that. Which brings us to our next characteristic:

Someone with Common Sense

An Armchair Millionaire is a skeptic. Not a cynic, mind you, but a skeptic—someone who likes to know the facts before jumping to any conclusions. And someone who knows there probably aren't any quick and easy fortunes headed our way. Armchair Millionaires know the idea of getting rich quickly is a waste of our time. For that reason, we probably won't be spending our hard-earned money on lottery tickets. (Not unless the prize is really big.)

But Armchair Millionaires know that it is possible, and even likely, to get rich slowly.

One quick look at the growth of a single dollar at a 10 percent annual rate of return over two centuries ($190 million!) will show us that time and compounded returns—as you'll learn in Step 5—are very powerful tools for making a lot of money. More powerful tools than expensive brokers, or elaborate investment theories. In other words, an Armchair Millionaire is . . .

A Do-It-Yourselfer

After all, how else are you going to know that your investment plan is being done right? Sure, we'd love to have it done for us, but when it comes to the really important things, it's worth knowing how to do it ourselves—especially if we are going to rely on it.

There's another advantage to running your own plan. One of the most common investing mistakes, so common that it's legendary in investing circles, "is selling into a panic." Everyone's heard a story (or has one of their own) in which someone sold their stocks or mutual funds when the market was in a downward spiral—only to see the market quickly rebound.

When you understand how your investing plan works and how the stock market has worked historically, then you'll understand why selling into a panic is irrational. Armchair Millionaires know how their investing plans work. And they never invest in anything they aren't comfortable with.

By bringing the control over your financial freedom into your own hands, you achieve ultimate security. It's captured best in the old saying, "Give a man a portfolio and he'll invest for a day. Teach a man to invest and he'll eventually become a millionaire." (Okay, so maybe the saying doesn't go *exactly* like that, but you get the drift.)

Someone with a Plan

There isn't an Armchair Millionaire out there without a saving and investing plan that's intended to build their wealth over the long term. That's a given. But what really sets an Armchair Millionaire apart from other investors is that an Armchair Millionaire's plan can run on autopilot. The plan requires some planning, a little implementation, and then basically you never have to think about it again. Of course, if your personal style is to spend time researching investments and plotting your course, you can do so. But an Armchair Millionaire's plan works reliably and on its own while you sleep, when you're on vacation—all the time. You don't ever have to break a sweat. Just sit back and relax. Once you master the basic skills and disciplines—emotional and intellectual—that you need to build wealth, then you can use the twin levers of short-term desires vs. long-term gains to build your portfolio at any pace you want. So every Armchair Millionaire is . . .

Someone with a Portfolio
There's one last thing that any Armchair Millionaire will eventually have. It's the inevitable result of a lifetime investing program: a seven-figure portfolio.

What an Armchair Millionaire Is Not
Okay, so now you know more about what an Armchair Millionaire is. Here's a brief rundown on the things an Armchair Millionaire is not:

One thing that all Armchair Millionaires are not is perfect. When we asked our community members if they live below their means, only half said they do. If you're thinking that you lack the discipline to become an Armchair Millionaire, think again. Just starting to sort out your financial life is enough to designate you an Armchair Millionaire.

Armchair Millionaire Member Poll
Do you live below your means?
50% yes   30% no   20% sometimes

A Cheapskate
Yes, it's true that the less money you spend, the more money you'll have. But that doesn't mean you have to deny yourself anything that could be construed as a luxury. After all, it isn't unreasonable to want

to enjoy the well-deserved fruits of your labors. Modern life is demanding and we all deserve to pamper ourselves now and again. What you'll learn as you develop your plan is that you can create a personalized balance between short-term desires—such as the desire for an expensive cup of coffee, or a cushy new couch—and long-term goals, such as financial freedom. This balance will decide how fast your portfolio will grow. So you can still be an Armchair Millionaire and spend money on nonessential items; you'll just take a little longer to reach your goal. The choice is entirely up to you. If you're deep in debt as you read this, your story may be a little different—but we'll cover that shortly.

An Extravagant Spender

When you hear the word *millionaire*, chances are you imagine someone with deep pockets, eating fancy dinners, ordering custom-made shirts, and flying on the Concorde for dinner in Paris. In other words, someone who never worries about money.

This image of a millionaire is so firmly entrenched in American mythology that it's hard to shake. But as we've said before, even millionaires can spend their way into the poorhouse. The first way to become an Armchair Millionaire is to curb your frivolous spending. But before you panic and say you'll never be able to do it, please finish reading this book. The Armchair Millionaire Five Steps to Financial Freedom can help you overcome your preconceived notions about money and build a commonsense savings plan that will make you rich. In other words, you'll learn how to make money work for you, not against you.

> "The most popular watch among millionaires is a Seiko, a fine timepiece, moderately priced. This is also the most popular brand among CEOs of Fortune 500 companies."
> —From *The Millionaire Next Door*
> Bet you were expecting a Rolex, weren't you?

Someone with a Perfect Credit Report

Many Armchair Millionaires were once in debt. And they never want to be there again. Some have never been in debt, because the idea of owing just isn't for them. Still others are digging themselves out of the hole one bill at a time. As far as being an Armchair Millionaire is concerned, where you are when you start isn't important—it's where you're headed that matters.

The real beauty of the Armchair Millionaire's plan to help you achieve financial freedom is that it can work for anyone. So take a deep breath and repeat after us: "I'm ready to be a millionaire!" And turn to the next chapter. . . .

CHAPTER 2

Financial Freedom Can Be Yours

What Have You Heard in the Past About Making Money?

When you close your eyes and imagine what a successful investor looks like, what do you see? A man in a business suit chomping a cigar behind an impressive desk? A frenzied person on the floor of a stock exchange, motioning wildly and screaming "Buy!"? A genteel woman going about her daily business while her broker handles all her financial affairs behind the scenes?

There are many preconceived notions associated with investing. Mainly, that you have to be classy, smart, and wealthy, and either have a lot of time to monitor your portfolio constantly, or a near-genius broker to do all your legwork for you.

Would you believe that none of these notions is even the slightest bit true?

Wall Street is shrouded in myth and secrecy. It can seem that the only way you'll make money is if you've got "insider information" or a "hot tip." Well, friends, huddle up and get ready to hear a white-hot tip about making it in the market: You can be a complete schlub, never get out of your jammies, and still rake in the money. You can have only $100 a month to invest. You can be completely ignorant about complicated investment theories. You can be stranded on a desert island. But the point is, you (yes, you!) can achieve all your financial dreams.

Want to see what a successful investor looks like? Try picking up a mirror.

There are any number of ways you can rationalize to yourself that investing just isn't for you. But the fact is, no one else cares as much about your financial security as you do. So no one is better suited to make it happen than you are. Because if you don't take care of your own portfolio, chances are you won't have one. There's no need to panic. You can do this.

The fact of the matter is, investing and personal finance are rarely explained and taught in the real world—not in schools, not at the family dinner table, and certainly not among friends. This lack of discussion creates a situation in which the average person assumes that investing must be so difficult that it is out of his or her reach. Here, two Armchair Millionaire members talk about investing ignorance and how to get over it.

Are We Pathetic?

Q: "My husband and I are, I think, educated, intelligent people, except when it comes to money. We have close to $50,000 in a checking account, because we don't know what to do with it, or how, so we just leave it there. I am almost ashamed to admit this—who on earth doesn't know how to invest money? Is this a common problem, or so pathetic it doesn't warrant a reply?"

—Armchair Millionaire member Judi33

Start with a Change in Perception

A: "Investing money is like any other skill—it has to be learned. Many of us find that while we are growing up, money is presented to us as a substitute or symbol for all kinds of things, especially personal worth. We are made to feel guilty or greedy if we pay too much attention to it, and too stupid to understand all the complexities of managing it if we don't [pay enough attention to it]. In reality, money is a tool to express our values and what we want to do with our lives. Once you realize that, then all the rest of this starts to make sense. Congratulations on getting started."

—Armchair Millionaire member Jones_Ch

What You Will Learn in This Book

The best thing you could do to start your new life as an investor is to take all the ideas you have about investing and throw them right out the window. What you'll come to understand as you read this book is that investing is not only easy, it's boring. Kind of like brushing your teeth. Once you figured out how to brush your teeth, you never thought much about it again, did you? But you still brush every day, right? (If you answered "No," that's okay—your Armchair Millionaire portfolio will grow even on those days when you don't brush your teeth.)

MEET RICH

Rich is the official mascot of ArmchairMillionaire.com on the World Wide Web. Don't let appearances deceive you, though—Rich is much more than just a two-dimensional cartoon character. Throughout this book (as well as on ArmchairMillionaire.com), you'll occasionally find Rich explaining basic concepts of personal finance. He'll help to describe some of the strategies that lie behind the Armchair Millionaire philosophy. Above all, Rich is

here to remind you that saving and investing don't have to be
complicated.

So how is it possible that everything you've learned about the
stock market is wrong? The Armchair Millionaire Five Steps to
Financial Freedom are designed to alleviate all your worries about
investing as well as help you build a seven-figure portfolio. Here are
some of the mondo-sized myths that Armchair Millionaires tell us
they used to hold to be true, lock, stock, and barrel (before they saw
the light, of course).

BIG MYTH NO. 1:
You have to have money to make money.

REALITY CHECK: Well, of course you have to start with some
amount of money. But it's never too early to start saving, even if it's
$25 per paycheck. The thing about money you invest is that it grows.
Over time, it begins to grow upon itself so no matter how much you
start with, you're going to end up with a lot more.

Sure, there are lots of planners who won't accept a client unless
she has thousands and thousands of dollars. Many brokerage firms
require an initial minimum investment of $1,000 or more. Some
mutual funds make you invest up to $10,000 or more in order to
open an account!

But just because some companies cater to people who already
have money doesn't mean that they all do. In fact, you can start your
saving and investing plan with less than the cost of this book. There
are mutual funds that will accept an initial investment of $25 or less.
There are brokers with whom you can open an account with no minimum investment. (For a complete list of such funds and brokers,
refer to the Appendices B and C.) Armchair Millionaires know that
it doesn't require a fortune to get started investing. When you make
yourself a priority, it's just a matter of time.

BIG MYTH NO. 2:

You have to have a lot of time to invest wisely.

REALITY CHECK: Once you've set up your portfolio—a process we'll cover soon enough—*you don't have to do anything else*. Except watch your money grow. Instead of sweating over stock reports, take up a fulfilling hobby. Knowing that you've got your finances in order is probably going to give you a greater sense of well-being, and you're going to need an outlet to let all those good feelings flow. Catch up on all the letters you've meant to write but haven't. Volunteer some time at the hospital, or learn to tap dance.

Of course, if you're in need of a hobby, then learning how to analyze stocks might be a good one. Most hobbies can end up costing you a bundle, but investing in stocks is a hobby that can potentially make you money. But this book isn't about that—we're only going to cover how to build your core portfolio using the Armchair Millionaire's approach to investing. Researching and investing in individual stocks would be a separate piece of your overall investment strategy, and entirely optional.

When you invest as an Armchair Millionaire, time actually becomes your friend, allowing your money to grow exponentially. We'll talk more about that in Chapter 9, "Start Today—Put the Power of Compound Interest to Work for You."

BIG MYTH NO. 3:

You need a degree in business, or you must be a math whiz, or you should be able to understand complicated formulas in order to be a successful investor.

REALITY CHECK: While we said that you could become an Armchair Millionaire without the aid of a professional, it's also true that you don't need any special knowledge of math or business. You won't need any of the algebra you've forgotten since high school. You won't need to take accounting classes at night, or even know how to use a computer if you don't want to (although we believe this book will make a case for how using a computer to tap into a community of like-minded investors can enhance your investing experience).

A friend of ours likes to tell a story about how he nearly didn't graduate from high school because of a mishap in calculus class. Two terms of failing grades meant that he needed to pass the final in order to pass the class, and he needed to pass the class in order to have enough credits to graduate. On the final, he achieved a D⁻ (whether through study, luck, or the teacher's sympathy he'll never know) and proceeded to graduate on schedule.

His bad math experience behind him, our friend successfully completed a liberal arts education, and never took another mathematics course in his four years of college. He embarked on a career in the performing arts, and later took up investing for his retirement and to support his growing family. And you know what? His mathphobia hasn't impeded his investing success whatsoever. His portfolio continues to chug right along—because he invests sensibly as an Armchair Millionaire, and not strictly by the numbers.

Contrary to popular belief, complexity is not a necessary component of a financial plan. Once you understand how the market works—and you will, after you read Chapter 8, "Use the Armchair Investing Strategy"—you'll see that the simplest investment plans are best. So you can earn just as high a rate of return as the most famous investment gurus. And you don't have to pay anyone else to make your portfolio decisions for you.

BIG MYTH NO. 4:

Once you hit it big in the markets, you will have a wonderful, extravagant life and nothing bad will ever happen to you again.

REALITY CHECK: Financial security is a beautiful thing, but it's not going to make you a fairy princess or a movie star. You will achieve financial security through common sense and a serious—though low-maintenance—commitment to financial responsibility. If, once you achieve the portfolio of your dreams, you forget about common sense and commitment and start spending money willy-nilly, you will lose it. Money can help us live the lives we want to lead, but it can't fix all of our problems.

BIG MYTH NO. 5:

It's too hard to figure out how the stock market works.

REALITY CHECK: The stock market in the United States is actually older than our country itself. The New York Stock Exchange, the largest stock exchange in the world, began in downtown Manhattan in the early 1700s when a bunch of guys stood around on a street corner buying and selling pieces of paper. These pages represented shares in companies, and the price of each share was set by negotiation between the buyer and the seller. Pretty simple!

Believe it or not, the stock market today works exactly the same way. Of course, today we have brokers and computers and big investment banks who buy and sell millions of shares each day, but the price of each trade is determined by the negotiation between the buyer and the seller. Sure, you could delve into the details of how the market works, from the operations of an auction exchange to learning the intricate hand signals used by traders on the trading floor. But just as you don't need to be trained as a gourmet chef in order to appreciate a fabulous meal at a four-star restaurant, understanding the intricacies of the stock market isn't a prerequisite for becoming a successful investor.

In fact, the single most important thing you need to know about the stock market can be summed up in a few words: It goes up over the long term. In the history of the modern stock market, it's easy to see that the market goes up in seven out of every ten years. Sure, it goes down, too—the market has declined 10 percent or more fifty-three times since 1900. You can expect the stock market to see a drop of 10 percent or more every two years, on average. And the market has seen declines greater than 25 percent fifteen times in the past one hundred years, or an average of once every six years.

But here's the key: The market has a 100 percent success rate in bouncing back every single time it has fallen—if you just give it enough time. With odds like those, what more do you need to know about how the market works?

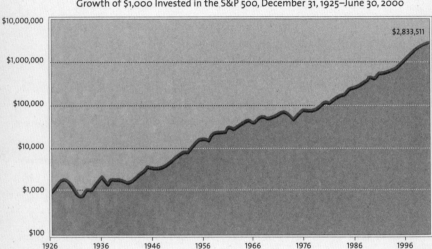

Growth of $1,000 Invested in the S&P 500, December 31, 1925–June 30, 2000

BIG MYTH NO. 6:

If you want to be a successful investor, you have to stay on top of the market each day.

REALITY CHECK: Chances are that you can turn on the television right now and have your choice of several financial television programs or entire channels devoted to money. There are thousands of Web sites devoted to the topic of investing. In New York City, there's even a radio station that exclusively broadcasts business and investing news twenty-four hours a day. It's easy to succumb to the belief that you *need* to be on top of every blip in the market, that you can't afford to miss any piece of news that might affect your portfolio.

We believe that the information revolution has brought great things to our world. You can tune in to TV stations, radio programs, and Web sites from all over the world, and learn new things and be introduced to new cultures. Unfortunately, the sheer amount of information that's constantly bombarding us presents another problem: How do we figure out what's important when we try to take in all this information?

There's a term that Armchair Millionaires use when describing information overload: "noise." Nearly all of the "news" that we hear on a daily basis is absolutely useless in managing a sensible long-term financial plan. And investors who listen to this noise and try to react quickly will nearly always find that they lose out. There are hyperactive traders, including day traders, who are equipped to profit from all the bouncing around the stock market may do in the short term. Day traders try to capitalize on ultra-short-term gyrations in the market by making big bets on where a stock is headed in the next few minutes. It's fruitless for most individual investors to try to focus on active trading strategies such as these, for a couple of reasons. Most of us just can't spend hours a day glued to our computer monitors— we have jobs to do! And taxes and commissions take away big chunks of any profits that you might make as a hyperactive trader.

The Armchair Millionaire's plan for financial success doesn't require you to pay any attention whatsoever to the daily influx of "news" and information you may hear or read about the markets. You can safely ignore your portfolio for months and still be successful! In these busy times, don't you have better things to do than try to outfox the pros? Especially when the odds are stacked against you if you do try.

BIG MYTH NO. 7:

You're better off working with a stockbroker or financial advisor than trying to invest yourself.

REALITY CHECK: Let's just get this out of the way right now: There are plenty of people who can benefit from the services of a smart and sensible broker or financial advisor. If you've got lots and lots of money, or have a lot of your net worth tied up in your own business, or have some other particularly complicated financial situation, then you should find a good financial planner—and pronto. Planners often provide important services such as tax planning, estate planning, and life insurance evaluations, and the good ones can even help you build a portfolio that's profitable.

But one of the financial industry's dirty little secrets is that most pros can't even beat the market averages, so don't expect your broker to have the inside track to investing success. There's a classic investing book from the 1930s, *Where Are the Customers' Yachts?*, that takes its title from a visit the book's author made to a Manhattan yacht club with the president of an investment firm. The esteemed financier was pointing out all the yachts that belonged to partners in the firm, obvious symbols of their success. The young author's response upon seeing these expensive toys was, "Where are the customers' yachts?" This is a not-so-subtle reminder that financial professionals don't necessarily generate their personal wealth from their investing prowess, but from what they're paid by their clients.

If you're the type of person who tries to fix the leak yourself before calling the plumber, then you can be a successful investor *without* a broker. You'll be no better or worse off than someone in your same situation who hired a planner—and chances are good that you'll come out ahead since you'll save on fees and commissions.

The Armchair Millionaire's financial freedom plan is one that you can implement all by yourself, without professional assistance.

BIG MYTH NO. 8:
Rich people are the only people who have the connections and the resources needed to invest successfully in the stock market.

REALITY CHECK: One Armchair Millionaire member, Candis K., said it best: "The market doesn't care about the color of my skin, my ethnic background, my weight, my clothes, how much money I have, or whether I even have a college or high school degree." Here's a little mathematics quiz to prove the point (yeah, we know we said you wouldn't have to know much math, but don't worry, this isn't too hard):

Which investor had a greater return—the one who invested $1,000,000 and made a profit of $100,000, or the one who invested $100 and made a profit of $15?

Sure, $100,000 is a heckuva lot bigger than $15, but that $100,000 is only a 10 percent return on the million-dollar investment. On the other hand, $15 is a 15 percent return on an investment of $100. That's 50 percent better than the million-dollar investor did. In dollar terms, there's a big difference, but in percentage terms, the smaller investor did better.

So, don't worry about the size of your portfolio, or how much you can afford to invest. You don't have to be a millionaire to invest like one, and chances are you'll eventually end up a millionaire yourself if you follow our advice. Remember, it's not how much you start out with, it's how much you end up with.

BIG MYTH NO. 9:
Saving money is too hard.

REALITY CHECK: Lots of things in life are hard. Climbing Mount Everest is hard. Programming a VCR is hard. Saving money, though, *isn't* hard—once you know the secret.

So what's the secret? Too many people think of savings as what's left over after you pay for all the essentials in life—things like food, drink, clothes, and shelter. The truth is, budgeting is nearly impossible to do successfully—if you wait until you've paid all your expenses to save money, chances are there won't be any cash left to save. Every month, unexpected expenses can arise, whether it's new tires or a shoe sale. And then, poof! Your budget is shot.

Later on in this book, you'll find out how to start a savings plan that takes care of itself once and for all just as soon as you get it started. It comes down to this: Stop thinking about ways to build your net worth, and just get started.

BIG MYTH NO. 10:
Since the stock market can crash at any time, it's best to avoid it altogether.

REALITY CHECK: There are two truths about the stock market: It goes down and it goes up. Sometimes it booms, and sometimes it crashes. But see BIG MYTH NO. 5—the market *always* recovers, over time.

This simple bit of knowledge can fortify you to withstand any downturns as long as you have time as your ally. If you don't have five years or more until you need the money that you've invested, then you'll take other measures, including keeping some of your money out of the market. But for long-term investing, you simply can't beat the stock market.

People who avoid the stock market for this reason have a big misunderstanding about how "risk" and "reward" work when it comes to investing. Any time you invest, even if it's in a bank savings account, you put your money at risk. But the good thing about risk is that as you increase the risk you're willing to take on, you have the potential to receive better returns on your investment.

Academic researchers have discovered that in order to obtain the highest rate of return on your portfolio, you need to be invested in the stock market. And if you have the power of time on your side, you can invest 100 percent of your portfolio in stocks. A portfolio that only includes stocks may go up and down in value more than a portfolio that might include bonds and/or cash, but over the long term it grows more and faster than other assets, such as bonds, CDs, or real estate. If you want to become an Armchair Millionaire, you need to invest in the stock market. Period.

BIG MYTH NO. 11:

You can make lots of money fast in the stock market—if you know the secrets.

REALITY CHECK: Thomas O'Hara, Chairman of the National Association of Investors Corp. (NAIC), a leading investor education group in the United States, likes to say that "if there was a secret way to quickly achieve wealth, wouldn't someone have figured it out by now and wouldn't the U.S. be a country of millionaires?"

The truth is, the biggest secret about the stock market is that there are no secrets. There's nothing new about the Armchair Millionaire's plan to help you achieve financial freedom—no previously undisclosed strategy or recent academic discovery that's changed the world of finance. In fact, many professional financial advisors and institutional investors use the Armchair Millionaire approach to investing. But no one has brought together all of these steps in such a sensible, easy-to-implement way. Until now.

It is possible for the average person to get a grip on their finances. And the best part is, you don't have to do it alone. There are thousands of other Armchair Millionaires who are making their financial security a reality, one year at a time.

The Gallery of Armchair Millionaires

Meet Candis—Suburban Housewife and Investor Extraordinaire

Get ready to meet a real live member of the Armchair Millionaire community. She didn't know much about investing when she started out. She had been discouraged by brokers. But now she's right on track to retire in fifteen years.

Armchair Millionaire Member Name: Candis
From: Michigan
Age: 46
Occupation: Queen of Domestic Chaos, Liege of the Laundry Room, Kid Wrangler. (I used to be in sales, I now teach National Association of Investors stock selection classes on a volunteer basis through the local adult education program.)
Family Status: Married with two children
Financial Goals: To be able to retire (extremely, very, lazily) comfortably in fifteen years or fewer. I also want to be able to afford to send my boys to Harvard if they choose to go.

What got you started investing?
I became disgusted and frustrated with:

1. The lousy rate of interest from passbook savings.
2. The lousy advice and treatment I received from a stockbroker when I was in my twenties and wanted to invest $700. He said, and I quote, "You don't have enough money to invest." This was around 1975. If I had invested that $700 in stocks then ... twenty-two years later ... *sigh*.
3. After some experiences I had, in addition to those mentioned above, I realized that stockbrokers were not my friends, no matter how much I paid them, and that I had best just learn how to invest because no one cared more about my future than I did.

What were your misconceptions about investing before you started?
That I had to stay glued to the television or ticker tape to be able to make a profit in the market. I remember when I was pregnant with my first child and I was learning, really learning, about the market at the same time; I would sit on the couch and watch the ticker tape on the telly for hours on end, convinced that an eighth or a quarter of a point would make a big difference in my financial future twenty years hence. Of course the fact that I was pregnant, full of those

wonderful things called pregnancy hormones, didn't help the clarity of my thought a great deal.

Biggest investment blunder you've made?
Selling Sun Microsystems after I had tripled my money in it. That was two splits ago. I paid $3,900 for it less than ten years ago. I sold it for $12,000. It would be worth $84,000 now had I kept it. (Sob, sob, sob, sob, boo hoo!)

What did you learn from this blunder?
Never, and I mean never, sell a stock if the fundamentals say "hold." I listened to the talking heads on the television nattering on about doomsday scenarios for the stock. Trust yourself—look at the fundamentals of the company and if the talking heads say "sell," don't sell the stock, buy more.

What do you want the world to know about investing?
You can do it! It is not rocket science. Heck, you just need to be able to do fifth grade math, and if you can afford a cheap calculator, you don't even need to know how to do the math. You just need to be able to listen with both ears, study with both eyes, and use your one brain. If you can follow a cookie recipe, you have all the skills you need to invest in the stock market successfully.

Get Ready for a Fantastic Voyage

You have a great journey ahead of you on the road to financial freedom. Some of it will be hard, but for the most part, it's ridiculously easy. And with just a small amount of determination and open-mindedness, the hard parts won't be hard at all.

Just as with any new undertaking—such as, say, learning to ski—the first few steps toward implementing a financial plan can be scary.

The first time you take a little chunk of your paycheck and stash it away in an investing account, it might seem like there's no way you'll make it to the next payday.

The emphasis on that last sentence is on the word *seem*, because once you make it to that next payday, you'll realize that "paying yourself first" is not only good for you, it's relatively painless and richly rewarding.

Getting your financial plan in motion may be two of the hardest things you've ever done on a voluntary basis. But once you get started, it's all downhill from there (and that goes for skiing too!). Imagine the day, a year from now, when you check the balance in your investment account and see that your money has grown without any mental anguish or effort on your part. You'll find that you are well on your way to making a down payment on a house, sending your kids to college, or financing that trip around the world you've always fantasized about.

Can't you just see yourself in a beautiful home, with a lot of money in the bank? (Or insert your own goal here.) Just by reading this book, you're already on your way.

ADVICE FROM RICH

It doesn't pay to put off starting your saving and investing plan, even for only one year. If you start today and invest $100 a month in a portfolio that gives you an average return of 10 percent a year, you'll have $72,399 in twenty years, tripling your total investment of $24,000.

However, if you put off starting for another five years, and then invest $100 a month for fifteen years, you'll end up with just $40,162, a bit more than double your total investment of $18,000. It doesn't take a math whiz to see that ending up with $72,399 (three times your initial investment) is more attractive—a lot more attractive—than just barely doubling your investment and ending up with $40,162.

But what if you wait until one year from now to start your plan? In nineteen years, you'd have $64,668. Not too shabby, but significantly less than $72,399. To be exact, the penalty for waiting one year turns out to be $6,531. When was the last time you turned down a gift of $6,531?

Chapter 2 Action Items

Before you start your full-fledged plan, it's important to make sure what your goals are. This chapter should help you see that financial freedom is possible. Chapter 3 can help you get your head and heart straight to define those goals, and to give you the wherewithal to achieve them.

- Think about what stereotypes you associate with successful investors. Then forget them.
- Read Chapter 3.

Preparing Your Head and Heart for Achieving Financial Success

Are you ready—really ready—to become a millionaire? You can have all the knowledge in the world about investing, but if you don't have the right frame of mind for success, you're likely to end up making the same mistakes over and over again.

Let's face it—resolving to invest for your future is one of the most "grown-up" decisions you'll ever make, no matter how old or young you are. In the face of all the conflicting information you may see and hear from friends and colleagues, in the media, and even from financial professionals, you might feel like you're back in grade school trying to learn how to write letter *E*'s that aren't backward.

One of the reasons that investing seems like such a "grown-up" activity is that you have to be eighteen years old before you can legally own stocks or mutual funds (you can start investing before that age, you'll just need a custodian to oversee your account). Add this to the list of life's little ironies: You can legally drive a one-ton mass of steel, aluminum, chrome, and rubber at 65 miles an hour down an interstate highway years before you can legally own a share of stock.

But the real reason investing is a grown-up decision is because it means assessing your goals, analyzing your current status, and formulating a plan that will turn your goals into a reality. You're going to have to use both parts of your brain—the rational half to determine your steps, and the emotional half to give yourself the resolve to take those steps. This is not necessarily hard to do, but it is big. Not quite as big as having a baby, but definitely bigger than switching long-distance carriers.

What will have to happen in order to make you fully committed to starting an investment plan? It varies from person to person. For one Armchair Millionaire, sitting down to define her goals with her husband helped her see the light. For another, it took tracking every little expense to see exactly where her money was going. Here and on the next pages, Armchair Millionaires talk about what gives them the resolve they need to take control of their financial lives.

We are going to do it!
"My husband and I together have over $50,000 in debt. We both make relatively good money, but the burden of these debts is almost unbearable. We sat down last night and really assessed our goals. We want to be homeowners. We want enough land to have a healthy garden. We want dogs and cats. We want to be able to live on one income when we decide to have little ones. We want to travel before we have these kids. All of this takes patience and saving and good habits.

"We are learning now, at a young age, that anything worth having requires patience and saving. So often we buy things to appease our urges for instant gratification. It feels good for a few minutes, but then the weight of knowing that money could be better spent paying off a card or going into a savings account sinks in. Ugh. That is an awful feeling."

—Armchair Millionaire member ali_w

Armchair Millionaires realize that they can bring together both sides of their brains into the process of carrying out a sensible saving and investing plan. They let their dreams and goals empower their path to success (as defined by having an investment plan that provides them with more money than they need to survive), tempered with realism and a good dose of skepticism.

If It Isn't Hard, Why Doesn't Everyone Invest?

Investing seems intimidating until you've done it the first time. Many people get nervous about the prospect of buying their first car or house, applying for that first mortgage or car loan, filing their first tax return, getting their first job. After the initial haze of the experience clears, they have a better idea of what to expect the next time.

But unlike tax returns and mortgages, investing doesn't have a deadline, making it seem easy to put off. How many times have you said, "Next year, I'm really going to get my finances in order"? But the sooner you invest, the more time your money has to grow. Starting today versus starting next year can have a big impact on your future financial situation.

But before you start thinking that you've already waited too long and all hope is lost, remember that whenever you set out toward financial freedom for the first time, your age doesn't matter. You could be a thirty-year-old entrepreneur, a twenty-two-year-old college grad, or a sixty-five-year-old retiree—the decision to work toward financial freedom means taking personal responsibility. It means taking positive action to meet your goals. It means acting like a "grown-up."

Once you get going, it's important that you are comfortable with your investment plan. If you wake up in the middle of the night in a cold sweat because you're worried about your portfolio, you've got a problem. If you're biting your fingernails to the quick because you're worried that you might be missing out on the stock market's big moves, you've also got a problem. The trouble may be with your plan, or it may be that you're just not clear about your financial goals and how you'll reach them. Either way, you need to get intimate with your investing plan. Take the time to snuggle up with your portfolio. Unburden all your personal secrets. Become good friends. Because if you're not 100 percent satisfied with your personal financial plan, it just isn't going to work.

ADVICE FROM RICH

Don't confuse skepticism with cynicism. It's good to use a bit of restraint and caution when it comes to investing. When we were kids, we were taught never to jump into a lake or swimming pool until we knew how deep or shallow the water was, and what might be lurking beneath the surface. Likewise, you should never, ever invest in anything that you don't understand until you know all the risks and the potential rewards and the most likely outcome.

Investing is a lot like an important relationship. Your investing plan and your relationships will both work only if you're willing to stick together through ups and downs, for better and for worse. It's only natural that you may get emotional at times, or that you'll make a stupid mistake, or get caught doing something you shouldn't have done—whether it's forgetting to take out the trash or taking a flier on an IPO you hear about from some broker who calls you up while you're eating dinner. That's when you'll kiss and make up, and move on. It's the grown-up thing to do.

If only it were that easy to separate your emotional attachment to money from what you *know* in your mind is the right thing to do. Unfortunately, we're all human, so it's unreasonable to expect us to act like investing robots. You might misjudge your tolerance for the occasional ups and downs of a portfolio, and react to short-term news when you should be holding on to a long-term vision—even if you know the truth that comes from looking at the facts. Coming to terms with your own ability to make mistakes requires a great deal of maturity. The better you know yourself and your own bad habits, the more successful you'll be.

So, are you ready for a system of saving and investing that:

- Is easy to implement?
- Is easy to understand?
- Makes sense to you?
- Empowers you?
- And best of all, will make you rich?

Then read on!

Regaining Control of My Money!

"I can identify with anyone who has a feeling of desperation about their finances. I was in the same boat until a friend advised that I take control of my money and gave me some hints on how to begin. The first thing I needed to do was to see, on paper, how much money was coming in versus how much was going out, and then to track down where any unaccounted-for money was going. These two steps were real eye-openers for me! The first revelation was that I definitely didn't need to be as broke as I was. By beginning to write down every little expense, I have begun to see where the extra spending has caused so many problems for me. Another benefit of writing down each penny spent is that it makes me think twice about spending it—do I really need that magazine just because Brad Pitt is on the cover of it?! From here I hope to establish a firm budget that will help me save for my retirement and my kids' college educations. I had thought that it was too late for either of those things, but now, with a plan in front of me I can see that it can be done."

—Armchair Millionaire member jujubee71

Beginning Your Journey

You wouldn't get into your car and drive across the country on your summer vacation unless you had mastered a few basic skills and had a good idea of where you were going and how you'd get there. For instance, before you back out of the driveway, you need to know:

1. How to drive a car. You don't need to know how a four-stroke engine works, but to be a successful driver you do need to know how to steer, brake, accelerate, and turn.
2. Where you are headed. If you don't know where you're going when you start your trip, you'll never get there—it's guaranteed!
3. How you'll get there. A good road map is essential for a cross-country car trip. You even might map out your route with a highlighter before getting started. Or you might start off with a general sense of how to get to your destination, knowing that you could stop and ask for directions if you really needed to (obviously, if you're a man you'd never do that, but women always see it as a viable option).

Those are the basic requirements for taking a road trip in your car. They're not so different from how you'll go about building your savings and investing plan.

1. You don't need to understand how the stock market works in its most mundane details in order to profit from investing in stocks.
2. You do need to identify the reasons or goals that you're working toward. It could be that you're saving for retirement or college for the kids or a summer home or a boat or to start a business or even to allow you to retire at forty-five. Defining a goal not only gives you something to shoot for, it also determines how much time you have to get there. If you don't have a goal, or if your goal is something vague like "I want to be rich" or "I want to make money fast," chances are you'll never get there.

Some people keep a postcard from a tropical island, or a photo of their dream home tacked up on their refrigerator or bulletin board, just to help keep a mental picture of the goals they're working toward.

3. You need a plan to get you toward your goals. However, you don't have to create a plan that budgets all the fun out of life. There will be detours along the way, but a sound plan will get you to your destination in time.

In order to make the right preparations to make the transformation to an Armchair Millionaire, you need to empty your brain of everything you've ever been told about investing and personal finance. You need to forget everything you've heard on television, everything you've read in financial magazines, every piece of junk mail you've seen that's tried to sell you an investing newsletter, and every Web site that's promised you the secrets to quick wealth. Forget all those infomercials and advertisements.

And while you're reading this book, ignore what your sister-in-law or fishing buddy has told you about hot stock picks. If someone tries to wow you with investing stories at a cocktail party, change the subject to pets, or the weather.

And as you read, every time you hear yourself saying "But . . . ," try keeping your mind (both sides of it) open.

The Last 10 Percent

There's an old saying that "success is 90 percent perspiration and 10 percent inspiration." You can break down successful investing in much the same way. You'll get 90 percent of the way to financial freedom using the knowledge and tools in this book. But the last 10 percent comes from the heart. And that's often the hardest part. Your own bad habits can get in the way. You'll need to stop being afraid of money, and start taking control of your own financial future.

You deserve to feel financially secure, and you are the only person who can make it happen. Don't let that nay-saying voice in your head keep you from investing. Combat that voice by listening to your heart instead.

Simple, but not EASY

"Losing weight is simple: eat less, exercise more. But many of us know, it's not easy. Only when motivation overcomes resistance do we make progress. Likewise, 'spend less, save more' is simple, but not easy. Savor the struggle that will make you stronger. Try to find others who would be interested in forming a support group. Hang in there and make your financial plan work. After all, what's the alternative?"

—Armchair Millionaire member habitatmom

Getting Ready to Be a Successful Investor

To help you start down the road toward becoming an Armchair Millionaire, here are some practical tips.

JOIN AN ONLINE INVESTMENT COMMUNITY, SUCH AS THE ARMCHAIR MILLIONAIRE. There is strength in numbers. On the Armchair Millionaire Web site (http://www.armchairmillionaire.com), you can meet many of the investors profiled in this book, as well as others who are on their own journeys to financial freedom. Chances are that you will meet someone who's in the same place in their life right now as you are, or someone who's been there already and can lend a helping hand. Best of all, everything at the Armchair Millionaire is free.

JOIN OR FORM AN INVESTMENT CLUB. Many investors find that investment clubs are a great way to learn about investing, as well as to invest in the stock market. You could even start one with a few friends and get the support you need to further your investment education.

For more information about investment clubs, contact the National Association of Investors Corp. (NAIC):

NAIC

P.O. Box 220

Royal Oak, MI 48068

877-ASK-NAIC (toll-free)

248-583-NAIC

248-583-4880 (fax)

http://www.better-investing.org

service@better-investing.org

Another resource for investment clubs is a Web site called Investment Club Central. They feature a directory of investment club Web sites, as well as tutorials and articles:

http://www.iclubcentral.com.

REASSURE YOURSELF. If you don't have a computer, yet, get one! But you don't need a computer to get the reassurance you need to get started. Instead, write reassuring notes to yourself and paste them on your bathroom mirror or refrigerator or on top of your checkbook—anyplace where you'll see them regularly. Come up with a few messages that will remind you of your goals, like "I want to retire a millionaire!" or "Pay yourself—you're worth it!" Or tear out a picture of your dream house, or mountain cabin, or your alma mater (where Junior will surely want to matriculate) and tape it up as well. These reminders of your dreams and goals will inspire you to make them come true.

TAKE THE NEXT STEP. We think you're ready now to take the next step toward financial freedom, so turn to the next chapter.

Chapter 3 Action Items

- Make up your mind—the rational half and the emotional half—that financial freedom can be yours.
- Find ways to keep that resolve, either by joining an online investing community, starting an investment club, or writing yourself encouraging notes. Experiment and discover what works best for you.

Dealing with Your Debt

Americans love to borrow money. We've racked up over a trillion dollars in consumer debt in this country, all so we can live in big houses (paid for with 20 percent down and thirty years of paying off the mortgage) and drive big cars (paid for with a four-year auto loan). We can buy anything we want, whether we can afford it or not, just by whipping out a piece of plastic and telling the cashier to "Charge it!" Have you ever seen a commercial for a credit card in which people aren't smiling, laughing, and doing fun things? It's fun to spend when it all just goes on the card!

On second thought, maybe *love* isn't the right word to describe our fatal attraction to borrowed money. Perhaps *obsession* is a better description of the "buy now, pay later" habits of Americans. There was once a time when personal bankruptcy was looked upon with scorn. Now, the stigma is gone, and more people are filing for bankruptcy than ever before. According to the American Bankruptcy Institute, a record number of people, 1,398,182, filed for personal bankruptcy in 1998—an increase of 94.7 percent since 1990. What's worse, some people have made a habit of bankruptcy, spending themselves into an enormous hole, then begging for protection from the bankruptcy courts, only to repeat the whole process all over again.

When You're in Too Deep: The Five Warning Signs
ADVICE FROM RICH

How can you tell when your debt is out of control? Answer the five questions below. If you answered "yes" to any of these questions, you may be losing the credit card battle.

- Do you only make the minimum monthly payment required on your cards?
- Is your credit limit maxed on most of your cards?
- Do you use credit cards for day-to-day purchases like groceries, movie tickets, or fast food?
- Do you use cash advances on one card to pay off another?
- Do you ever make a purchase just to earn frequent flier miles?
- Do you routinely spend more than you earn?

Sure, there's nothing like the feeling you get from whipping out a credit card and taking home that new book or CD or computer gadget. At least, that is, until the bill arrives. It's easy to shake the credit card hangover, though, by making the minimum payment and forgetting about the whole mess until next month, when another bill arrives.

The feeling of despair that comes as you charge down the credit card highway is bad enough. The deeper you fall into debt, the more helpless you feel about ever getting out.

The worst part of this vicious circle, though, is it's downright impossible to save when you're barely making the minimum payments on your credit cards each month. Many wannabe Armchair Millionaires ask "How can I start my saving and investing plan when I'm mired in debt?"

The good news is that it's not impossible. No matter how much debt you have, you *can* get out. If you're in debt over your head, it can certainly *seem* like all your financial goals are way out of reach.

But it's not impossible to reverse directions and get started on the path to financial freedom. And you don't have to be one of those 100 percent debt-free, pay-cash-for-everything superhumans, either. All you need to do is take charge of your personal debts. With the right plan, you can defeat the debt monster while building your nest egg.

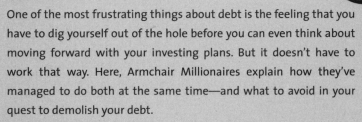

How Armchair Millionaires Save and Pay Off Debts at the Same Time

One of the most frustrating things about debt is the feeling that you have to dig yourself out of the hole before you can even think about moving forward with your investing plans. But it doesn't have to work that way. Here, Armchair Millionaires explain how they've managed to do both at the same time—and what to avoid in your quest to demolish your debt.

Put Your Savings to Work

"My husband and I have a goal to pay off our credit card debt. We have opened a savings account, and every time we have $1,000 accumulated we take $500 and put it toward the credit card. (We have consolidated our debt onto one card.) The 'cushion' $500 is always there in case we have an emergency and that way we should not have to charge anything."

—Armchair Millionaire member dkdk123

What Not to Do

"We just cashed out my husband's 401(k) to pay off debts, and the taxes and penalties killed us! The debt is gone, but now so is every penny we ever saved, and a lot of it we never saw. There's usually a 10–15 percent penalty fee for taking it out before retirement on top of the taxes, so we only saw two-thirds of what was once ours."

—Armchair Millionaire member JacJ.

Of course, if you're truly the type who already pays off your credit card bills each month, and are happy with your current mortgage and auto loan, you can skip this chapter entirely. Otherwise, it's time to get motivated!

From the Armchair Millionaire's Gallery— A Look at Real People Who Really Invest

One feature of the Armchair Millionaire Web site is the Armchair Millionaire's Gallery—where you can meet real people and learn their stories and ideas about investing. Here are two excerpts from Gallery, featuring two people who were once about to tear their hair out over their debts. Not only have these folks been there, but they've managed to pull themselves out of debt and become successful investors. Before you decide there's no way you can ever demolish your debt, read on.

Up from the Depths

Armchair Millionaire Member Name: Steve J.

From: Florida

Age: 33

Occupation: Medically retired military personnel

Family Status: Married with children

Investment Goals: To enjoy a comfortable retirement and to be able to handle emergencies in the meantime.

Background: I have a chronic disease, and due to medical bills, I lost everything that I had—I even lived in my car at one point. But I have worked my way back up to a point where I'm seeing the benefits of saving and investing and will continue until I reach my goal! My wife and I always used to spend all of our money, until we started having money automatically deducted from our checking account and added to our investment account. It took me a long time to get smart about money because I was always trying to keep up with my neighbors in having the newest, most expensive of everything. I spent it all. Now my wife and I discuss our investments for all of our goals. We do it as a team. We just didn't realize that a little financial planning goes a long way. Now I'm teaching my kids to start saving every month, and how to compare prices, and shop clearance.

Just Starting Out

Armchair Millionaire Member Name: Nondas S.

From: New York

Age: 32

Occupation: Administrative assistant

Family Status: Divorced

Investment Goals: To pay for son's college education, stay out of debt, and have money to retire.

Background: No one in my family saves. They are into buying the most expensive clothes and jewelry. I used to have huge credit card bills, then I lost my job and couldn't pay any creditors, much less put savings in the bank. I thought because I had so little money I couldn't start my financial plan. Now I go to the 99-cent stores and always buy things on sale. I contribute to my 401(k) at work and my company matches the funds and now I take $1,000 a month and put it in savings to invest. I have only started to work toward my goals, and I wish I had more time to follow my portfolio. But I am on the right track, and that feels good.

Putting Your "Defeat Your Debt" Plan into Place

One piece of advice that's often given to debt-laden investors is to pay down *all* your debts before you start saving. The rationale for this bit of wisdom is that paying off a credit card that charges you an interest rate of 18 percent is like getting a guaranteed rate of return of 18 percent on your money. That's a better return than you'll get on just about any investment.

It sure sounds like a good deal. But the success of this approach depends on a complete and total change of your money behavior patterns. If you could eliminate your bad habits that quickly, you probably wouldn't be in such bad shape in the first place!

The Armchair Millionaire approach to paying down your debt is both practical and effective. You can put your plan into effect using our arsenal of five "Debt Busters." They'll take some work (and some time), but the rewards will be more than worth it. By sticking to the plan, you *will* become debt free, and you will get your saving and investing plan started, as well.

DEBT BUSTER #1: KNOW YOUR ENEMY. Before you begin the battle, you have to know what you're up against. And that means getting intimate with your credit cards, loans, and any other debts.

How much do you really know about your debts? Without looking, can you name all the credit cards in your wallet or pocketbook, and the interest rate each one charges? Do you know the balances you're carrying from month to month? And do you even know what a "grace period" is, not to mention how long it is for each of your credit cards? How much of your auto loan payment goes to interest and how much actually pays for your car?

It's pretty easy to get to know more about all your debts. All you need to do is make a list. You can use the worksheet in the sidebar on pages 44–45 to help you get organized.

Debt Buster #1 in Practice—Tips for Dealing with the Day of Reckoning

Think you can skip this step? Think again. Here, two Armchair Millionaires talk about how important it was to take stock of their debt.

The Debt Hit List
"My husband is a spender—he never met a new gizmo or gadget he didn't feel he needed to have and saving was a totally foreign concept

to him. I, on the other hand, am a saver and can pinch a penny until it begs for mercy. I handle all the finances, and I would feel guilty if I had to tell him, 'No, we can't afford it,' or 'Money is tight.' But I was about to tear my hair out, because I would pay off a bill only to find out he'd charged it back up again.

"To finally get him to participate and pay attention, I made up a 'Debt Hit List.' I listed all the debts, balances, monthly payments, and interest rates. I wrote down everything, even mortgage and utilities. I also included income compared to expenses. Then I showed him the list. He was in absolute and total shock and finally understood why there was no cash flow. He finally turned over all his credit cards, and with his newfound cooperation we were finally able to make progress. Last year we paid off eleven debts in twelve months and this year we have paid off six. We now have cash flow and he is much better about his spending habits. It just took the shock of it all in black and white to wake him up. I wish I had thought of the hit list idea five years ago."

—Armchair Millionaire member debsan

Psych Yourself Up

"I started reducing my debt by writing down everything I owe. When I did it, I was appalled at my situation. It helped me realize that I will never learn to be responsible for my finances if I don't act. I got myself in this mess. I will feel so proud and accomplished once I get myself out of it."

—Armchair Millionaire member MsJoeCool

Now, gather up all your credit card statements for the past few months, your car loan, student loan, and mortgage payment books, and any other related paperwork. Make a list of all your debts, including the balance of each debt, the minimum payment due right now, and the interest rate.

If you're unsure of any of these items, call the toll-free number that you'll find on your statement to get all the information.

Have you ever seen your own credit report? For a serious reality check, you might want to get a copy of the information that's been reported by credit card companies to various credit reporting companies. If you've been having trouble making payments on time, or have built up a mountain of debt, it could be sobering to see it all on paper in black and white. Some Armchair Millionaires get really motivated after they've seen the hard evidence of overspending.

It typically costs about $8 to get a copy of your report from one of the major agencies, and you can get one free if you've been denied credit for any reason. For more information, or to order a copy of your report, contact one of these agencies:

Experian
P.O. Box 2104
Allen, TX 75013-2104
888-EXPERIAN
http://www.experian.com

Equifax
P.O. Box 740241
Atlanta, GA 30374-0241
800-685-1111
http://www.equifax.com

Trans Union
P. O. Box 403
Springfield, PA 19064
800-888-4213
http://www.transunion.com

Another good resource for information on obtaining and understanding credit reports is available on the Quicken.com Web site:
http://www.quicken.com/banking_and_credit/credit_reports

Why is this step so important? You won't win this battle unless you know exactly what you're up against. Besides giving you a baseline reading of your personal debt situation, this information will be essential for planning your investing strategy.

One more note: This is a time of reckoning, so try to be completely and totally honest with yourself.

Defeat Your Debt Worksheet

Go ahead—write in this book! This isn't second grade, so there's no teacher to reprimand you. If you'd like, go ahead and make a copy of this page (you might need more than one), or recreate it with a spreadsheet program in your computer. Then, gather up those monthly statements, and fill out this form. You'll use this list later during Step 6 to help plan your strategy.

DEBT NAME: Credit Cards, Loans, etc.	CURRENT BALANCE	MINIMUM PAYMENT: Monthly	INTEREST %	COMPANY INFO
Visa	$5,000	$125.00	13.9%	MBNA VISA 123 Debtfree Way Wilmington, DE 67890 800-800-0000 Acct. # 123-1234-12-1234
Car Loan	$2,250	$300.00	7.7%	ABC FINANCE 456 PayLater St. New York, NY 12345 888-800-0000 Acct. # 123-1234-12-1234

Once you've completed your list, you may find it completely overwhelming. But please don't despair. Standing face to face with the enemy may be intimidating, but it's necessary.

Now let's figure out how to knock this mountain of debt down to size.

DEBT BUSTER #2: INVEST IN YOUR DEBT. If you sit down and add it all up, you'll probably be surprised to realize how much you're paying in interest every year, just from carrying balances on your credit cards from month to month. Starting right now, however, you're going to think about your monthly payments in a different light. Instead of being an albatross around your neck, think of those monthly payments as an investment in your future. We call this "investing in your debt."

Even though it might hurt when you write out that check to the credit card company, you need to speed up repayment of your debts. Figure out how much money you can invest in your debt each month, over and above the regular monthly payments you are making now. It could be a single lump sum payment, or an extra monthly payment on your auto loan or mortgage. Chances are that you'll probably need to make a commitment to paying a higher amount for several months, or even for a year or two. Commit as much as you absolutely can. Even if you can only find an extra $10 a month you will be able to make a difference.

Debt Buster #2 in Action—Making a Molehill out of a Mountain

Here are some ideas from Armchair Millionaires to help make those aggressive payments just a little easier.

The Methodical Method

"After you've come up with your list of debts, pick one card (I usually pick the one with the smallest balance) and concentrate on paying it off. When it is paid off, close it out, and work on the next one. The fewer bills you have coming in, the less stressful it is and the easier it is to keep track of what you owe so you can plan."

—Armchair Millionaire member Kitkatson

Make Your Payments Online

"I have signed up for online bill payment. I've got a lot of debt. I hate paying bills, so I was often late with the payments. Last year I paid almost $600 in late charges alone. Now with the online payments, I just set up recurring payments and all I have to do is log on once in a while and all my credit cards (as well as some of the other bills) are paid."

—Armchair Millionaire member vizsla

Really Assess Your Priorities

"Very often we think about getting out of debt as requiring huge sacrifices—cutting back on things that you enjoy or feel you need. When things feel like a sacrifice, we naturally don't really want to do them. I have found that once I start to think about getting out of debt not as a sacrifice but as a priority, something I truly want to do, the whole picture changes. Suddenly when I choose to not buy something, it doesn't feel like I'm denying myself anything, but instead like I'm investing in myself, and in the dream of being debt-free. I think this attitude shift has really made me feel like I'm much more in control of my debt and my financial future, rather than feeling like a victim."

—Armchair Millionaire member bandl

Why is it important to invest in your debt? If you make only the minimum payments on your cards, your progress on paying them down will be very, very slow and expensive. If you have a $3,000 balance on your credit card and only make the minimum payment of $10 each month (or 2 percent of the total, whichever is higher), it will take you almost thirty-eight years to pay it off! And it will cost you $7,931 just in interest.

DEBT BUSTER #3: LESSEN THE BURDEN. You may have been surprised to see the interest rates charged by your credit cards when you filled out the chart. Credit card companies are great marketers, but you'll never hear one tell you how much one of their "exclusive preapproved titanium" cards will really cost you if you carry a balance from month to month.

But you'd better pay attention to the rates on cards you carry. Just think about that $7,931 you could potentially owe on a $3000 balance with an 18 percent interest rate. If you switch to a card with a 9.9 percent interest rate, you'll pay down the debt three years sooner, and pay just $1,935 in interest—a savings of nearly $6,000.

It just doesn't make sense to carry a balance on a card with a high rate if you can transfer the balance to a card that charges a more reasonable interest rate. You may also be able to consolidate your credit card debts by combining the balances of two or three cards onto a single card with a lower rate.

You may be able to get your credit card company to knock down your interest rate a point or two. How do you get them to do this? Simple—just ask. A phone call to your credit card provider with a request for a lower rate is often all it takes to pay less in interest each month. If you want to find a card with a lower rate, that's pretty easy, too—try using the Web. You can search on the Web for a credit card with the right rate for you:

BankRate.com
11811 U.S. Highway 1
North Palm Beach, FL 33408
561-627-7330
http://www.bankrate.com

BanxQuote
305 Madison Avenue, Suite 5240
New York, NY 10165
212-499-9100
http://www.banx.com

ABC Guides Credit Card Rates Guide
http://www.abcguides.com/creditcards

Also, magazines such as *Money* regularly publish lists of the best credit card rates.

Usually, you apply for a new card with a phone call, or even online. Just remember that card companies sometimes offer a lower "teaser rate" at the beginning, but the rate may balloon to as much as 21 percent after the teaser period ends. As always, check the details before you sign up.

Debt Buster #3 in Action—Minimizing the Credit Card Bite

Credit card companies can be sneaky, but that's no reason not to enlist their help. Below are ideas from the Armchair Millionaire community on using credit card companies to your advantage, as well as some warnings about what to look out for.

It Works!

"I called four creditors today and two of them lowered my interest just because I asked them to."

—Armchair Millionaire member LittleEd

Some Words of Caution

"Once credit card companies catch on that you're paying them down they'll increase your credit line and decrease your minimum payments. Don't fall for it. Once you put your plan together, stick with the original payments. One card chopped my minimum in half! They also happen to be one of my highest interest balances. I just keep jabbing away at it using the same payment amount I started with."

—Armchair Millionaire member gbchriste

Terminate Unnecessary Cards

"You don't have to wait until your card is paid off to close the account. By closing the account, or 'suspending account privileges' as they might say, you still make your payments each month but you won't be able to charge and you won't see a renewal card show up in the mail one day. One less temptation to face! A nice side effect of attempting to close your credit card account might be more favorable terms. When they ask why you are closing, tell them the interest rate is too high. If they transfer you to a special accounts representative, you've got them on the hook. Most likely, they will offer either a permanent or temporary rate reduction. Great! Take the lower rate and cut up your card anyway."

—Armchair Millionaire member cstephenso829

And remember: Signing up for more credit cards doesn't mean that you get to spend more. In fact, you should cut up your old cards right away, and notify the credit card companies that you're canceling your account. Holding on to unused credit cards can limit the amount of credit you can get in the future, and it might make it too easy to succumb to temptation if some big-ticket item catches your eye. One warning is in order: Don't try to do the credit card shuffle. Some people are constantly switching from card to card in search of low rates. When the teaser rate expires, they switch to a new card. If you do this too frequently, the card companies will catch on, and you might find a dark spot on your credit report.

Refinance Your Mortgage

Another strategy for reducing your debt is to refinance your home mortgage. Armchair Millionaire member Marla M. and her husband had an adjustable rate mortgage (commonly known as an ARM) on their South Carolina home. As the name implies, the interest rate on an ARM is adjustable—but you don't get to change the rate, only your bank can. And, as Marla discovered, your bank is likely to raise it at any chance they get.

When Marla purchased her house, her rate was an affordable 6.25 percent. Three years later, her rate had increased to 7.87 percent, significantly increasing her monthly mortgage payments. So she went mortgage shopping. Using the Web, she found a fixed-rate thirty-year mortgage that would lock her in to a 6.87 percent rate.

While that 1 percent difference doesn't sound like much, it came out to $83.33 a month for Marla, a savings that can really add up over the years. Over the thirty-year duration of the loan, the savings will amount to $8,143.

But the really amazing thing about that $83.33 is that it could have a big impact on that monthly house payment. If Marla applied that amount directly to the principle on her home, she could pay off the loan in twenty-two years instead of thirty! An even more exciting prospect is the idea of investing the monthly savings in a long-term saving and investing plan. If Marla invested according to the strategies laid out by the Armchair Millionaire, and can achieve a 10 percent annual return on her portfolio, that $83.33 per month would grow to $173,267 at the end of the thirty years!

Sure, it's a hassle to refinance your mortgage. But when interest rates are low, it can also be a very smart thing to do. You can reduce your overall debt load and free up some cash to pay down other debts, or to save and invest for your future.

Don't Be Driven by Car Loans

The funny thing about buying a new car is that as soon as you drive it off the dealer's lot it becomes a used car. And its value drops by as much as 30 to 40 percent! Meanwhile, you're still facing four years of monthly payments.

Unfortunately, you won't be able to refinance your auto loan like you can with your home mortgage loan. You might be able to make additional payments on the loan, paying it down as quickly as possible.

The real opportunity to save comes when you make the purchase in the first place. There are a few rules that Armchair Millionaires use before making one of the biggest purchases of their lives—an automobile.

- Always buy used. Since a new car becomes used as soon as you buy it, why not just buy a used car at the start? You'll save lots— and you won't have to go so deeply in debt (if at all).
- Go for practicality, not style. That sport utility vehicle may make you feel great, but a sensible sedan will get you to your destination at the same time without burning a hole in your wallet.
- Buy with cash, not with credit (as much as possible). Whenever you are able to save in order to make a big purchase you'll come out far ahead of borrowing.

DEBT BUSTER #4: GIVE UP PLASTIC FOR ONE WEEK—AND FOR GOOD. So the real clincher of this debt-reducing strategy is that once your debt is gone, *you can't go out and rack up new debt.* This is not a one-time deal. Your attitudes about spending have to change. This all sounds very scary, but to get started, all you have to do is give up plastic for one week. Still sound scary? Many Armchair Millionaire members thought so too—they all decided to give up their credit cards for the same week during the "Declare War on Your Debt" Community Challenge. And you know what? Nobody died from a lack of recently charged consumer goods. In fact, a lot of people got really excited about the possibility of life without debt—permanently.

You can try this too. Make a promise to yourself to give up credit cards for one week. Take the cards out of your wallet, and lock them up. Some people put all their credit cards into a bowl of water and then put the bowl in the freezer. Now, if you want to buy something with your card, you really have to think about it while the ice is thawing!

Without easy access to your credit cards, how do your spending habits change? For most people, the realization that you *can* live without credit cards is somewhat shocking, but also a step in the right direction.

Debt Buster #4 in Action—Make Your Experiment a Success

Okay, so you're not carrying around your credit cards. Congratulations! However, there are still other pitfalls to avoid. Here, Armchair Millionaires explain how they've made the most of going without credit.

Beware the Debit Card

"I finally had a lightbulb go on over my head. We stopped using our credit cards some time ago and have been using checks and a debit card for everything. It finally occurred to me that we were having trouble paying the bills, not because we don't make enough money, but because we haven't been careful about where we were spending it. We weren't charging things, but the debit card was a little too convenient. We started figuring out how much money we need to put aside each payday for the bills (including saving) and take out the rest in cash. So after we pay bills, there's not a whole lot of money left each week. That money is used for groceries, entertainment, and miscellaneous expenses. Once the money is gone, it's gone and we have to make do until the next payday. It doesn't leave much room for error, but we have our savings account for backup."

—Armchair Millionaire member lucifie

Eliminate Temptation

"If you can't control yourself at the store, don't go. The more you shop, the more you think you need. Find another source of entertainment. Take pride in going without things; it makes you feel good. You can handle this."

—Armchair Millionaire member judycater

Whatever It Takes

"When I was paying down my credit cards, I would remind myself that credit cards are not our friends. Think of them as little plastic gremlins sitting in your wallet. While you sleep at night those little plastic gremlins come to life with razor-sharp teeth and a huge appetite and gobble up all the cash in your wallet and checkbook. When I kept that image in my mind, it made me think twice about reaching into my wallet to pull out a credit card and charge something. I know it's silly, but it worked for me—I couldn't wait to get those hungry little gremlins out of my wallet."

—Armchair Millionaire member debsan

Once you've learned that you can live without your credit cards for a week, try it for two weeks. Then try it for a whole month. Before too long, you'll break the credit spending habit altogether.

It can take time to really change your spending habits, but there are some tricks you can use to help rein in your urges. One way is to mentally add the amount of interest you're likely to pay on top of each purchase you make. That stack of new CDs might cost you $79.99 at the music store checkout. However, if you carry a balance on your 18 percent-rate credit card and make only the minimum monthly payment, the real cost of those CDs might be closer to $110. It would take you thirty-two months of making the minimum 3 percent payment to pay off that purchase, and you'd pay about $30 in interest. Are those CDs worth $110?

DEBT BUSTER #5: PLAN YOUR STRATEGY Now you're ready to really move into action. There are two plans of attack to paying down your credit card debts, and it's your choice which to use.

Using the list you made on page 44, find the card with the highest interest rate, and the one with the highest outstanding balance (after you've made any transfers or balances). Some Armchair Millionaires prefer to get rid of as many of their debt-laden cards as quickly as possible, so they choose the card with the smallest outstanding balance and direct their monthly "debt investment" (from Debt Buster #2) toward that card each month until it's entirely paid off. Then they cut up that card, notify the credit card company that they want their account cancelled, and proceed to the next smallest outstanding balance. You would proceed in this fashion until you've entirely eliminated all your credit card debts.

Armchair Millionaire Member Poll
How much credit card debt do you have?
45% Less than $1,000
22% $1000–$5000
15% $5000–10,000
18% More than $10,000

The average balance on a credit card in America is $7,000. Armchair Millionaires are beating those odds—with 45 percent carrying $1,000 or less in credit card debt. Where do you stand? If you're not one of those 45 percent, don't panic. Reading this book is your first big step toward getting there.

Others prefer to pay off the card with the highest interest rate first. Once you've paid down that card, move to the card with the next highest interest rate, and continue until you've eliminated all your debts.

If you've completed Steps 1 through 5, then you're ready to make a long-term commitment to reducing your spending, reducing your debts, and increasing your savings. But you also should not delay starting your own Armchair Millionaire Five Steps to Financial Freedom plan while you work down your debts. Even if you can put aside only $10 a week for your long-term savings plan, that's enough to get started.

Debt Buster #5 in Action—Other Benefits of Setting Goals

While all these steps to becoming debt-free may sound overwhelming, the word from Armchair Millionaires is that taking these steps can help change your whole attitude about the process of eliminating debt. And once you can see your debts in a different light, doing what you must to get rid of them isn't so hard after all. Here some Armchair Millionaires share their insights:

Attitude Adjustment

"My wife and I have discovered that assessing our situation has helped change our attitude toward spending. In fact, it is completely changed now that we have a set of clearly defined goals. We actually have these written down and I chart our progress on a set of graphs every month. Our top priority is to be debt-free in three years. We now use the phrase 'in three years' as a point of humor in our house. Whenever anybody says, 'I need such and such . . . ,' my wife or I will pipe up with, 'in three years.' It's amazing. Our sofa has a tear in it. My wife looked at it and said, 'I guess that can wait three years.' The VCR broke. 'We'll get another in three years.' The list goes on. Now that we realize what the benefits will be, three years just doesn't seem that far off."

—Armchair Millionaire member gbchriste

The Most Important Step

"I seriously thought about bankruptcy at one point—I was behind on my car loan, my rent, my credit cards. But I found that once I made my mind up that I was not going to let it all defeat me, I began to succeed in reducing my debt."

—Armchair Millionaire member brianpearcy

Where to Go If You Still Need Help

If you have tried the Armchair Millionaire plan for defeating your debt and still feel like you need more help, don't worry. There are a number of wonderful national nonprofit organizations devoted to assisting those with debt problems. The National Foundation for Consumer Credit and Myvesta are two excellent groups that will work with you and your creditors to allow you to pull yourself up out of debt. If you do sign up for one of their services, though, don't be surprised if the advice they give you sounds a lot like our advice in this chapter!

National Foundation for Consumer Credit
8611 Second Avenue, Suite 100
Silver Spring, MD 20910
800-388-2227
http://www.nfcc.org

Myvesta.org
P.O. Box 8587
Gaithersburg, MD 20898
800-680-3328
http://www.myvesta.org

The Final Piece—Finding the Support You Need

Perhaps the best part of the Armchair Millionaire Web site community is the inspiration you'll receive from the other people there who are also dedicated to getting their finances in order. Best of all, they are there at any time of the day or night so you can boost your resolve whenever you need to.

You Don't Have to Do It Alone

"My husband and I are working on overcoming our debt. At first we were very excited at the prospect of being debt-free. But then I started thinking it would take forever and I got depressed. But what has really helped to keep me on track is coming back to the Armchair Millionaire message boards on a regular basis. Every time I come here it helps me to realize my goals again, and I usually get off-line and write out another check to a credit card company."

—Armchair Millionaire member Junebugs

Chapter 4 Action Items

In this chapter, you have learned how to defeat your debt, a necessary step before starting to build your long-term savings plan. Here are the steps you need to get started.

- Make a list of all your debts, including credit cards, the amount owed on each, the interest rates you pay, and other details about the loans and cards. Set aside a monthly dollar amount to be directed at your debts.
- Reduce your debt burden by transferring balances to a credit card with a lower interest rate, or refinancing your mortgage, or consolidating your debts into a lower interest rate loan.
- Set aside a week when you won't make any charges on your credit card whatsoever. Don't carry them with you (not even "in case of emergency").

- Make a monthly payment to your creditors, starting either with the debt with the highest interest rate, or the debt with the largest outstanding balance. Then continue until you're debt-free!
- Finally, start your saving and investing plan right now, even if you're deep in debt. Learning to save can be hard, but it gets easier once you see your portfolio start to grow. To find out how to get started, go on to Part II: Five Steps to Financial Freedom.

Part II

....

Five Steps
to Financial Freedom

In the first part of this book, you heard from the real experts—the people who make up the Armchair Millionaire community—who attest that building a successful portfolio doesn't take a lot of luck or require a great deal of money. And you've learned that beginning your portfolio will require patience and discipline; it will be one of the most grown-up decisions you'll ever make.

Now that your head and your heart are ready for the road ahead, all that remains is finding out *how* to invest.

The five steps to building an extraordinary portfolio, even on an ordinary income, are the subject of Part II. As with Part I, you'll learn the tips, tricks, and wisdom from real Armchair Millionaires, but you'll also learn about a specific plan—the Five Steps to Financial Freedom. These five simple steps have been culled from the experiences of thousands of investors. They are the five most successful, powerful, and reliable saving and investing strategies ever. And they have been battle-tested by teachers, doctors, financial advisors, men and women, novices and experts alike. In short, these five steps can make you a millionaire.

The Five Steps break down like this:

- The first two steps, *Max Out Your Tax-Deferred Savings* and *Pay Yourself First,* are simple savings techniques that will show you how to hold on to enough of your income using tax-advantaged investing and simple budgeting tricks to begin investing.
- Step three, *Invest Automatically,* and step four, *Use the Armchair Investing Strategy,* show you how to invest your savings in the stock market using the strategies that have made investors wealthy for decades. Pay special attention to Chapter 4 where we reveal specific portfolios and investments that can be tuned to your personal investing goals and time frame. With these model portfolios, you can put your plan into action today with confidence and knowledge.
- Finally, in step five, *Start Today,* we reveal the most important secret to building wealth. Without a doubt, this is the one strategy that all successful investors have in common. And best of all, it's easy to implement.

You're only five steps away from financial freedom. Take a deep breath, and get ready to take your first step now. . . .

CHAPTER 5

STEP 1:
Max Out All
Tax-Deferred Savings

There is a revolution going on. One that you, yourself, may be part of. And you might not even know it.

It's a retirement savings revolution. Millions of Americans are behaving like savvy investors by using special savings plans to build a substantial nest egg that will fund their retirement years. These investors are saving vast wealth (to the tune of an estimated $4.5 trillion) using retirement plans sponsored by their employers or the government (or both). They are taking advantage of government programs that are designed to help them save money and reduce their taxes at the same time.

We all know that Americans tend to gripe about the government. And we all want to reduce our taxes. Armchair Millionaires know that the first, most important step toward building a nest egg is to max out all the tax-advantaged retirement plans available to them. If you decide to take the government up on one of these plans, you're getting in on a terrific deal. Not only will you be saving for your own future, the government will give you a break on your taxes, or at least let you postpone paying some of them for twenty or thirty or forty years. Just think how much your money could grow in that time!

There are a number of different retirement plans that you might be eligible for depending on whether your company offers a plan to its employees, whether you're self-employed, what your annual income is, and other factors.

What Makes a Retirement Account a Retirement Account?

The first thing you need to know is that many of these government-approved plans all use something called "tax-deferred" investing.

Hold it right there. What does tax-deferred mean, you ask? "Tax-deferred" is actually an accountant's term, and it means that you can get out of paying some taxes now, though you will have to pay them later. With tax-deferred accounts, you get to kick in money on a regular basis, let it grow, and postpone ("defer") any taxes you might have to pay until your retirement years.

All these plans share at least one of the following characteristics:

- Ability to make pretax contributions, meaning whatever money you put into a retirement account is put in before taxes are taken out. Therefore, retirement account contributions lower your tax bill right away.
- "Tax-deferral," the postponement of all taxes on earnings in the plan until retirement. At retirement, when your income will probably be lower, you'll pay taxes at a lower rate.
- Elimination of all taxes on earnings in the plan. You may never pay taxes on the earnings in some retirement plans!

Of course, the downside of these specialized retirement plans is that you have to be willing to put the money away until you're almost sixty years old.

If that seems like a long time, don't worry, because you get plenty of benefits from retirement accounts in the short term, too. For example, by taking money out of your paycheck and socking it into a 401(k) or traditional IRA, your monthly tax bite will go down. That's because the IRS looks at tax-deferred money as if it weren't really earned, and therefore, no taxes are owed. Overall, the benefits of tax-deferred savings are mighty substantial.

How much will all this save you? Lots. Here's an example using a 401(k), a company-sponsored retirement plan that might be one of your options:

Let's say you contribute $2,000 to your regular (as in not tax-deferred) saving and investment plan at the beginning of each year. If your account can grow just 10 percent a year, you'll end up with $596,254 in thirty-five years. But you'll have to pay taxes along the way on all the dividends, interest, and capital gains that you earn in this account. Those taxes could take a formidable bite out of your portfolio's performance. If taxes eat up just 1 percent of your return each year, your nest egg in thirty-five years turns out to be just $470,249 (say goodbye to $126,005—yowza!).

So what happens if you put $2,000 into a tax-advantaged retirement account instead? First of all, you can kick that expected return back up to 10 percent, ending up with $596,254, since you won't have to worry about paying taxes each year in the account. But it gets even better when you add in the savings you'll get on your federal income taxes. If you're in the 28 percent tax bracket, a $2,000 contribution to your retirement plan could save you $560 a year in taxes. For the same out-of-pocket cost to you of $2,000 a year, you could be putting aside $2,560 into a retirement plan. So once you factor in the growth of that $560 you save each year, the end result of all this accelerated saving is a grand total of $763,205 in thirty-five years.

ADVICE FROM RICH

"Think of retirement account investments as a gift from Uncle Sam. If you contribute $2,000 to a tax-deferred account, you not only get $2,000 working for you, but you save $560 on your tax return. So it's as if you received $560 for free. And how can you turn down free money?"

When you retire, it's true that you'll have to pay taxes on the money as you withdraw it from your account, but the assumption here is that you'll be living on an income that's smaller than when you were working, and therefore you'll be in a lower tax bracket.

From the Armchair Millionaire's Gallery—
Meet Crystal R., Who Learned to Love Her Retirement Plan the Hard Way

Instead of lecturing you about how important retirement savings are, we're going to let one of our community members show you how learning to save for retirement is an important part of growing up.

Armchair Millionaire Member Name: Crystal R.

Age: 27

Hometown: Brooklyn, NY

Occupation: Proposal writer for management consulting firm

Family Status: Married

Financial Goals: Comfortable retirement, financing kids' college educations

How Did You Get Started Investing?

Very simply, my company offered a 401(k) program. I was so impressed by the company's matching agreement of 14 percent. And I thought, "Wow, this can't be real!" So I did the max. I was twenty-four at the time. I chose the fund that was most aggressive. I felt that I had little or nothing to lose and I felt like I was of the age where I could invest a sizable amount and if things didn't work out in the first couple of years, eventually things would balance out and I'd be okay.

What happened when you noticed your paycheck was less when you began your 401(k) program?

Once I did it, I forgot about it. I'd get my statements and check the balance and get excited, but that's pretty much it. What impressed me the most was that I could invest a certain amount of money but it wouldn't result in an equal amount decrease from my paycheck because it was a pretax investment. So I could invest just over $200 and only feel the difference of maybe $180 plus the company matching. It was incredible.

What's the Biggest Investment Mistake You've Made?

I made a huge one. When I changed jobs, I never rolled over the money I had put away into my 401(k). Instead, I spent it all. I don't even remember what I spent it on. Don't get me wrong, I enjoyed spending it. But I should have been more serious about what that money was intended for. I won't be doing something like that again.

What Did You Learn from That Mistake?

I wish I had more discipline back then. I have it now. A lot of the realities of life have sunk in over the last few months. Saving money has become much more important to me. My father had a stroke recently. Watching him go through both physical changes and financial strain from not being able to work have made me realize that you've got to be prepared for anything. That event made me much more serious about saving and investing.

What Do You Want Others to Know About Starting to Invest?
There's a huge difference between just saving and saving to invest. My philosophy used to be, "Let me save so I can spend." But that's not what investing is all about. Unless you can connect it to a larger event—like retirement—you sort of miss the point. People know this, but there's a difference between knowing and doing.

A Short History of Retirement Plans in America

Before we get into the specific plans and how each one could work for you, here's a short history of how these plans came about in the first place.

One of the first people to suggest an all-encompassing retirement plan in America was Revolutionary War figure Thomas Paine, way back in 1795. (It's just a coincidence that Paine's best known work is titled "Common Sense," the phrase that Armchair Millionaires use to describe their investing strategy.) Paine proposed a 10 percent inheritance tax to fund a program that would pay annual benefits of ten pounds sterling to each citizen after turning fifty.

Paine's plan was never enacted, of course. But in 1935, another government-sponsored plan was created to provide for the security of older Americans, aptly named "Social Security." The goal of the system was to "give some measure of protection to the average citizen and to his family against the loss of a job and against poverty-ridden old age," as President Roosevelt said when he signed the legislation that passed the Social Security Act into law.

Social Security was never intended to allow retirees to live "high on the hog," however. It was meant to keep those who were no longer able to work off the soup lines, and as a result only provides a very modest income. (Those of you who are expecting Social Security to carry you through your retirement years may be in for a rude shock.)

The Future of Social Security?
ADVICE FROM RICH

In a recent survey of Americans aged eighteen to thirty-four, 46 percent believed in the existence of extraterrestrials while only 28 percent believed Social Security will still be around when they retire. But what are the facts? Andrew Hacker, author of *Money: Who Has How Much and Why*, explains it this way: "Figuring out whether Social Security will be able to support you when you retire is a simple thing. How many workers are there per retiree? Because Social Security is taken from your check, it spends three months in Maryland, and then it goes out to your grandfather. When Social Security started, there were something like twelve workers to every retiree. We're getting dangerously close to two to one. And that's the wake-up call for individual investors to plan on being responsible for their own incomes when they retire."

In decades past, employees could count on their companies to provide for a comfortable retirement. After a lifetime of service, a "company man" was sure to receive a gold watch and a pension that would see him and his wife through their golden years.

Corporate pension plans are known as "defined benefit plans" because they pay out a fixed amount to retirees, based on a formula that considers the person's salary history, age, and number of years of service. The company puts up the money that funds the pension plan for all its employees, and then invests that money until it's needed.

But back in the 1980s, some big companies were having trouble with their pension plans. Specifically, they weren't putting enough money in the plans to cover the payouts they'd need to make to their current employees upon retirement.

Of course, companies that engaged in the practice of underfunding their retirement plans were faced with the wrath of their employees—and, in many cases, the powerful unions who represented those workers. What could be worse than reaching retirement age and learning that there's nothing left in your company's pension fund for you?

As a result, a new type of company-sponsored retirement plan began to emerge in the 1980s. A corporate benefits consultant named Theodore Benna pored over the U.S. tax code trying to figure out ways that employers could provide cash bonuses or profit-sharing plans to highly paid executives without discriminating against low-level staffers. Benna discovered a loophole in paragraph (k) of section 401 that could be used to turn profit-sharing plans into tax-deferred savings plans, and the "401(k) plan" was born.

401(k) plans are retirement plans offered by companies to their employees. In these plans, the workers must make contributions to the plan from each paycheck (from their pretax salary, thereby lowering their tax bill). The company may or may not make an additional matching payment, too.

Companies like 401(k) plans, and one reason is because they shift the cost of retirement plans to the employees. As a result, fewer companies are offering pension plans these days, and more companies are offering 401(k) plans.

If your company doesn't offer a 401(k) plan, don't worry. In 1974, the U.S. tax law was modified to allow individuals who weren't covered by a company pension plan to save for retirement and still get a tax break. These plans are known as Individual Retirement Accounts (or IRAs).

Millions of Americans have established IRA accounts, which offer the opportunity to set aside money before taxes, like a 401(k) does. The money you invest in the IRA account gets to grow free from taxes until you retire, just like a 401(k). You can open an IRA at just about any bank, brokerage firm, or mutual fund company. When you retire, you can begin to take money out of your IRA, paying taxes as you go.

Congress introduced a variation on the IRA in 1998—the Roth IRA. The Roth IRA, like a "traditional" IRA, lets your money grow free from taxes until you retire. But unlike a traditional IRA, the money you withdraw from a Roth IRA is completely tax-free! Of course, the U.S. government isn't going to give up on collecting taxes altogether, so you won't get a tax break up front when you contribute to a Roth IRA (like you get when you fund a regular IRA).

Armchair Millionaire Member Poll
Which Retirement Account Is the Fairest of All?

We aren't the only ones who think that 401(k)s are great. When we asked the Armchair Millionaire community where they had their retirement funds, here's what they had to say:

Where will most of your retirement income come from?

43% 401(k)

25% IRA

23% Pension

8% Social Security

MAKING THE MOVE TO MAXIMUM SAVINGS

With all these retirement plan options available, how do you figure out which is best for you?

When it comes to retirement and tax-related investing, there's a lot of information to consider. So we've brought it all together into one special section.

This will make it easier to learn about the topic—when you're ready. If you're not prepared to dig into this information just yet, feel free to jump ahead to Chapter 6. There, you'll be able to continue learning the simple steps you need to take in order to achieve financial independence the Armchair Millionaire way.

When you've finished the book, you can return to this section to learn how to maximize every last dollar of your tax-advantaged savings and investing and put your plan into action!

Uncover the Right Retirement Plan for You

Do you have a job? Then your first stop on the retirement plan highway should be to march into your company's human resources department to find out if they offer a retirement plan for employees—and if you're eligible! Chances are good that your company has a 401(k) plan available to its employees.

Signing up is as simple as filling out an enrollment form that tells your company how much you want to have withheld from each paycheck and deposited into your 401(k) account. That's it! (Well, you'll also have to figure out how to invest your funds, but we'll cover that in Chapter 8.)

The Beauty of the 401(k) Plan

401(k) plans are an Armchair Millionaire's best first choice for long-term savings, for a couple of reasons:

1. Once you establish your account, your company will handle all the details of putting money into the plan—automatically! You won't have to remember to write a check or transfer money each month.
2. 401(k) plans provide tax savings from federal income taxes by letting you fund the account from pretax earnings. In other words, the money you contribute to your 401(k) will be taken out of your paycheck before any other deductions or taxes, so you'll see the

tax savings in each paycheck. If you decide to set aside $50 from each week's paycheck for your 401(k), and you're in the 28 percent tax bracket, your check will only be $36 smaller—not $50!

3. You won't have to pay any taxes on the earnings and gains in your 401(k) until retirement. This will allow your portfolio to increase in value over time at a much faster rate.

A Real Life Look at the 401(k)

Think the money that you stash away in a 401(k) won't amount to much? Here, Armchair Millionaires explain how the money can add up, and how to make the most of your 401(k) funds.

401k All the Way

"A 401(k) plan is an excellent way to save for retirement. Nothing yet (except winning the lottery) can beat it. I know! I've been in my 401(k) since 1983 and I can't believe how it's grown—way up there in the six figures! All I can tell you is, do it!"

—Armchair Millionaire member arnawaz

Maxing Out from the Get Go

"When I became eligible for my 401(k), I took the plunge and went for 15 percent right away instead of trying to work up to it. I had to work a moonlighting job for a while, but now I am accustomed to less money in my hand. I have learned to love paying myself first!"

—Armchair Millionaire member caugros

4. Many companies will match the contributions that employees make to their 401(k) plans. Your employer might kick in fifty cents for every dollar you contribute up to a certain point, or they might even match you on a one-to-one basis. Armchair Millionaires have a name for this—it's called "free money"! When you think about it, you'll find few opportunities in your life when people

will pay you for taking care of yourself, so you should never pass up an offer like this from your employer. In fact, a cardinal rule of 401(k) saving is to always contribute at least enough to your plan to get the maximum match (if your company offers one).

Many companies have specific "sign-up" periods for 401(k) plans, such as once a quarter. That's one reason it's important to get started in your 401(k) as soon as possible. If you miss the sign-up period, it might be another three months before you'll be able to get started.

Many companies have a waiting period of six months or a year before employees are eligible to participate in their 401(k) plans. If you're waiting to become eligible, there's no reason you can't start saving now, though. Figure out how much you'll contribute to the 401(k) and then set that money aside in a separate savings and investment account when you receive each paycheck.

How Much Can You Contribute to Your 401(k)?

You can contribute up to 15 percent of your pretax earnings, to a maximum of $10,500 a year (in 2000—the amount is adjusted for inflation each year). Some company plans will even allow you to make extra, nondeductible contributions to your 401(k) above and beyond that 15 percent limit. Generally, though, you'd want to make sure that you have taken advantage of any other tax-advantaged retirement plans that you are eligible for before making nondeductible contributions to a 401(k).

One final thought for those of you who might be wary of locking up your money for the next forty years: Many 401(k) plans will allow you to borrow money back from your account, and then repay yourself with interest. You might be able to borrow up to 50 percent of the value of your account, and repay the loan with your regular contributions. Just remember that borrowing from your 401(k) means that you'll have less money working toward meeting your ultimate retirement goals, so consider this as a last resort if you really need

the cash. It might provide some peace of mind, though, if you antici-
pate the need to come up with a down payment for a home or cover
big tuition bills for your kids.

But just don't plan to take the money out of your 401(k) before
age fifty-five. If you do, you'll be subject to a 10 percent federal
penalty tax, probably a state penalty tax, and payment of the income
taxes that you deferred when you put the money into the plan in the
first place. This can take a hefty bite out of your total proceeds.

Learning the Hard Way

The thing about retirement plans is that you really need to
wait until you are legally retiring to dip into that money. Is it really
so bad if you don't wait? See what this Armchair Millionaire has to
say:

The Best Laid Plans . . .
"Word to the wise: Don't withdraw from your retirement plan!
Everyone advised me against it, but I'm hardheaded and had to do it
my way. Now, I'm slapped with a huge tax bill. I had my reasons for
making the withdrawal at the time, and had my plan worked out, I
would've been able to pay this tax bill. But, as we know, the best-laid
plans don't always work out. Anyway, just take my advice and DON'T
DO IT!"

—Armchair Millionaire member donyale99

Company-Sponsored Alternatives to the 401(k)

If your company doesn't offer a 401(k), they might offer a 403(b) or
457 account instead.

A 403(b) account is very similar to a 401(k), except it's offered to
employees of schools, universities, and nonprofit organizations. 403(b)
accounts are somewhat more limited than 401(k)s in the types of
investments they can hold—403(b)s have to be invested in mutual

funds or annuities (a type of insurance plan). They are sometimes known as tax-sheltered annuities (TSA).

A 457 plan is a deferred compensation plan offered to government employees, and offers the same pretax advantages as a 401(k). The maximum amount is 33⅓ percent of your predeferral taxable compensation or $8,000 (in 2000). It's possible that you might have a 401(k) and 457 plan available to you and can contribute to both.

If you work for yourself, or for a small company, your employer might offer you a retirement account such as a SEP-IRA, SIMPLE IRA, or Keogh plan. The principle behind all these plans is exactly the same—you and/or your company can contribute pretax money to your retirement account, getting a tax break and allowing your money to grow unimpeded by taxes.

A Keogh plan (also known as a Qualified Retirement Plan, or QRP) is designed for a self-employed individual or small business. There are two kinds of Keogh plans, "Profit Sharing" and "Money Purchase." If you establish a Money Purchase Keogh for your business, contribution is mandatory—you must make the same percentage contribution each year (up to 20 percent of your income, up to a maximum of $30,000)—whether you have profits or not. In a Profit Sharing Keogh, contributions are limited to the lesser of $30,000 or 13.04 percent of your self-employment income. The contribution percentage can change each year. Individuals can contribute to both types of plans in the same year.

A Savings Incentive Match Plan for Employees (SIMPLE), allows companies with 100 or fewer employees to offer a SIMPLE IRA plan. With this plan, employees can defer a portion of their salary as with a 401(k), up to $6,000 annually, and may receive an employer match or contribution as well.

In a Simplified Employee Pension (SEP) IRA, employees can make generous tax-deductible retirement contributions (up to $24,000 per year) for themselves and any employees. This is the easiest and most economical business retirement account to set up in most cases.

In fact, if you have a moonlighting job, or have any self-employment income at all, you ought to consider establishing a SEP-IRA or other retirement plan specifically designed for small businesspeople. A SEP-IRA is easy to set up with just about any brokerage firm or mutual fund company. Even if you have a 401(k) at your day job, you can contribute to a SEP-IRA. And since SEP-IRA plans let you stash away much more each year than in a 401(k) plan, that $24,500 limit is something to strive for.

Other Retirement Plan Options—
The Individual Retirement Account

Once you've contributed the maximum to any company-sponsored retirement plans such as the ones we've just described, it's time to take a look at some other options that might allow you to shelter your money from taxes. If your company doesn't offer any retirement plan for its employees, then you'll definitely want to take a look at Individual Retirement Accounts (IRAs).

An IRA is a special account that you establish with a bank, mutual fund company, or brokerage in which you can save funds for retirement.

The tax-cutting benefit of an IRA makes it particularly appealing to many investors. If your adjusted gross income (AGI, the amount of your annual income that the IRS uses to determine the taxes you owe) is below a certain level, and you aren't covered by a pension plan or a retirement plan at work, then you can deduct your IRA contributions from the amount of your income that's subject to federal income taxes, lowering your tax bill.

The amount that you are allowed to put into your IRA is also determined by your AGI. If your AGI in 2000 is less than $30,000 for a single taxpayer or $50,000 for a married couple filing jointly, you can deposit up to $2,000 (each, if married) as a deductible contribution. The amount that can be contributed and deducted is scaled down for single people who make up to $40,000 and for couples who earn up to $60,000.

Making Contributions the Easy Way

One reason a personal IRA isn't quite as alluring an investment vehicle as a 401(k) is that no one is going to make automatic contributions for you. So you could get to the end of the year and have to make a lump contribution of $2,000, and not everyone has $2,000 sitting around. Here, two Armchair Millionaires tell us how they got around that:

Funding an IRA the Easy Way

"I have found that using direct deposit from my employer helps me to save for retirement. I have $166 taken automatically from my account monthly and put into an IRA (multiply that times 12 and it adds up to $2,000). Some employers will let you split the direct deposit (money market and checking, for example). Just ask; even if they don't tell you, they may offer it."

—Armchair Millionaire member mtnspirit

You Don't Need Cash to Open an IRA

"Some of the fund companies, such as Fidelity or Scudder, for example, let you open IRAs with stocks instead of just putting cash in. I have bought stocks and used the dividend reinvestment provision. The results have been excellent."

—Armchair Millionaire member rfd21

If you're not eligible to make a deductible contribution to an IRA, it is possible to make a contribution to a "nondeductible IRA." Nondeductible contributions still grow tax-deferred in the IRA, but withdrawals after the age of 59½ are taxable only on the gains in the portfolio—you already paid the taxes on the original contributions. In a fully deductible IRA, contributions and earnings are entirely taxable because 100 percent of the original contributions provided a tax deduction to the individual.

When Can You Withdraw Funds from an IRA?

The main advantage of an IRA is that you pay no taxes on gains in the account until you retire. This is why IRAs are referred to as "tax-deferred" accounts. Taxes on dividends, interest, and capital gains are all deferred, in the case of an IRA, until retirement. When you eventually do retire, you can begin to withdraw money from the account and use it to augment your income from Social Security and other retirement plans. At that time, you'll pay taxes on the funds you take out at the IRS's "regular income" tax rate.

One warning about IRA withdrawals: Generally, if you take out funds from your IRA before the age of 59½, you'll pay a penalty. However, you can withdraw funds from a regular IRA without penalty for the following reasons:

- You buy a first home (up to $10,000)
- You need to pay for qualifying higher education expenses (for you, your spouse, your children, or your grandchildren, to pay for tuition, fees, books, supplies, and equipment)
- You need to pay medical expenses that are greater than 7.5 percent of your AGI
- You need to pay health insurance premiums because you are unemployed
- You become permanently disabled
- You roll over the distribution to another IRA
- You are withdrawing funds using a special schedule of early payments made over your life expectancy (IRS rules allow you to begin withdrawing funds prior to age 59½ in the form of an annuity that is paid at least once a year. The amount of that annuity is set by IRS rules based on your life expectancy and cannot be changed once payments have begun.)

There are many complicated rules about IRA accounts, but the bottom line is that by letting your funds grow tax-free over a long period, you can build a substantial nest egg for your retirement.

Remember, IRAs are designed to help you plan for a comfortable retirement—they lose their benefits if you tap into the account too soon.

A New IRA Option—The Roth IRA

In 1998, Congress introduced the Roth IRA. This is an IRA with a twist—the funds you deposit into a Roth IRA grow on a tax-free basis in the account until you withdraw them, but when you do take out the money, you won't have to pay any taxes on the earnings you've accumulated. In a regular IRA, funds grow on a tax-deferred basis, but when you withdraw money from a regular IRA, you have to pay taxes on the withdrawal as regular income.

How is this feat accomplished? The initial contributions you make to a Roth IRA are made with after-tax dollars—they are nondeductible. You don't get a break on your tax bill when you put money into a Roth IRA as you do when you contribute to a regular IRA. The break comes later, when you don't have to pay any taxes on the money you take out.

ARE YOU ELIGIBLE? If your 2000 AGI (adjusted gross income) is more than $160,000 (for a married couple, filing jointly) or $110,000 (for a single individual), you can stop reading right now; you're not eligible to make any contributions to a Roth IRA this year.

If your AGI is $150,000 or less (married, filing jointly) or $95,000 or less (filing singly), then you can contribute $2,000 per spouse to a Roth IRA. You can contribute to a Roth IRA even if you or your spouse is covered by a pension plan or by a company retirement plan like a 401(k).

If your AGI is between $150,001 and $160,000 (married, filing jointly) or between $95,001 and $110,000 (filing singly), the amount you can contribute is gradually phased out.

While Roth IRAs allow you to withdraw money before retirement under certain circumstances, there are special rules that govern when you can take money out and what you can use it for. If you don't follow the rules, you could be liable for a penalty tax.

Every IRA is made up of two types of funds: *contributions,* the money you put into the account, and *earnings,* the amount of any investment gains that your contributions have made while in the account (sometimes known as accumulated earnings). Earnings that you withdraw from the IRA are known as *distributions.*

You can take out *contributions* at any time from a Roth IRA without penalty and without any tax liability. Not that you'd want to take out those contributions—after all, it's the power of compounding that can really build up your portfolio over a long period of time. But, it's nice to know that you have access to some cash in case of a big emergency.

After a five year period, you can withdraw the *earnings* that have accumulated in your account without taxes or penalty, but only for the following very specific "life changes":

- You reach the age of 59½
- You (or your spouse, children, or grandchildren) buy a first home (up to $10,000 only)
- You become disabled
- You die

One difference between a Roth IRA and a traditional IRA is that upon your death, your heirs would receive your Roth IRA proceeds entirely free from federal income taxes, whereas, in a regular IRA, your heirs would be liable for taxes on the total amount of your account.

Any earnings taken out of your IRA for the above reasons and after the five-year period are known as a *qualified distribution.*

If you withdraw earnings for any reason other than those listed above, you'll have to pay federal taxes at your regular income tax rate and a 10 percent premature withdrawal penalty. This is called an *unqualified distribution.*

PENALTY-FREE DISTRIBUTIONS. You can avoid the premature withdrawal penalty in some instances. Roth IRAs have provisions that give you a break on the penalty in the case of some other "life changes." You are exempted from the penalty, but not from the taxes, if you take out earnings from the account for the following reasons:

- You need to pay medical expenses that are greater than 7.5 percent of your AGI
- You need to pay health insurance premiums because you are unemployed
- You need to pay for higher education expenses
- You buy a first home (for amounts over the $10,000 tax-free allowance)

POTENTIAL PITFALLS. Another point is worth mentioning here: Any withdrawals you make are treated as coming first from your contributions. You can't choose whether to withdraw earnings or contributions—you must take out the money you put in first, and then take out the earnings. While this isn't a problem in most cases (since your contributions can be accessed without penalties and taxes), it may make a difference when planning withdrawals in some circumstances.

One more thing. States don't always follow changes in federal law, so there may be state taxes on accumulated earnings that are withdrawn from a Roth IRA, whether or not they are free from federal taxes. You'll need to check with the department of taxation in your state to see how they handle these distributions.

The bottom line is that Roth IRAs offer a totally tax-free way to save for retirement. In addition, in many instances you can have access to the money in your account prior to retirement with no penalty and little or no tax liability. With the Roth IRA, Uncle Sam has given Americans a nice break and an important new retirement planning tool—with the flexibility to help you handle important life events along the way if you need to.

How to Choose

So how do you choose the retirement vehicle for you? Remember, there are really three options when choosing an individual retirement account: a deductible IRA, a nondeductible IRA, and a Roth IRA. Your total annual contributions to any single type of IRA or a combination of a Roth IRA and deductible IRA can be no more than $2,000, subject to AGI (Adjusted Gross Income) limits. And you must have earned income to contribute to any IRA (meaning that you must have gotten your income from a job, and not an investment portfolio).

SHOULD YOU CHOOSE A DEDUCTIBLE IRA OR NONDEDUCTIBLE IRA? If you are eligible for a deductible IRA, it's always a better choice than a nondeductible IRA because the contributions provide a tax deduction in the current year. Nondeductible IRAs are okay for people who have already contributed the maximum to all other retirement plan options and still want to put money away for the long term.

SHOULD YOU CHOOSE A ROTH IRA OR NONDEDUCTIBLE IRA? A Roth IRA will always be a better choice than a nondeductible IRA (an IRA that is funded with after-tax dollars). Contributions in both accounts grow on a nontaxed basis, but the earnings distributed from a nondeductible IRA when you retire are taxable at your regular income tax rate. Remember, your distributions from a Roth IRA are tax-free.

SHOULD YOU CHOOSE A ROTH IRA OR DEDUCTIBLE IRA? Roth IRAs have fewer limitations on participation than deductible IRAs. It's possible that you might have an AGI that's too high to allow you to contribute to a deductible IRA, or that you're covered by your employer's pension plan or 401(k). In either case, a Roth IRA will be an obvious choice.

However, the choice between a Roth IRA and a deductible IRA is less clear for many people. Some experts claim that you should always take a tax deduction when it's available to you—which means choosing a deductible IRA, rather than a Roth IRA.

The issue of "getting your tax benefit up front" is what most differentiates a Roth IRA from a regular IRA. The Roth IRA is described by the Internal Revenue Service as a "back-loaded IRA," because its tax benefits are only fully realized when money is withdrawn from the account. A regular IRA is "front-loaded" because you realize a tax deduction in the year in which you contribute to the fund.

The problem with figuring out which IRA is best for you is that you need to determine whether the "back-loaded" tax benefits of a Roth IRA (which you'll realize twenty or thirty or forty years down the road) outweigh the "front-loaded" benefits of a regular, deductible IRA. Here are a few things that you should consider when making your choice.

If you're feeling confused about whether a Roth is for you, join the club. When we asked the Armchair Millionaire community if they converted to a Roth, there was no one clear winner.

Did you convert to a Roth IRA?
Yes 45%
No 55%

Ben Franklin's famous words, "Nothing is certain but death and taxes," are certainly true. But there's no way to be absolutely sure of the tax rates to which you'll be subject when you retire. One thing you can be sure of is that our elected representatives will continue to fiddle with the tax code, raising and lowering the tax rates over the years.

Leaving the uncertainty of changes in the tax code aside, the major consideration in choosing between the two types of IRAs is what tax bracket you expect to be in when you retire, and if that is higher or lower than your current bracket.

How Others Have Made the Decision

You may be scratching your head right now, wondering how you'll be able to figure out which IRA is best for you. Here, two Armchair Millionaires share their insights on how to decide.

Run the Numbers

"Anyone who is considering a Roth needs to contact a financial advisor and have them run the numbers. How much will your future wealth increase by switching to a Roth? More importantly, how much will it cost to switch, and can you afford the current tax liability? My wife and I both have traditional IRAs worth about $35,000 each. My financial advisor ran the numbers and found that by the time we reach fifty-nine and a half our savings would be twice that of a traditional IRA if we switched to a Roth, but that it would cost about $15,000 in current taxes to switch. That's money we don't have, and to take it from the IRAs as they currently stand would defeat the purpose of the IRA. The good news is you don't have to switch all of your money to a Roth, you can convert as much or as little as you like. Regardless, the best retirement planning advice is to get started right away."

—Armchair Millionaire Loco

You Could Keep Your Old IRA and Put Future Funds into a Roth— Avoiding the Taxes Due in a Roth Conversion

"It's tough for a lot of people to come up with the taxes due in a Roth conversion. But if you are saving money for retirement every year anyway, putting new money into a Roth IRA has some tremendous advantages over the long haul, since the earnings are all tax-free. Even if you can afford to only put a few bucks a year into a Roth IRA, just do it. You won't regret it ten or twenty years from now."

—Armchair Millionaire member Larry

IF YOU EXPECT YOUR TAX BRACKET TO BE LOWER IN RETIREMENT.
One of the assumptions that has made a deductible IRA such an attractive retirement planning vehicle in the past is that your federal income tax rate will be lower when you retire than when you are working. Say you are currently in the 28 percent federal income tax bracket. When you retire, it's likely that you will be living on a reduced, fixed income, and that your tax bracket will drop to the 15 percent level. The distributions you take from that IRA are taxed at 15 percent instead of the 28 percent you might have paid prior to retirement, a significant savings.

For that reason, if you and your spouse expect to be in a lower tax bracket during retirement, the traditional IRA will generally be a better deal than a Roth IRA. You'll get big tax deductions now while you are in a high bracket, but pay much lower taxes on your IRA distributions later when you are in a low bracket.

The presumption in this recommendation is somewhat unrealistic, however. First of all, taxpayers in a "high tax bracket" (at the top of the 28 percent bracket and above) are unable to contribute to a deductible IRA, and so aren't getting "big deductions."

Secondly, comparing a Roth IRA and a deductible IRA is a bit like comparing apples and oranges, since one provides you with a tax benefit today, and the other provides you with a tax benefit when you retire. In order to make a fair comparison between the two types of IRAs, some mathematical adjustments are necessary.

One complication comes when you compare a Roth IRA and a regular deductible IRA. When you calculate how much you'll be able to contribute before taxes to a deductible IRA, you should plan to invest the money you "save" on taxes in a separate, non-tax-advantaged brokerage account or mutual fund. That's because you'll eventually have to pay taxes on your contributions to your IRA. With a Roth IRA, it's too easy to forget that you've already paid taxes on the money you've deposited into your account, but those taxes are a real expense. By investing the "tax savings" from a deductible IRA, you may find that you will come out ahead with a deductible IRA. Unfortunately, investing those tax savings is something that most people won't do.

If you expect your tax bracket to be lower in retirement, and you don't invest the tax savings provided by the deductible IRA contributions each year in another account, and you still want to maximize your after-tax retirement income, a Roth IRA will likely be a better choice.

IF YOU EXPECT YOUR TAX BRACKET TO BE HIGHER IN RETIREMENT. If your retirement planning has been moving along nicely, it's probably not hard to imagine a scenario in which your income when you retire may actually be higher than it is now, moving you into a higher tax bracket. If you expect to be in a higher tax bracket at retirement, then a Roth IRA is probably the better choice. You'll get to lock in the tax rate you pay right now. Later, when you're sitting pretty in a higher bracket, you won't have to worry about the tax man at all!

What's Your Tax Bracket?
ADVICE FROM RICH

You'll hear lots of talk about "tax brackets" whenever retirement plans are discussed. But do you know what your tax bracket is, or how to figure out what it is? It's simply the federal income tax rate you'll pay to the IRS each year, based on your AGI (that's your Adjusted Gross Income, your taxable income base). The following table outlines the federal income tax brackets from 2000; someone who is in the "28 percent tax bracket" has an AGI of between $25,351 and $61,400 (if they're single) or $42,351 and $102,300 (if they're married and filing jointly).

2000 Taxable Income Brackets and Rates

Single	Married Filing Jointly	Federal Tax Rate
$0–$26,250	$0–$43,850	15%
$26,251–$63,550	$43,851–$105,950	28%
$63,551–$132,600	$105,951–$161,450	31%
$132,601–$288,350	$161,451–$288,350	36%
Over $288,350	Over $288,350	39.6%

IF YOU EXPECT YOUR TAX BRACKET TO BE THE SAME IN RETIREMENT. The choice becomes less clear, however, if you expect to be in the same federal tax bracket at retirement. In most cases, identical amounts invested in a Roth IRA and a regular IRA that achieve the same rates of growth will end up roughly the same value after taxes. In such cases, you'll probably prefer the Roth IRA, since you'll get tax-free instead of simply tax-deferred earnings. In addition, Roth IRA holders have an increased accessibility to funds in the account under certain circumstances. That advantage may tip the scales further in favor of the Roth IRA.

Wrapping Up IRAs

Many brokerage firms and mutual fund companies provide IRA calculators on their Web sites, and sometimes offer workbooks and other materials that can help determine what plan is best for you. Often they'll send you a complete retirement savings kit along with the application forms you'll need. Check the Appendices at the back of this book for phone numbers and Web site addresses to get in touch with these firms.

One terrific online source of information about IRAs is the Roth IRA Web site (http://www.rothira.com). This site has articles, links, and calculators to help you figure out all the details of retirement plans.

While all this talk about Roth IRAs and traditional IRAs may be confusing, just remember this: It's far more important that you are putting money aside into some kind of retirement plan than which plan you're using. Banks, brokerages, and mutual fund companies are among the most common places to have an IRA. You can also invest your IRA in CDs, bonds, stocks, mutual funds, limited partnerships, and certain types of real estate. (We'll give you the lowdown on the best investing approach for Armchair Millionaires in Chapter 8.)

You have until April 15th to open or deposit money into an IRA for the prior tax year. Even so, you should try to make your annual IRA contributions as soon as possible at the beginning of the year, not at the end of next March. Better still, you can set up an automatic transfer to have money sent electronically from your bank account to your IRA account each month or each quarter. This ensures that you'll never have to remember to write a check or worry about coming up with a big chunk of money for your annual IRA contribution.

Chapter 5 Action Items

In this chapter, you've learned why you should max out all your tax-deferred savings plans. Here are the steps you need to take to get full advantage of all the options available to you.

- Talk to your boss or human resources department about the company retirement plans they may offer employees.
- Sign up for your 401(k) or other company plan, and make it your goal to contribute the maximum amount that's allowed.
- Set up an IRA or Roth IRA account, if you're eligible. You can open an account at just about any bank, brokerage firm, or mutual fund company.
- Establish an automatic investing plan to have money sent to your IRA account each month.

CHAPTER 6

STEP 2:
Pay Yourself First

A Method to Save Big Money Without Budgeting All the Fun Out of Your Life

If you make an annual salary of $35,000 a year, and work for thirty years, you'll have earned more than one million dollars (even if you never get a raise). But the big question is, how much of that million will you be able to save?

There's a simple method that will help you to hold on to some of that cash painlessly. By the end of this chapter, you will have learned the secret to becoming a world-class saver. And don't worry, you won't have to take a vow of poverty in order to begin building your savings. But you will have to adapt how you approach saving for the future. You see, the problem with thinking that you don't have enough to start your savings plan is that you've put the most important person in your life—yourself—at the bottom of your list of priorities.

But What About the Bills?

This is a common complaint that we hear from people who haven't started their own savings plan yet. "Sure, I'd like to build up my savings account," they say. "But after I put food on the table, pay my mortgage, make the car payment, and take care of all the monthly bills, there's barely anything left for the fun stuff. If I started saving money, I'd have to live like a monk."

ADVICE FROM RICH

Every schoolkid knows that Ben Franklin wrote "A penny saved is a penny earned." While that simple bit of advice is usually used to admonish people to start stashing pennies in the piggy bank, that's missing the point. The real gist of this maxim is that if you spend every cent you bring home, you aren't really earning anything because you end up giving all your money to someone else. Only when you pay yourself can you really consider that money "earned."

Sure, all those things like rent or the mortgage, groceries, the electric bill, medical bills, the car payment, the gas bill, the water bill, property taxes, and so on are important. Nobody's saying you should skip the phone bill in order to put a few extra dollars in the bank; in fact, telephone companies tend to look askance at customers who don't pay their bills, to put it mildly.

And yes, you should be able to buy yourself a new sweater, or CD, or whatever, from time to time. But the thing about saving money is that it's not about deprivation. If you put aside money that you would normally spend on something else (say those frothy, tasty, and expensive cappuccinos you indulge in every day on your way to work), then you're substituting cappuccinos now for a big, juicy bank account later. A bank account that you can use to buy something big—like a house. Or a second house. Now doesn't that make up for all those missed cappuccinos?

Repeat After Us: Budgeting Stinks

The second problem most people face when trying to start saving comes from listening to the standard advice they get from investment books and financial advisors. According to these "experts," before you do *anything* else with your financial plan, you should sit down and come up with a monthly budget. List all of your expenses on one half of a piece of paper (this is the long list) and all your income on the other half (this is the short list). Add up all your monthly expenses, and subtract them from your monthly income, and the result is the amount of money you should be able to save each month. If you end up with a negative number, then reduce your expenses in appropriate places until you end up with more income than expenses.

Now (or so the theory goes), you have a plan to follow for all of your monthly spending. Many experts recommend that you carry around a little notebook and write down every dime that you spend each month. At the end of the month, add up all you've spent and you'll know exactly where all your money went.

While this exercise is supposed to provide you with a road map for building up your savings, all too often it proves to be *only* an exercise, and a futile one at that. Human nature always seems to get in the way. Despite all their good intentions, too many people fall flat on their faces. Within a few weeks, they've abandoned their budgets altogether. Now, besides being right where they were when they started, they've concluded that they are destined for financial failure and will never be successful at this saving thing. Nothing could be further from the truth—at least if you take a few tips from the Armchair Millionaires.

Real Life Ways to Get a Grip on Spending

You can sit in your chair reading this book and say to yourself, "That's it! From now on, I'm saving money!" This would be fine if you were going to spend the rest of your life sitting in that chair. But sometime soon, probably today, you're going to find yourself in some sort of store. It may be a grocery store, it may be the mall, it might even be Neiman Marcus. And then the resolve you've just built up may waver—even the tiniest bit—and the next thing you know, you've dropped a wad of bills on a new, improved razor, or fabulous pair of shoes. . . . Here, fellow Armchair Millionaires share their strategies for taming the spending monster.

How Many Hours Will It Cost?

"One thing that does work for me is to calculate how many hours it will take to earn the after-tax and post-pay-yourself-first money to buy the item I'm pining for. When I realize that an item will take a month to earn, I often reconsider."

—Armchair Millionaire member kimberly

The Waiting Game

"What works well for me is to write down the price of every item I am tempted to buy. I then slip the list back into my purse. I review it every week. Occasionally, I realize that something on the list will truly enhance my quality of life, so I go ahead and buy it. (Two examples of this are my computer and my treadmill, both of which I use daily.) However, most of the items on the list I find that I really don't want once the initial impulse is gone. I have actually saved thousands by using this method."

—Armchair Millionaire member Mew

An Enveloping Financial Plan

"We are paid twice a month so I write two checks each month for cash. The cash goes into envelopes for school lunches, allowances for the children and my husband and me, and for entertainment (such as movies and dinners out). When the set amount of money is gone, it is gone. But I always feel satisfied because we have enjoyed ourselves without wrecking our financial plan."

—Armchair Millionaire member anonymous

Numbers Don't Lie

"My biggest temptation is clothes. I have a closet crammed full of them, but always feel I have nothing to wear. Here's how I reined myself in: I reviewed my credit card bills for the past five years, and added up the cost of every single piece of clothing I'd ever bought (I always bought on credit). I could not believe how many thousands of dollars I'd spent on clothes, yet I hardly liked anything I owned! I calculated what that money would be worth if I'd put it into a mutual fund and got really depressed. But it helps me put my spending into perspective and makes clothing sales a lot less tempting."

—Armchair Millionaire member anonymous

You can understand why Armchair Millionaires have a motto that they proclaim often and loudly: "Budgeting stinks!"

Believe it or not, you don't need a budget to be able to build up your savings. You don't have to write down every dime you spend in a little notebook (even though some people find this a good deterrent to overspending). In fact, you probably already have a very good idea of your own spending habits.

How to Pay Yourself First

To get yourself headed in the right direction, you need to do one thing: Move yourself up the priority list. In fact, you should move yourself all the way to the top of the list, right to the number one position. Each month, before you pay all the essential and nonessential bills in that stack on your desk, write a check to yourself earmarked for your future. Make it out in the amount of 10 percent of your monthly take-home pay (take-home pay is the amount of your paycheck after taxes and all other deductions). And put this in the memo field on the check: "For my financial freedom plan."

Then, send that check to a separate account—preferably a saving account that you can't access through an ATM machine—before you have a chance to spend it. We call this "paying yourself first," and it's the Armchair Millionaire's alternative to not paying yourself last. In time, your savings will grow and help you become a wealthy person.

Getting back to that 10 percent, you may wonder why you should set aside 10 percent of your paycheck, as opposed to 8.5 percent or 15 percent? Well, it's a nice round number and it's easy to calculate, to be sure. But when you really think about it, would giving up 10 percent of your salary really cramp your lifestyle? Check out the chart to see what you would have to give up in a typical month in order to reach eventual financial success. Most people find—much to their surprise—that they can get by quite comfortably on a salary that's 10 percent lower.

What would you have to give up to "Pay Yourself First?"

If you make $45,000 a year, and pay roughly 30 percent of your salary in taxes and other payroll deductions, your take-home pay would be about $2,625 a month. Ten percent of your monthly take-home pay comes out to $262.50.

So what does that mean in the real world? Here's what you'll have to give up in a month in order to pay yourself first and begin your path to financial independence:

$2.25	3 Cups of coffee or tea
$6.00	3 Muffins to go with that joe or tea
$3.00	3 Chocolate chip cookies from local bakery
$3.00	6 Hershey chocolate bars
$9.00	2 Big Mac Value Meals at McDonald's
$8.00	1 Latest Mary Higgins Clark or Tom Clancy paperback
$25.00	1 Latest Danielle Steel or John Grisham novel (hardcover)
$3.50	1 Latest issue of *Maxim* or *Elle* magazine
$4.00	4 Bottles of Bud (watching the game, at home)
$6.00	2 Bottles of Bud (watching the game, at a bar)
$6.00	4 Espressos

$25.00	2 Latest Faith Hill or Moby CDs
$50.00	1 Newest shoot 'em up computer game on CD-ROM
$12.00	3 Pay-per-view movies on cable
$16.00	2 Movie tickets at the nearest multiplex
$17.50	5 Video or DVD rentals at Blockbuster
$15.00	1 Large Papa John's pizza with the works, delivered
$7.00	2 Gallons of ice cream (the cheap stuff)
$7.00	2 Frappuccinos at Starbuck's
$6.00	2 Bags of Oreo cookies
$6.00	1 Dozen Krispy Kreme doughnuts
$8.00	2 Bags of chips and french onion dip
$6.00	2 Fruit smothies
$11.00	11 Instant lottery tickets

$262.25   Total

How much beer, ice cream, and magazines would you have to give up each month in order to save 10 percent of your paycheck? You can see for yourself on the Armchair Millionaire Web site, at: http://www.armchairmillionaire.com/fivesteps/step_2app.html

Plug in your take-home pay, and the calculator will do the rest!

The not-so-highly-technical term for this strategy is, "Pay Yourself First." Once you understand the concept, it makes perfect sense, right?

At the very beginning, you might find it hard to adjust to living without the money you're saving and investing. Over time, though, most people discover that they don't really miss the money that's being whisked out of their account each month. It's hard to miss something when you haven't even seen it in the first place. And if you should happen to run out of money at the end of the month, you'll have already set aside the money for your saving plan.

Tips for Putting "Pay Yourself First" into Place

Paying yourself may make a lot of sense logically, but when the time comes to actually take that money out of your checking account, it can seem like a crazy idea. Below, Armchair Millionaires share their tricks for making sure that you don't miss that 10 percent.

I'm Just a Bill

"As soon as I get paid, I put money away for my bills. I also have to pay myself just as if I had gotten a bill in the mail. Add yourself to your monthly or weekly bills and soon it will be second nature to pay yourself."

—Armchair Millionaire guest

No Pain, All Gain

"When you get used to paying yourself first, the plan seems to run itself, unlike dieting or exercise. All you have to do is start. I hate exercise because of the true motto—no pain, no gain. With 'Pay Yourself First,' once you start, that's really all you have to do."

—Armchair Millionaire member Sean

There is one warning that comes along with paying yourself first. Just because you're not living within the constraints of a monthly budget that's been configured to the penny doesn't mean you have free rein to spend all you want. This is especially true when you're just getting started, before you've accumulated a lot of money in your account. Later on, when you've accumulated a few hundred— or a few thousand—dollars in your account, you'll see how your money grows and grows. That can be a real motivator when you're tempted to buy that king-size candy bar—just think about how every dollar contributes to your financial future.

As one Armchair Millionaire pointed out a few pages back, one way to change your spending habits is to stop thinking about the dollar amounts. Instead, think about how long you have to work before you'd make enough to pay for a particular item out of your "Pay Yourself First" plan.

Here's how it works. If you make $45,000 a year, your weekly paycheck of $865 is probably only worth $600 or so after taxes. Ten percent of your weekly take-home pay is $60, the amount you should aim to put into your pay-yourself-first plan.

Now, if you're thinking of buying a stereo that costs $300, how long would it take to pay for it? It would take five weeks' worth of paying yourself first in order to get your hands on that stereo. Dinner and a movie for two wipes out half a day's worth of savings. Opting for the $30,000 luxury car instead of a vehicle with a more reasonable price tag $18,000 might give you a flashier ride, but the extra $12,000 will cost you two hundred weeks' worth of paying yourself first.

Being Financially Responsible Doesn't Have to Be Boring

You don't need to budget all the fun out of your life, but you just might find out that you like the idea of spending less. There's a movement in this country of people who are dedicated to the idea of living well on less. For these folks, "frugal living" and "cheapskate" aren't derogatory terms, but labels that celebrate the notion of simplifying their lifestyles. These people have reevaluated their priorities, and decided that "simple" is better. They've figured out that they get around town in a 1995 Ford Taurus just as well as they would in a brand-spanking-new $49,000 luxury sedan. Or, they think it might be nicer to retire at age forty-five than to buy a big fancy house in a country club development (with a big mortgage to match) and toil away in their job until they're sixty-two just to pay off the home loan.

Having Fun with Less Money

Still think paying yourself first means you'll have to live like a monk? Try to look at it in a different light. This Armchair Millionaire member has found a way to do just that.

Reassess Your Priorities

"It helps to slow down and think about what you really want out of life. The answer for most people is not more stuff, but quality time and experiences with family, friends, and self. So skip the Saturday trip to the mall for clothes that you probably don't really need, and take the kids for a bike ride instead. Don't spend $20–$30 on a trip to the movies, go to the park and fly kites. Save the money and use it to get out of debt or to invest in your future and your children's futures. Choose to live more simply and you may just find that can save money *and* be happier."

—Armchair Millionaire member anonymous

The Difference Between Paying Yourself First and Saving for Retirement

It's also important to note that your "Pay Yourself First" plan is not a replacement for your retirement savings plan. You still need to be saving and investing in a tax-deferred retirement account, such as an IRA or 401(k). The money in your own savings plan can help you save for your other goals, whether it's the education of your child, a new home, an early retirement, or for any other dreams you may have.

"Paying Yourself First" is a layaway plan for your future—and you owe yourself a good future. And best of all, "Pay Yourself First" will grow your nest egg without changing your lifestyle.

From the Armchair Millionaire's Gallery— Three Folks Who Are on Their Way

Still need a little inspiration to start your savings plan? Meet three Armchair Millionaires who not only talk the talk, but walk the walk. They don't live like monks, they weren't born with trust funds, but they *are* working toward achieving all their financial dreams—just like you will when you start paying yourself first.

Looking to the Future

Armchair Millionaire Member Name: Glenda J.

From: California

Age: 45

Occupation: City government worker

Family Status: Divorced

Investment Goals: To invest for the long term and accumulate enough money to retire comfortably so I can travel, spend time with my kids and grandkids, and just have fun and not worry!

Background: I have never been a saver. I wish now that I'd started saving in my twenties—now that I'm in my mid-forties, retirement is making me nervous. I would like to retire by the time I'm sixty but I'm not sure that's feasible.

I had $10,000 in cash three years ago and it went to my head. My children and I just went on a spending spree. We had always had such a hard time—never having money, never being able to do fun things. So we bought new TVs, I fixed my ailing car, I bought another car (bad move—had to sell it later at a loss!), paid off bills, fixed my daughter's car, pretty much just frittered the money away. After eighteen months, it was gone like the wind. Now, in hindsight, I should have purchased stocks or mutual funds. I'll probably never have that much cash in my hands again.

I got started investing six years ago by putting money each payday into the tax-deferred program available through my work. Since then, I have seen my account go from $6,000 to $50,000. Several quarters I saw earnings of over $1,000 each. That was nice!

My daughter is now a single parent in her mid-twenties and I stress to her to save, save, save. She has opened a money market account at her bank. I tell her that if I had saved beginning at her age, I would probably have close to $500,000 instead of the $50,000 I have now.

I'd like to tell everyone who hasn't started their investment plan that you need to look to the future. Twenty years has a way of just going by and before you know it, you could be seriously thinking of retirement and worrying that you may wind up living on the street.

Some people are disciplined and save. I have never been that way. It has been a long time coming—but putting my money away on payday before I have a chance to spend it has really helped my portfolio grow.

Living Frugally But Still Having Fun

Armchair Millionaire Member Name: Mark P.
From: Oregon
Age: 28
Occupation: Mechanical Engineer
Family Status: Single
Investment Goals: Retire from the corporate world at 40
Background: Working in the high tech-industry, I make a good salary. But I live well below my means. I drive an inexpensive car and I don't eat out a lot. I get a kick out of being frugal, but I still dedicate funds to my favorite hobbies—windsurfing, snowboarding, and world travel. My goal is to remain debt-free until I make the inevitable decision to buy a house.

My dad was a real saver and taught us to do the same. My company offered a class called "The Road to Financial Independence" that I attended when I was twenty-four. That got me started investing. Before that, I thought that buying things would make me happy. I get a lot more enjoyment now out of watching my portfolio grow with companies I like than I do buying more stuff that I don't really need. I see that my friends have lots of debt that they can't seem to shed because they live consistently above their means. I've learned it's important to live simply and challenge yourself to be frugal . . . but not at the expense of having fun.

Setting Attainable Goals—and Reaching Them

Armchair Millionaire Member Name: Greg F.

From: Florida

Age: 44

Occupation: Salesman

Family Status: Married

Investment Goals: Retire at 52

Background: Pay yourself first. That's all you need to know. My father was a banker who grew up in the Depression. He taught me to live within my means, never carry a balance on credit, and encouraged me to go into business for myself, starting when I was eight years old selling pachysandra plants that I had grown, door to door. I still have a copy of the first paycheck I received.

I figured out how much I need to retire on and what my anticipated return is and then decided what I needed to save in order to accomplish that. I've tried to pass along what I've learned about saving and investing to my two kids, and recently gave them each a copy of *The Millionaire Next Door* to help them learn more about the subject. Probably the biggest event that has happened recently is my one-year-old marriage. I now have somebody I want to play and retire with. My wife, Gail, is helping to motivate me toward my goal.

Putting Your "Pay Yourself First" Plan into Place

Unfortunately, while the concept of paying yourself first sounds great, we all know how hard it is in reality to write that check to yourself each month. Let's face it. Budgeting, like dieting, just doesn't work.

If we all had that kind of willpower, America would be a country of healthy and wealthy folks.

Does that mean you should give up? No way. Here's how you can make sure you take care of your plan each month.

First of all, whatever you do, don't put your weekly or monthly 10 percent payment in a savings account that's linked to your checking account. That makes it too easy to transfer money back to your checking account, or to withdraw funds using an ATM card on the spur of the moment.

Ideally, you should open another, completely separate account, at a bank or other financial institution (we'll cover this in detail later in this chapter). If you think you might be tempted to withdraw money for some frivolous purchase, open an account at an altogether different bank from your regular bank, one that's on the other side of town or inconvenient for you to get to. You can mail your monthly check to the bank to have it deposited into your account. Don't get an ATM card, either. If your bank insists on sending you one, cut it into pieces right away or add it to that credit card sorbet in your freezer.

An Honest-to-Goodness Foolproof Plan to Pay Yourself First

There is one even easier way to pay yourself first each month—a method so foolproof that hardly anyone could mess it up. If you can't discipline yourself to pay yourself first each month, you don't have to stand alone. Call in the reinforcements!

Here's all you need to do: Get in touch with a brokerage firm or mutual fund company and open an account. That's not all, though. You need to ask the institution to help you pay yourself first, in what most financial institutions call an automatic deduction plan. (We like to call it the "Pay Yourself First Plan for Real People.")

Once you've set up your plan, your bank will send a specific sum each month to your mutual fund or brokerage firm. Automatically. Your broker or fund manager will then invest that amount on your behalf. Automatically.

Setting up an automatic investment plan is easy. Nearly all brokerage firms and mutual fund companies will help you. First, you need to have an account with a broker or mutual fund. If you already have an account, ask for an application form for their "automatic deduction plan." If you don't have an account, you can set up an automatic plan when you establish your account.

Complete the form and indicate how much you want transferred each month. Then return the form—you will generally be asked to enclose a voided check from your checking account.

Don't be confused about requests for the "routing number of your current financial institution" or other gobbledygook. A phone call to your bank or the financial institution can help fill in any blanks on the application.

One Automatic Plan Caveat

One of the great things about taking part in an investing community such as Armchair Millionaire is that you can benefit from others' mistakes. Here, an Armchair Millionaire community member explains one possible Pay Yourself First pitfall:

Don't Forget to Keep Track of Your Deduction

"You do, of course, have to remember to write the money that is automatically deducted in your checkbook each month so you don't bounce a check. Believe me, paying yourself is so easy. It is totally painless. Just sign up and you will naturally adjust your spending to accommodate the missing amount."

—Armchair Millionaire member Judy D

Chances are that you already have an automatic deduction plan in place to pay your monthly health club dues or life insurance premiums. Your 10 percent plan is no different.

It may take a month or so before your transfers start happening.

But after that, it's smooth sailing. Each month, your 10 percent will be electronically transferred from your bank account to your saving and investing account.

Let Your Employer Help

Many companies offer a savings plan for their employees, and this can be another good way to get started with your savings plan. Each week, your company will take a certain percentage from your paycheck and deposit it into a special account. Sometimes, you'll have the option of buying your company's stock in the savings plan. Other times, your money will simply collect interest or be available for investment into mutual funds. Check to see if your company offers such a savings plan.

Pay Yourself First Worksheet

After you've decided to pay yourself first, you need to figure out exactly how much you should be saving each month. Use this simple worksheet to determine your own monthly saving goal. A calculator might be useful if you're mathematically challenged, as many of us are.

ONE WEEK'S TAKE-HOME PAY $ _____

Take a look at your paycheck from last week. Try not to wince at the thought of all the taxes you paid. Now write the amount of the check, after taxes and deductions, on the above line. (If you get paid on some other basis rather than weekly, you'll have to make an adjustment.)

MULTIPLY BY 4.33 (x 4.33)

Seems like a strange number, doesn't it? Let us explain: Have you ever noticed how there are 52 weeks in the year, and 4 weeks in a month, but 12 months in a year? If you multiply 4 times 12, you end up with 48 weeks—not 52. That explains why you get your weekly paycheck 5 times in some months and 4 times in other months—the average month is actually 4.33 weeks long.

AVERAGE MONTHLY TAKE-HOME PAY = $ _____
If you multiply your weekly take-home pay times 4.33, the result is your average monthly take-home paycheck. Since we want to establish a monthly saving plan, this number is crucial.

MULTIPLY BY 10 PERCENT (X 10%)
Now, multiply your monthly take-home pay by 10 percent.
Monthly Amount to Pay Yourself First $ _____
The result is the amount you should be setting aside each month in a separate saving and investing plan, on top of your contributions to an IRA and/or 401(k).

If 10 percent of your weekly paycheck seems comfortably within your reach, try increasing your monthly contribution to 15 percent. Also, when you get a pay raise, the first thing you should do is increase your weekly savings amount to 10 percent of your new paycheck.

There's no limit to how much you can save and invest, and the more you can put away on a regular basis, the better off you'll be when it comes time to reap the rewards.

Chapter 6 Action Items

In this chapter, you've learned the importance of "Paying Yourself First." Here are the steps you need to get started on your own "Pay Yourself First" plan.

- Set up a separate saving or investing account with a financial institution.
- Determine the dollar amount you will contribute each month. It's okay to start out small—but keep aiming to contribute at least 10 percent of your take-home pay in the plan.
- Establish an automatic deduction plan to transfer money each month from your bank to your saving and investing account.

CHAPTER 7

STEP 3:
Invest Automatically—
and Benefit from
Dollar Cost Averaging

Now that you've learned some of the basic tools for saving money, it's time to get to the real meat of the matter—what to do with the money you've saved in order to achieve the maximum benefit for your long-term goals. While you might *feel* comfortable letting your money sit in the bank collecting interest, the danger in stashing your cash in savings accounts and certificates of deposit is that your money will only grow by 3 percent or maybe 5 percent a year. That's simply not enough to turn you into a millionaire.

Armchair Millionaires know that they need to do something with their cash besides putting it in the bank. But it's not good enough to simply "invest"—you need to invest in the most sensible fashion possible. So what are the options?

Coming to the decision to invest means knowing the answers to three simple questions.

1. **Where should you invest?** ("Stocks, bonds, or Treasury bills"?)
2. **When should you invest?** ("Is now the right time? Will the market go down soon?")
3. **What should you invest in?** ("If stocks, which ones?")

In this chapter, you'll learn the answers to the first two of these questions (we'll save the last question and the specific investment plan you should consider for the next chapter, Chapter 8). So let's take a look at deciding where you should invest.

Where should you invest?

As you might have guessed by now, Armchair Millionaires are partial to investing in the stock market. But stocks aren't the only place you can invest.

Experts divide the universe of potential investments into different categories called "asset classes." These groupings are just a way to lump together investments that have similar levels of risk and return. The three major asset classes are cash, bonds, and stocks. (Some people consider real estate, precious metals, and other natural resources as assets, too, but we'll stick with the first three classes.)

You're probably familiar with cash, even though you may never have thought of it as an asset class. Cash is just as good as, well, money in the bank—as long as you keep it in the bank and not under your mattress. The good thing about cash is that you can safely earn a little bit of a return in a bank account. The bad thing about cash is that you can only earn a little bit of a return in a bank account.

If your grandfather had put $1 in the bank on the first day of 1926, he'd have ended up with $16.06 by June 30, 2000. That's a 3.8 percent rate of return over 74 years. That's pretty dismal, but wait—it gets worse when you add in the effects of inflation. Inflation is nothing more than the rising costs of goods and services. Inflation is a loaf of bread that costs $1.79 today, the same loaf that your mom used to buy for a dime or a quarter when you were a kid. Over time, inflation in the U.S. has grown at an average rate of 3.1 percent, and it impacts your investments just as it impacts the cost of bread. Adjusted for inflation, that dollar that your granddad invested in 1926 is now worth only about $1.67.

Armchair Millionaires know that it's a good idea to have some cash on hand for emergencies, but if you're working toward a goal that's twenty or thirty years down the road, it's better to seek out a better rate of return in another asset class. On the risk and return scale, cash offers little risk and little return compared to other investments.

So what about bonds? A bond is nothing more than a promise to repay a loan. The borrower can be a company (a corporate bond), a local government agency (a municipal bond), and even the federal government (a Treasury bond).

While many people think of bonds as "safe" investments, the riskiness of a particular bond depends on many factors, most importantly, who issued the bond. For instance, bonds issued by a company that's desperate for cash will pay a high interest rate, but that's because anyone who buys their bonds is taking the risk that the company will welch on the debt (this is known as "defaulting" on the bond). These are also called junk bonds. On the other hand, a bond issued by a company like IBM carries much less risk of default than a junk bond, so they can pay a lower interest rate. At the high end of the safety scale, bonds issued by the federal government carry little risk of default, since they are "backed by the full faith and credit of the United States government."

Are bonds a good idea? If your grandmother had persuaded her husband to buy long-term government bonds in 1926, their $1 would have grown to $44.24 by 2000, an average return of 5.2 percent. If she could have persuaded him to buy long-term corporate bonds instead, their $1 would have grown to $60.10, returning 5.7 percent annually. That's better than cash, for sure (way to go, Grandma!), but after inflation it's hard to imagine that they could have really gotten ahead if they had stuck purely with bonds.

That leaves the third major asset class—stocks. Stocks are sometimes known as equities. These are shares of corporations that are bought and sold by investors in a public market. When you own shares of stock in a corporation, you become a part-owner of that company.

So let's say that Granddad invested in the stock market in 1926. Perhaps you're familiar with the history of the stock market and know about a not-so-minor event that happened in 1929 when the stock market crashed. What you may not know is that 1929 wasn't the worst of it. Over the next three years, the market continued to decline, making paupers out of millionaires. Granddad's $1 investment in 1926 would have been worth $2.20 at the end of 1928 (doubling his money in two years), but that $2.20 would have been worth just 79 cents at the end of 1932. Ouch!

But your granddad was smart. He didn't get spooked by the market, and he remained invested in stocks, even though there were many more times when the market would jump and fall dramatically. By mid-2000, his $1 investment would have been worth $2,833.51. We'll do the math here—that's an 11.2 percent annual return on his investment over the seventy-four-year period.

When you compare these three asset classes, the question about where to invest is a no-brainer. The stock market offers much higher returns over the long term, so most Armchair Millionaires invest their long-term savings in stocks. When we say "long-term" we mean five years or longer.

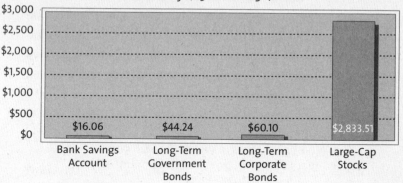

Growth of $1.00 Invested in Various Assets
January 1, 1926–June 30, 2000

But simply knowing that stocks are the place to be if you want to be a millionaire doesn't really go far enough. You still need to know when to invest in the stock market, and what stocks you should buy!

When should you invest?

Once you've made the decision to invest in the stock market, you need to know when is the best time to invest. When you look at the market from a historical perspective, you can see that it's very common for the market to experience some serious downturns. From 1928 through 1999, the Standard & Poor's 500, a leading index used to gauge the performance of the stock market (we'll tell you more about indexes in Chapter 8), declined in 20 of those 74 years. In 8 of those years, it declined more than 10 percent, and more than 20 percent in 4 of the years—and that's not even counting the times that the market has declined more than 10 percent or even 20 percent in the middle of a year and then recovered.

The stock market goes up and down in the short term without any apparent pattern or regularity, and it can be pretty painful to watch 30 percent of your portfolio disappear in the course of a couple of months. So what happens when the market falls through the floor?

Nothing.

The key to investing in the stock market is to remember that over time it always tends to go up. In 54 of the last 74 years, the S&P 500 has ended the year higher than it started out. In 43 years, the S&P 500 ended more than 10 percent higher, and in 29 years, it closed the year with a 20 percent or greater gain. As long as you're willing to wait it out, your portfolio should survive.

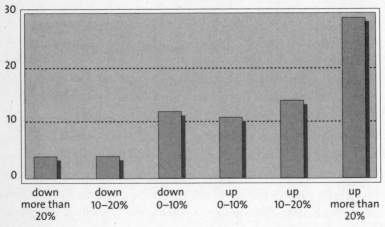

**Number of Years in Which the S&P 500
Ended Year Higher or Lower than Beginning of Year
1928–1999**

"So when is the best time to invest in the stock market?" you may be wondering. "When the market is high? Or when the market is low? And why can't I just sell right before the market drops and then buy back right before the stocks go back up again?"

Obviously, you'd love to be able to time your investments so that you only put money into the market when it's low. That way, when the market reaches new heights you'd make a fortune, right?

If only it were that easy. Unfortunately, there is no way of knowing when is the absolute best time to invest. Believe us, thousands of people have searched and searched for the magic formula that would predict the direction of the stock market over the next day, week, month, or longer. All have failed. This is called "timing the market," and it's a waste of time. The truth is that no one is able to correctly guess the future direction of the market. Not your broker. Not the professionals of Wall Street. Not your Uncle Sid. No one.

Think about it: if there were a foolproof way of knowing exactly when you should buy into the stock market and when you should get out, we'd be a nation of millionaires already.

Another problem with trying to buy stocks in a falling stock market is that it sounds easy, but many people don't have the stomach for it. In fact, the stock market is the only place we know of where people get more interested when the prices are being raised. They seem to lose interest when stocks are "on sale."

Where does that leave you, if you'll never know when it's the best time to invest? Actually in a very good place. Armchair Millionaires understand that while the market can't be predicted in the short term, it does go up over the long term. And so the best thing to do with your long-term savings is to invest in the stock market all the time. Because stock markets, while having bad days—even bad years—tend to go up over time.

So resolve yourself right now to never knowing the absolute best time to invest in the stock market.

Yet you do know that you want to earn that 11 percent return (like your grandfather did) by being invested in the stock market. So when should you invest? All the time! Meaning that each month, you should invest the same amount of money in stocks. No worrying, no wondering, just the same old boring investment every month.

This approach to investing is called "dollar cost averaging." When you put dollar cost averaging to work in your financial plan, you invest all the money you're saving each month into the stock market, no matter how high or low the market is. (Remember, we'll cover the question, "What should you invest in?" in Chapter 8.)

When you invest a set amount each month—say $90—your money will buy you fewer shares when the market is high, and more shares when it's low. You'll put dollar cost averaging to work and sleep well every night, knowing that, over time, you're buying the number of shares that's just right for your budget.

	Monthly Investment	Share Price	Number of Shares	Cumulative Cost	Total Worth of Investment
Month 1	EACH MONTH YOU INVEST $90	$9	10	$90	$90
Month 2	$90	$3 OUCH! BIG DROP!	30	$180	$120
Month 3	$90	$6	15	$270	$330 WOW! A PROFIT!

The reason dollar cost averaging works is that it forces you to buy fewer shares when the stock market is high and more shares when the market is low. You can think of it as automatically buying more shares any time the market is on sale. Plus, since it helps you to "buy low" every time you invest, dollar cost averaging boosts portfolio performance, even when the stock market fluctuates. In time, a regular investment plan like this helps to smooth out the market's ups and downs. The bonus is that this strategy boosts your return over time, and takes away your day-to-day worries about the normal swings in the market.

Dollar cost averaging is easy to understand, even easier to do, and the long-term effect it will have on your portfolio will bring tears (of joy!) to your eyes. To quote John Bogle, one of Wall Street's most successful money managers, "As far as investing is concerned, dollar cost averaging suggests that slow-and-steady will likely win the race."

Does It Work?

Sure, it sounds great in theory, but does it really work?

A lot of it depends on whether you can stomach the market's ups and downs. Even though time is on your side, there may be months—even years—when your investments will be worth less than you paid. This can test the mettle of the most knowledgeable investor. Tools like dollar cost averaging can protect you, but only if you're ready to stick to a plan in good times and bad.

Imagine this: You return from vacation, log on to your computer and discover that the market has crashed and your $10,000 portfolio is now worth $5,000. Do you sell? Or do you keep buying every month using dollar cost averaging?

a. Sell it all
b. Stick to the plan

Armchair Millionaires know that it's best not to panic when the market falls. In fact, dollar cost averaging can be your friend in declining markets if you stick to the plan.

Dollar Cost Averaging in Retrospect

To really see how dollar cost averaging works, we have to go back in time a bit. Let's compare how it would have worked with your investment during the worst bear market in history—the Great Depression.

Assume for a minute that you started investing near the beginning of the Depression. If you had made a lump sum investment on January 1, 1928, you would have *lost* an average of 0.9 percent every year through 1938 (ouch!). On the other hand, with regular monthly investments throughout the Depression, your average annual *gain* would have been 7.4 percent.

Regular Investing Is a Winner in Bull and Bear Markets

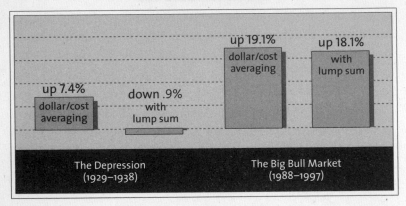

But dollar cost averaging also works in rising markets. Consider the greatest bull market in history—1988 through 1997. If you had invested a lump sum on January 1, 1988, your average yearly return through the end of 1997 would have been 18.1 percent. Regular monthly investments made during that same time would have returned you an average of 19.1 percent.

(This calculation assumes that your savings were invested in the stock market in the S&P 500 index. It also assumes that you reinvested all your interest, dividends, and capital gains.)

As you can see, dollar cost averaging really helps you maximize your return during the down markets, but still lets you enjoy the great returns of bull markets. Over time, it can make a huge difference in your portfolio's value.

If you've ever asked yourself, "Is this the right time to get into the stock market?" or said, "The market's too high now. I've missed my chance," you'll soon forget those words after you've learned about the power of dollar cost averaging every month.

Investing in the stock market regularly gives your money the force of a one-two punch: You have the best long-term investment, along with a powerful tool—dollar cost averaging—that will bolster the worth of your investment during good and bad markets.

Perhaps the Best Part of Dollar Cost Averaging—Peace of Mind

Another very powerful aspect of dollar cost averaging is its ability to let you relax. No matter what happens in the market, or how you're feeling about your finances, dollar cost averaging insures that your investment plan keeps marching on undisturbed. And this positive impact on your emotional health is what makes the Armchair Millionaire plan so livable, and so successful. Because if you become stressed out over a dip in the market, you could panic and sell your shares when prices are low (and all Armchair Millionaires know that is a quick way to lose money). With dollar cost averaging in the arsenal of investment tools, Armchair Millionaires have the emotional security of being able to keep their wits about them no matter what's happening in the market. Here, some Armchair Millionaire members explain exactly how investing on a regular schedule helps them sleep at night.

The Long-Term Payoffs

"One of the best reasons for dollar cost averaging is that, over time, you'll pay less for your fund shares than if you'd bought in big blocks every year or so. You get the peace of mind knowing that you're ensuring a good return over the long term without ever trying to time the market (which is nearly impossible for even the experts to do consistently)."

—Armchair Millionaire member bandl

No More Waiting for Lady Luck

"Think about it this way: Each year, you set aside $1,000 to buy shares of mutual fund X. You decide to wait and watch until the shares are as low as you think they'll go. If you did this, you would be trying to time the market. And timing the market is not the kind of thing an amateur can do. Frankly, I'm skeptical that even the pros can do it. If you know someone who has timed the market and made a lot of

money that way, don't be seduced. They were lucky. I don't like luck
being a part of my investing strategy. That's why I go to Vegas."

—Armchair Millionaire member Rose

The Bigger Picture

"Here's why dollar cost averaging and indexing are so smart. They don't
assume any single narrow investing strategy will be the one and only
one that works. Instead, dollar cost averaging takes a really broad view
of the markets and merely predicts that the markets will continue, on
average, to rise in the future. It's hard to dispute the evidence of more
than a century's worth of stock market data. People have to understand
what risk is and not just turn away some good ideas because there is an
element of risk. Not investing intelligently is the biggest risk of all."

—Armchair Millionaire member Matt

From the Armchair Millionaire's Gallery—
Meet Armchair Millionaire Member AMDave, Dollar Cost Averager Extraordinaire

AMDave is an official community leader for the Armchair Millionaire Web site. Dave's exuberance for the Armchair Millionaire plan
and his ability to encourage conversation make him a natural at helping everyday folks start their investment plan. Here, Dave explains
how he got started investing, and why dollar cost averaging is such
an important part of his financial plan.

Armchair Millionaire Member Name: AMDave
From: Horsham, Pennsylvania
Age: 33
Occupation: Networking Consultant
Family Status: Married, with daughter (17 months) and another child
on the way

Financial goal: Retirement, college for children
How far along are you? On track so far

What was your biggest misconception before you started investing?
I used to think that investing in the stock market was no different from going to the casino. I still believe that's true in the short term. In the long term however, the market eventually works its way upward, making it a good place to put money (on a regularly timed basis) that won't be needed for several years.

How does dollar cost averaging help you achieve your goal?
By having equal 401(k) plan contributions automatically deducted from my paychecks each month, I buy more shares when the price is low, fewer shares when the price is high. Rather than being upset during the summer of 1998 market correction, I was enjoying buying a greater number of fund shares "on sale" with each payroll deduction. I also don't have to worry about investing a large lump sum just before a market crash, or about procrastinating because of that fear.

What do you want the world to know about investing?
Invest as much as you can as early as you can. Make periodic (preferably automatic) investing part of your life early on, and you'll have a good chance at meeting your financial goals.

Making Dollar Cost Averaging Work for You

Once you've decided on how much you will "Pay Yourself First," you can use that amount to dollar cost average into the stock market. In Chapter 8, you'll learn exactly how to invest in the stock market in order to maximize your returns and minimize your risks.

But instead of writing a check each month, there's an even easier way to put dollar cost averaging to work. You should set up an

Automatic Investment Plan (AIP), which will withdraw that money from your checking account and invest it automatically.

Nearly all brokers and mutual funds offer an AIP option. Why not? It's a great way to make sure their customers keep sending them money. In fact, brokers and financial institutions like AIPs so much they don't even charge for the service.

Beware of Hidden Fees

While dollar cost averaging can make the most of your money, if your account or your chosen investment requires a transaction fee, dollar cost averaging won't be nearly as effective. Below are some words of wisdom from Armchair Millionaires on this topic:

Buyer Beware

"You definitely don't want to get into a relationship with a broker or a mutual fund company that charges you a fee for each automatic investment as if it's a stock transaction. You need to find plans and companies that let you make your automatic investments for free or for annual account charges. In other words, if you dollar cost average $100 a month, don't pay a $25 or $30 transaction fee each time. That would be crazy. If the investment you want to buy can only be bought for a transaction fee, then you might want to consider making one large investment once a year, rather than each month. (Or you might want to change brokers.)"

—Armchair Millionaire member Jes

"I agree. If you think taxes retard your investment's growth, stock transaction fees are deadly. Don't even think about dollar cost averaging if you are paying stock transaction fees every time."

—Armchair Millionaire member Marty

At some brokerages, you'll have to complete two sets of forms, one to authorize the transfer of money each month, and the other to authorize the monthly investment in your chosen mutual fund or other security.

To sign up, request forms for the company's automatic investment plan. You'll probably have to send a cancelled check from your bank account along with the form, and you may need your bank's routing number, but your bank's customer service desk can tell you that in a jiffy.

The beauty of an automatic plan like this is that you'll never have to worry about whether the market is high or low—and you'll never have to put investing on your list of "Things to Do." Your plan will run itself.

In good times or bad, dollar cost averaging is the smartest way to build a portfolio's value for long-term investing. Historically, stock market investments have done better than any other kind of investment over a long time. It's only when you stick with stocks through good and bad that you can earn that 11 percent annual return.

That brings us right up to the third part of our investing decision, "What should I invest in?" Keep on going to Chapter 8 for the answer.

Chapter 7 Action Items

- Determine the fixed amount of money you want to invest each month.
- Open an account at a brokerage firm or mutual fund company, one that has an option to receive automatic payments from your bank account.
- Fill out your AIP forms and send them to the financial institution where you've chosen to open your monthly savings account.

CHAPTER 8

STEP 4:
Use the Armchair
Investing Strategy

So far, we've examined the first two parts of the investing process, knowing 1) where to invest (in the stock market) and 2) when to invest (always, so you can take advantage of dollar cost averaging). For many people, the toughest part about investing is the last part of the equation: 3. **What should you invest in?**

Knowing that the stock market is where you *need* to be regularly investing if you want to become an Armchair Millionaire isn't enough. How do you analyze investments? What stocks or mutual funds should you buy? And when should you sell?

Many Wall Street professionals have spent millions of dollars testing various theories on which stocks to buy and how long to hold them. Fortunately for you, the Armchair Millionaire has developed a simple, yet highly effective approach to long-term investing in the stock market. It incorporates decades of academic research done at some of the greatest universities, as well as some ideas from the sharpest investing minds of all time.

We call our program the Armchair Investing Strategy. While it includes investing methods that have been around, and have been used successfully for years, they have never been brought together into one comprehensive strategy. What's more, you can put the plan to work at lots of brokerage firms and mutual fund companies without having to pay lots of fees or commissions. It's elementary enough so you won't need an MBA or a degree in accounting in order to put it to work. And it won't require that you spend hours a day (or hours a week—or even hours a month) managing your portfolio once you've got it up and running. For people with busy lives, the Armchair Investing Strategy is a way to invest without giving up your hobbies or family time.

Part A—Why the Armchair Investing Strategy Works

For most investors, the Armchair Investing Strategy will be the perfect way to make your money work for you over the long term. But the fact that the Armchair Investing Strategy is near-Nirvana didn't happen by accident. When we developed this approach to the stock market, we started out by studying what all the experts had to say about what works, and looked for a strategy that meets eight basic criteria.

Eight Criteria for a Near-Perfect Investing Strategy

1. THE STRATEGY MUST BE EASY TO START. We looked for an investing method that anyone could implement quite simply, with any amount of money, from $50 to $50,000.

2. THE STRATEGY MUST BE EASY TO MAINTAIN. Once you're up and running with your portfolio, it shouldn't require hours of work each day, or each week, or even each month. You shouldn't need to spend all your free time researching stocks and mutual funds, or spending hours on the phone with your broker, or reading the stock tables in the newspaper, or doing calculations in a spreadsheet.

3. THE STRATEGY MUST BE EASY TO UNDERSTAND. What good are complicated investing strategies that require you to wade through financial textbooks or to go back to college for an advanced degree? "Easy to understand" doesn't mean "unsophisticated," however.

4. THE STRATEGY MUST BE INEXPENSIVE TO IMPLEMENT AND TO MAINTAIN. In this instance, we're not talking about the amount of money that you actually invest—we're referring to the fees, commissions, and expenses some investment plans require that can add up to a small fortune over the years. In fact, one of the two biggest factors that can kill long-term gains in a portfolio is the cost of management. Investors who are consistently trading stocks and funds, buying and selling on a daily or weekly basis, risk watching their returns become seriously reduced by the amount they pay in commissions (not to mention the taxes on all those short-term gains). If you have to pay hundreds of dollars for data and reports and subscriptions, then all these expenses will also reduce your returns.

5. THE STRATEGY MUST BE TAX-EFFICIENT. Taxes are the other item that can put a big dent in the long-term gains in a portfolio. Whenever you have profits in your portfolio, either from dividends, interest, or capital gains (when you sell a stock or mutual fund), you'll have to pay taxes to the IRS. What's worse is that frequent traders have to pay higher taxes, since gains on stocks you've owned for less than a year don't receive the lower capital gains tax rate of 20 percent. Instead, short-term capital gains are taxed at your ordinary income rate—if you're in the 28 percent tax bracket, you'll pay taxes of 28 percent on your short-term earnings. If you want to be a millionaire, you'll definitely want to pay less in taxes over the years.

6. THE STRATEGY MUST BE WIDELY AVAILABLE. What good is an investing plan that you can't use in your 401(k), or with the broker of your choice? The Armchair Investing Strategy can be used in some form or other at just about any mutual fund company or brokerage firm in the country.

7. THE STRATEGY MUST HAVE A LOT OF HISTORY TO JUDGE IT BY. If you're investing for the long term, you'll want a plan that's been proven over the long term. At the end of the twentieth century, the U.S. stock market was in one of the biggest bull markets in its history. In the 1990s, the stock market grew tremendously, and most investors will barely remember the minor blips in 1997 and 1998 (as they will likely forget the turbulence in the spring of 2000). But things won't always look so rosy, if history is our guide. A lot of mutual funds and investment advisors advertise great track records over the past five years, but anyone can look like an investing genius in a bull market. When the market turns south, and experiences a few years of declining returns, how will those portfolios perform?

Instead, we looked for a strategy that has worked well through bull and bear markets, going back to at least 1970. Why 1970? Well, the U.S. stock market had one of its worst bear markets in the 1970s, so evaluating a portfolio based on its performance since then can give us a good idea how it will likely perform in the next bear market.

8. FINALLY, THE STRATEGY MUST MAKE A LOT OF MONEY (NATURALLY!). After all, who wants an easy, understandable, inexpensive, tax-efficient, widely available investing plan with a long history if it doesn't generate a good rate of return! And the winner is . . .

There's only one way to invest in the stock market that meets all those criteria—and it's called "Indexing." Indexing is a way of investing so that you match the returns of an entire stock market index, guaranteed. An indexed portfolio provides every single one of the advantages outlined above.

In fact, one of the finest investors of our time, Warren Buffet, says that indexing is the best approach to the stock market for 99 percent of all investors. But before we can tell you why indexing is so great, we first have to take a detailed look at what indexing is. Bear with us—there's a lot of information to go over, but we promise it all fits into one cohesive, easy-to-understand package. Honest.

What Is a Market Index?

In order to understand the Armchair Investing Strategy, you must first know what a stock market index is. You've probably heard of one of the most common stock market indexes, the Dow Jones Industrial Average (also known as "the Dow" or the "Dow 30"). The Dow is a collection of thirty stocks that represent some of the biggest companies in American business. Every day, the prices of all thirty stocks are used to determine the value of the Dow Jones Industrial Average. Investors look at the value of the Dow and use it as a gauge of the entire market—if the Dow is up, the market as a whole is usually up. If the Dow is down, the rest of the market is usually down as well.

Another common index is the Standard & Poor's 500. The S&P 500 includes five hundred companies of all sizes and from all industries, chosen by S&P to represent the full spectrum of American business. It includes computer companies, utilities, transportation companies, manufacturers, restaurants, stores—you name the industry and it's probably represented by the S&P 500. While the S&P 500 contains small and large companies, the largest companies dominate the index because it's weighted by market capitalization. That means that S&P first considers the size of a company relative to other companies (in financial speak, this is known as a company's "market capitalization" or "market cap"). Then, it adds enough of that company's shares to the S&P 500 so that it is represented in the index in the same proportion. Or, to put it more simply, bigger companies have more shares in the index than do smaller companies.

The Dow 30 and the S&P 500 aren't the only indexes of the stock market. There are indexes that range from the obvious (such as the Dow or S&P 500) to the obscure (such as the Bloomberg Football Club Index, which represents the performance of publicly traded

British soccer teams). There are indexes that track the performance of particular industries and of the stocks in particular countries. There are indexes for small companies, large companies, and those in between.

Investors and mutual fund managers like to measure their own results against the performance of a particular index. For instance, a mutual fund that invests in large companies might use the S&P 500 as a benchmark by which they can let the world know just how well they're doing.

What Is a Mutual Fund?

Mutual funds are one of the most popular investments available. A mutual fund is a pool of money that's been contributed by investors, is actively maintained by a manager (a single person or a team of investment analysts who invest all the contributions of investors in a single portfolio), and is invested in companies the manager handselects. A mutual fund can hold stocks, or bonds, or cash, or other assets, and there are funds that are devoted to specific investing strategies, countries, or regions of the world. Among stock funds, there are those that invest in technology stocks and those that invest in utility stocks and so on. No matter what your financial flavor is, chances are there are funds that fit the bill.

The main advantages of mutual funds are that your money is managed by professionals, you can easily build a diversified portfolio, and you can invest relatively small amounts without paying a lot in fees and commissions.

ADVICE FROM RICH

A lot of investors like to invest in stocks directly, without going through a mutual fund. Although the Armchair Investing Strategy is based on investing in mutual funds, it doesn't mean you have to give up your stock-picking habit entirely. Many Armchair Millionaires use what's called the "core and explore" method of building a portfolio.

They use the Armchair Investing Strategy for their "core" portfolio, investing at least half of their total assets using our approach. Then they use the other portion of their portfolio to "explore" the world of stocks and other investments.

Standard mutual funds aren't all peaches and cream, though. One of the main disadvantages to mutual funds is that they often charge fees to offset the cost of the manager's salary. Along the same lines, because managers are directly responsible for a fund's performance, they can quickly change the makeup of a mutual fund to boost earnings (or cut losses), meaning that the fund you buy into isn't necessarily the fund you'll end up with at any given point in time. And finally, even if you find a mutual fund with a manager whose track record you respect, that manager may leave, again opening you up to the possibility that the fund you buy into won't be the same one you end up with.

The Beauty of an Index Fund

An index fund allows you to enjoy the good parts of a mutual fund with little of the bad by buying stock in all the companies of a particular index. That's how an index fund can reproduce the performance of an entire section of the market. An index fund builds its portfolio by simply buying all of the stocks in a particular index—in effect, buying the entire stock market, not just a few stocks. The most popular index of stock index funds is the Standard & Poor's 500. There are index funds that track twenty-eight different indexes, and more are added all the time.

An S&P 500 stock index fund owns five hundred stocks—all of the companies that are included in the index. This is the key distinction between stock index funds and "actively managed" mutual funds. The manager of a stock index fund doesn't have to worry about which stocks to buy or sell—he or she only has to buy the stocks that are included in the fund's chosen index. A stock index fund has no need for a team of highly paid stock analysts and expensive computer equipment to pick stocks for the fund's portfolio. So the hardest part of running a mutual fund is eliminated.

That's great because an index mutual fund is much cheaper to run than an active fund. Eliminate those analysts' salaries and an index fund can cut its costs tremendously. Those savings can be passed along to investors in the form of higher returns. Remember, reducing commissions is an easy and powerful way to boost your investing returns.

ADVICE FROM RICH

The average time that an index used in the Armchair Investing Strategy has existed is 35.3 years. This is good news for people who believe that the more information you have, the more intelligent decisions you can make. Investors in index funds are more comfortable investing with the benefit of decades of information.

Since index funds diversify by buying all the companies in an index rather than by trying to pick winners and losers, they aren't going to "beat the market." But they're guaranteed not to underperform their benchmark index either (at least by a significant margin).

If that sounds like a plan that guarantees mediocrity, it is—and that's good!

You see, the main advantage of stock index funds is that they perform better than actively managed funds. Some investors find it incredible when they learn that most mutual funds are flops, at least when it comes to generating returns for their shareholders. From 1995 to 1999, for instance, nearly 85 percent of all mutual funds that were set up to beat the S&P 500 failed to meet that goal in any particular year. When you think about it, that's an incredible statistic—8 out of 10 mutual funds can't beat the market. If the investors in those funds only knew what Armchair Millionaires know, they'd be much better off. Investing in an index fund guarantees that you'll always match the performance of the overall market.

EXTRA! EXTRA! Read all about it! Index Funds Clobber Actively Managed Funds

Sure, investing in a stock index fund also guarantees that you'll never outperform the overall market, but fewer than 20 percent of all professional mutual fund managers can reach that goal in any given year. Even armed with this knowledge, some investors are convinced they can pick out one of the funds that will be in the rare 20 percent club. Armchair Millionaires, though, know that this sounds easy in theory but is actually much harder in practice. If you look at a list of the top-performing mutual funds for the last several years, you won't likely find many of the same names on more than a few lists. It's not uncommon for a fund to have a "hot" year, but it's very uncommon for a fund to consistently turn in above-average performance.

Back in Chapter 7, you learned how the stock market has generated better returns than just about any other kind of investment. When you invest in stock index funds, you get the same kinds of returns as the whole market in your own portfolio. And when you consider the failure rate of active funds, being doomed to an "average" performance in your portfolio doesn't seem like such a bad deal, does it?

Modern Portfolio Theory—A Fancy Way of Saying "Minimize Risk, Maximize Returns"

By now, you've probably guessed that the Armchair Investing Strategy uses index funds as its primary investment vehicle. But you don't have to take our word on the benefits of passive investing through the use of index funds. The Armchair Investment Strategy is really an extension of a well-respected school of thought called the "Modern Portfolio Theory."

The Modern Portfolio Theory was first developed by an economics student named Harry Markowitz in the early 1950s. Working on his doctoral thesis at the University of Chicago, Markowitz figured out that it is possible to build a portfolio that will generate above-average returns but with below-average risk. That's good news for Armchair Millionaires.

Markowitz defined risk as going hand-in-hand with returns in an investment portfolio. Investors always like to reduce the risk of their stocks falling drastically in price, but rather than worry about the risk level of individual stocks, Markowitz suggested that investors look at the risk of their overall portfolio.

ADVICE FROM RICH

One of the basic concepts of the Armchair Millionaire approach to investing is the "asset class." We've discussed asset classes before, but it bears repeating. An asset class is a way experts group different types of investments that share common characteristics. For instance, all of the following are asset classes: real estate, precious metals (gold, silver), stocks, bonds, cash. Making the decision about how much of your portfolio to invest in any of these asset classes is known as "asset allocation" or "asset class investing."

HOW DO YOU FIGURE OUT THE RISKS IN A STOCK OR PORTFOLIO? Markowitz says that you should look at how the different stocks or different "asset classes" move in price relative to one another. For instance, the stock of an umbrella manufacturer and the stock of a suntan lotion company are both dependent on the overall climate. And while a rainy season is a blessing for the umbrella manufacturer, it's a curse for the suntan lotion business. In academic terms, these two companies have a low "correlation." If you own either stock in your portfolio, you might expect wild swings in their share prices depending on the weather—a high-risk proposition.

But what if you owned both stocks? Then, no matter whether the sun shone or the clouds poured, your portfolio would have one stock that would be doing well. This reduces the risks in your overall portfolio. The good news, according to Markowitz, is that these two companies don't entirely cancel each other out. By adding more and more companies to your portfolio, you can decrease the risk and increase your returns.

Armchair Millionaires know that when you put all this together, it's entirely possible to build a portfolio that has a much higher average return than the level of risk it contains. When you build a diversified portfolio and spread out your investments among stocks that have a low correlation, you're really just managing risk and return. That's not so complicated, is it? Well, it was pretty radical for Wall Street back in the 1950s, and it took some time for Modern Portfolio Theory to take hold in the minds of professional investment managers. By 1990, Modern Portfolio Theory was considered so important to investing that Markowitz received the Nobel Prize for Economics.

The Efficient Market Hypothesis, or Why Picking Individual Stocks Doesn't Work

Building on Markowitz's work, a researcher named Eugene Fama developed a theory about the market in the 1960s that claimed it was impossible to pick individual stocks that were undervalued or overvalued at any particular time. Fama explained that at any point in time, the prices of all stocks reflect all the available information about those stocks. Since the prices of stocks are always "correct," it's fruitless to try to pick individual stocks that you think will go up in price—any future price movements are due to factors that you can't predict.

Fama's theory is called the "Efficient Market Hypothesis," and it was a pretty radical idea for the scores of investment analysts who make their living by telling clients what stocks to buy and sell. Unlike buying a car, where you can negotiate a price that's better than the sticker price, you can't buy stocks at a near-wholesale price. Since the stock market prices a stock "efficiently," you'll never be able to get a bargain when you try to buy individual stocks.

What's more, Fama demonstrated how price movements of individual stocks do not follow any trends or patterns at all. Past price movements cannot be used to predict future prices—stock prices always move randomly. This is known as the "Random Walk Theory," named after the zigzagging path a drunk might make as he walks down the sidewalk. (Burton Malkiel popularized the Random Walk Theory in his classic book, *A Random Walk Down Wall Street*.) All this academic research points to just one conclusion: It's impossible to build a portfolio based on individual stock picking, if you want to reduce your risk and still maintain a decent return.

The Armchair Investing Strategy—Many Investing Theories Distilled into One

So how do you invest? The answer is clear—instead of picking stocks, you should invest in an entire stock market. That way, you'll get the benefits of diversification and noncorrelating markets and asset classes, and you won't sidetrack your portfolio by making mistakes in the stocks you pick. And you can invest in the entire stock market by investing in a stock market index fund.

Institutional investors, often referred to as "smart money," have always favored an indexing approach to their portfolios. These managers of pension funds and other large investment portfolios put an average of 40 percent of their assets into index funds. Individual investors, however, are just catching on, and only invest 5 percent of their assets in index funds. But since individuals are putting $10 of every $15 they put in mutual funds into index funds, some experts foresee that individuals could have 50 percent of their assets in index funds within the next decade, finally catching up to the "smart money."

Part B—The Nuts and Bolts of the Armchair Investing Strategy

As you can see, investing in index funds is a smart choice for most investors. The next component is to determine which indexes you should invest in—or, to put it another way, which sub-asset classes you should invest in.

Remember that asset classes are the major categories of investments that you can make in a portfolio. Stocks, bonds, cash, real estate, and precious metals are examples of assets that you can own as an investor. The Armchair Investing Strategy aims to invest primarily in a single asset class—the stock market. It is the stock market alone that has grown the fastest over this century.

Investment Returns: Stocks, Bonds, & Bills: 1926–2000*	
Asset Class	**Average Annual Total Return**
Stocks (S&P 500 Index)	+11.2%
Bonds (Long-Term U.S. Government)	+5.2%
Cash (U.S. Treasury bills)	+3.8%
*As of June 30, 2000	

But just knowing that you want to invest 100 percent of your portfolio in the stock market isn't very specific. You need to get more targeted than just picking an asset class. You need to pick a sub-asset class. For instance, should you buy U.S. stocks or stocks from other countries? Large companies or small companies? These are all sub-asset classes, and deciding which of these groups you want to invest in and how much you should invest in the selected groups is the key to the Armchair Investing Strategy.

How Does the Armchair Investing Strategy Work?

Once you've settled on the concept of investing in index funds (a historically superior choice, Armchair Millionaires believe), your next step is to find the right mix of funds that will help you meet your goal of becoming a millionaire without the slightest risk of becoming a pauper in the interim.

The Armchair Investing Strategy requires that you invest your portfolio in index funds that track the indexes of three sub-asset classes:

- One that invests in large companies in the U.S.
- One that invests in small companies in the U.S.
- One that invests in large companies outside the U.S.

Bigger and Better: The S&P 500

The first mutual fund in the Armchair Investing Strategy is any mutual fund that mimics the Standard and Poor's 500 Stock Index (also known as the S&P 500).

Here is a list of some of the index funds that follow the S&P 500:

> Advantus Index 500 Fund A (ADIAX)
> Aetna Index Plus Large Cap A (AELAX)
> Aon S&P 500 Index (ASPYX)
> California Investment Trust S&P 500 Index (SPFIX)
> Dreyfus S&P 500 Index (PEOPX)
> E*Trade S&P 500 Index (ETSPX)
> Evergreen Select Equity Index A (ESINX)
> Fidelity Spartan Market Index (FSMKX)
> First American-Equity Index A (FAEIX)
> Galaxy II Large Co. Index (ILCIX)

Harris Insight Trust Index (HIDAX)

Invesco S& P 500 Index (ISPIX)

Kent Index Equity (KNIDX)

MainStay Equity Index A (MCSEX)

Munder Index 500 A (MUXAX)

Northern Stock Index (NOSIX)

One Group-Equity Index A (OGEAX)

PIMCO Stocks PLUS Fund A (PSPAX)

Schwab S&P 500 Index (SWPIX)

Scudder S&P 500 Index (SCPIX)

State Street Global Advisors S&P 500 Index (SVSPX)

Strong Index 500 (SINEX)

T. Rowe Price Equity Index (PREIX)

Transamerica Premier Index (TPIIX)

USAA S&P 500 Index (USSPX)

Vanguard Index Trust 500 (VFINX)

Wachovia Equity Index A (BTEIX)

Wells Fargo Equity Index A (SFCSX)

(You can find complete contact information for these funds in Appendix B.)

The S&P 500 is a collection of 500 of the biggest and best companies in America. The stocks in the S&P 500 are determined by the S&P's Index Committee, who choose companies that can serve as a proxy of American business.

Growth of $1.00 Invested in the S&P 500, January 1, 1972–June 30, 2000

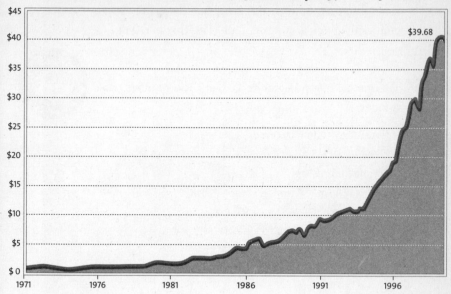

Most of the companies in the S&P 500 are quite big, so their stocks are known as "large-cap" (large-capitalization) stocks. The companies in the S&P 500 range from GE (the largest company in America, worth more than $572.3 billion) to the five-hundredth company, Owens Corning (a building materials manufacturer with a value of $277.4 million). It is safe to say that if America is doing well, you can tell it from the rise in the S&P 500. And if America is doing poorly, so is the S&P 500.

Even though the Dow Jones Industrial Average is the "index" most widely reported to the public, it is the S&P 500 that is the most widely followed by professional investors. If you had invested $1,000 in the S&P 500 at the end of 1925, it would be worth $3 million at the end of 1999! Since 1972, the S&P 500 has gone up an average of 13.79 percent annually.

Small Is Good, Too

The second mutual fund in the Armchair Investing Strategy is one that mimics the popular index called "The Russell 2000."

These mutual funds follow the Russell 2000 or other small-cap index:

> AXP Small Company Index A (ISIAX)
> Federated Mini-Cap C (MNCCX)
> Fund Information
> Galaxy II Small Company Index (ISCIX)
> Gateway Small Cap Index (GSCIX)
> Merrill Lynch Small Cap Index D (MDSKX)
> Schwab Small Cap Index (SWSMX)
> Vanguard Index Trust Small Cap (NAESX)

(You can find complete contact information for these funds in Appendix B.)

The Russell 2000 is a proxy of small businesses in America, and is maintained by the Frank Russell Company. Historically, small businesses grow faster than the big ones. This makes sense. It takes a lot to radically affect the business of the biggest companies, whereas sometimes the future prospects of a small company can be impacted, positively or negatively, by one new client or a single business opportunity.

This brings us to our next point. The small companies (we call them "small-cap stocks") in the Russell 2000 tend to go up and down a lot more (this is known as volatility) than do the biggest companies. That's why it makes sense to diversify, by buying an index of all the small companies in America. This index will incorporate the good news and the bad news into one big picture, providing an average performance experienced by all of the small companies in the index.

Growth of $1.00 Invested in the Russell 2000, January 1, 1972–June 30, 2000

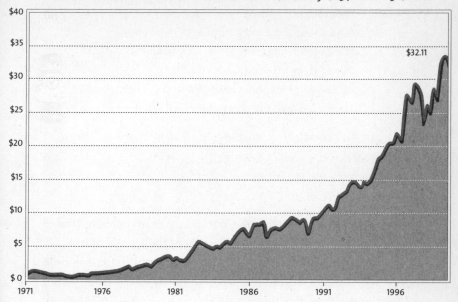

$32.11

Since 1972, small-cap stocks, as represented by the Russell 2000, have returned an average annual gain of 12.94 percent.

Going Global with EAFE

An idea as good as the Armchair Investing Strategy only gets better. The third and final mutual fund in our plan follows another index fund, Morgan Stanley's Europe, Australasia, Far East Index, often referred to as the EAFE index and pronounced "eefah."

These mutual funds follow the EAFE Index:

      Dreyfus International Stock Index (DIISX)

      E*Trade International Index (ETINX)

      First American International Index A (FIIAX)

First American International Index B (FIXBX)
Merrill Lynch International Index D (MDIIX)
One Group Intl Equity Index A (OEIAX)
One Group Intl Equity Index B (OGEBX)
One Group Intl Equity Index C (OIICX)
Schwab International Index (SWINX)
Vanguard Total Intl Stock Index (VGTSX)

(You can find complete contact information for these funds in Appendix B.)

The EAFE Index mimics the performance of publicly traded stocks around the world, with the exception of the United States.

Investing internationally has gotten a bad rap in the last decade because the strength of America's economy has left so many other countries in the dust. But this wasn't always so. From 1983 through 1988, the Morgan Stanley EAFE Index easily outperformed the S&P 500 each year.

Growth of $1.00 Invested in EAFE January 1, 1972–June 30, 2000

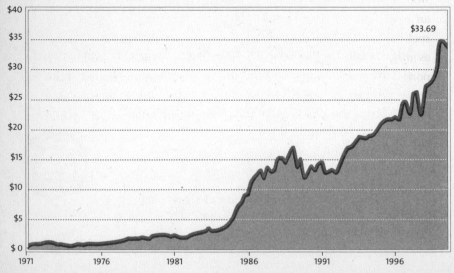

If you're investing for the long haul, it makes sense to participate in growth all over the world, not just in your own country. And don't even think of trying to figure out when the right moment is to invest internationally. That's called "market timing" and it's a sucker's game. Even if you get it right, it's probably more due to luck than to brains. The average annual return of the EAFE index has been 13.14 percent since 1972.

Why Does the Armchair Investing Strategy Work?

There are three very good reasons for the Armchair Investing Strategy's success.

First, it's important to note that the Armchair Investing Strategy invests entirely in the stock market. Over the past fifty years, not only have equities outperformed the government bond market, but they have also easily outpaced inflation, which is the minimum standard of performance for all investors. If you want to become a millionaire, you need to be invested in the stock market. Each of the index funds in our strategy invests solely in stocks.

Second, index funds provide broad diversification at a very reasonable price. Rather than trying to pick winners and losers in the stock market (usually a fruitless endeavor), an index fund invests in an entire market, and therefore always matches the benchmark it seeks to beat. Financial experts tell us that no matter the time frame, as much as 90 percent of the success of the Armchair Millionaire portfolio comes from picking the right asset class for the job. The other 10 percent will come from investing at the right time and choosing the right individual investments. In other words, while most people spend their energy looking for the next Microsoft and worrying about the next market top, the largest part of your long-term portfolio's return will come from just choosing the stock market as your investing vehicle of choice.

It is true that some people can pick the winners in any market some of the time, but it is rare that anyone can do it all of the time. It's so rare, in fact, that in the ten-year period ending in mid-1995, the S&P 500 Index beat 83 percent of all actively-managed general stock mutual funds. That's where diversification comes in—by spreading your money around several different sub-asset classes, you can always make sure you've got the big winner in your portfolio.

Perhaps the Best Part of the Armchair Investing Strategy

Throughout this book, we've been telling you that the Armchair Millionaire plan is great not only because it can make you rich, but because it can actually take a load off your mind. We're not going to say it again here. Instead, we're going to let one of our members say it for us.

Running on Auto-Pilot

"I have learned to pretty much leave my portfolio alone. It seems I was always tweaking it and trying to figure out a good investment strategy, racking up a lot of commissions and headaches for myself in the process. I've since learned an excellent and easy strategy since coming to the Armchair Millionaire site. I have my automatic exchanges set up for all my investment accounts and now all I need to do is watch my money grow."

—Armchair Millionaire member MarcusJN

Third, the Armchair Investing Strategy benefits from the advantages of a long-term perspective.

As John Bowen, expert financial advisor, explains, "The minimum expected investment period for any portfolio containing equity securities is five years. This five-year minimum investment period is important in that the investment process must be viewed as a long-term plan for achieving the desired results. This is because one-year volatility can be significant for certain asset classes. However, over a five-year period, volatility is greatly reduced."

Finally, each of these index funds represents a different segment of the stock market. The S&P 500 is representative of the U.S.'s largest companies, while the Russell 2000 includes much smaller companies. Academic research shows that the largest and smallest companies' stocks have a low correlation with each other. In other words, when one of these asset classes is not performing well, the other ones may likely be going strong. This further minimizes the risks associated with volatility.

The EAFE Index represents stocks from Japan, the United Kingdom, Europe, and the Pacific Rim. It's important to invest in these markets because international and U.S. stocks have a low correlation.

"Building a portfolio containing asset classes with low correlation to each other results in greater long-term performance for the investor while reducing risk through diversification," says Bowen.

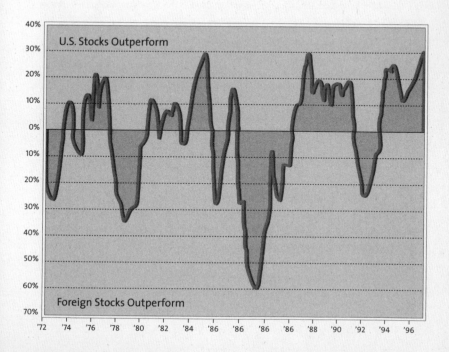

ADVICE FROM RICH

In the graph on page 143, you can see the periods since 1972 when U.S. stocks outperformed foreign stocks (as represented by the S&P 500 and the Morgan Stanley EAFE), and vice versa. If these markets had a close correlation, the peaks and valleys on both sides of the zero percent line would have been fairly close to the line. As you can see, however, these two markets have tended to have big swings in their returns when compared to each other.

Investing using the Armchair Investing Strategy takes advantage of two sets of noncorrelating markets: big U.S. companies versus small U.S. companies, and American companies versus international ones. There's no guarantee that they won't all do badly at the same time, but statistically speaking, it doesn't happen that way very often.

Growth of $1.00 from January 1, 1972–June 30, 2000 in the Armchair Millionaire Strategy

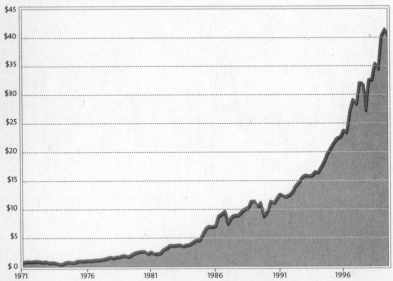

The Numbers Speak for Themselves

If you had invested $1,000 according to the Armchair Investing Strategy back on January 1, 1972, you would have had $35,156 on June 30, 2000. That's an annual rate of return of 13.3 pecent on your initial investment—not bad at all. Imagine what your return would be if you continually put a little money into the Armchair Investing Strategy every month by Paying Yourself First!

ADVICE FROM RICH

As you use the Armchair Investing Strategy, there will doubtless be times when it seems like some hot sector of the market is zooming right by you. Or some friend will boast about the market-besting returns she's gotten in some mutual fund or stock. While it's only human nature to second-guess your investment decisions, it's vital to remember that Armchair Investing is about long-term performance, not short-term profits. Over the long term, the Armchair Investing Strategy works. For a little reality check, the next time a friend brags about his stock-picking skills, ask him to tell you some tales about his losing picks, too.

These results assume an initial investment of $333.33 in the S&P 500, the Russell 2000, and the Morgan Stanley EAFE (in equal thirds) on January 1, 1972, with all subsequently paid dividends reinvested each quarter. The annual returns of each of the indexes in the Model Portfolio for the period are:

Morgan Stanley EAFE: 13.14%
Standard & Poor's 500: 13.79%
Russell 2000: 12.94%

Note: Since the Russell 2000 was created in 1984, and back adjusted to 1979, results are based on DFA 9 & 10 prior to December 1978.

Part C—From the Armchair Millionaire's Gallery—

*Founder Lewis Schiff and His Lovely Wife, Lynette,
Set Up Their Armchair Investing Plan*

As the founder of the Armchair Millionaire, I don't just talk about the Armchair Investing Strategy. My wife, Lynette, and I use the strategy in our real lives—we pay ourselves first, and every month we use dollar cost averaging to purchase shares of three different index funds, just as you've seen in this chapter. Best of all (for you), we post the actual numbers regarding our regular contributions, account balances, and rates of return at www.ArmchairMillionaire.com. We call this the Armchair Millionaire Model Portfolio—it's how we put our money where our mouths are.

If you're sitting there wondering to yourself, "What does an account that actually uses the Armchair Investing Strategy look like, and how do I make mine happen?" this is where it all becomes clear.

What Is the Model Portfolio?

The Model Portfolio takes all the tenets of Armchair Millionaire-style investing and puts them to work. The portfolio follows us as we rebuild our existing portfolio using the Five Steps to Financial Freedom and the Armchair Investing Strategy. Working with John Bowen, the Armchair Millionaire's official portfolio advisor, we figured out a new approach to saving and investing. The Model Portfolio allows you to follow along and eavesdrop on our discussions and see the plan unfold.

First, the Background

Before we get into the nuts and bolts of the portfolio, let's meet the main characters—Lewis and Lynette

He: Born and raised in New York City

Age: 31

Occupation: Executive Producer and Creator, *The Armchair Million-aire.* Previously worked at *Worth* magazine, launched Worth OnLine in 1995.

Investing Background: Started saving and investing at age 21

She: Born in Chicago; has lived in New York City for 13 years

Age: 35

Occupation: Graphic designer for magazine industry

Investing Background: Began saving and investing soon after meeting Lewis in order to impress him

Where They Are Now: Married in Big Sur, CA, in the summer of 1996, Lynette and Lewis then moved into a co-op apartment on New York's Upper West Side. They met at *Worth* magazine, but both left to start their own businesses. They have a yellow Labrador named Homer.

Their Goals: Lynette and Lewis want to get their respective businesses rolling, then they plan to begin a family and raise their kids in the New York area. In the long term, they plan to save and invest for the next twenty years, then move to a coastal summer community and open a café.

Meet John Bowen, Armchair Millionaire Model Portfolio Advisor

John Bowen worked with us to set up our very own Model Portfolio using the Armchair Investment Strategy. He was the CEO of a financial planning company and is the author of *The Prudent Investor's Guide to Beating the Market.* For many years, Bowen dispensed the usual advice to clients about how to invest their dollars, making specific recommendations about stocks, bonds, and mutual funds after developing a full-blown financial analysis for each client. "These analyses can be a great, great benefit to traditional financial planning," explains Bowen, "but quite honestly, many of these financial plans didn't deliver. It was very frustrating."

At the same time, John was teaching Investment Theory at Golden Gate University's Graduate School. A regular part of his curriculum was why financial products that involved active stock picking and market timing just don't improve performance. In fact, taught Bowen, these strategies subtract from the returns that an advisor can achieve for clients.

But one year, a graduate student raised his hand and said "John, I understand what you're teaching. Are you doing it for your clients?"

At that moment, Bowen had an epiphany. "No, I'm not," he admitted. "Professionals who advise individuals don't encourage passive investing because it doesn't cost a lot to implement and requires very little advice from a broker." And thus the transformation of John's financial advisory firm began. For an entire year, John and his partners went without paychecks as he sought counsel from some of the top minds in academia and finance. In the end, they metamorphosed from a traditional financial planning firm to one on the frontier of investment knowledge.

Soon the firm created a network of financial advisors with a uniform investing approach, thus impacting a greater number of retail clients and changing the way investors invest.

John has worked closely with us to make sure that our Model Portfolio follows the simple Armchair Investing Strategy. He has used his twenty years of experience to make our Model Portfolio one that can help anyone—with any amount of money and time—reach, and even exceed, their financial goals using simple, understandable, commonsense strategies.

STEP 1—DEFINING YOUR FINANCIAL OBJECTIVES. In order to come up with an appropriate financial plan, the first step is always to figure out your financial goals—what's important to you about money and what you want for your future. John Bowen sat down with us to discuss these issues and begin building the Model Portfolio.

John: Working with a couple to help them achieve their investment goals is very different from working with an individual. Finding out who is the dominant personality in the financial relationship is important. Often, the longest and most important conversation is about values and finding out the answer to this one question: Why are you trying to build up this money?

Lewis: I can definitely assure you that Lynette and I have different views on money.

Lynette: [Laugh] That's true.

John: Lynette, what's important to you about money?

Lynette: It's important that I always have enough—and there's no real number value. But if something ever happened to my graphic design business, it'd be important to know that there was enough money to survive.

John: What about you, Lewis?

Lewis: Above all, I would like to avoid worrying about money as much as possible.

John: What would it mean to have enough money, so that you wouldn't worry about it anymore?

Lynette: I never really thought about what's going to happen to me in forty years or anything like that. Then three years ago, I started putting money into an IRA. It all started to take shape for me. Prior to that, I think the details of planning a financial future escaped me. I probably wouldn't be in really great shape if I hadn't met Lewie.

Lewis: I was the exact opposite. I started saving and investing when I was twenty-one years old. I've always been an active investor— that was pretty much my hobby. Now it's clear to me that investing successfully is much simpler than I thought it was, but I took a very roundabout route to figure that out.

So Lynette and I come at this from very different angles. She's sort of new to it and is now putting her first financial plan together. And I've been doing this for over ten years, and now I want to redo my entire portfolio to reflect all the things I've

learned by researching investment strategies and creating the
Armchair Millionaire program.

John: Making a decision about how to invest is easier than most people think. Much of it is determined by the length of time you are
investing for. For example, money that's to be used in the immediate future (up until five years from now) should be treated differently from money that won't be needed for a lot longer. In
reality, you need to set your time frame, and then we can begin to
examine the risks that are appropriate to the lifestyle you are trying to achieve. Let's separate the risks into two parts. The first is
the resources that you're going to need in the next few months or
next year or so. These have to stay in some form of cash with
some rules of thumb about how much cash you should have in
reserve.

Lewis: We've already set aside cash in an emergency fund. I think
the most common rule of thumb is to have between two and six
months' salary available in a savings account, right?

John: Right. The second part is the money that you're ready to set
aside for at least five years. You'll be able to put these funds into
inexpensive mutual funds using the Armchair Investing Strategy.

STEP 2—ASSESSING YOUR TOLERANCE FOR RISK. Really thinking about how much risk you can tolerate will greatly affect the outcome of your portfolio. If you don't seriously think about how you
might react to a dip in the market, you could panic and sell when the
market is low. Selling when stock prices are low is deadly to a portfolio. A little soul-searching will help us understand our attitudes
toward risk.

John: Lynette, you describe yourself as a little bit more conservative
than Lewis, so I'm going to start out with you on this. One of the
things we believe strongly is that the stock market tends to grow
over the long term. And I have all the reasons and all the data in
the world to prove that. However, there are occasional short-term

corrections. A good example is the Asian market. Japan had trouble during most of the 1990s.

So, if we look at any money you are going to invest for the next five, ten years, or for the rest of your life, you have to be prepared for setbacks along the way. Emotionally, each of us can handle a different amount of uncertainty. Because you two have a long-term investing horizon—more than twenty years—the effect of compounding returns on your portfolio will be much larger the more risk that you're willing to take. (See Chapter 9, Step #5 of the Five Steps to Financial Freedom, for more on compounding.) It's important to remember that the occasional setbacks in this strategy will be more severe than a portfolio that's not invested entirely in stocks.

Have you ever thought about your tolerance for a short-term setback like that?

Lynette: To be honest, it scares me. But I would certainly try to do it in a smart, comfortable way that was somewhere between minimum and maximum risk.

Lewis: I would also like to raise the issue of the danger of being too conservative. Someone once told me that investing for growth is really about making sure your money grows farther and faster than the shrinking effect that inflation has on your money.

John: That's why we're going to use an investing strategy, the Armchair Investing Strategy, that takes full advantage of the long-term growth of the market, given your discomfort with risk.

Lynette: So, what do we do next?

STEP 3—OPENING AN ACCOUNT AND SETTING UP THE INVESTMENT.

John: Now it's time to transform your portfolio to match everything we've been talking about. It's not so hard to invest intelligently and with common sense. I love the term "Armchair Investing" because it accurately describes how simple it is to implement

Armchair Investing Strategy. What it fails to do is capture the amount of data, academic research, and long-term success that lies behind this basic strategy. Without exception, when I tell people what the Armchair Investing Strategy is, they are underwhelmed. But they become totally satisfied as time goes by.

Lewis: I know that researching your brokerage firm is another vital step in setting up a successful portfolio—also deciding what services you need out of a firm, and what you are willing to pay for them before you shop around.

If the financial industry wants to know why more people don't invest, they should look no further than the process of opening a new brokerage account. There are several different components to starting a saving and investing plan. Looking back, any one of them could have derailed us from getting our plan started.

Lynette: By far the most intimidating and confusing moment was actually getting the plan started.

Lewis: We decided to change our brokerage because we wanted to take advantage of some of the new features and services other brokerages were offering. Since we already had our strategy mapped out (the Armchair Investing Strategy), we wanted to find a brokerage that had access to all of our mutual fund choices and would allow us to make periodic purchases without a fee. Our new broker will allow us to implement the Armchair Investing Strategy using no-load mutual funds. In addition, since we ended up using a broker and not just a mutual funds company, we'll have a wider array of investment choices in the future. Finally, their Web access is fast and easy to use, something that's important to us.

Lynette: We checked out brokers and companies where we can make ongoing, regular investments without transaction fees.

Lewis: Thirty-five pages of application forms later (yes, 35—that's not a misprint), I was ready to transfer our main, taxable brokerage account, my two IRAs (one contributory IRA and one rollover IRA from my previous job) and Lynette's two IRAs (one contributory IRA and one SEP-IRA, a type of retirement account for self-employed individuals).

By the time we were done, we had switched over a total of five new accounts, set up a password for Web access, chosen another password for phone access, filled out signature cards, set up "money links" between our local bank and our brokerage, and, finally, arranged for direct deposits between our employers and our bank. As if all that weren't enough, we decided to get brand-new credit cards that would give us frequent-flier mile rewards.

Lynette: All I can say is, this better be worth it.

Lewis: [Gulp] It will all work out, honey. I promise.

And? How Is the Portfolio Performing?

The Model Portfolio finally came to be on March 9, 1998—we launched a real money portfolio. The following chart shows that we are right on track to hit our goal—$1 million by April 1, 2015.

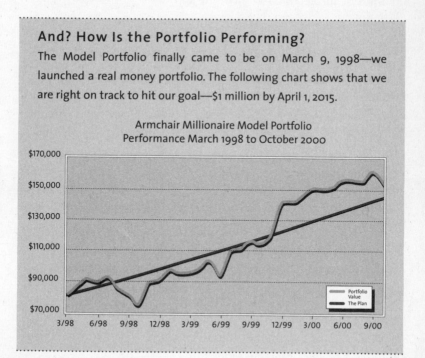

Armchair Millionaire Model Portfolio
Performance March 1998 to October 2000

How You Can Get Started in the Armchair Investing Strategy

The Armchair Investing Strategy is a great way to build your nest egg. We've selected three mutual funds that represent large U.S. companies, small U.S. companies, and large foreign companies, and invest a third of our portfolio in each. What's more, the funds we've chosen are index funds, and each one tracking a particular index that represents one of the segments of the market listed above.

You can emulate the Armchair Investing Strategy at just about any brokerage or mutual funds company. You can use it in your own 401(k) account, or in an IRA or Roth IRA, or in a regular taxable nonretirement account—or all of the above.

How to Choose a Broker: Look at the Funds They Offer

If you'd like to use the Armchair Investing Strategy at a brokerage firm (either a discount, full-service, or online firm) or at a mutual fund company, you should look at a few things to help you make your decision. Since you won't need the advice of a stock broker to help you implement the Armchair Investing Strategy, you won't need to pay the high commissions of a full-service broker. A full-service broker might offer three funds that match the Armchair Millionaire Strategy, but those funds may carry a "load," a commission that you'll pay when you buy or sell the fund, or both.

The first criterion, of course, is to look for a company that offers the three funds that we use in the Armchair Investing Strategy:

- Large U.S. Company Index Fund
- Small U.S. Company Index Fund
- Large Foreign Company Index Fund

Once you've found a firm that offers the funds you need, then check that the firm has reasonable transaction fees for buying and selling funds. Some brokerage firms charge $25 or more every time you buy a mutual fund. If you were investing $100 a month, a $25 transaction fee would wipe out a big chunk of each monthly investment. Many have no fees at all, at least for most of the funds in their program. These are often called "no-transaction fee" funds, and these are perfect for Armchair Millionaires. Here's a list of firms that are ideal for implementing the Armchair Investing Strategy:

- Charles Schwab
- E*Trade
- Fidelity
- Vanguard
- Waterhouse Securities
- Strong Funds
- T. Rowe Price
- TIAA-CREF

Each of these firms has a variety of index funds available and commission structures that make the Armchair Investing Strategy very inexpensive. (Complete contact information for these firms is available in Appendix C.)

Look for Asset Allocation Funds
ADVICE FROM RICH

Some mutual fund and brokerage companies offer mutual funds that invest in the stock market according to an asset-allocation strategy that is similar to the Armchair Investing Strategy. For instance, the Charles Schwab Market Track Portfolios and the Fidelity Four-in-One Index Fund are alternatives Armchair Millionaires might use instead of buying three separate mutual funds. Generally speaking, these "funds of funds" have slightly higher expenses, but the advantage is that the fund maintains its asset allocation so you can invest in one fund instead of three.

Other Products and Services Offered by Brokerages

There are many other services that brokerage firms may offer that can affect your decision to work with that particular company. Lynette and Lewis outline a number of factors that they considered in selecting their broker:

- Availability of local branch offices. Some investors like knowing that their broker has a nearby office where you can turn if you ever have problems. While online brokers are very convenient, they don't maintain bricks and mortar offices in towns and cities across the country.
- Toll-free telephone support available twenty-four hours a day. Many financial services firms are cutting back on customer support, which could mean limited office hours or that you would have to make a long distance telephone call when you need help.
- Fees and expenses. Many brokers charge hefty fees for opening or closing an account, transferring shares in or out of the account, or maintaining an account that's below a certain minimum balance (often $10,000 or $25,000). Every dollar you pay in fees reduces your overall return, and it doesn't take much for the fees to add up to a sizable chunk of a new investor's portfolio.
- Types of accounts. Most investors need retirement and non-retirement accounts, so make sure your broker offers the types of IRA, Roth IRA, SEP-IRA (if you're self-employed), and other accounts you'll need. One advantage of consolidating your accounts at one brokerage is that the firm may offer additional services or lower fees if the total value of all your accounts is greater than a certain amount, say $100,000. Sticking with one broker can also be more convenient for you when it comes to record-keeping and managing your portfolio.

If You Don't Have a Lot of Money to Invest

Many firms require an initial deposit of $1,000 or more in order to open an account. But if you don't have that much in the bank already, don't panic. Some firms will waive the minimum initial deposit requirement if you sign up for automatic deposits. Here, an Armchair Millionaire describes how he cleared this obstacle.

Getting Started with a Minimum Investment

"T. Rowe Price will allow you to start a mutual fund with no minimum deposit—all you have to do is promise to deposit at least $50 a month via direct deposit. The form they send you to open the account doesn't mention this feature, however. To open the account with no initial deposit, leave the initial deposit section blank, and simply fill out the automatic deposit section, attach your blank check, and you're ready to go. T. Rowe Price has several index funds to choose from. There are probably other mutual fund companies that waive the initial minimum if you agree to automatic deposits. I found out about this from an article on Morningstar.com (the mutual fund rating company)."

—Armchair Millionaire member khuyck

Working with Your Current Brokerage or Fund Company

You may already have an account at a brokerage firm or mutual fund company—does that mean you have to transfer your accounts to a new place? Not at all. While the paperwork required to transfer your portfolio to a new firm isn't particularly complex, it's still *paperwork*— and nobody loves paperwork. In fact, one of the advantages of the Armchair Investing Strategy is that you can do it just about anywhere, including in a company-sponsored retirement account, such as a 401(k).

Emulating the Armchair Investing Strategy

In order to put the Armchair Investing Strategy to work in an exist-ing account, you'll need to find three funds that come closest to the Armchair approach. Check to see if your 401(k) plan, fund company, or broker offers index funds that track the same indexes the Arm-chair Millionaire uses: the S&P 500, the Russell 2000, and the Mor-gan Stanley EAFE.

If your plan doesn't offer index funds that are based on those exact same indexes, next check to see if your plan has any index funds that follow a different large company, small company, or international index not used in the Armchair Investing Strategy. For instance, you may be able to find a small-cap stock index fund that tracks the S&P Small Cap 600 instead of the Russell 2000.

ADVICE FROM RICH

If you want to use the Armchair Investing Strategy and your 401(k) plan just doesn't seem to offer the right funds, talk to the people in your company who manage the 401(k) program and see if they will consider adding some more funds to the plan.

Alternatives to Index Funds: Using Active Funds

If your plan comes up short on offering index funds, next turn to actively managed funds. You'll want to look for no-load mutual funds that meet these three criteria:

1. Select funds that invest in the same kinds of companies as the Armchair Investing Strategy suggests. Here's a table of the corre-sponding categories used by various mutual funds rating and research services to describe the same underlying approaches to the three indexes used in our plan:

Type of Companies	Underlying Index	Category
Large U.S.	S&P 500	Large Growth, Growth & Income, Large Cap
Small U.S.	Russell 2000	Small Cap, Small Blend
Large Foreign	EAFE	Foreign Stock, Non-U.S. Equity

2. Look for funds that have low expense ratios—this is the percentage of the fund that its managers keep to pay for expenses. All other things considered, a fund that has lower expenses should provide a higher rate of return for shareholders.

Here are the average expense ratios for actively managed funds in the three categories used in the Strategy, according to the Investment Company Institute:

Fund Category	Average Expense Ratio
Growth & Income (Large Growth)	1.30%
Small Cap	1.62%
Non-U.S. Equity	1.89%

It's worth noting that the average S&P 500 Index fund has an expense ratio of 0.7 percent, nearly half the cost of an actively managed fund. That's money in your pocket!

3. Look for funds that have a good track record over the past five and ten years. Don't worry about what funds may have been "hot" last year. Look for funds that have performed well over the long term, since you'll be holding your funds for the long term as well.

Putting the Pieces Together
"If you're wondering how all the pieces of your portfolio fit together, think of them as a whole unit, rather than separate com-

ponents. For instance, my 401(k) is invested in an S&P 500 fund, so I have all my 401(k) money going into that. I have my IRA and Keogh money in small caps (Russell 2000). I currently have my taxable investments in the S&P 500, but am in the process of switching it to an EAFE Index. Look at your portfolio as a whole, not in pieces."

—Armchair Millionaire member am_bo

Now that you know how the Armchair Investing Strategy works, you need to know how much money to invest in each of the three stock index funds that make up the portfolio. This is the simplest part of the Armchair Investing Strategy—you just invest an equal portion in each. For every $1,000 that you invest in the Armchair Investing Strategy, you should put $333.33 into each index fund. For many people, the decision to invest in the stock market is fraught with anxiety. The Armchair Investing Strategy is so simple to use—and so effective—that it helps take the worry out of managing a portfolio. It doesn't matter what long-term goals you might be striving to reach, whether it's a comfortable retirement, college education for your kids, a forty-foot sailboat, or a summer home in the mountains—the Armchair Investing Strategy is your key to becoming a millionaire.

Composing Your Portfolio by Time Horizon

The Armchair Investing Strategy is a long-term approach to the stock market. You should only use it for money that you're willing to set aside for at least five years. If you have short-term goals, such as paying for college tuition for your kids, or a first home, or a big wedding, then you should implement a modified version of the Armchair Investing Strategy.

First, examine your time frame—how long until you will need your funds? For every year fewer than five, put 15 percent of your investments into a more conservative investment, such as a bond index fund, or a money market fund. That way, that percentage of your money won't be hurt if the stock market takes a hit. So if you are going to need your money in a year, make sure 60 percent (15% x 4 years) of your money is out of the stock market.

If you're sixty-five and already retired, you're probably looking forward to ten or more years of golden living, so you should still set aside part of your portfolio in a five- or ten-year plan like the Armchair Investing Strategy.

Chapter 8 Action Items

- Find a brokerage firm that you like, that has low fees, and that offers index funds in different sub-asset classes.
- Set up an automatic investment plan.
- Invest one-third of your long-term portfolio in stock market mutual funds that track these (or equivalent) indexes:

  Standard & Poor's 500
  Russell 2000
  Morgan Stanley EAFE

- If your financial institution doesn't offer index funds that match the Armchair Millionaire approach, you should invest in three actively managed funds that match the Armchair Investing Strategy.
- Breathe easy, knowing that your investment plan is running on autopilot.

STEP 5:
Start Today—Put the Power of Compound Interest to Work for You

By now, we hope you've learned the importance of saving your money and investing it regularly in the stock market. You've also learned why it's so important to "Pay Yourself First," and to take advantage of tax-deferred retirement plans like 401(k) accounts and IRAs. What could possibly be left to know about investing, you may wonder?

Well, there is one more step, one last action that you have to undertake before you can reach your million-dollar goal. In fact, we've saved the single most important step of the Armchair Millionaire plan for last. This is the true secret to building wealth, and perhaps the most important bit of financial advice that you may ever receive.

What is the key to financial freedom? It's this:

START TODAY.

Sounds like a no-brainer, right? But actually, there's a formidable stack of academic research, mathematical calculations, and supercharged thinking that have gone into the development of this key piece of the Armchair Investing Strategy. All of this knowledge has been crystallized into these two words, the two most important words you should remember even if you forget everything else we've told you in this book (though we certainly hope you'll remember a bit more).

The Power of Compound Interest

How can an uncomplicated command like this be so critical to the building of a million-dollar portfolio? It comes down to the power of time. You should put your money to work in a sensible investing plan so that eventually you won't have to work. Time is money, as the saying goes, but the opposite is also true—money is time. The sooner you put your money to work for you, the greater it will grow. This is because of the miracle of *compound interest.*

One of the greatest minds of the twentieth century, Albert Einstein, pondered the many secrets of the universe (including that famous formula about relativity that every school kid can recite). But even Einstein was supposedly astounded at how compound interest worked. Legend has it he called it "the eighth wonder of the world." (There's been some question about whether Einstein ever said any such thing, but it's such a good story that we had to include it here.)

What's so amazing about compound interest? Compound interest is simply what happens when you put some money in a bank account that earns interest. After the bank makes the first interest payment in the account, that interest begins to earn interest. Sure, at first your interest seems pretty puny, but over time, all that interest earning interest causes your account to grow at a higher rate.

Suppose you invest $1.00 and leave it alone for ten years at 10 percent interest. After a year, your dollar would be worth $1.10. In the second year, that 10 percent interest would be calculated on $1.10, not $1.00, so you'll have $1.21 after the second year, After a decade, you would have $2.59—more than double your original investment—and with no additional savings put in. The effects of compounding simply grow stronger over time. After two hundred years, your original dollar would be worth $190 million!

In an investment account, the same thing happens, only we call it "compound returns." Your investments will grow and earn interest, dividends, and capital gains. And then those returns start to earn returns, etc., etc. Sure, it sounds simple, but over the course of time, the effects are nothing short of awesome.

Here's a quiz that might help you understand the amazing powers of compounding.

You are offered a temporary job for thirty days. You have to choose between two different payment plans:

1) $1,000 a day for thirty days, *or*
2) A penny for the first day, two cents the next day, four cents for the third day, and your pay would double like that every day for thirty days.

Which do you choose? If you chose the first payment method, that's too bad. The good news is you'll make $30,000 for 30 days' work (nice work if you can get it!).

Here's the bad news: If you chose the second payment plan, you're going to take home over $10 million ($10,737,418.23, to be exact) instead of the $30,000 that you would have made with choice #1. That's the power of compounding at work!

Check out the math.

Payment plan 1
$1,000 a day for 30 days
$1,000 × 30 days = $30,000

Payment plan 2
A penny for the first day, two cents the next day, four cents for the third day, and your pay would double like that every day for thirty days. Here's how it would look:

Day	Payment	Cumulative Total
1	.01	.01
2	.02	.03
3	.04	.07
4	.08	.15
5	.16	.31
6	.32	.63
7	.64	1.27
8	1.28	2.55
9	2.56	5.11
10	5.12	10.23
11	10.24	20.47
12	20.48	40.95
13	40.96	81.91
14	81.92	163.83
15	163.84	327.67
16	327.68	655.35
17	655.36	1,310.71
18	1310.72	2,621.43
19	2,621.44	5,242.87
20	5,242.88	10,485.75
21	10,585.76	20,971.51
22	20,971.52	41,943.03
23	41,943.04	83,886.07
24	83,886.08	167,772.15
25	167,772.16	335,544.31
26	335,544.32	671,088.63
27	671,088.64	1,342,177.27
28	1,342,177.28	2,684,354.55
29	2,684,354.56	5,368,709.11
30	5,368,709.12	10,737,418.23

TOTAL: $10,737,418.23

Now, do you still think that it's not worth it to invest a small amount of money? We didn't think so.

A *Tale of Two Teenagers*

Nicole is a smart kid. Her parents have explained compound interest to her, and so she knows how to invest a gift of $2,000 that she receives on her eighteenth birthday. Nicole puts the entire amount in an Armchair Millionaire portfolio of mutual funds that returns 10 percent each year.

Then she keeps investing $2,000 each year for three more years. Then she stops to join a rock and roll band. Nicole's total investment: $8,000. At age sixty-five, Nicole will have $615,063 from her original investment of $8,000. *Nicole's parents love her.* Especially after she quit the band and went back to college.

Charlie wasn't loved as a child . . . Charlie's parents didn't teach him the value of compound interest. He doesn't start investing until he's thirty. But when Charlie does finally start investing, he invests $2,000 each year. Just like Nicole.

Charlie keeps investing $2,000 *for the next thirty-five years*. Unfortunately, even if Charlie keeps putting away $2,000 every year, for the next thirty-five years—**for a total of $70,000 invested**—he'll still have *less* than Nicole.

After thirty-five years, Charlie will have $596,254. Almost $20,000 less than Nicole, even though he invested nearly eight times as much as she did. Time really is money.

The Lesson: Understand the power of compounding interest. Worship it. Show it how much you love it by starting your investing plan today. Oh, and be nice to your kids.

Compound Interest in Action

Okay, okay, so compounding interest is great. But what if you're well past your early adulthood? Of course, you can't turn back the clock—so if you didn't start investing at an early age, there's nothing you can do about it now. But you can decide to not let any more time go by before you begin your financial plan. That's why "Start Today" is so beautiful—you can heed its advice at any age. To help you take the plunge, listen to these real life Armchair Millionaires.

A Real Life Someone Who Started Early . . .

"I started saving money at the age of sixteen. At twenty-three, I bought my first house with a cash deposit of 25 percent (about everything I had in the bank account). Now, I'm thirty and have almost paid for my house. At the bank, I have the same amount of money I earn in a year. At forty-five, if everything goes right, I'll have enough money to retire. The only thing I would not do if I had to do it all again, I wouldn't have paid for my house that fast, so that the money I put into the house could have grown more."

—Armchair Millionaire member Let it grow!

Versus a Real Life Someone Who Didn't

"I enjoyed my twenties, but I wish I had saved more instead of spending money on clothes, cars, bar-hopping, and such. I lived rent-free until I was twenty-six. Had I plunked even $250 a month into an investment vehicle, I would have a substantially larger sum of money tucked away than I do now. I started to invest at age twenty-eight, and currently at age thirty-two have a portfolio worth $44,000. I kick myself thinking about what I could have if I had gotten smart a few years earlier. I now have a well paying job but I also have a wife, child, and mortgage. It's harder to find the money to save now than it would have been ten years ago."

—Armchair Millionaire member Michael

A Ray of Hope

"I think a lot of us buy into the fairy tale that things will work out all right in the end. We grew up in a mad advertising world of 'buy now, cry later.' So we are all paying for it with no freedom, as many of us—regardless of income—struggle to make it to the next paycheck.

But now that we know how to save and invest, we can do something about it. Even if it is a minimal amount at first, we must all begin somewhere. I started with $20 per paycheck and proceeded to pay off all my debts. I am down to one loan that will be paid off in a few months, and I am planning on buying a condo next spring. Not bad for someone who could not afford the rent three years ago."

—Armchair Millionaire member Raymond D.

From the Armchair Millionaire's Gallery

How Compound Interest Has the Power to Turn You into an "Accidental Millionaire," with Special Guest Star, Professor Andrew Hacker

There is more to making compounding interest work for you than simply starting now. The second half of the final step in the Armchair Millionaire plan is to leave the money that you have invested where it is. Because if you dip into those funds, you'll not only reduce your immediate returns, but over time your compounded returns will suffer. However, if you leave those funds whole, you can harness the true power of compound interest. Take for example the story of Professor Andrew Hacker. The author of *Money: Who Has How Much and Why* started his career as a humble college instructor who never imagined that he had the astuteness needed to make money in the market (if only he had had the Armchair Millionaire program to follow!). All he did in regard to investing was to steadily deduct a percentage of his paycheck and put it into his university retirement account at Teachers Insurance and Annuity Association-College Retirement Equities Fund, known as TIAA-CREF (TIAA-CREF is a leading provider of retirement plans for educational institutions). He didn't even look at his balance until it came time for him to retire. What he found when he finally did look is nothing short of astounding.

Name: Professor Andrew Hacker

Age: Late 60s

Occupation: I'm a college professor. I'm officially retired, but I'm still teaching a full load of classes because I like to.

How long have you been investing?

Well, I've never officially invested on my own—all I have done is had a certain percentage deducted from my paycheck into my pension fund. I started that over forty years ago, when I started teaching.

Was it difficult for you to give up that portion of your paycheck?

My first salary as an instructor was $4,500 a year. And my deduction into my pension was 7.5 percent, and the university matched another 7.5 percent. Even though I wasn't making that much money, not having that 7.5 percent felt just ordinary, like any other payroll deduction.

When you started out what were your financial goals?

As a college professor, I knew I wasn't going to get rich. Until I went to my first job at Cornell and I was taken under the wing of a professor who did outside writing. With his help, I discovered that you can be a college professor, which is a nice, worthy occupation, and still become quite comfortable. The goal was always not wealth but comfort.

How far along are you now?

I've reached my goal. That is to say, more comes in than I need.

How did you realize that your financial goals had been met?

Now I am a professor at the City University of New York, and a few years ago I was eligible for retirement. At the time, they were having a budget crunch. And of course, when they cut positions, they cut from the bottom, even when it might make more sense to take aim at full professors sitting on fat salaries. I'm not Saint Andrew, but I realized I was getting a salary that was the equivalent of three junior people's. So I called up my fund administrators, and found out that the total in my retirement account was $1.1 million dollars. I was flabbergasted! This shows you the value of compound interest—not just the investments—but forty years of compound interest. Wow.

How did your life change after you realized that your years of investing had paid off?
My generation, I call it the Eisenhower generation, we got on an escalator and we just moved up. I'm a pretty good guy, but I didn't deserve everything I got. It was just a historical happenstance. So I set up a trust fund for my daughter and her husband because I felt I should share.

And there's only been one other real change: I now fly to Europe in business class. And I have flown the Concorde once. It was fun. There were about sixty other people on it. And I realized that all these people were regulars—they knew the stewardesses, they were busy working on their laptops. We landed at Kennedy airport at 9 A.M., and there was no one else there because no other flights had arrived yet. And there were fifty-nine limousines lined up to pick the regular Concorde passengers up! My wife and I were the only ones who took a cab.

What advice would you give someone who wants to begin investing?
Speaking as an outsider, if I were to invest, I hope I would be prudent enough to put it all into an index fund. I'm smart, but in no way am I smart enough to beat the market. I know some people do, but there isn't that much smartness around. And my second piece of gratuitous advice is to get married and stay married. Two can live as cheaply as 1.7, so you will have extra money. And if you don't get divorced, you don't have child support, you don't have a second household to keep up, all those things. I was married for more than forty years, and it was important.

Put Compounding to Work Today

The secret ingredient of compounding isn't skill, nor is it luck or knowledge. It's nothing more than time. By starting now, you can put its mighty force to work.

But, there's a catch (there's always a catch). The longer you procrastinate on your investment plan, the less effective the law of compounding becomes. If you don't believe it, turn back to page 165 and see what your total pay would have been if you had only worked twenty-five days. Those first five days didn't seem that important (after all, you only brought home 31 cents). But without them, you'd only have $335,544.31 after twenty-five days instead of the whopping $10,737,418.23 you'd accrue after thirty. That's why you need time on your side—and why you must *start today*.

When you put money into an investment, you earn returns in the form of interest, dividends and capital gains. The value of your investment compounds when these returns themselves start to earn returns. *Over time, this compounding will be the most important ingredient to building your fortune.*

ADVICE FROM RICH

When calculating the returns of your portfolio, you may have gains from any or all of three sources. *Interest* is the money you earn on cash that's held in a bank or money market account. *Dividends* are a share of the profits that a company may pay its stockholders, usually four times a year. *Capital gains* are the profits from stocks or other securities that have appreciated (increased) in price since you first purchased those shares. If you own a stock or security that has increased in price, you are said to be holding "unrealized capital gains"; you "realize" the gains when you sell the shares (and in the process create a tax liability, since realized capital gains are subject to taxes.)

When you add up all three of these, dividends, interest, capital gains (realized and/or unrealized), you can determine the **total return** of an investment.

The secret ingredient to compounding is no more than time—so the sooner you start your investment plan, the longer you have for compounding to work its powerful magic. *Start today*!

ADVICE FROM RICH

Here's a nifty trick for figuring out the impact of compounding on your investments, known as the Rule of 72. Here's how it works: Divide 72 by your expected annual rate of return. The result is the number of years until your investment doubles. So, suppose you expect to get an average yearly return of 10 percent. 72 divided by 10 equals 7.2. Your investment would double in just over seven years. How's that for an enjoyable math problem?

Putting It All Together

So let's take a look at just exactly how the Five Steps work together to help you to reach your million-dollar goal.

Consider Fred, the prototypical Armchair Millionaire. He's thirty years old, and earns a salary of about $45,000 a year, taking home about $3,000 a month after taxes.

Fred has been saving a bit here and there, and has saved up about $10,000 in the bank. He also knows enough to be investing in his 401(k) at work, and is now contributing $300 each month to the plan. Over the past few years, his 401(k) has grown to be about $10,000.

In order to become a millionaire, here's what Fred needs to do:

Step #1. Fred needs to max out his 401(k) plan each month. He should increase his monthly contribution to $562, which is 15 percent of his pretax monthly salary. This will allow him to contribute $6,750 a year to his 401(k) plan. If he gets a pay raise of 3 percent a year, he should increase his 401(k) contribution accordingly. In twenty-one years, Fred will have contributed a total of $203,394 to his plan.

Step #2. Fred needs to pay himself first. Each month, before paying any other bills, Fred should set aside 10 percent of his after-tax income for his Armchair Millionaire plan, which comes out to $300 a month. Assuming his salary increases on average about 3 percent a year, he should increase his "Pay Yourself First" contribution by the same amount—more if he can afford it. And if he signs up for a money-link program with a bank or brokerage, that money will be automatically withdrawn from his account each month, saving the hassle of remembering to write a check. In twenty-one years, these savings will come to a total of $113,235.

At this point, Fred will have saved a total of $316,629. While that's not chicken feed, it's far short of a million dollars. But that's okay, as you'll see once we invest that money for Fred.

Step #3. Fred should invest each month, both in his 401(k) account and in a taxable account at a brokerage firm or mutual fund company (using his "Pay Yourself First" money). He shouldn't let the money sit around, or try to "time" the market. He needs to invest each and every month, regardless of how high or low the market may be. His broker or mutual fund can handle this, automating the process.

Step #4. Fred should invest according to the Armchair Millionaire Investing Strategy, dividing up his investments into three pieces. He will invest a third into a U.S. large-cap stock index fund (like an S&P 500 index fund); a third into a U.S. small-cap stock index fund (one that imitates the Russell 2000, for instance); and one-third into a foreign large-cap stock index fund (one that tracks the EAFE index). This will provide him with the proper diversification and optimum return at the least risk.

Step #5. Fred should let his portfolio ride. He should continually add more money to his accounts and let the returns compound continuously.

If Fred can manage these five steps, and if his portfolios are able to grow just 10 percent a year on average, the value of his investments will be a million dollars in twenty-one years. Fred didn't need to win the lottery, or be a genius investor. Investing sensibly, the Armchair Millionaire way, is all it takes.

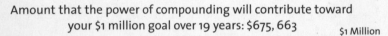

Amount that the power of compounding will contribute toward your $1 million goal over 19 years: $675, 663

$1 Million

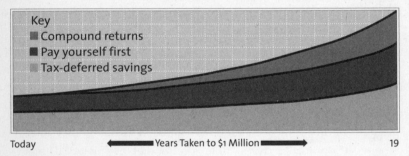

Key
■ Compound returns
■ Pay yourself first
■ Tax-deferred savings

Today   ◄■■■■Years Taken to $1 Million■■■■►   19

- Fred's current tax-deferred savings: $10,000
- Fred's ongoing investments: $800 each month; amount in Fred's tax-deferred investment accounts in nineteen years: $251,122
- Amount Fred pays himself each month: $300 (10 percent of his take-home pay); total saved in nineteen years: $100,421.
- Amount that the power of compounding will contribute towards Fred's $1 million goal over nineteen years: $675,663.
  GRAND TOTAL: $1,000,000

This is what the power of compounding will do for your investments on the way to your million-dollar goal. Time is the secret ingredient for accomplishing your goal. So start now, already!

Chapter 9 Action Items

In this chapter, you've learned how compound returns are the secret of a million dollar portfolio.

It's imperative that you start your plan today. Follow the steps in this book, and you can join the ranks of Armchair Millionaires from all around the world.

CHAPTER 10

Fulfilling Your Dreams

Now you've read all about the five steps that can help you to achieve all your long-term financial goals and provide you with the confidence that you'll need to build real wealth. Up until this point, we've talked about all the work you'll have to do in order to achieve your financial dreams. Of course, according to the Armchair Millionaire plan, all this striving won't really *feel* like work. But while you're on your way, it's important to remember that as you get older and your portfolio grows, your time frame shrinks. Someday, you will arrive at the target you've been aiming at for many years. How will you know when you've gotten there? What will that be like? And what will you know then that you don't know now?

Before we fast-forward and start answering these questions, there's just one thing left to do. In order to imagine your dreams fulfilled, you first have to know exactly what those dreams are. After all, if you don't know what you want, you're never going to get it. Take some time to daydream about how you want your life to be after you've accumulated enough wealth to live comfortably. Do you want to travel the country in a Winnebago? Or start the business you've always dreamed about? Whatever it is, get a good image in your mind of what you look like doing it. This picture will help carry you through any rough times you might experience along the way.

While Visions of Armchair Millionaires Danced in Their Heads

Are you curious to see how your financial goals compare to others'? Here members of the Armchair Millionaire community talk frankly about where they want to be in twenty years.

Looking at the (Very) Long Term

"I'm going to retire from my job as a firefighter in eight years (at age fifty-six) with a good pension. Once I retire I plan to work at jobs that I enjoy, such as a flight instructor, a helicopter pilot for tour operators in exotic locations, or a river guide. I also plan on living to one hundred! So I don't plan on withdrawing money from my tax-deferred accounts until I'm seventy and a half. By that time I should have a very big nest egg that should allow me and my wife to live a most comfortable final thirty years."

—Armchair Millionaire member Knucklehead

Aiming to Live Stress-Free

"I would like the ability to retire by the age of forty-five but would love to continue working until sixty. Providing for my son and traveling are my highest goals. Freedom from stress is all I need."

—Armchair Millionaire member Isaac

A Call to Action

"My long-term goal is to be in a financial position to be able to enjoy life to its fullest, and be free from the job that controls my life as I trade hours for dollars. My short-term goals are to reach financial independence working for myself, and showing others how to do the same. It's a wondrous world out there. Let's get out from behind those desks, choose the hours that we want to work (or not work), spend our time making ourselves wealthy (instead of our companies), and see this world at our leisure (instead of on the week-long "vacations" our bosses allow us to take)!"

—Armchair Millionaire member Cindy

FAST-FORWARD

Let's pretend that it is twenty years from now. You've been following your Armchair Millionaire plan for financial freedom. How will you know when you start to reach the goals you've been striving for for so long? Of course, it depends on how you define those goals— either your portfolio will reach a designated number, or the income from your investments will be such that you can stop working for a living. Maybe you'll finally be able to fund a new business enterprise without jeopardizing your standard of living. Or you'll be able to quit your job and dedicate your time to a charitable cause. There are many ways to see your dreams coming true.

In very basic terms, you'll know you've reached your destination when you don't have to worry about money anymore. This doesn't mean that you'll have a lavish, indulgent lifestyle. In true Armchair Millionaire fashion, you'll have a peace of mind that comes from being satisfied with what you have, and with having more than you need.

A Day in the Life of a Millionaire

Let's take a closer look at the future and see what it's really like to live your life as a millionaire.

The first thing you'll do every morning is wake up in a house that you have already paid for. This house will most likely be in a very nice, but not flashy, neighborhood. The house itself will have more room than you absolutely need without being a sprawling testament to the size of your bank account.

Over breakfast, you can read the paper for ideas on where to take your next vacation. You may look for news about your investments, or you may skip the financial section altogether, knowing that your portfolio is still functioning on autopilot. Perhaps your daughter will call from college—where she is enjoying a paid-for education (and if she's the offspring of an Armchair Millionaire, chances are she's working a little on the side to help minimize her living expenses and to get a head start on her own portfolio.)

After breakfast, you'll climb into your reliable, debt-free car and drive to the job you've taken because it's so much fun you'd do the work for free. Perhaps it's a new business that was spawned out of a hobby, or a part-of-the-year job that also gives you the flexibility to travel. Or maybe you'll take up painting, and furnish all your relatives' homes with original works of art.

You'll be able to do all this without any worry, because your finances are completely in order. You said good-bye to credit card debt long ago. You're well insured to protect against emergencies. And you have a will set up to insure that your hard work will continue to pay off even after you're gone. And of course, your investment portfolio is still growing, generating interest and a favorable rate of return.

It sounds pretty nice, doesn't it?

More Than Just Money

While you're thinking about your goals, keep in mind your ideals. Here, an Armchair Millionaire who is also an actual millionaire talks about how money is not all there is.

Think Outside the Box

"I am thirty-seven and made it into the millionaire club last year, but now I realize that money alone cannot give you happiness, you need more in life. That certain extra something will differ from person to person. It may take some time and a lot of conviction to achieve it, but the name of the game is to know what you want and then go for it."

—Posted by FAIZAN

From the Armchair Millionaire's Gallery—
Looks Like He's Made It

Armchair Millionaire Member Name: CanQuitAnytime
From: Gainesville, Florida
Age: 48
Occupation: Construction Manager
Family Status: Married
Financial goals: Complete financial independence with a middle-class lifestyle. My secondary goal is to use my estate to help future generations of my family.

How far along are you?
Actually, I am there but every day I work improves the quality of my lifestyle when I do retire. Also, there will be that much more for my kids.

How long have you been investing?
Since May 1980

What got you started?
The year after I got married, I had to pay taxes on two incomes. The tax bite was horrible and it took both my wife's and my paychecks and what little savings we had. Ever since, I have been budgeting, saving, and investing.

What was your biggest misconception before you started investing?
I thought that investing was for rich people. I thought little guys like me just had savings accounts.

What was the biggest investment mistake you ever made?
I got into day trading and options. I confused an 'up market' with investing savvy. I programmed my computer to analyze all types of

stock and option combinations, covered calls, spreads, and so on. When the market turned down, I lost *big time*. It set me back over a year.

What did you learn from that mistake?
The only real way to create wealth is to make a business plan for yourself. Know what your expenses are. Not just from month to month, but for the next five, ten, and twenty years. This includes the next car you will need when the old one finally dies, college and weddings for kids, and so on. Understand how much you have to sell in order to realize the extra income you need to pay for all these expenses and still save for investments.

What milestones do you most remember about your financial journey?
I remember the first time I realized the plan was working and I could look forward to early retirement. I can't explain the change it made in my mental disposition. My outlook was altered forever. I also remember when it dawned on me that my estate could be a wonderful legacy for my family. With the right planning, my kids' kids' kids one hundred years from now will go to college and have advantages that others will not, based on investments I am making now.

How is your life different now that you are so much nearer to your financial goals?
I like to say I am married to my wife, not my job. Most of my friends can't say that. When I was in the military, very early on in my career, everyone wanted to just make it twenty years and then retire. I swore that [kind of obligation to a job] would never happen to me. And guess what! By saving and investing, it never did.

What advice would you give to someone who is just beginning to plan for attaining her financial goals?
1. Get control of your cash flow (track every penny).

2. If you are not saving at least 10 percent of your salary as well as maxing out your retirement plans, you are living above your means.
3. Understand what you invest in (educate yourself) and invest for the long term.
4. Money and work isn't everything. If you aren't having fun, you are in the wrong job.

Listening to Your Future Self

Now that you can see what life will be like as a millionaire, can you imagine what kind of advice the millionaire-you would give the now-you? It might go something like this:

"I know it seems like a long road to get to where you don't have to worry about money. But the sooner you start, the easier it will be, and the sooner you can start to enjoy it. Trust me, the things you have to give up to invest are definitely worth the security you'll have later in life. What's a fancy new piece of stereo equipment or pretty new dress compared to a worry-free retirement? That dress will be out of style in less than a year, and the stereo equipment will be obsolete in two. Get your plan set up today and it will work for you for years to come. I can tell you that you are really going to love financial freedom. Sorry I can't talk more, but I'm late for my tee time!"

This might seem like a silly exercise, but a little forethought will only make your plan stronger.

What I Wish I Had Known— Armchair Millionaires Share Their Tips

Luckily, you don't have to rely solely on your imagination to get advice from those who have already achieved their financial goals. Below, Armchair Millionaires share the wisdom they know now and wish they had known then.

Do Your Research

"The one thing I wish I knew when I started investing was to read, read, read. Books, magazines, and newspapers give you the full picture—the kind of info you'll never get all on your own."

—Armchair Millionaire member Pamela

Investigate Your Sources

"You have to be very aware of whom you take advice from when it comes to money. Most people have agendas when it comes to financial advice—brokers are especially guilty of this."

—Armchair Millionaire member Inanka

'Nuff Said

"I wish I'd never listened to my brother-in-law."

—Armchair Millionaire member Clain

Talk to Other Like-Minded Investors

"I wish I had been on the message boards of sites like Armchair Millionaire before I started investing. When you get a lot of different opinions, you learn how to form your own."

—Armchair Millionaire member Ash

Stop Looking for the Pot of Gold

"I wish I had known to invest for the long term in well-known blue chips versus trying to hit the home run with penny stocks and losing all my money year after year."

—Armchair Millionaire member Sharon

Don't Wait

"I wish I'd understood how even a small amount saved and invested each month would grow into a substantial amount over time. I would have started sooner."

—Armchair Millionaire member Katie

Action Items for Chapter 10

- Get a good image of your future self enjoying the benefits of years' worth of investing. What will you be doing? And what advice will you be giving to folks about investing?
- Get started on your investment plan today. Dreams will still only be dreams if you don't start now.

Appendices

APPENDIX A

How to Use the Armchair Millionaire Web Site and This Book

This book was born on the Internet! It's a companion to Armchair-Millionaire.com (http://www.armchairmillionaire.com), a Web site that was founded in 1997 in order to help ordinary people learn commonsense strategies for saving and investing. Every month, thousands and thousands of people visit ArmchairMillionaire.com looking for advice and information. Like you, they're all trying to find their way toward a better financial future.

Together, they make up a community of people just like you—people who want to become financially independent without budgeting all the fun out of their lives.

When you visit Armchair Millionaire on the Web, you'll find plenty of information that we just couldn't fit into this book. Here's a taste of what you'll find there . . .

The Five Steps to Financial Freedom

Learn even more about the five simple steps that can make you a millionaire. We've even got a cool interactive tool that will help you create your own customized plan for saving and investing. Enter a few details, and we'll explain it all, step by step, and give you an action plan at the end that you can use to get started. Thousands of people in the Armchair Millionaire community have already put these time-tested principles to work, and you'll meet some of them here. You'll also find the essential tools and information you'll need to get started on your own path to financial freedom.

The Model Portfolio

Countdown with Lewis and Lynette as they invest their real money and turn it into a million-dollar portfolio using the Five Steps to Financial Freedom. You'll get current updates and tips as their portfolio grows and grows.

Armchair Millionaire Communities

We've created several areas on our site, each devoted to a different topic. We call them our "communities," and it's here that you'll find more specific answers to questions on many of the concepts we've covered in this book. Here are the three main communities:

GETTING STARTED

The name says it all. Paying off debt? Just beginning to set aside a few bucks? Jump in and get started!

SAVVY INVESTING

Here you'll learn all about the options that will help you save and invest in the stock market.

FUND-AMENTALS

You'll find all you need to know about mutual funds, from the basics of fund investing to advanced asset allocation strategies.

Finally, be sure to check out **The Armchair Millionaire's Gallery.** Here you can meet real people on their way to financial freedom— and a few who have already arrived.

Index Funds You Can Use in the Armchair Investing Strategy

Standard & Poor's 500 Index Funds

The first component of the Armchair Investing Strategy is to invest in U.S. large cap stocks, preferably in an S&P 500 index fund.

Fund Information	Initial Investment	
	Regular	IRA
Advantus Index 500 Fund A (ADIAX) 800-665-6005 http://www.advantusfunds.com	$250	$250
Aetna Index Plus Large Cap A (AELAX) 800-367-7732 http://www.aeltus.com/aetnafunds	$1,000	$500
Aon S&P 500 Index (ASPYX) http://www.aon.com	$1,000	—
Bankers Trust Pyramid Equity 500 Index (BTIEX) Bankers Trust and its affiliated companies have been acquired by Deutsche Bank	$2,500	$500
California Investment Trust S&P 500 Index (SPFIX) 800-225-8778 http://www.caltrust.com	$5,000	$5,000
Dreyfus S&P 500 Index (PEOPX) 800-221-1793 http://www.dreyfus.com	$2,500	$750

Fund Information	Initial Investment	
	Regular	IRA
E*Trade S&P 500 Index (ETSPX) 800-786-2575 http://www.etrade.com	$1,000	$250
Evergreen Select Equity Index A (ESINX) 800-225-2618 http://www.evergreen-funds.com	$1,000	$1,000
Fidelity Spartan Market Index (FSMKX) 800-544-6666 http://personal300.fidelity.com/products/funds	$10,000	$500
First American-Equity Index A (FAEIX) 800-637-2548	$1,000	$250
Galaxy II Large Co. Index (ILCIX) 877-289-4252 http://www.galaxyfunds.com	$2,500	$500
Harris Insight Trust Index (HIDAX) 800-982-8782 http://www.harrisinsight.com	$1,000	$250
Invesco S&P 500 Index (ISPIX) 800-675-1705 http://www.invesco.com	$5,000	$2,000
Kent Index Equity (KNIDX) 800-633-KENT http://www.kentfunds.com	$1,000	$100
MainStay Equity Index A (MCSEX) 800-624-6782 http://www.mainstayfunds.com	$1,000	$1,000
Munder Index 500 A (MUXAX) 800-438-5789 http://www.munder.com	$500	$250
Northern Stock Index (NOSIX) 800-595-9111 http://www.ntrs.com	$2,500	$500
One Group-Equity Index A (OGEAX) 800-338-4345 http://www.onegroup.com	$1,000	$250

Fund Information	Initial Investment	
	Regular	**IRA**
PIMCO Stocks PLUS Fund A (PSPAX) 800-227-7337 http://www.pimcofunds.com	$2,500	$1,000
Schwab S&P 500 Index (SWPIX) 800-435-4000 http://www.schwab.com	$1,000	$500
Scudder S&P 500 Index (SCPIX) 800-225-2470 http://www.scudder.com	$2,500	$1,000
State Street Global Advisors S&P 500 Index (SVSPX) 800-647-7327 http://www.ssgafunds.com	$10,000	$250
Strong Index 500 (SINEX) 800-359-3379 http://www.strong-funds.com	$2,500	$1,000
Transamerica Premier Index (TPIIX) 800-892-7587 http://www.transamerica.com	$1,000	$250
T. Rowe Price Equity Index (PREIX) 800-225-5132 http://www.troweprice.com/mutual/index.html	$2,500	$1,000
USAA S&P 500 Index (USSPX) 800-382-8722 http://www.usaaedfoundation.org	$3,000	$2,000
Vanguard Index Trust 500 (VFINX) 800-860-8394 http://www.vanguard.com	$3,000	$1,000
Wachovia Equity Index A (BTEIX) 800-994-4414 http://www.wachovia.com	$250	$250
Wells Fargo Equity Index A (SFCSX) 800-552-9612	$1,000	$250

You could also purchase S&P Depository Receipts, known as SPDRs or Spiders. These are exchange-traded funds that own the same stocks in the S&P 500 as an index fund, and have very low expenses. SPDRs trade on the American Stock Exchange under the ticker symbol SPY, and you can purchase them at any brokerage firm.

Small-Cap Stock Index Funds

The second component of the Armchair Investing Strategy is to invest in a small-cap index fund, one that tracks the Russell 2000 (or other small-cap) index as a benchmark.

Fund Information	Initial Investment	
	Regular	IRA
AXP Small Company Index A (ISIAX) 800-328-8300 http://www.americanexpress.com/advisors	$2,000	$50
Federated Mini-Cap C (MNCCX) 800-341-7400 http://www.federatedinvestors.com	$1,500	$250
Galaxy II Small Company Index (ISCIX) 800-628-0414 http://www.galaxyfunds.com	$2,500	$500
Gateway Small Cap Index (GSCIX) 800-354-6339	$1,000	$500
Merrill Lynch Small Cap Index D (MDSKX) 609-282-2800 http://www.ml.com	$1,000	$100
Schwab Small Cap Index (SWSMX) 800-435-4000 http://www.schwab.com	$2,500	$1,000
Vanguard Index Trust Small Cap (NAESX) 800-871-3879 http://www.vanguard.com	$3,000	$1,000

Morgan Stanley EAFE Index Fund

The third piece of the Armchair Investing Strategy is to invest in a global mutual fund, one that uses the MSCI EAFE as its benchmark. MSCI EAFE stands for "Morgan Stanley Capital International—Europe, Australasia, and the Far East," and it tracks stocks in those countries. It's a bit harder to find an index fund that follows the EAFE, so you may have to use an actively managed fund with low expenses instead of an index fund.

Fund Information	Initial Investment	
	Regular	IRA
Dreyfus International Stock Index (DIISX) 800-645-6561 http://www.dreyfus.com	$2,500	$750
E*Trade International Index (ETINX) 800-786-2575 http://www.etrade.com	$1,000	$250
First American International Index A (FIIAX) First American International Index B (FIXBX) 800-637-2548	$1,000	$250
Merrill Lynch International Index D (MDIIX) 800-456-4587 http://www.ml.com	$1,000	$100
One Group Intl Equity Index A (OEIAX) One Group Intl Equity Index B (OGEBX) One Group Intl Equity Index C (OIICX) 800-480-4111 http://www.onegroup.com	$1,000	$250
Schwab International Index (SWINX) 800-435-4000 http://www.schwab.com	$2,500	$1,000
Vanguard Total Intl Stock Index (VGTSX) 800-662-7447 http://www.vanguard.com	$3,000	$1,000

APPENDIX C

Brokerage Firms and Mutual Fund Companies

Here are some of the top brokerage firms and mutual fund companies. Call or visit them on the Web to get information on opening an account.

Charles Schwab
800-225-8570
http://www.schwab.com

E°Trade
800-ETRADE-1
http://www.etrade.com

Fidelity
800-544-6666
http://www.fidelity.com

Strong Funds
800-359-3379
http://www.estrong.com

TD Waterhouse
800-934-4448
http://www.tdwaterhouse.com

TIAA-CREF
800 842-2776
http://www.tiaa-cref.org

T. Rowe Price
800-225-5132
http://www.troweprice.com

Vanguard
800-871-3879
http://www.vanguard.com

401(k) Plan: A tax-deferred defined contribution retirement plan offered by an employer.

403(b) Plan: Similar to a 401(k) plan, but offered by nonprofit and educational organizations.

457 Plan: A savings and retirement plan for local and state government employees.

Adjusted Gross Income: The amount of your annual income that the IRS uses to determine the taxes you owe. Certain deductions, known as "adjustments," are subtracted from your total income to determine your AGI. Your AGI is calculated prior to taking itemized or standard deductions.

Armchair Millionaire: An investor who uses commonsense saving and investing methods in order to attain financial freedom.

asset: Anything that an individual or a corporation owns that has economic value to its owner.

asset class: A high-level classification of an investment. Examples of asset classes include stocks, bonds, cash, and real estate.

automatic deduction plan: Offered by brokers and mutual fund companies, whereby funds are transferred each month from a bank account and invested automatically.

back-end load: A commission or sales fee that is charged upon the redemption of mutual fund shares.

bond: A legal obligation of an issuing company or government to repay the principal of a loan to bond investors at a specified future date.

broker: An individual or firm that charges a fee or commission for executing buy and sell orders submitted by another individual or firm.

buy and hold: A long-term investing strategy in which an investor's stock portfolio is fully invested in the market all the time.

capital gain: An increase in the value of a capital asset such as common stock. If the asset is sold, the gain is a "realized" capital gain. A capital gain may be short term (one year or less) or long term (more than one year).

common stock: A class of stock in a company, normally with voting rights. Corporations may have several classes of common stock, as well as preferred stock, or they may have a single class of common stock. Common stock–holders are on the bottom of the ladder in a corporation's ownership structure, and have rights to a company's assets only after bond holders, preferred shareholders, and other debt holders have been satisfied.

compound interest: The way that fairly small amounts of money can grow substantially over time, as interest earns interest. Over time, the effect compounds to speed up the growth of your savings. The principle of "compound returns" refers to profits earned and reinvested in an investment portfolio.

contributions: Cash deposited into a retirement plan.

diversification: A risk management technique that mixes a wide variety of investments within a portfolio, thus minimizing the impact of any one security on overall portfolio performance.

dividend: A share of profits paid by a company to its investors. Not all companies pay dividends.

dollar cost averaging: The practice of steadily contributing a regular amount of money into an investment rather than one lump sum at once. Studies have shown that dollar cost averaging lowers risk and increases return over time.

equity: Another word for stock, or similar securities representing an ownership interest.

financial planner: An investment professional who helps individuals delineate financial plans with specific objectives and helps coordinate various financial concerns.

front-end load: A mutual fund commission or sales fee that is charged at the time shares are purchased. The load is added to the net asset value of the shares when calculating the public offering price.

index: A group of stocks that represents a market or a segment of a market. The Standard & Poor's 500 is the most well-known index, which measures the overall change in the value of the 500 stocks of the largest firms in the United States.

index fund: A mutual fund that only invests in the securities that make up a particular index.

investment: The process of buying property or securities with the intention that your holdings will increase in value.

IRA: Individual Retirement Account. A plan for retirement saving that allows assets to grow on a tax-deferred basis until the holder reaches retirement age.

Keogh plan: A qualified tax-deferred retirement plan for persons who are self-employed.

large-cap: Shorthand for "large capitalization," referring to very big publicly traded companies.

market capitalization: The total dollar value of all outstanding shares, calculated by multiplying the number of shares by the current market price.

mutual fund: An investment company that continuously offers new equity shares in an actively managed portfolio of securities. All shareholders participate in the gains or losses of the fund. Shares are issued and redeemed as per demand, and the fund's net asset value per share (NAV) is determined each day. The shares are redeemable on any business day at the net asset value. Each mutual fund's portfolio is invested to match the objective stated in the prospectus.

no-load fund: A mutual fund whose shares are sold without a commission or sales charge. The shares are distributed directly by the investment company.

portfolio: Any group of investments.

qualified distribution: A withdrawal from a retirement plan which is not subject to any penalties.

realized capital gain: A profit made on the sale of securities.

reinvestment: Using dividends, interest, and/or capital gains earned in an investment to purchase additional shares rather than receiving the distributions in cash.

return: The percentage of gain or loss for a security in a particular period, consisting of income plus capital gains relative to investment.

ROTH IRA: A type of Individual Retirement Account that doesn't offer a tax deduction on contributions, but allows the withdrawal of funds on a tax-free basis upon reaching retirement age.

routing number: Used by banks to identify where checks should be sent for processing and clearing.

SEP IRA: Simplified Employee Pension (SEP) IRA. A retirement plan for self-employed individuals and small companies.

small-cap: Shorthand for "small capitalization," referring to small publicly traded companies.

take-home pay: The amount of your paycheck after taxes and other withholdings.

unrealized capital gain: An increase in the value of securities that you currently own and have not sold.

INDEX

Page numbers in *italics* indicate charts.